The Story of Stile
That Began In . . .

SPLIT INFINITY

"In terms of the great body of Anthony's work, I would have to say that **Split Infinity** is his best novel so far. It is a treat to follow Stiles' adventures . . . and after a time one tends to develop distinct liking for the hero. There is a curious gentleness to him, reminiscent of Valentine Michael Smith in Heinlein's **Stranger in a Strange Land.**"   —*BEST SELLERS*

And Continued In

BLUE ADEPT

"This phase of the triptych is called **Blue Adept** and deals with a planet divided by a 'curtain.' On one side science works and magic doesn't. On the other side magic works and science doesn't. Though I've always admired Piers Anthony's competence, I never realized before how serious, how penetrating his thoughts can be."   —*Theodore Sturgeon*

". . . the story maintains its exciting pace with many unexpected twists, and Anthony's humorous touches continue to delight the reader."
—*Library Journal*

Comes To A Grand Conclusion In

JUXTAPOSITION

By Piers Anthony
Published by Ballantine Books:

THE MAGIC OF XANTH

THE APPRENTICE ADEPT

INCARNATIONS OF IMMORTALITY

Juxtaposition

Piers Anthony

A Del Rey Book

BALLANTINE BOOKS • NEW YORK

TABLE OF CONTENTS

CHAPTER 1

Clef

"I could give you some sleepfog," the lady robot said. "You stayed awake all night researching, and the Game is this afternoon. You have to rest."

"No drugs!" Stile snapped. "Better to be keyed up than fogged out."

"Better yet to be rational," she said.

He shook his head, looking at her. She was so exactly like a woman that most people never realized the truth. Not only could she function in all the ways of a living human female, she was extremely well formed. Her hair was a sun-bleached brown, shoulder length; her lips were full and slightly tinted, kissable; her eyes were green behind long lashes. She was the sort of creature rich, lonely men obtained to gratify their private passions more perfectly than any real woman would. But Stile knew her for what she was, and had no passion for her. "This is one time I wish I could just click off the way you can."

"I wish I were flesh," she said wistfully. She was programmed to love him and protect him and she was absolutely true to her program, as a machine had to be. "Come on—I'll put you to sleep." She took Stile's head in her lap and stroked his hair and hummed a lullaby.

Oddly enough, it worked. Her body was warm and soft, her touch gentle, and he had complete faith in her motive. Stile was close to few people and he tended to feel easier around machines. His tensions slipped away and his consciousness followed.

He found himself dreaming of the time several days before, when he had passed the Platinum Flute on to the musician Clef and guided the man across the curtain. In this dream he followed Clef's consciousness, not his own.

1

Somehow this did not seem strange. Stile had felt an instant and deep camaraderie with the man when they played music together. Stile himself was highly skilled with a number of instruments, but Clef's musical ability amounted to genius. It had been impossible to remain aloof from a person who played that well.

Clef had never been to the frame of Phaze. He stared at the lush tufts of grass, the tremendous oaks and pines, and the unicorn awaiting them, as if he were seeing something strange.

"This is Neysa," Stile informed him, perceived in the dream as a different person. The unicorn was black, with white socks on the rear feet, and was as small for her species as Stile was for his. Clef towered over them both, and felt awkward. "She will carry thee to the Platinum Demesnes."

What affectation was this? Stile had spoken normally until this moment. "I don't even know how to ride!" Clef protested. "And that's a mythical creature!" He eyed the long spiraled horn, wishing he could touch it to verify that it was only tacked on to the horse. He had been told that this was a land of magic, but he found that hard to credit.

"Well, I could conjure thee there, but—"

"Absolutely not! Magic is—incredible. Wherever I have to go, I'll walk."

Stile shrugged. "That is thy business. But I must insist that Neysa accompany thee. Until thou dost reach the protection of the Little Folk, this region is not safe for thee."

"Why are you suddenly talking archaically?" Clef demanded.

"This is the tongue of this frame," Stile explained. "Now must I conjure clothing for thee."

"Clothing!" Clef exclaimed, daunted. "I am a serf, like you, forbidden to—I can not—"

Stile had recovered a package of clothing from a hiding place and was putting it on. "Here in Phaze, thou art a man. Trust me; clothe thyself." He paused, then said in a singsong voice: "An ye can, clothe this man."

Suddenly Clef was clothed like a Citizen of Proton, with

silken trousers, shirt, jacket of light leather, and even shoes. He felt ludicrous and illicit. "If anyone sees me in this outrageous costume—" He squinted at Stile. "You were serious about magic! You conjured this!"

"Aye. Now must I conjure myself to the Blue Demesnes, to report to the Lady Blue. Neysa and the Flute will keep thee safe, methinks. Farewell, friend."

"Farewell," Clef responded weakly.

Stile sang another spell and vanished. Clef contemplated the vacated spot for a while, absorbing this new evidence of enchantment, then felt his own clothing. Blue trousers, golden shirt—what next? "And I'm supposed to travel with you," he said to the little unicorn. "With thee, I should perhaps say. Well, he did warn me there would be tribulations. I don't suppose you know the direction?"

Neysa blew a note through her horn that sounded like an affirmation rendered in harmonica music. Clef had not realized that the animal's horn was hollow, or that she would really comprehend his words. He followed her lead.

The scenery was lovely. To the near south was a range of purple-hued mountains, visible through gaps in the forest cover. The immediate land was hilly, covered with rich green turf. Exotic birds fluttered in the branches of the trees. No path was visible, but the unicorn picked out an easy passage unerringly.

"Are you—art thou able to play music on that horn?" Clef inquired facetiously, feeling a need to assert himself verbally if not physically.

For answer, Neysa played a merry little tune, as if on a well-handled harmonica. Clef, amazed, fell silent. He would have to watch what he said in this fantastic frame; more things were literal than he was inclined to believe.

The pace became swift, as Neysa moved up to her limit. Clef had always liked to walk, so was in no discomfort, but wondered just how far they were going. In Proton, with the limitation of the domes, it was never necessary to walk far before encountering mass transportation. Obviously there was no such limit here.

The animal perked up her small ears, listening for something. Clef knew that horses had good hearing, and presumed unicorns were the same. It occurred to him that a

world of magic could have magical dangers and he had no
notion how to cope with that sort of thing. Presumably
this equine would protect him in much the way Stile's
distaff robot protected him in Proton; still, Clef felt nervous.

Then, abruptly, the unicorn became a petite young
woman, wearing a simple black dress and white slippers.
She was small, even smaller than Stile, with lustrous black
hair that reminded him of the mane or tail of—

Of course! This was, after all, the same creature, in a
different shape. She even had a snub-horn in her forehead,
and her shoes somehow resembled hooves, for their slipper
tops tied into thick, sturdy soles.

"Stile is getting married," Neysa said. There was the
suggestion of harmonica music in her voice. "I must go
there. I will summon a werewolf to guide thee."

"A werewolf!" Clef exclaimed, horrified.

But the girl was a unicorn again. She blew a loud blast
on her horn.

Faintly, there was an answering baying. Now Neysa
played a brief harmonica tune. There was a responding
yip, much closer. She changed back into the girl. Clef tried
to ascertain how she did that, but it was too quick; she
seemed simply to phase from one form to the other with
no intermediate steps. Perhaps that was why this frame
was called Phaze—people phased from one form to another, or from nudity to attire, or from place to place.

"A bitch is coming," Neysa said, startling Clef again; he
had not expected such a term from so pert a miss. "Farewell." She changed into a firefly, flashed once, and zoomed
away to the north. There seemed to be no conservation of
mass here.

A dark shape charged toward him, low and furry,
gleaming-eyed and toothed. Clef clutched the Platinum
Flute—and suddenly it was a fine rapier. "Will wonders
never cease!" he exclaimed. This was a weapon with which
he was proficient. He stood awaiting the onslaught of the
wolf with enhanced confidence, though he was by no
means comfortable. He did not relish the idea of bloodshed, even in self-defense.

But the creature drew up short and metamorphosed into

a woman. This one was older; in fact, she looked grand-motherly.

Clef was catching on to the system. "You—thou art the werewolf the unicorn summoned?"

"Aye. I am the werebitch available, man-creature. I have seen weddings enow; since my old wolf died I care not overmuch to see more. I will guide and guard thee to the Elven Demesnes. Put thou that blade away."

"It is not a blade; it is a rapier," Clef said somewhat primly. But now it was neither; it was the Flute again. "Neysa told you all that in one brief melody?"

"Aye. She was ever economical of speech. What is thy name, man?" the bitch inquired as she walked east.

"Clef, from the frame of Proton. And thine?"

"Serrilryan, of Kurrelgyre's Pack. We range mostly southeast of the Blue Demesnes, up to the Purple Mountains. Good hunting here."

"No doubt," Clef agreed dryly.

"If thou art walking all the way to the Platinum Demesnes, thou wilt have to step faster, Clef-man. We have forty miles to go."

"My legs are already tiring, Serrilryan."

"We can help that. Take thou a sniff of this." She held out a little bag of something.

Clef sniffed. The bag emitted a pungent aroma. "What is this?"

"Wolfsbane. For strength."

"Superstition," he muttered.

"Have ye noted how fast thy walk is now?"

Clef noticed, with surprise. "I'm almost running, but I don't feel winded at all!"

"Superstition," she said complacently.

Whatever it was, it enabled him to cover distance with wolflike endurance. Serrilryan shifted back to canine form to pace him.

Still, they were only partway there as night came on. The bitch became the woman again. "Do thou make a fire, Clef-man. I will hunt supper."

"But—" But she was already back to bitch-form and gone.

Clef gathered what dry wood he could find, along with

bits of old moss and straw. He formed a neat tepee, but had no idea how to ignite it. Presumably the denizens of this frame could make fire with simple spells, or perhaps they borrowed fire-breathing dragons. Such resources were not available to him.

Then he had a notion. The Platinum Flute had become a rapier when he wanted a weapon; could it also become a fire maker?

He held it near the tepee. It had formed into a clublike rod. From the tip a fat spark jumped, igniting the mass. He had discovered how to use this thing! He was almost getting to like magic.

When the bitch returned with a freshly slain rabbit, the fire was ready. "Good enough," she said gruffly. She roasted the rabbit on a spit.

This type of meal was foreign to Clef, but he managed to get through it. Stile had warned him there would be privations. But he was ready to suffer anything to obtain legitimate possession of the Platinum Flute, the most remarkable instrument he could imagine. Only the Little Folk could grant that; it was their Flute.

Serrilryan showed him where there was a streamlet of fresh water, so that he could drink and wash. Out of deference to his human sensitivity, she refrained from lapping her own drink until he was sated.

Now all he had to worry about was the night. He really wasn't equipped to sleep in the wilderness. "Serrilryan, I realize that for your kind this is no problem, but I am not accustomed to sleeping outside. I am concerned about bugs and things." Though in fact no bugs had bothered him here; perhaps the reek of the wolfsbane kept them away. "Is there any domicile available?"

"Aye," she said. She brought out a small object. Apparently she could carry clothing and objects on her person even in wolf form, though none of it showed then.

Clef looked at the thing. It appeared to be a tiny doll's house. "I'm afraid I don't quite follow."

"It is an amulet," she explained. "Invoke it."

"Invoke it?" he asked blankly.

She nodded. "Set it down first, man."

He set it on the ground. "Uh, I invoke thee."

The amulet expanded. Clef stepped back, alarmed. The thing continued to grow. Soon it was the size of a doghouse, then a playhouse. Finally it stood complete: a small, neat, thatch-roofed log cabin.

"Well, I never!" Clef exclaimed. "A magic house!"

Serrilryan opened the door and entered. Clef followed, bemused. Inside was a wooden table with two chairs and a bed with a down quilt. Clef contemplated this with a certain misgiving, realizing that there were two of them and only one sleeping place. "Um—"

She phased back to canine form and curled herself up comfortably on the floor at the foot of the bed. That solved the problem. She needed no human props and would be there if anything sought to intrude during the night. Clef was getting to appreciate werewolves.

He accepted the bed gratefully, stripped away his ungainly clothing, lay down, and was soon asleep.

Stile's consciousness returned as Clef's faded. Sheen was still stroking his hair, as tireless as a machine. "I never realized he would have so much trouble," Stile murmured. He told her of his dream. "I'm used to Phaze now, but it was quite an adjustment at first. I forgot all about Clef, and I shouldn't have."

"Go back to sleep," she told him.

"That amulet—that would have been fashioned by the Red Adept. She's gone now, because of me. I really should see about finding a new Adept to make amulets; they are too useful to be allowed to disappear."

"I'm sure you will," Sheen said soothingly.

"Phaze needs amulets."

She picked up his head and hugged it against her bosom, smotheringly. "Stile, if you don't go to sleep voluntarily—"

He laughed. "You're a bitch."

"A female werewolf," she agreed. "We do take good care of wayward men."

They did indeed. Stile drifted back to his dream.

Next morning Serrilryan brought some excellent fruit she had foraged. They ate and prepared to resume the march. "This cabin—can it be compressed back into its token?" Clef asked.

"Nay. A spell functions but once," she said. "Leave it; others may use it after us, or the Blue Adept may dismantle it with a spell. Most likely the Little Folk will carry it to their mountain demesnes."

"Yes, of course it shouldn't be wasted," Clef agreed.

They walked. His legs were stiff from the prior day's swift walk. The wolfsbane had worn off, and Serrilryan did not offer more. It was dangerous to overuse such magic, she said. So they progressed slowly east, through forest and field, over hills and through deep gullies, around boulders and huge dense bushes. The rugged beauty of the natural landscape was such that it distracted him from his discomfort. What a special land this was!

In the course of the day he heard something to the east. Serrilryan's wolf ears perked. Then he observed a column of thick, colored smoke rising from the sky. There had been a bad explosion and fire somewhere.

"That is Blue fighting Red," the bitch said knowingly. "She killed him; now he is killing her."

"I realize this is a frame of magic," Clef said. "Even so, that does not seem to make an extraordinary amount of sense."

"Adept fighting Adept is bad business," she agreed.

"How could they take turns killing each other?"

"There are two selves of many people, one in each frame," she explained. "One self cannot meet the other. But when one dies, there is a vacuum and the other can cross the curtain. Blue now avenges the murder of his other self."

"Oh, I see," Clef said uncertainly. "And must I avenge the murderer of mine other self?"

"Mayhap. Where wast thou whelped?"

"On another planet," Clef said, surprised. "I signed for Proton serf tenure as a young man—"

"Then thy roots are not here. Thou hast no other self here, so art not barred from crossing."

"Oh. Fortunate for me, I suppose. Dost thou also have another self in Proton?"

"Nay. But if I crossed, I would be but a cur, unable to were-change. And the hunting is not good there."

Clef had to laugh agreement. "All too true! Proton, beyond the force-field domes, is a desert. Nothing but pollution."

"Aye," she agreed, wrinkling her nose. "When men overrun a planet, they destroy it."

"Yet Stile—the Blue Adept—he is also a serf in Proton, like me."

"He was whelped on Proton. His root is here."

Clef watched the dissipating grotesqueries of the cloud of smoke. "I'm glad I'm not his enemy!" He resumed slogging forward. At this rate he would be lucky to travel ten miles by dusk.

Actually, he realized, it might be just as well to take several days before reaching the Little Folk. There was a tremendous amount to learn about Phaze, and this slow trek was an excellent introduction. When he finally did arrive, he would have a much better comprehension of the frame, and know how to deport himself. With all the pitfalls of magic, he needed that experience.

The werebitch paced him uncomplainingly. She shifted from form to form at need, conversing when he wished, scouting when there was anything suspicious in the vicinity. Finally he asked her: "Is this not an imposition, Serrilryan, for thee, shepherding a novice while thy Pack is active elsewhere?"

"I am oath-friend to Neysa the unicorn," she replied. "For her would I shepherd a snow-demon halfway to Hell."

"Halfway?"

"At that point, the demon would melt." She smiled tolerantly. "Besides which, this is easy duty for an old bitch. I am sure the Blue Adept has excellent reasons to convey thee to the Mound Demesnes." She considered. "If I may inquire—?"

"I am to play the Platinum Flute for the Mound Folk, to enable them to ascertain whether I am the one they call the Foreordained. That is all I know—except that my life will have little purpose if I can not keep this ultimate instrument."

"The Foreordained!" she exclaimed. "Then is the end of Phaze near!"

"Why? I consider it to be a pretentious, perhaps non-sensical title, to say the least, and of course there is no certainty that I am the one they seek. I am merely a fine musician and a rather good fencer. What have I to do with the fate of a land of magic?"

"That is all I know," she admitted. "Be not affronted, Clef-man, if I hope thou art not he."

"I take no affront from thee, bitch." He had long since realized that the term he had considered to be uncomplimentary was the opposite here.

"Thou dost play the flute well?"

"Very well."

"Better than Blue?"

"Aye. But I decline to play this particular instrument in the frame of Phaze until I meet the Mound Folk. It is said the mountain may tremble if—"

"Aye, wait," she agreed. "No fool's errand, this."

"Dost thou like music, Serrilryan?"

"Some. Baying, belike, at full moon."

"Baying is not my specialty. I could whistle, though."

"That is music?" she asked, amused.

"It can be, properly executed. There are many types of whistles. Hand-whistling can resemble a woodwind."

"Aye, with magic."

"No magic, bitch. Like this." He rubbed his hands together, convoluted his long fingers into the appropriate configuration, and blew. A fine, clear pipe note emerged. He adjusted his fingers as if tuning the instrument and blew again, making a different pitch. Then he essayed a minor melody.

The sound was beautiful. Clef had not exaggerated when he claimed to play well; he was probably the finest and most versatile musician on the planet. His crude hands produced prettier music than that of most other people using fine instruments.

Serrilryan listened, entranced, phasing back and forth between her forms to appreciate it in each. "That is not magic?" she asked dubiously when he paused.

"I know no magic. This is straight physical dexterity."

"Never have I heard the like!" she exclaimed. "The Blue Adept played the Flute at the Unolympics, and methought that was the most perfect melody ever made. Now I think thou mightest eclipse it, as thou sayest. Canst thou do real whistling too?"

Clef smiled at her naïveté. He pursed his lips and whistled a few bars of classical music eloquently. She was delighted.

So they continued, and in the evening he serenaded her with a whistle concert. Squirrels and sparrows appeared in nearby trees, listening raptly. Clef had discovered how to relate to the wild creatures of this lovely wilderness world.

This night the werebitch had located a serviceable cave to sleep in. They piled straw and fern for a bed, and she curled up by the entrance. It was a good night. He was getting to like Phaze.

Stile woke again. "Time to go for the Game," he mumbled.

"Not yet. Sleep," Sheen said. She was a machine, indefatigable; she could sit up and hold him indefinitely and was ready to do so. She was his best and perhaps his only personal friend in this frame. She had saved his life on several occasions. He trusted her. He slept.

The third day Clef found his muscles acclimatizing, and he traveled better. But the world of Phaze seemed restless. There was the sound of horse or unicorn hooves pounding to the east, and a lone wolf passed nearby. "What's going on?"

"The Red Adept has sprung a trap on the Blue Adept," Serrilryan said, having somehow picked up this news from the pattern of baying and the musical notes of the distant unicorns. "He is badly injured but can not cross the curtain for magic healing, for that a basilisk has hold of him. It is very bad." Indeed, she was worried and, when she returned to bitch-form, her hackles were ruffled. Clef, too, was concerned; he had known Stile only a few hours before their parting, but liked him well and wished him well. There seemed to be nothing he could do, however.

But later the situation eased. "They have saved him," Serrilryan reported. "He is weak, but survives."

Clef's own tension abated. "I am exceedingly glad to hear that. He lent me the Platinum Flute, and for this marvelous instrument I would lay down my life. It was the sight of it that brought me here, though I am wary of the office it portends."

"Aye."

In the afternoon they heard a sudden clamor. Something was fluttering, squawking, and screeching. The sounds were hideous, in sharp contrast to the pleasure of the terrain.

Serrilryan's canine lip curled. Quickly she shifted to human form. "Beast birds! Needs must we hide."

But it was not to be. The creatures had winded them, and the pursuit was on. "Let not their filthy claws touch thee," the werebitch warned. "The scratches will fester into gangrene." She changed back to canine form and stood guarding him, teeth bared.

The horde burst upon them. They seemed to be large birds—but their faces were those of ferocious women. Clef's platinum rapier was in his hand, but he hesitated to use it against these part-human creatures. Harpies—that was what they were.

They gave him little opportunity to consider. Three of them flew at his head, discolored talons extended. "Kill! Kill!" they screamed. The smell was appalling.

Serrilryan leaped, her teeth catching the grimy underbelly of one bird. Greasy feathers fell out as the creature emitted a shriek of amazing ugliness. Immediately the other two pounced on the wolf, and two more swooped down from above.

Clef's misgivings were abruptly submerged by the need to act. There seemed to be no chance to reason or warn; he simply had to fight.

Clef was aware that the werewolf had taken his remark about his skill at fencing to be vanity, for he was hardly the warrior type. However, he had spoken the truth. The rapier danced before him. In seven seconds he skewerd four harpies, while Serrilryan dropped the fifth, dead.

The remaining beast birds now developed some crude

caution. They flapped and bustled, screeching epithets, but did not charge again. Their eyes were on the gleaming platinum weapon; they had suddenly learned respect.

Clef took a step toward them, and the foul creatures scattered, hurling back one-syllable words fully as filthy as their feathers. This threat had been abated.

"Thou art quite a hand with that instrument," Serrilryan remarked appreciatively. "Never saw I a sword stab so swiftly."

"I never used a rapier in anger before," Clef said, feeling weak and revolted now that the brief action was over. "But those horrible creatures—"

"Thou didst withhold thy strike until they clustered on me."

"Well, I couldn't let them—those claws—"

"Aye," she said, and went canine again.

But there was something wrong. She had tried to conceal it, but his reaction to this combat had made him more perceptive to physical condition. "Wait—thou hast been scratched!" Clef said. "Thy shoulder's bleeding!"

"Wounds are nothing to wolves," she said, phasing back. But it showed on her dame-form too, the blood now staining her shawl. "How much less, a mere scratch."

"But thou didst say—"

"Doubtless I exaggerated. Bleeding cleans it." She changed back again and ran ahead, terminating the dialogue.

Clef realized that she did not want sympathy for her injury, at least not from the likes of him. Probably it was unwolflike to acknowledge discomfort. Yet she *had* warned him about the poisonous nature of harpy scratches. He hoped nothing evil came of this.

That night they camped in a tree. Clef was now more accustomed to roughing it, and this was a hugely spreading yellow birch whose central nexus was almost like a house. Serrilryan curled up in bitch-form, and he curled up beside her, satisfied with the body warmth she radiated. The papery bark of the tree was slightly soft, and he was able to form a pillow of his bent arm. Yes, he was coming to like this life.

"This frame is just a little like Heaven," he remarked as

sleep drew nigh. "My frame of Proton is more like Hell, outside the domes, where nothing grows."

"Mayhap it is Proton-frame I am destined for," she said, shifting just far enough to dame-form to speak, not bothering to uncurl.

"Proton? Dost thou plan to cross the curtain, despite thy loss of magic there?"

She growl-chuckled ruefully. "Figuratively, man-person. When I die, it will be the real Hell I will see."

"Hell? Thee? Surely thou wilt go to Heaven!" Clef did not believe in either region, but neither did he believe in magic.

"Surely would I wish to go to Heaven! There, belike, the Glory Hounds run free. But that is not the destiny of the likes of me. Many evils have I seen since I was a pup." She shifted back to canine and slept.

Clef thought about that, disturbed. He did not believe this was an immediate issue, but feared that she did. He was bothered by her growing morbidity and her low estimate of self-worth. She might have seen evil, but that did not make her evil herself; sometimes evil was impossible to escape. It had been that way with the harpies. Yet what could he do to ease her depression?

Troubled, he slept.

"Strange dream," Stile said. "Every time he sleeps, I wake. But I'm dreaming in minutes what he experienced in days."

"How much farther does he have to go?" Sheen asked.

"He should reach the Elven Demesnes in two more days."

"Then you sleep two more times. I want to learn how this ends." Her fingers stroked his eyes closed.

Serrilryan's wound was not healing. It was red and swollen, the blood refusing to coagulate properly. She limped now, when she thought he wasn't looking, and her pace was slower. She was suffering—and he couldn't comment for fear of embarrassing her.

The terrain became more hilly. Huge trees grew out of the slopes, some of their roots exposed by erosion. But the eager grass was covering every available patch of ground, and the turf was thick and spongy. Clef was soon breathless, ascending the steep, short slopes, drawing himself up by handholds on trees and branches and tangles of roots. Serrilryan followed, her familiarity with this region making up for her weakness, shifting back and forth between forms to take advantage of the best properties of each.

Something tugged at his hair. It was not the wind. Clef paused, fearing he had snagged it in a low branch—but there was no branch. He put his hand up, but there was nothing. Yet the tugging continued, and now there were little touches on his skin.

"Something's here!" he exclaimed, alarmed.

The bitch sniffed the air and cocked her ears. She phased into woman-form. "Whistle," she said.

Perplexed, he whistled. Oddly, the touchings abated. He whistled louder and with more intricacy, a medley of classical themes. He enhanced it with trills and double notes, warming to it, serenading the landscape.

Slowly, shapes appeared. They were little people, perching on branches and on the slope and even floating in air. All were listening raptly.

"Aye, the sidhe," Serrilryan said, pronouncing it *shee*. "The Faerie Folk. They cause no harm, just idle mischief."

Discovered, the sidhe moved into a dance, whirling in air. Their little lasses were, in the archaic measurement of this frame, about four feet tall, the lads not much larger. They moved prettily and smiled often—happy folk.

But when Clef stopped whistling, they faded out of sight again. "The sidhe associate not overmuch with other folk, but they do like music," the werebitch said. "I am destined to see them three times before I die."

"How many times hast thou seen them so far?"

"This is the third time."

"Then I should not have whistled them into sight!"

She made a gesture of unconcern. "I am old; my pace is slowing. My teeth are no longer sharp. The Pack will not let me live much longer anyway. Glad am I to have seen the lovely Faerie Folk once more."

"But this is barbaric! The other wolves have no right—"

"Question not the way of the Pack. I have killed others

in my day; always I knew my turn would come. Perhaps it would have come ere now, had I not been fated to guide thee. I am content, Clef-man."

Clef shook his head, not commenting further. Obviously there was violence along with the beauty and literal magic of this frame.

They marched on. Later another phenomenon occurred —a kind of sweeping of an unbreeze through the forest, dissipation of nonexistent clouds in the sky, and revivification of things that had not been dead. A hidden tension had been released, an obligation expiated. "What is it?" Clef asked.

"The lifting of a geis," Serrilryan said.

"I don't think I understand."

"The abatement of an oath. It hung over the forest; now it is done."

"What oath is this?"

"The Blue Adept swore vengeance against the Red Adept."

"Um, yes. But I thought he was getting married. He is also moving through the Proton Tourney. Isn't this an awful lot of activity for such an occasion?"

"There is no comprehending the ways of Adepts."

That seemed to be the case. The Blue Adept evidently had a lot more power, and was involved in more great events, than Clef had realized. It was mildly odd that so small a man had so large an impact on this frame.

By nightfall they reached the marker for the Platinum Demesnes, indicated by a sign saying *PT 78*.

"The path within is treacherous," the werebitch said. "Morning is better for it."

"Yes, certainly." Clef wasn't sure, now that he was this close, that he really wanted to reach these mysterious elves. If he were not the Foreordained, they would take the Flute from him, for it belonged to them.

Serrilryan knew of an existing shelter nearby, and they spent the night there. "I want thee to know," he told her, "how I appreciate the trouble thou hast taken on my behalf. This all may come to naught, yet it has been worthwhile for me."

"I thank thee, man," she said. "It has been nice talking

with thee and hearing thy music. Few among the Pack have time or courtesy for the old."

She did not look well at all. It was evident that pain was preventing her from relaxing. Clef whistled, filling the air with melody, and after a time the werewolf fell into a troubled slumber. Then Clef himself relaxed.

"I didn't know there were harpies in that vicinity," Stile said, waking. "I should have given him better protection. Though the way he used that rapier—" He shrugged and returned to sleep himself, secure in the robot's embrace.

In the morning Clef woke before the werebitch. She was breathing in pants and whining slightly in her sleep. The bad shoulder bulged with swelling, and the fur was falling out. This was obviously a severe infection. A good antibiotic could abate it—but this was Phaze, the frame of magic, where antibiotics were not available and perhaps would not work anyway.

Magic was what was needed—but he could not perform it. Unless the Flute—but no, he had resolved to play it only for the Mound Folk, because of the potential significance of the rendition. Still, maybe its magic could help. He laid the instrument against her body, as close to the wound as he could.

Her whining stopped; she was drawing comfort from the propinquity of this powerful talisman. Still, she was shivering, though the morning was warm. He had nothing with which to cover her.

Clef began to whistle again; it was all he could do. This time he selected a merry folk-song melody. He whistled it well; the joyous notes rippled through the forest, abolishing sadness. The bitch's shivering eased, and she slept peacefully at last.

For an hour he whistled. At last she turned and woke. She made a growl of displeasure at the lateness of the hour, but Clef wasn't fooled. She had needed that extra rest.

Breakfast was no problem. Squirrels and birds had dropped nuts and berries as offerings of appreciation, and these were excellent. This was a world that liked music.

Clef, in return, was becoming quite fond of this world. Yet it had its dark side, as Serrilryan's ailment showed.

They mounted the steep trail leading to the Mound Demesnes. Clef was now better able to manage than the werewolf. He wished he could help her, but all he could do was slow his pace to make it easier for her, leaving her pride intact.

Deep in the mountains there was a thin, suspended bridge crossing a chasm. Clef eyed it dubiously, but Serrilryan proceeded on across without hesitation. She was so unsteady he hastened to follow, so he could catch her if she started to fall.

Halfway across he looked down. The chasm yawned so deep and dark it made him dizzy. He did not enjoy the sensation. Fortunately the chasm was narrow, and in moments they were across.

At last they came in sight of the Mound. Serrilryan sank in a heap before it, her waning energy exhausted. She had done her job; she had delivered him safely.

But there was no one about. The sun shone down brightly and the hills were alive with small animals and birds—but no people. Clef, worried about the werebitch, did not care to wait overlong for an introduction. "Ho there!" he called. "I must meet with the Platinum Mound Folk."

There was no answer. Could he have come to the wrong place? "Serrilryan—" he began.

She changed with difficulty to dame-form. She was haggard. "This is the place, music man. The Mound Folk go not abroad by day. At night thou wilt see them."

"I don't think thou canst last till night," he said. "We must have healing magic for thee now."

She smiled weakly. "It is too late for me, friend. My day is done. One favor only I beg of thee—"

"Anything!"

"I would hear the Flute ere I die. Canst thou play an epitaph for me?"

He knew this was final. She would expire within the hour. He was at the realm of the Little Folk; he was no longer obliged to wait. "Yes, it is time," he agreed. "There

can be no better use for this instrument." He brought out
the Flute.

He played an ancient folk song that he felt was appropriate to this occasion: *Tumbleweeds*. It was the sort of
theme a wolf could appreciate, for it related to the freedom of the great outdoors, the rolling bushes called tumbleweeds drifting in the wind across the plain, cares of the
world left behind. Perhaps it was not that way, here in
Phaze, but he felt confident the mood would be conveyed.

From the first note, the Platinum Flute was potent, the
finest instrument he had ever played, enhanced by its
magic so that the sound transcended mere physics. The
music rippled, it flowed, it resonated; it was as if he were
flying, expanding, encompassing the landscape, the world,
the universe, the split infinities that were the frames of
science and magic. The sound loomed loud enough to
embrace all of Phaze, yet delicate enough to touch the
soul.

And the mountain trembled. The ground shook, but not
in the manner of an earthquake. It started shuddering
where he stood, and vibrated outward rhythmically, responding harmonically to the music of the Flute. The
effect intensified as he continued playing. Leaves fluttered
on trees, pine needles shook free of their moorings, and
the green grass of the slopes stood up tall and quivered like
the tines of tuning forks. The clear sky thickened; clouds
formed from nothing, flinging outward in rainbow-hued
bands. The sunlight dimmed; dusk coalesced.

Clef played on, caught in the wonder of the animation
the Flute was working. Serrilryan's fur stood out from her
body, charged. There was a canine smile on her face.
Washes of color traversed her, causing her human and
canine aspects to mingle aesthetically.

The ground shook harder. Branches fell from trees. The
roof of the Mound collapsed. The mountains in the Purple
range peeled off segments of themselves and settled substantially. Dust rose up. Animals fled. The sky swirled
nearer and nearer.

The Little Folk appeared, for now there was no direct
sunlight to shrivel them. They stood in the twisting dust
and fog, staring while their Demesnes collapsed about

them. Yet such was the power of the Flute that no one protested.

An avalanche formed and crashed downward. No one moved. The rocks and debris coursed past them all, avoiding living creatures, and advanced like a channeled flow of water until they piled up in a cairn over the body of Serrilryan, the werebitch. She had died smiling. She had heard the Platinum Flute; she had expired. Now she had been buried.

Still Clef played. From the cairn a spirit diffused, billowing and tenuous, extricating itself from the piled stones. Now it looked like a wolf, and now like a woman. It was Serrilryan's soul, departing her tired body at last.

Barb-tailed, horned, fire-clothed man-form devils hurried across the slope to intercept that soul. Suddenly Clef realized that the werebitch had spoken literally of Hell; she had known her spirit would be taken there. But Clef recoiled from the concept. She had helped him loyally and given her life in consequence. Surely that helped counterbalance whatever prior evils there might have been in her life. If he had any say at all in the matter, she would go to Heaven, where she wanted to be. He owed her that much. He shifted his playing, questing for the tune that would carry her soul upward.

Now from the troubled sky came wolves, flying without wings, their fur shining, so that they seemed possessed of light auras like halos. The music brought them down, showed them the way they might otherwise have missed, and marked the cairn.

The devils reached the soul first. But the angel-wolves arrived in time to balk the conveyance of the soul to Hell. A battle ensued, the half-visible humanoid figures against the half-visible canine figures. Spiritual fog and cloud and dust roiled along with the physical. But the theme of the Flute strengthened the wolves and weakened the devils. In a moment the angel-wolves wrested the bitch soul from the minions of Hell and loped up into the turbulent sky.

Yet before they departed entirely, the soul of Serrilryan paused. She looked back toward Clef, and he knew she was thanking him for a gift as unexpected as it was gratifying. Her sinful human component had been juxtaposed with her pure wolf component in death, nearer perfection than they had been in life, and the forces of Heaven had prevailed. She sent to earth one glance of purest appreciation that made the air about Clef sparkle. Then she turned again and loped on toward Heaven with her divine companions.

The Purple Mountains continued to shake and settle. Dragons flew up from the southern marches; creatures stirred all over Phaze. But Clef would not stop playing until the bitch was safely ensconced in Heaven. He would permit no loophole, no reversal.

Stile woke in alarm. The building was shaking!

"There seems to be an earthquake in progress," Sheen said. "The Purple Mountain range is settling."

"That's no natural phenomenon! That's the Foreordained!" Stile cried. "Now I realize that Clef is indeed the ultimate magician, with power to level mountains and delicacy to send souls to Heaven."

"The Foreordained," Sheen repeated. "Clef is the one destined to save Phaze?"

"He played the Platinum Flute, and the mountain trembled and tumbled. That's the signal. I saw it in my dream —and now I know it's true. My vision has caught up to the present and affirmed it."

Sheen checked the newsscreen. "There has certainly been a shake-up in Proton. Power has been disrupted all along the southern range. Mine shafts have collapsed. If that's the result of one melody on one flute, it means magic is spilling over into the science frame."

"So it seems. I'm sure my encounter with Clef was not coincidental. It was—foreordained. And my dream of his progress—there has to be some reason for that. I suspect he and I are destined to meet again."

"You could never stay out of mischief," she agreed. "Now it's time to get ready for your Tourney match."

"Did anyone ever tell you you are inhumanly practical? The end of the split infinity may be in the offing, and you pack me off to a Game."

"Your match is foreordained too," she said complacently.

CHAPTER 2

Backgammon

It was Round Thirteen of the annual Tourney. Only three players remained, two with one loss each. These two had to play each other; the loser would be eliminated from the Tourney, and the winner would meet the single undefeated player.

The two who played were as different as seemed possible. One was a huge, fat, middle-aged man in voluminous and princely robes inset with glittering gems. The other was a tiny naked man, muscular and fit, in his thirties.

"Ah, Stile," the clothed man said affably. "I was hoping to encounter you."

"You know of me, sir?"

"I always research my prospective opponents, serf. You have been extremely busy recently. You have been chasing around the landscape, crashing vehicles, and disappearing between Rounds."

Stile was noncommittal. "My time between Rounds is my own, sir."

"Except for what that girl robot demands. Is it fun making time with a sexy machine?"

Stile knew the Citizen was trying to rattle him, to get him tangled up emotionally so that he could not concentrate properly on the Game. It was a familiar technique. Stile could not return the favor because all Citizens were virtually anonymous to serfs, and in any event a serf could not treat a Citizen with disrespect. So Stile would have to take it—and play his best regardless. He was experienced at this sort of thing; the Citizen would probably rattle himself before he got to Stile.

It was time for the grid. Each man stood on one side of the unit, looking at the screen. There were sixteen boxes facing Stile, labeled across the top: 1. PHYSICAL 2. MENTAL 3. CHANCE 4. ARTS, and down the side: A. NAKED B. TOOL C. MACHINE D. ANIMAL. Stile's panel was lighted by the letters.

"That was a very neat stunt you worked, last Round," the Citizen remarked. "Making that Amazon throw away her win. Of course you know you won't be able to trick *me* that way."

"Of course not, sir." Stile touched the TOOL indication. That was his line of greatest strength.

The subgrid showed: 3B, Tool-Assisted Chance. Stile groaned inwardly. The CHANCE column was the bane of good players. It was difficult to make his skill count here.

"You don't like it, huh?" the Citizen taunted. "Figure it to come up another slot machine, wash you out painlessly, eh?"

This man really had researched Stile's prior Games of the Tourney. The lone Game Stile had lost had been just that way. "I am not partial to it, sir." As long as he handled the needling without heat, he was gaining.

"Well, I'm partial to it! Know why? Because I'm lucky. Try me on poker, Stile; I'll come up with a full house and tromp you. Try me on blackjack; I'm all twenty-ones. The breaks always go my way! That scares you, huh?"

The Citizen protested too much. That could indicate weakness—or could be a ruse. Stile actually could handle himself in games of chance; often there was more skill than showed. He would try for a suitable variant. "Luck is impartial, sir."

"You believe that? You fool! Try me on dice, if you doubt!"

Stile made his selection. The Citizen had already made his. The third grid showed: Board Games of Chance.

"Okay, sucker, try me on Monopoly!" the Citizen urged.

But when they played it through, it came up backgammon. "My favorite!" the Citizen exclaimed. "Dice and betting! Watch me move!"

Stile thought he was bluffing. That bluff would be called. Stile was expert at backgammon. It was only technically a game of luck; skill was critical.

They adjourned to the boardroom. The table was ready.

There was no physical audience; the holograph would take care of that.

"Now you know this game represents a year," the Citizen said. "Twenty-four points for the hours of the day, thirty pieces for the days of the month, twelve points in each half-section for the months in the year."

"And the seven spots on the opposites of a die are the days of the week," Stile said. "The two dice are day and night. It hardly matches the symbolism of the ordinary deck of playing cards or the figures of the chess set—sir."

They were playing a variant deriving in part from Acey-Deucy, traditionally a navy game. The games of Mother Earth had continued to evolve in the fashion of human society, with some variants prospering and others becoming extinct. In this one, no pieces were placed on the board at the start; all started from the bar.

It was not necessary to enter all fifteen pieces on the board before advancing the leaders. Yet it was still backgammon, the "back game," with pieces constantly being sent back to the bar while they ran the gauntlet of opposing pieces. People were apt to assume that a given game had an eternally fixed set of rules, when in fact there were endless variations. Stile had often obtained an advantage by steering a familiar game into an unfamiliar channel.

The Citizen was, as he claimed, lucky. He won the lead, then forged ahead with double sixes, while Stile had to settle for a two-to-one throw of the dice. Doubles were valuable in backgammon, because each die could be used twice. Thus the citizen's throw enabled him to enter four men to the sixth point, while Stile entered only two. This continued fairly steadily; the Citizen soon had all fifteen men entered and well advanced, while Stile was slower.

Soon the two forces interacted. The Citizen hit the first blot—in layman's language, he placed one of his men on the spot occupied by one of Stile's men. That sent Stile's man home to the bar, the starting place. "Sent you home to your slut machine, didn't I?" he chortled. "Oh, let there be no moaning at the bar!"

That was a literary allusion to an ancient poem by Tennyson of Earth. Stile was conversant with historical literature, but made no response. The Citizen was showing pseudoerudition; he was not the type to know any but the most fashionable of quotes, and he had gotten this one wrong. The correct line was, "and may there be no moaning of the bar." Yet, mentally, Stile filled in the remainder: "when I put out to sea." Tennyson had then been late in life, knowing he would die before too long. That poem, *Crossing the Bar*, had been a kind of personal epitaph. When he put out to sea, in the figurative fashion of the Norse boats for the dead, he hoped to see his Pilot, the Deity, face to face. Those left behind in life should feel no sorrow for him, for he, like the werewolf, had found his ideal resting place. It was generally best to read the full works of past literary figures, and to understand their backgrounds, rather than to memorize quotes out of context. But it was no use to go into all that with this great boor and bore of a Citizen.

Well, Stile intended to send this obnoxious Citizen out to sea. It was already apparent that the man was not a top player; he depended on his luck too heavily, and on a basic strategy of "making" points—of setting up two or more men on a point, so that the opponent could neither land there nor hit a blot. Luck and conservative play—a good enough strategy for most occasions. Three out of four times, a winning strategy.

But Stile was not an ordinary player. He depended not on luck but on skill. Luck tended to equalize, especially on an extended series, while skill was constant. That was what gave the superior player the advantage, even in a game of chance. It was necessary to take risks in order to progress most efficiently. There would be some losses because of these risks, but, overall, that efficiency would pay off. Stile was already grasping the weakness of the Citizen's mode of play. Probably the man had an imperfect notion of the strategy of the doubling cube—and that could make all the difference, regardless of his vaunted luck.

Soon the Citizen had a number of men in his home board, ready to be borne off. The first player who bore off all fifteen men would win the game, but not necessarily the Round. This modification was scored by points; each man left in play when the opponent finished was one point. One hundred points was the Game. It could take several games to accumulate the total. The key was to minimize one's losses in a losing game, and maximize one's winnings in a winning game. That was where the doubling cube came in.

Best to test the man's level, however. Stile needed to have a very clear notion of his opponent's vulnerability, because the Citizen was not a complete duffer; he was just good enough to be dangerous. Luck did play an important part in backgammon, just as muscle did in wrestling; it had to be taken into account.

Stile rolled 3–2. As it happened, he was able to enter two men and hit blots on the second and third points. It was a good break, for the Citizen left few blots he could possibly avoid. Thus Stile's 2 and 3 dice canceled the effect of cumulative scores of twenty-one and twenty-two on the Citizen's dice. Stile was making his limited luck match the effect of his opponent's good luck. It was a matter of superior management.

But the Citizen was hardly paying attention to the moves. He was trying to undermine Stile's confidence, convinced that even in a game of chance, a person's certainty counted most. "A number of people have been wondering where you disappear to between Rounds, little man. You seem to walk down a certain service corridor, and never emerge at the far end. Hours or even days later you emerge, going the opposite direction. It is a food-machine service corridor, yet you show no sign of feasting. Now how can a man disappear from the board, like a piece being sent to the bar? It is a mystery."

Stile continued playing. "People enjoy mysteries, sir."

The dice rolled; the men advanced. The Citizen's luck held; he was gaining despite imperfect play. "Mysteries exist only to be resolved. It is possible that you have discovered something fantastic, like a curtain that separates fact from fantasy? That you pass through this invisible barrier to a world where you imagine you are important instead of insignificant?"

So the man had done fairly thorough research into Stile's Phaze existence too. Still, Stile refused to be baited. "No doubt, sir."

"And can it really be true that in that fantasy you ride a

unicorn mare and associate with vampires and were-wolves?"

"In fantasy, anything is possible," Stile said.

"Double," the Citizen said, turning the doubling cube to two.

Now the game drew to a close. The Citizen finished first; Stile was left with eight men on the board. Doubled, that was sixteen points against him.

They set up for the second game, since they were not yet close to the one hundred points necessary for the finish. The Citizen was obnoxiously affable; he liked winning. Stile hoped he would get careless as well as overconfident. With luck, the Citizen might even distract himself at a key time by his determined effort to unnerve Stile.

Still, the Citizen's luck held. The man played indifferently, even poorly at times, but the fortune of the dice sustained him. When he had a clear advantage, he doubled, and Stile had to accept or forfeit the game. Then Stile had a brief run of luck—actually, skillful exploitation of the game situation—and doubled himself. "Double!" the Citizen said immediately when his own turn came, determined to have the last word and confident in his fortune. Now the doubling cube stood at eight.

"I understand a little squirt like you can use magic to snare some mighty fine-looking women," the Citizen said as they played. "Even if they're taller than you."

"Many women are," Stile agreed. References to his height did irritate him, but he had long since learned to conceal this. He was 1.5 meters tall, or an inch shy of five feet, in the archaic nomenclature of Phaze.

The Citizen's infernal luck continued. There did seem to be something to his claim about being lucky; he had certainly had far superior throws of the dice, and in this game, supervised by the Game Computer, there could be no question of cheating. He was winning this game too, by a narrower margin than the last, but the eight on the doubling cube gave every piece magnified clout. The Citizen liked to double; maybe it related to his gambling urge.

"I guess there could be one really luscious doll who nevertheless married a dwarf," the Citizen observed with a smirk. "I guess she could have been ensorcelled."

"Must have been." But despite his refusal to be baited about his recent marriage to the Lady Blue, Stile was losing. If this special ploy did not work, he would wash out of the Tourney. If only the luck would even out!

"Or maybe she has a hangup about midgets. Sort of like miscegenation. Some people get turned on that way."

The Citizen was really trying! But Stile played on calmly. "Some do, I understand."

"Or maybe pederasty. She likes to do it with children."

But the effect of that malicious needle was abated by the Citizen's choice of the wrong concept. It was generally applicable to the sexual motive of a male, not a female. Still, Stile would gladly have dumped this oaf down a deep well.

Stile lost this game too, down six men. Forty-eight more points against him, a cumulative total of sixty-four. Another game like this would finish him.

The luck turned at last and he won one. But he had only been able to double it once, and only picked up six points. Then the Citizen won again: eight men, redoubled, for thirty-two points. The score now stood at 96–6. The next game could finish it.

Still the Citizen's amazing luck held. Had he, after all, found some way to cheat, to fix the dice? Stile doubted it; the Tourney precautions were too stringent, and this was an important game, with a large audience. The throws had to be legitimate. Science claimed that luck evened out in the long run; it was difficult to prove that in backgammon.

Stile's situation was desperate. Yet there were ways. Stile knew how to play the back game specialty, and now was the time. When his position looked good, he doubled; when the Citizen was clearly ahead, *he* doubled. But the Citizen retained a general advantage, so Stile's doublings seemed foolish.

Stile used the back game to interfere with the Citizen's establishment on his home board. Because most of Stile's men had been relegated to the bar, he had them in ready position to attack the Citizen's men as they lined up for bearing off. This sort of situation could be a lot more volatile than many people thought. "Double," Stile said, turning the cube.

"You're crazy," the Citizen said, redoubling in his turn. Stile hit another blot. He needed more than this to recover a decent position, but it helped.

The Citizen threw double sixes. That moved his blotted man all the way from the bar to one space from the end. His luck was still more than sufficient to swamp whatever breaks Stile managed.

Stile doubled again, though he was still obviously behind. The Citizen, when his turn came, laughed and doubled once more. Now the cube stood at sixty-four, its maximum. "You really want to go down big, tyke!"

They were reduced to five men each; the rest had been borne off. The game was actually much closer than the Citizen realized. Stile had already won the advantage he sought. If the game had proceeded with only Stile's first doubling, and he won by two men, all he would have would be four more points. If he lost by the same margin, however, the Citizen's four points would put him at one hundred for final victory. But now the cube stood at sixty-four, so that a two-man win by the Citizen would give him the same victory by an unnecessary margin—while the same win by Stile would give him 128 points, at one stroke enough for his final victory. So he had in effect evened it up. Instead of being behind by ninety points, he had only to win two points. The Citizen had been foolish to permit the doubling to go to this level; he had thrown away a major advantage.

"I hear some of these animals can change to human form," the Citizen said. "I guess an animal in the form of a woman could be a lot of fun to a lonely man."

Was there anything this slob did not know about Phaze, or any limit to his crudity of insinuation? Stile allowed a little ire to show, deliberately. "It is a different frame, sir, with different natural laws. Those animals have human intelligence."

The Citizen gleefully pounced on this. "So you *have* sampled the wares of the mares and the britches of the bitches!" He was hardly paying attention to the backgammon game in his voyeuristic lust. He wanted to make Stile angry and, in seeming success, he was letting the means preempt the ends. This was always ethically prob-

lematical, and often strategically unsound. The Citizen
was setting himself up for a fall. If only the luck evened
out!

Stile had a good roll of the dice. He hit two blots, and
the Citizen hardly noticed. "I don't see that it is any of
your business, sir, no disrespect intended."

"With animals!" the Citizen exclaimed, smiling broadly.
"You admit it!"

"I don't deny it, sir," Stile said, obviously nettled.

"And did they bother to change form each time?" the
Citizen demanded, almost drooling. He was hardly looking
at the board, playing automatically and poorly. "Maybe
sometimes a bitch stayed in her dog-form, just for the
novelty?"

Stile wondered just what sort of bestiality lurked in the
secret dreams of this nasty man. Perhaps this was the
phenomenon of projection, in which a person with illicit
desires projected the realization of certain acts onto others.
The Citizen was giving himself away without realizing it.

Stile continued to parry him verbally, taking the worst
of it, though he had the ability to reverse the onus at any
time. He was tacitly egging the man on. Meanwhile, he
exploited the rolls of the dice skillfully, and soon had
gained a net advantage. The Citizen could have prevented
this, had he been paying similar attention. But his morbid
fascination with Stile's supposed exploits with shape-chang-
ing females had done him in. By the time he became
aware of the trap, it was too late; even his amazing luck
could not make up for his squandered opportunities.

They entered the final stage, and both resumed bearing
off men. For once Stile had better throws of the dice, and
finished two men ahead.

It took a moment for the Citizen to absorb the significance. He had been so far ahead, he knew subjectively
that it would take a prohibitively massive turn of fortune
to deprive him of victory. No such turn had occurred.
Now his eyes fixed on the number 64 at the top of the
doubling cube, and he saw that this narrow margin of two
pieces had at one stroke washed him out of the Tourney.

"You must visit Phaze some day, sir," Stile said brightly.
"I know just the bitch for you."

CHAPTER 3

Honeymoon

Stile crossed the curtain at the usual place, emerging from the food-servicing hall to the deep forest of Phaze. In a moment a unicorn trotted up. But it wasn't Neysa. This one was slightly larger, male, and his coat was deep dark blue except for the two red socks on his hind feet.

"Clip!" Stile exclaimed, surprised. "I expected—"

The unicorn metamorphosed into a young man garbed in blue shirt, furry trousers, red socks, floppy hat, gloves, and boots. His resemblance to the unicorn was clear to anyone conversant with the forms. "She's off getting bred, at long last. The Herd Stallion's keeping her with the herd until she foals. That's S.O.P."

"Yes, of course," Stile agreed, disappointed. He found his hidden clothes and dressed quickly; it would not do to travel naked here, though there was really no firm convention. He wanted only the best for Neysa, his best friend in this frame, yet he felt empty without her company. But he had made a deal with the Herd Stallion to release her for breeding when his mission of vengeance was finished; now that he had dispatched the Red Adept, it was time. Time for relaxation, recovery, and love. Time to be with the lovely Lady Blue.

"That was the funniest thing," Clip said, evidently following the thrust of Stile's thoughts. "Thou didst marry the Lady, then skipped off without even—"

"An idiosyncracy of the situation," Stile said shortly. He had departed without consummating the marriage because of a prophecy that he would have a son by the Lady Blue; he knew he would survive the dangerous mission ahead of him if he only waited to generate that child thereafter, since such prophecies had the force of law. But

31

now the barbs of the ugly Citizen were fresh in his mind, making this subject sensitive. "You're volunteering to be my mount?"

"Neysa intimated gently that I'd get horned at the wrong end if I didn't," Clip admitted. "Besides, thou dost have interesting adventures."

"I'm only going to honeymoon with my wife."

"That's what I mean." Clip shifted to his natural form, his horn playing with the sound of a saxophone—a bar of the wedding march, trailing into a tune with risqué connotations.

Stile jumped on the unicorn's back, landing deliberately hard. Clip blew out one more startled note and took off. The velocity of the unicorn was greater than that of the horse because it was enhanced by magic; yet the two types of creatures were closely akin. As Clip himself had put it, once: as close as men were to apes. Stile was uncertain what freighting accompanied that statement, but had never challenged it. Man had intelligence and science the ape lacked; unicorns had intelligence and magic the horses lacked.

Soon they emerged from the forest and were racing over the fields toward the moated castle that was the heart of the Blue Demesnes. "Dost thou happen to know how Clef from Proton fared?" Stile inquired. "I gave him the Platinum Flute and sent him to the Little Folk, but I've been too busy to follow further. I'm sure you're up on all the news."

Clip blew an affirmative note. He was the gossipy kind.

"Did Clef arrive safely?" Stile was interested in verifying the accuracy of his dream. The frames had always been firmly separated; if his dream were true, it meant that that separation was beginning to fuzz, at least for him.

The unicorn sounded yes again. His sax-horn was more mellow than Neysa's harmonica-horn, though less clever on trills. Like her, he could almost speak in musical notes, making them sound like yes, no, maybe, and assorted other words, particularly colloquialisms. Actually, unicorns could express whole sentences in chords, but this was a separate mode that owed little to archaic English.

Stile was coming to understand that language too, but his grasp of it was as yet insecure.

"Was he—is he by any chance the one the Platinum Elves called the Foreordained?"

Again the affirmative.

"Then that earthquake—we felt it in Proton—that was the shaking of the mountains when he played?" But this had become rhetorical; he had the answer. The frames had certainly juxtaposed in this respect. "I wonder what that means?"

Now Clip had no answer. No one except the Little Folk of the Mound knew the significance of the Foreordained. And the all-knowing Oracle, who answered only one question in the lifetime of each querist.

Yet the arrival of the Foreordained suggested that the end of Phaze was near, according to another prophecy. That bothered Stile; he had worked so hard to secure his place here. Was he to be denied it after all?

Well, he was determined to snatch what joy he might, in what time remained. On the cosmic scale, the end might be centuries distant. Magic prophecies were devious things, not to be trusted carelessly. People had died depending on misinterpreted omens.

That brought him back to the manner in which he had secured his own fortune by postponing his fathering of a son. He was eager to get on with it. He had loved the Lady Blue from the first time he had encountered her. He had never before met such a regal, intelligent, and desirable woman. But she was the widow of his other self, and that had made things awkward. Now she was his, and he would never leave her—except for one more necessary trip to the frame of Proton, to try for the final Round of the Tourney. It really was not as important to him as it once had seemed, but he had to give it his best try.

They galloped up to the prettily moated little castle. Stile vaulted off as they entered the courtyard. The Lady Blue, his vision of delight, rushed to his arms. She was of course garbed in blue: headdress, gown, slippers. She was all that he desired.

"Are we ready?" he inquired when the initial sweetness of the embrace eased.

"I have been ready since we wed, but thou didst depart in haste," she said, teasing him.

"Never again, Lady!"

"Hinblue is saddled."

"We have already traveled much of the eastern curtain. Shall we pick up at the Platinum Demesnes?"

She did not reproach him about his concern for Clef's welfare, the obvious reason to pass the region of the Little Folk. "As my Lord Blue desires."

"Wilt thou condone magic for the start?"

She nodded radiantly. "Magic is the substance of my Lord Adept."

They mounted their steeds, and Stile played his good harmonica, summoning his magic. His Adept talent was governed by music and words, the music shaping the power, the words the application. Actually, his mind was the most important factor; the words mainly fixed the time of implementation. "Conduct us four," he sang, "to the platinum shore."

Clip snorted through his horn: *shore?*

But the magic was already taking hold. The four of them seemed to dissolve into liquid, sink into the ground, and flow rapidly along and through it south-southeast. In a moment they re-formed beside the Mound of the Platinum Elves. There was the fresh cairn of Serrilryan the were-bitch, exactly as his vision-dream had shown it.

"Anything I visualize as a shore, is a shore," Stile explained. "There does not have to be water." But as it happened, there was some cloud cover here, thickest in the lower reaches, so that the descending forest disappeared into a sealike expanse of mist. They stood on a kind of shore. Almost, he thought he saw wolf shapes playing on the surface of that lake of mist.

"And we were conducted—like the electricity of Proton-frame," the Lady commented. "Methought thou wouldst provide us with wings to fly."

A dusky elf, garbed in platinum armor to shield his body from a possible ray of sunlight, appeared. He glanced up at Stile. "Welcome, Blue Adept and Lady," he said.

"Thy manner of greeting has improved since last we visited," the Lady Blue murmured mischievously.

"As well it might have," the elf agreed. "We know thee now."

He showed them into the Mound. Stile noted that the structure had been hastily repaired, with special shorings. Evidently the destruction wrought by the Foreordained's Flute had not entirely demolished it. Stile hoped there had not been much loss of life in the collapse. Clip and Hinblue remained outside to graze the verdant, purple-tinted turf.

A deeply darkened and wrinkled elf awaited them inside. This was Pyreforge, chief of this tribe of Dark Elves. "Thy friend is indeed the Foreordained," he said gravely. "Our trust in thee has been amply justified."

"Now wilt thou tell the meaning?" Stile inquired. "We are on our honeymoon. Yet my curiosity compels."

"Because thou art on thy honeymoon, I will tell thee only part," the old elf said. "Too soon wilt thou learn the rest."

"Nay! If it is to be the end of Phaze, I must know now."

"It be not necessarily the end, but perhaps only a significant transition. That much remains opaque. But the decision is near—a fortnight hence, perhaps, no more than two. Take thy pleasure now, for there will come thy greatest challenge."

"There is danger to my Lord Blue?" the Lady asked worriedly.

"To us all, Lady. How could we survive if our frame be doomed?"

"We can not head it off?" Stile asked.

"It will come in its own time. Therefore put it from thy mind; other powers are moving."

Stile saw that Pyreforge would not answer directly on this subject, and the elf could not be pushed. "The Foreordained—what is his part in this? A title like that—"

"Our titles hardly relate to conventional human mythology or religion. This one merely means he was destined to appear at this time, when the curtain grows visible and tension mounts between the frames. The great Adepts of the past foresaw this crisis and foreordained this duty."

"What duty?" Stile asked. "Clef is merely a musician. A

fine one, granted, the best I know—but no warrior, no Adept. What can he do?"

"No Adept?" Pyreforge snorted. "As well claim the Platinum Flute be no instrument! He can play the dead to Heaven and crumble mountains by his melody—and these be only the fringes of his untrained power. Once we have trained him to full expertise—he is the Foreordained!"

So Earth mythology might not relate, but the implication of significance did. "So he is, after all, Adept? He seemed ordinary to me—but perhaps I did not hear him play in Phaze."

Pyreforge smiled wryly. "Thou didst hear him, Adept. Music relates most intimately to magic, as thou shouldst know."

So the elf knew of Stile's vision! "And Clef is the finest musician to come to Phaze," Stile said, seeing it. "But what exactly is he to do? May we say hello to him?"

"You may not," the old elf said. This usage always sounded incongruous to Stile here, where "thee" and "thou" were standard—but of course it was the correct plural form. "His power be enormous, but he be quite new to it and has much to learn and little time ere he master his art. We need no more shaking of our mountains! He be deep in study for the occasion he must attend and may not be disturbed."

"What occasion?" Stile asked with growing frustration.

But still the elf would not respond directly. "Thou shalt meet him when it be time, Lord Blue, and all will be clarified. Leave us to teach the Foreordained his music. Go now on thy honeymoon; thou must recuperate and restore thine own powers for the effort to come."

So it seemed. They were teaching Clef music? This was either humor or amazing vanity! Disgruntled, Stile thanked the diminutive, wrinkled elf and departed. "I don't feel comfortable being ignorant of great events, especially when there are hints they relate intimately to me," he muttered to the Lady.

"How dost thou think I felt, cooped up in the Blue Demesnes whilst thou didst go out to live or die?"

"I don't recall thy staying cooped long—"

"Let's ride, my Lord."

Stile smiled. She had the feminine way of changing the subject when pressed. She was not a woman to let fate roll over her unchallenged, and her present deference to him was merely part of the honeymoon. Had he desired a creature to honor his every foible, he would have loved Sheen. The Lady Blue would always be someone to reckon with.

They mounted and rode. Pyreforge was right: the curtain was brighter now, faintly scintillating as it angled across the slopes of the Purple Mountains. It followed the contours of the terrain in its fashion; the curtain extended vertically until it became too faint for them to see, and evidently continued below the ground similarly. As the land fell away, it exposed more of the curtain. There was no gap; the curtain was continuous.

That was what intrigued Stile—that ubiquitous transition between frames. The landscapes of Proton and Phaze were identical, except that Proton was a barren, polluted world where science was operative, while Phaze was a fresh, verdant world of magic. Only those people who lacked alternate selves in the other frame could cross between them. No one seemed to know why or how the curtain was there, or what its mode of operation was. It just served as the transition between frames, responsive to a wish from one side, a spell from the other.

They intended to follow the curtain in its generally westward extension until it terminated at the West Pole. Stile had been increasingly curious about the curtain, and the West Pole held a special fascination for him because it didn't exist on any other world he knew. Now he had an excuse to satisfy both interests—by making them part of his honeymoon.

As the Blue Adept, he was one of the most powerful magicians in Phaze; riding a unicorn—ah, he missed Neysa!—he had some of the best transportation and protection available; and in the company of the lovely Lady Blue—oh, what an occasion this would be!

"I want to make a map," he said, remembering. "A map of Phaze, as I know it now and as I will discover it, and of the curtain in all its curvatures."

"The curtain is straight," the Lady said.

"Straight? It meanders all over the frame!"

"Nay, Lord, it is the frame that meanders," she assured him. "When we follow the curtain, we bear due west."

Stile decided not to argue. After all, she was his new bride and she was heart-throbbingly delightful, and an argument at this time would be awkward. Nevertheless, he would map Phaze as he perceived it.

He played his harmonica, bringing the magic to him. Then he set the instrument aside and sang: "Place on tap a contour map."

True to his visualization, the map appeared—a neatly folded pseudo-parchment. He opened it out and contemplated its lines and colors. There were the White Mountains to the north, the Purple Mountains to the south, the sites of the Blue, Black, Yellow, White, Brown, and—former—Red Demesnes, and the curtain winding around and between them. Contour lines indicated the approximate elevations.

But there were sizable blank areas. This map covered only the territory Stile knew. He had traveled around a lot of Phaze recently, but there was more to explore. He expected to enjoy filling in the rest of this map. The plotting of the curtain should take care of much of it, since it meandered—went straight?—past most of the significant establishments of this frame.

"No one uses a map in Phaze," the Lady protested, intrigued.

"I am not from Phaze," he retorted. He showed her the map. "Now as I make it, the curtain should bear west a day's leisurely travel, then veer north here to pass the palace of the Oracle and on by the Yellow Demesnes near the White Mountains. That will be a couple days' ride. Then it must curve southwest to intersect the Black Demesnes here—"

"The curtain is straight," she repeated.

"Humor me, beloved. Then on until we reach the West Pole, somewhere over here. The whole trip should take a week, which will leave us—"

"Thou art a fool," she said pleasantly. "Little thou knowest of Phaze."

"That's why I'm exploring it," he agreed. "Thou art wife of a fool, fool."

She leaned toward him, and her mount obligingly closed the gap. They kissed, riding side by side, while Clip played another suggestive tune. Stile gave the unicorn a sharp little kick in the flank with his left heel. Clip emitted a blast of musical laughter with an undertone of Bronx cheer and flicked his tail across Stile's back in the familiar fly-swatting gesture.

"Now let's move," Stile said as the kiss ended.

The two steeds broke into a canter, following the curtain down the hill, through a valley, and up a wooded slope. Stile loved riding; it was the thing he did best. The Lady paralleled him, balancing smoothly, her hair flying out in a golden splay. She, too, was a fine rider and she had a fine steed, though no horse could match a unicorn in full exertion. Stile probably could have borrowed another unicorn from the herd, but there had been no point. This was no dangerous mission, but a gentle romance. Hinblue was a very good mare, the offspring of the Blue Stallion and the Hinny—the best equine heritage in Phaze. Stile remained sorry his friend Neysa was not here to share the trip with him—but realized that Neysa might be jealous of the Lady Blue, with some reason. Maybe Neysa's breeding had been mostly a pretext to separate herself from this excursion. Well, Clip was good, if spirited, company.

Time passed. The curtain veered to the south, forcing them to cross over the height of the Purple range, rather than at any natural pass. Their steeds slowed to a walk, and the air became chill. There was no snow here, but the vegetation turned bluish as if from cold, and then full purple. That was what gave the range its color, of course; he should have known. Finally Stile cast a spell to make them warm—himself and the Lady and the two animals—so that no one would have to overexert to maintain body heat.

Then, on the steep downslope, he cast another spell to enable them all to float through the air, resting. A harpy popped out of a hole in a cliff, saw the two equines with their riders, all drifting blithely in midair, and popped hastily back into her hole. "Just as well," the Lady Blue remarked. "That creature's scratch is poisonous, and they oft resent intrusion into their demesnes."

Clip snorted. Unicorns were invulnerable to most magic and had no fear of harpies. Stile, remembering how the werebitch Serrilryan had died, knew that if the harpy had attacked, he would have reacted with ferocity perhaps unbecoming to this occasion.

Then they passed the cliffside nest of a griffin. Three cubs poked their beaks up to peer at the weird procession. In the distance there was the birdlike scream of an adult, probably the mother, aware that her babies were being disturbed. A griffin was a fighting animal, almost as fierce as a dragon; unicorns did not normally seek combat with this species. Stile, of course, could handle it—but he elected to hasten their descent, getting well away from the nest before the mother griffin appeared. Why seek trouble?

At the southern foot of the range an extensive plain commenced. Evening was approaching, and in the slanting sunlight they saw shapes in the sky like grotesque birds. "Dragons," the Lady Blue murmured. "This is dragon country."

"If any come for us, we'll simply step across the curtain," Stile said. Again it was easier to avoid than to fight; he had no desire to waste magic or to prove his power. A unicorn, a werewolf, or a vampire could change forms as often as it wished, because that was inherent in such creatures' nature, while Stile could use a particular spell only once. When he had to, he could accomplish more by magic than any other creature and could change one creature to another—but eventually he would run out of new spells. Magic was best saved for true emergencies.

"What of Hinblue?" the Lady asked.

"Um, yes. Maybe she can cross the curtain too."

"She could not survive in Proton-frame. There is no good air there, no grazing. And what of thine own mount?"

"Have no fear for me, Lady," Clip said, changing to man-form. "As a hawk, I can escape. But I cannot cross the curtain. In Proton I would be reduced to but a horse, and unable to cross back."

"Then I will use magic if the need arises," Stile decided.

"My lord, there is no time like the present," the Lady said. For a shape was winging toward them.

Stile had made up and memorized a number of spells, including some dragon restraints. In this case he would simply cause the dragon to forget it had seen anything interesting here.

But as the creature flew closer, Stile squinted at it. This was a peculiar dragon. The wings were wrong, the tail, the head—

"Why, that's no dragon," the Lady said.

Clip snapped his fingers. "That's a thunderbird! I didn't know there were any left in these parts."

"I don't have a specific spell for thunderbirds," Stile said dubiously. "I'll have to go to a general one."

"No need," the Lady said. "The bird is full of sound and fury—"

The creature swooped close, its wings spreading hugely, then sweeping together in a deafening clap of thunder.

"Signifying rain," Clip finished, as the drenchpour commenced.

Hastily Stile spelled into existence a large tent, already set up and guyed. The rain beat down on its canvas so heavily that he had to spell additional supports. Water seeped under the edges, and fog drifted through, coating them with condensation. A little frog appeared and croaked contentedly.

The other three were with him, but soon Clip returned to unicorn-form and moved outside to graze; the rain did not bother his equine form very much. Hinblue followed him out; grazing was always worthwhile, and the dragons would avoid this storm.

That left the Lady Blue. Stile turned to her. "I had thought of sunshine and sweet music for this occasion. Still—"

"Desist thy stalling," she said, and opened her arms.

Thereafter, the storm disappeared from his consciousness. It was a long, ecstatic night. In the morning he woke in a fine bed of hay and feathers, so concluded he must have done some incidental conjuring, but none of that

remained in his memory. He had only his awareness of the
Lady Blue—his woman at last.

There was a neat pile of assorted fruits at the tent
entrance; Clip had evidently scouted around in the night
and harvested what he thought was appropriate. At the top
of the mound was passion fruit, and below were apples,
cherries, and bananas. Symbolistic humor of the equine
kind. They had an excellent meal.

They resumed their ride. Clip had the sense not to play
any more ribald melodies on his sax-horn, but on occasion
he could not quite contain a faint musical snigger.

The curtain wandered back up the slope of the mountains, having no regard for the convenience of travelers—
as well it might not; Stile's party was probably the first to
make this particular trek. Here on the southern side, flowers of many colors abounded, and the bushes and trees
were highly varied. Birds flitted, and squirrels and rabbits
scurried. On occasion a grassy round trapdoor would open
and a little head would pop out—hermit-elves, harmless.

Then they came to a river. It cut across the curtain,
deep and swift—and a formidable steam-breathing water
dragon inhabited it.

They halted, eyeing the monster. The monster eyed them
back. Slowly a purple tongue came out and moistened its
chops. The mere sight of them made this creature salivate.
This hardly seemed a safe passage.

Stile pondered which spell to use. Immobilization
seemed best; he didn't want to hurt this animal. Yet that
was such a useful spell for emergencies that he hated to
use it routinely. Again he was up against the ad hoc nature
of magic; once any specific spell was used, it was gone. All
Adepts used magic sparingly, never squandering it. Stile, a
relative newcomer to the art, tended to use it more freely
than was wise; the novelty had not yet worn off. Until
recently, there had been so many challenges to his well-
being that he had hardly worried about wasting spells;
what use to save them for a nonexistent future?

Now he was a fairly secure married man, becoming
daily more conservative. So he pondered: Was there any
mundane way to pass by this dragon? The creature was

limited to the water, having flippers in lieu of wings and frogs' feet. This was, after all, a very restricted threat.

Again the Lady's thoughts were parallel to his own. She had an uncanny insight into his mind, perhaps because she had had much longer experience with him than he had had with her, odd as that might seem in any other frame than this. He had in fact been momentarily dismayed during the night by her almost-too-ready anticipation of his desires; none of this was really new to her. "It would be a long trek around the river, methinks, for the dragon would pace us. Clip could change to hawk-form and fly safely across, but Hinblue has no such magic."

"This becomes a challenge," Stile said. "For most of my life I existed without the benefit of magic. A year ago I would have found a way across without sorcery; I should be able to do it now."

"Though it take but a fortnight," she murmured, smiling.

"The curtain—" Stile began, but cut that off. He kept forgetting Hinblue!

"Put my steed not through that torture gratuitously," the Lady agreed.

Clip changed to man-form. "Thou wilt be all day on this. I can get us across now."

"Oh?" Stile asked, not entirely pleased. "How?"

"By decoying this dragon downstream while the three of you swim. The average dragon is not smart enough for that ruse."

Of course! Simplicity itself. "Thou are smarter than I, today," Stile said ruefully.

"Naturally. I'm a unicorn," Clip said generously. "I did not dissipate my strength all night in pointless heroics." He changed back to his usual form and snorted insultingly at the dragon, adding an obnoxious gesture with his horn. Unicorns could convey considerable freighting in this manner. The dragon oriented on him, steam pressure building up, measuring the distance it might strike.

Clip stayed just out of range, trotting downstream with a lewd swish of his tail. He played a few bars of music, and Stile could just about make out the words: "The worms crawl in, the worms crawl out . . ." Dragons were the

monarchs of the kingdom of worms, and were sensitive to
such disparaging references. This dragon followed Clip
briskly, hoping the unicorn would stray just within range
of fang or steam.

Soon Stile and the Lady stripped and swam safely
across with Hinblue, holding their garments aloft. They
were, after all, prevailing without magic.

"This is fun," Stile murmured, contemplating her body
in the clear water. "Shall we dally a bit?"

"Until the dragon joins the party?" she inquired sweetly.

They climbed out at the far bank and shook themselves
dry in the sun. Stile tried not to stare; this was a type of
motion he had never seen done by a woman of her construction, though he had lived most of his life in a society
of nudity.

There was a small coughing sound. Both Stile and the
Lady turned—and discovered the dragon was watching
too, its labile lips pursed into the semblance of a whistle.

Stile experienced a rapidly developing emotion. He tried
to control it, but in a moment it overwhelmed him. It was
mirth. He burst out laughing. "Oh, I'll bet that monster
doesn't see what I see!"

The Lady looked down at herself, frowning. "It
doesn't?"

"It sees the most delicious morsel in two frames. I
see—"

"Never mind what thou seest," she said with mock se-
verity. "I take thy meaning." She was neither self-
conscious nor angry. She had one of the finest bodies in
the frame and knew it.

A hawk arrived, swooping low and converting to
unicorn-form. Clip was ready to resume the journey.

Soon the curtain veered north, crossing the mountain
range again. Fortunately this occurred at a natural pass, so
they were able to get past expeditiously.

They emerged into the rolling countryside that was the
main grazing range of the unicorns. Now progress was
swift—but the distance was long. They were not yet near
the Oracle's palace before night overtook them and forced
another halt.

Again the animals grazed, and Stile was about to conjure another tent when the Lady stayed him. "Expend not thy magic superfluously, my Lord. Tonight the open sky suffices for us."

"If that is what thou dost desire, that is what thou shalt have," he agreed. He gathered straw and moss to fashion a bed, and they lay down side by side and looked up at the moons.

"Oh, see—the blue moon rises!" she cried, squeezing his hand.

"Our moon," he agreed. This was sheer delight, being with her, sharing her incidental pleasures.

"Oh, play, my Lord, play," she begged.

Obediently Stile found his harmonica and brought it to his mouth. But something stayed him—an ominous though not unpleasant feeling. He concentrated and placed it. "It was not far from here that I first found this instrument, or thought I found it. Here in the open, riding with Neysa. I conjured it without knowing."

"It is all that remains of my former Lord," she said. "His music and power have since found lodging in thee. Great was my grief at his loss, yet greater is my joy in thee."

"Still it bothers me how he died. Surely he could have saved himself, had he tried."

She stiffened. "I told thee how the demon amulet choked him, so that he could make neither music nor spell."

"Aye. But was not this harmonica always with him?"

"Always. But he could not play it, either, if—"

"And the golem did not remove it?"

"Nay. It was gone ere the golem came."

"Then how did it get out here in the fields for me to conjure? Or, if it were not here, how did it get wherever it hid? It remained not at the Blue Demesnes."

"True," she agreed thoughtfully. "Long and long I searched for it, but it was not with his body."

"Which is strange," Stile said. "He might have conjured it away from him in the instant he knew he would die— but why then did he not use his magic to protect himself? And why did he deny thee the inheritance of his prize possession? Such malice was not his nature, I am sure."

For Stile himself would not have done that. Not without excellent reason.

"He could not have conjured it!" she said, disturbed.

"Then he must have placed it in the field, or hidden it elsewhere, before he died. And that suggests—"

"That he knew he was slated to die!" she exclaimed, shocked. "He deprived himself of his most valued possession. But even without it, no one could have killed him, were he on guard!"

"Unless he intended to permit it," Stile said.

Her shock turned to horror. "No! Nothing I did, no will of mine should have caused him—"

"Of course not," Stile agreed quickly. "He would never have done it because of thee."

"Then what is thine import?"

"That perhaps he knew something, received an omen, that caused him to accept what was coming."

She considered that for some time, her hand clenching and unclenching in his. "Yet what could possibly justify— what was fated?"

"I wish I knew." For Stile's own passage across the curtain had been enabled by that demise of his alternate self. If the Blue Adept had sought to eliminate his brand of magic from the frame, he had acted in vain, for Stile performed it now.

That night they did not make love. They lay and watched the blue moon, and Stile played gently on the mysterious harmonica, and it was enough. Slowly sleep overtook them.

"Be at ease," a man's voice came from nearby. "We have met before, Adept."

Stile controlled his reaction. He still held the harmonica; he could summon his power rapidly. In a moment he placed the half-familiar voice: "Yes, at the Unolympics, Green Adept." He did not want trouble with another Adept —especially not when the Lady Blue was close enough to be hurt by the fallout. He was as yet unable to see the man; probably Green had employed a spell of invisibility, with related obfuscations. Otherwise he could not have gotten by the alert equines.

"I come in peace. Wilt thou grant truce for a dialogue?"

"Certainly." Stile was relieved. By custom verging on law, Adepts did not deceive each other in such matters. What in Phaze could this man want with him at this time?

The Adept became visible. He was a pudgy man of middle age, garbed in green. He looked completely in-offensive—but was in fact one of the dozen most powerful people of Phaze. "Thank thee. I will intrude not long."

A hawk appeared silently behind the Adept. Stile gave no sign. He did not expect treachery, but if it came, there would suddenly be a unicorn's horn in action. If Clip attacked the Green Adept, he risked getting transformed into a clod of dung, but Stile knew he would take that risk if necessary. "Surely thou hast reason."

"It is this, Blue: my sources give thee warning. Go not to the West Pole. Great mischief lies there."

"There is no mischief there," the Lady Blue protested. "It is a sacred place, under truce, like the palace of the Oracle."

"Dost thou think no mischief lies with the Oracle?"

Stile chuckled. "Excellent point, Green. But the Lady and I are on our honeymoon, and our excursion to the West Pole has private significance. Canst thou be more explicit?"

"Why shouldst thou care if mischief comes to a rival Adept?" the Lady demanded. "Thou didst evince no concern, Green, when the life of Blue hung in peril before."

That was an understatement. No other Adept had lifted a finger or made a spell either to warn or to assist the Blue Adept in his severe crisis that had left two Adepts dead or ruined. This sudden concern was suspicious.

"Needs must I then elaborate," Green said heavily. "My Demesnes lie athwart thy route. I would let thee pass unscathed, knowing thy mission—but by that acquies-cence I commit myself to thy fate. This is not my desire. I want no part of what befalls thee. Go not to the West Pole—but an thou must go, then go not through the Green Demesnes."

That made sense. The Green Adept had no personal interest in Stile; he merely wanted to make certain he was not implicated in what happened to Stile. If a prophecy decreed doom to all who might facilitate Stile's approach to the West Pole, this step exonerated the Green Adept.

"Now I seek no trouble with thee," Stile began. "But the Lady and I planned to follow the curtain to its terminus, and—"

"And we can bypass the Green Demesnes, in the interest of courtesy," the Lady Blue finished.

Stile shrugged. "The Lady has spoken. Set out warners at thy boundaries, and we shall there detour."

"I shall," Green agreed. "Since thou dost humor my preference, I offer one final word: my sources suggest that if thou dost go to the West Pole, thou wilt suffer grievously in the short term, and in the moderate term will incur the enmity of the most powerful forces of the frame. I urge thee once more to give up this quest. There are other suitable places to honeymoon. The Green Demesnes themselves will be opened to thee, shouldst thou care to tarry there instead."

"I thank thee for thy advice," Stile said. "Yet it seems the end of Phaze draws nigh, and powerful forces already dispose themselves in readiness. The Foreordained has appeared. What is fated, is fated, and I am ready if not eager to play my part."

"As thou dost choose." The Green Adept made a signal with the fingers of his left hand and disappeared.

"I mislike these omens," the Lady said. "Methought our troubles were over."

"Loose ends remain, it seems. I had hoped we could let them be for at least this fortnight."

"Surely we can," she agreed, opening her arms to him. The hawk flew quietly away. The weapon of the unicorn had not, after all, been needed.

Next day they resumed the ride north. Stile made a small spell to enhance Hinblue's velocity and let Clip run at full speed. They fairly flew across the rolling terrain. Fire jetted from the unicorn's nostrils, and his hooves grew hot enough to throw sparks. Unicorns, being magic, did not sweat; they ejected surplus heat at the extremities.

After a time they slowed. Stile brought out his harmonica and played, Clip accompanied him on his saxophone-voiced horn, and the lady sang. The magic closed about them, seeming to thicken the air, but it had no force without Stile's verbal invocation.

"We can camp the night at the Yellow Demesnes," Stile said. "The curtain clips a corner of—"

"By no means!" the Lady snapped, and Clip snorted.

Stile remembered. She didn't like other Adepts, and Yellow liked to take a potion to convert herself from an old crone to a luscious young maid—without otherwise changing her nature. Also, her business was the snaring and selling of animals, including unicorns. Stile had traded magical favors with Yellow in the past and had come to respect her, but he could understand why his wife and steed preferred not to socialize.

"Anything for thee," he agreed. "However, night approaches and the White Mountains lie beyond."

"Indulge thyself in a spell, Adept."

"How soon the honeymoon turns to dull marriage," he grumbled. Clip made a musical snort of mirth, and the lady smiled.

The ramshackle premises of Yellow appeared. Both animals sniffed the air and veered toward the enclosure. Hastily Stile sang a counterspell: "This will cure the witch's lure." That enabled them to ignore the hypnotic vapor that drew animals in to capture and confinement. Before long they had skirted those premises and moved well on toward the termination of the plain to the north.

At dusk they came to the White Mountain range. Here the peaks rose straight out of the plain in defiance of normal geological principles; probably magic had been involved in their formation.

The curtain blithely traveled up the slope at a steep angle. It would have been difficult to navigate this route by daylight; at night the attempt would be foolhardy. "And there are snow-demons," the Lady said as an afterthought.

Stile pondered, then conjured a floating ski lift. It contained a heated stall for two equines, complete with a trough filled with fine grain, and a projecting shelf with several mugs of nutri-cocoa similar to what was available from a Proton food machine. Clip could have converted to hawk-form and flown up, but the cold would have hindered him, and this was far more comfortable. Unicorn and horse stepped into the stalls and began feeding, while Stile and the Lady mounted for their repast. Eating and sleeping while mounted was no novelty; it was part of the joy of Phaze.

They rode serenely upward as if drawn by an invisible cable. "Yet I wonder where this magic power comes from?" Stile mused. "I realize that the mineral Phazite is the power source for magic, just as its other-frame self, Protonite, is the basis for that scientific, energy-processing society. But why should certain people, such as the Adepts, channel that power better than others? Why should music and doggerel verse implement it for me, while the Green Adept needs special gestures and the White Adept needs mystic symbols? There is a certain channelization here that can not be coincidental. But if it is natural, what governs it? If it is artificial, who set it up?"

"Thou wert ever questioning the natural order," the Lady Blue said affectionately. "Asking whence came the Proton objects conjured to this frame, like the harmonica, and whether they were turning up missing from that frame, making us thieves."

So his other self had speculated similarly! "I wonder if I could conjure a source of information? Maybe a smart demon, like the one Yellow animates with a potion."

"Conjure not demons, lest they turn on thee," she warned, and Clip gave an affirmative blast on his horn.

"Yes, I suppose there are no shortcuts," Stile said. "But one way or another, I hope to find the answer."

"Mayhap that is why mischief lurks for thee at the West Pole," the Lady said, not facetiously. "Thou canst not let things rest, any more in this self than in thine other."

That was quite possible, he thought. It was likely to be the curious child with a screwdriver who poked into a power outlet and got zapped, while the passive child escaped harm. But man was a curious creature, and that insatiable appetite for knowledge had led him to civilization and the stars. Progress had its dangers, yet was necessary—

Something rattled against the side of the gondola stall,

startling them. Clip shifted instantly to hawk-form, dropping Stile so suddenly to the floor that he stumbled face-first into the food trough as if piggishly hungry. Hinblue eyed him as he lifted his corn- and barley-covered face, and made a snort that sounded suspiciously like a snicker. "*Et tu, Brute,*" Stile muttered, wiping off his face while the Lady tittered.

Soon Clip returned from his survey of the exterior situation, metamorphosing to man-form. "Snow-demons," he said. "Throwing icicles at us."

Stile made a modification spell, and the chamber drew farther out from the mountainside, beyond reach of icicles. So much for that. "Yet this will complicate our night's lodging," Stile commented.

"Nay, I know a snow-chief," the Lady said. "Once the demons were enemies of my Lord Blue, but we have healed many, and this one will host us graciously enough, methinks."

"Mayhap," Stile said dubiously. "But I shall set a warning spell against betrayal."

"Do thou that," she agreed. "One can never be quite certain with demons."

They crested the high peak and followed the curtain to an icebound hollow in a pass on the north side. "Here, belike, can we find my friend," the Lady said.

Stile placed the warning spell, and another to keep warm—a warner and a warmer, as the Lady put it—and they rode out. There was a cave in the ice, descending into the mountain. They approached this, and the snow demons appeared.

"I seek Freezetooth," the Lady proclaimed. "Him have I befriended." And in an amazingly short time, they were in the cold hall of the snow-chief.

Freezetooth was largely made of snow and ice. His skin was translucent, and his hair and beard were massed, tiny icicles. Freezing fog wafted out of his mouth as he spoke. But he was affable enough. Unlike most of his kind, he could talk. It seemed that most demons did not regard the human tongue as important enough to master, but a chief had to handle affairs of state and interrogate prisoners. "Welcome, warm ones," he said with a trace of delicately

suppressed aversion. "What favor do you offer for the
privilege of nighting at my glorious palace?"

Glorious palace? Stile glanced about the drear, ice-
shrouded cave. It was literally freezing here—otherwise
the snow-demons would melt. Even protected by his spell,
Stile felt cold.

"I have done thy people many favors in past years," the
Lady reminded Freezetooth indignantly, small sparks
flashing from her eyes. That was a trick of hers Stile
always admired, but several snow-demons drew hastily
back in alarm.

"Aye, and in appreciation, we consume thee not," the
chief agreed. "What hast thou done for us lately, thou and
thy cohorts?"

"This cohort is the Blue Adept," she said, indicating
Stile.

There was a ripple through the cave, as of ice cracking
under stress. Freezetooth squinted, his snowy brow crust-
ing up in reflection. "I do recall something about a white
foal—"

Stile placed the allusion. His alternate self, the former
Blue Adept, had helped the Lady Blue rescue her white
foal from the snow-demons, who did not now realize that
the identity of the Blue Adept had changed. It hardly
mattered, really.

"That foal would have died with thy people, being no
snow-mare, though she looked it. But there was an avalanche—"

"An accident," Freezetooth said quickly.

"An accident," Stile agreed, though they both knew better. The demons had tried to kill the Blue Adept—and had
received a harsh lesson. Surely they did not want another.
But there was no need to antagonize them. "What favor
didst thou crave?"

Now there was a canny glint in the demon's frozen eye.
"Come converse privately, Adept, male to male."

In a private chamber the demon confessed his desire: he
loved a lovely, flowing, brilliantly hued fire-spirit. His
"flame" was literally a flame.

The problem was immediately apparent. Freezetooth
could not approach his love without melting. If she cooled

to his temperature, her fire would extinguish and she would perish. Forbidden fruit, indeed!

Fortunately the remedy was within the means of Adept magic. Stile generated a spell to render Freezetooth invulnerable to heat. The flames would feel as deliciously cold as they were in fact hot.

The demon chief departed hastily to rendezvous with his love. Stile and his party were treated well by the remaining demons, who were no longer chilled by the wintry glare of their lord. The finest snowbanks were provided for sleeping on, in the most frigid and windy of the chambers. Without Stile's warmth-spell, it would have been disaster. As it was, they started to melt down into the snow, and Stile had to modify his spell to prevent that. Once everything had been adjusted, the facilities were quite comfortable.

In the morning Freezetooth was back, and his icicles positively scintillated. No need to ask how his evening had worked out! He insisted that his close friend the Adept stay for a proper feast that evening.

It occurred to Stile that this hospitality could be useful. "Do thou remain here while I perform a necessary chore in Proton," he told the Lady. "I must attend the final Round of the Tourney, but should be back by noon."

"I know, my love. Is it selfish of me to hope that thou dost lose that Game and find thyself confined to Phaze?"

He kissed her. "Yes, it is selfish. Sheen depends on me."

"Ah, yes—I forget the Lady Sheen. Methinks I shall consider her options whilst thou art gone."

Stile wasn't certain what that would lead to. The Lady Blue could cross the curtain, but Sheen could not function in Phaze. "Until noon," Stile said, then spelled himself to his usual curtain crossing.

CHAPTER 4

Poem

Stile's opponent for the finals was a serf woman two years younger than he: Rue, a twenty-year-tenure veteran of the Game. Like himself, she had not qualified at the top of her age ladder; but also like himself, she was the best of her decade. She was one of the half-dozen serf players Stile was not eager to meet in the Tourney. He thought he could beat her, but he wasn't sure.

Rue had luck as well as skill, for she had lost no Rounds. That meant that a single victory for her would bring her the prize, while one for Stile would merely bring him even. To beat Rue twice in succession—that would be difficult.

They played the grid. Stile got the letters. Rue was good at all manner of tool and machine games, being in superb health; he was well skilled in these areas, too, and could take her in most tool games, but would be at a disadvantage in machine-assisted games. She would expect him to go for TOOL or ANIMAL, so instead he went for A. NAKED. If she went for 4. ARTS, as he expected, this would foul her up.

But she had done the unexpected too, going for 3. CHANCE. With two chances to his one, the advantage would be with her on the straight gamble—if that was the way she wanted to play it. As evidently she did.

They played the subgrid, and finished with a very simple guessing game; each had to pick a number, and if the total of the two numbers was even, Stile won. Even, in this coding, was male; odd was female. This game was so simple it would be played on the grid. Each would enter his/her number, the total flashing on both screens only when both were entered.

Would she choose her own code, an odd number? People tended to, unconsciously, feeling more at home with their own. If she chose odd and he chose even, she would win.

Obviously he should choose odd, to cancel her odd. But, as obviously, she would anticipate that and choose even. Then the result would be odd, and she would still win. It seemed she stood to win regardless.

It came back to the subjective. Given no advantage between alternatives, a person normally selected what pleased him emotionally. Rue, in doubt, should go for odd. Therefore Stile overruled his preference for even and chose the number of letters in his name: five. He entered this on the grid and locked it; no way to change his mind now.

Rue had not yet made up her mind. Now the onus was hers, and they both knew it, and the broadcast audience knew it. She could win or lose by her decision; Stile was passive. The pressure was on her.

"Ten seconds until forfeit," the voice of the Game Computer announced.

Rue grimaced and punched in her number. She was pretty enough, with auburn hair, an extremely fit body, and only a few age creases forming on face and neck. She was thirty-three years old, her youth waning. If she won this one, she would be eligible for rejuvenation, and Stile suspected she desired that more than the actual wealth of Citizenship.

The total showed eight. Rue had chosen the letters of her own name. Even—and Stile had won.

Stile kept his face impassive. He had been lucky—but was keenly aware of the fickleness of that mistress. Rue blanched a little, but knew her chances remained even. Now they were tied, with thirteen victories and one loss each.

There was no break between Rounds this time, since there were no complexities about scheduling. They played the grid again immediately.

This time Stile got the numbers. He certainly was not going for CHANCE, though it had just salvaged his drive. It had not won him anything beyond that, for as a finalist he had already achieved the prize of life tenure as a serf. The only real step forward he could make was to Citizenship, and now at last it was within his means. One single win—

He selected 4. ARTS, knowing that she would be playing to avoid his strong points elsewhere. The arts cut across other skills, and Rue was noted for her intellectual velocity and proficiency with machine-assisted games. Machine art would be a tossup, but he was willing to fight it out there.

But she surprised him again, choosing A. NAKED. So it was 1A, Naked Arts. Stile did not like this; he had had a very bad time in this box in his critical match with the Red Adept, and had pulled it out only by means of a desperation ploy.

They played the subgrids, and finished, to his abrupt delight, with EXTEMPORANEOUS POETRY. Stile had always fancied himself a poet; he had a ready flair for rhyme and meter that had served him in excellent stead in Phaze. But true poetry was more than this—and now he would be able to do something significant when and where it counted.

The Game Computer printed a random list of a dozen words. "Thirty minutes to incorporate these terms into poems," it announced. "Highest point scores given for the use of one key word per line, in order, in the terminal position, rhymed. Technical facility fifty percent; content fifty percent. A panel of judges, including one male Citizen, one female Citizen, male serf, female serf, and the Game Computer, will decide the rating of each effort on the basis of zero to one hundred. The higher composite score prevails. Proceed."

This was more restrictive than Stile liked, but he remained well satisfied. It was not that he thought he had an easy victory; he knew that Rue, too, had facility with words, perhaps greater than his own. She was an extremely quick-witted woman—which was of course one reason she had made it to the Tourney finals. She could cobble together a poem as readily as he could. But at least this particular contest would be decided on skill, not luck.

This was a fair encounter. If he won or if he lost, it would be because he had established his level. That was all he could ask.

Stile considered the words. They were: BITCH, CUBE, FLAME, SIR, SILENCE, LOVE, HORN, CHEAT, ROACH, CIVIL, FLUTE, EARTH. An anomalous bunch indeed! None of them rhymed with each other, so there were no free rides there. The only way to get a key term at the end of a rhyming line was to alternate with filler lines. "My female dog is a wonderful bitch; whenever she scratches she has an itch." That sort of thing would hardly win the Tourney; it was literal doggerel. It might be better to alternate terminal key words with mid-line key words, sacrificing the preferred terminal spot for the sake of the also-preferred, one-key-word-per-line arrangement. The Computer had not made it easy; the contestants had to choose between sacrifices. "My female dog is a wonderful *bitch*; she stands on a *cube* and does a twitch." That would garner a better technical score, but nothing extra on content.

He glanced at Rue. She was frowning, evidently displeased by the first term. Stile half smiled; he would have been similarly put out if the term had been RUNT. He was a runt and she was a bitch—but that was the kind of mischief random selection could do.

Because this was Naked Arts, they could use no implements, make no written notes. No rhyming dictionaries. They had to do it all in their heads, punching only the finished poems into the grid for judgment. If either had trouble with memory, he or she could place individual lines as they were worked out. But then those lines would be final, no changes allowed. Since both Stile and Rue were experienced Game players, both could hold the developing poems in memory until the time for presentation. No, the only problem was wrestling these awkward words into the most artistic and meaningful whole.

Stile wrestled a while, but was not satisfied. He could make rhymes and meter, certainly—but where was the meaning? One ignored the content portion of the poem at one's peril. Yet it seemed impossible to fit these unruly words into anything serious; the problem of rhyming and positioning turned his efforts to frivolous tangents, as with the antics of his female dog. What could a person do seriously with words like bitch, cube, and flame?

Time was passing. Rue was hard at work; her expression and concentration suggested she had developed a strategy of creation and was happily ironing out the wrinkles. She would probably come up with something very clever. He had to come up with something even more clever—or more significant. Sir, silence, love—what a headache!

He brought himself back to basics. There were really two types of poetry: the ornamental and the consequential. Ornaments were rhyme, meter, alliteration, pattern, humor, assonance, and technical cleverness. They were stressed in light verse, parody, the libretto for popular music, and such. Serious poetry de-emphasized such things, or dispensed with them altogether. Thus some people were unable even to recognize serious poetry, because it didn't necessarily rhyme. But ultimately any poetic appeal was to the deeper emotions, and the use of symbolism enabled it to evoke complex ramifications in the most compact presentation. As with Kipling's *Recessional*: "Far-called, our navies melt away; On dune and headland sinks the fire: Lo, all our pomp of yesterday Is one with Nineveh and Tyre!" Presented to Queen Victoria some centuries back, this poem did not find instant favor, for it signaled the decline of the Earth-wide British Empire. But what imagery was evoked by the names of those two ancient cities, foremost in their times, finally brought to ruin by the armies of Babylonia and Alexander the Great, drunkard though the latter might have been. Kipling's verse was superficially pretty; it rhymed nicely. But its real impact was its content, the somber warning for an over-extended empire. All too soon it had been London-town under the siege of weapons unknown in the time of Tyre, as the Germans sent their bombers and rockets over. How well Kipling had understood!

With that memory, Stile saw his way. Rhyme, meter, and the rest of the prettiness were encumbrances; he had to dispense with them all and concentrate on meaning and emotion. He would lose some technical points, but gain where it counted. Win or lose, he would do his best, his way.

Stile considered the first word—bitch. He knew of a noble bitch—the old female werewolf who had guided Clef to the Platinum Demesnes, sacrificing her life in the process. Stile could do worse than remember her in this poem!

Cube—there was one cube that was fresh in his experience, and that was the doubling cube of his recent backgammon game, which had enabled him to pull out a last-moment win.

Flame—well, it wasn't the most serious thing, but he had just enabled the chief snow-demon to have a liaison with his literal flame. That might not have any meaning to the Tourney judges, but this poem was not really for them but for Stile himself—his evocation of himself. The frame of Phaze was vitally important to him, and the flame related to that and to the notion of romance, which brought him to the Lady Blue. Ah, yes.

Sir—that was easy. This very poem was Stile's final effort to be called sir: to become a Citizen of Proton, and have similar stature and power in Proton as he did in Phaze as the Blue Adept.

But the remaining terms—they did not seem to relate. Now he was emotionally committed to this course, and had to use them in it—which meant he would have to improvise. That would be troublesome.

What was there to do except use the words as keys, perhaps as some psychic revelation that had to be clothed with syntax to become meaningful? If the first four terms brought him from the recent past to the present, the next eight might be taken as signals of the future. At least he would assume as much for the sake of the poem—insights to himself, now and to come. If the insights proved false, then this was a work of fiction; if true, of prediction. It was a worthy game, and he would take it seriously.

Stile bent to it with a will, and the lines fell into their places. No rhyme, no meter, no other ornamentation; just a series of statements like those of the Oracle, clarifying the significance of each key term. He found that there was not a great amount of mystery to it; the statements were mostly common sense, modified by what he already knew, and the whole was an affirmation of man's resignation to fate.

Suddenly time was up. Rue and Stile typed in their poems. Now it was up to the panel of judges.

In the interim, those judges had assembled. Each one sat in a separate booth facing a central holograph. They could view the holo and converse with each other at the same time. The Game Computer was represented by a booth containing a humanoid robot, its outer surface transparent, so that its wires, hydraulics, and electronic components showed. The thing was at first eerie, like an animated cross section of the human body, but soon the eye accepted it for what it was: an animation of a simplified representation of the far more complicated Computer.

"Display one poem," the Computer-figure said. "The serf Rue will commence her reading."

Rue looked at the printed poem in her grid screen and began to read. A holograph of her formed above the central table, where all the judges could see it plainly. It looked as if she were standing there, a woman on a pedestal, and her eyes made contact with those of whatever judge she happened to face.

"My poem is entitled *Cruel Lover*," she announced. Then she read, flouncing prettily and smiling or frowning to emphasize the meaning appropriately. As she read each line, it appeared on a simulated screen over her head, until the full poem was printed.

> Call me witch or call me bitch
> Call me square or cube
> By any name I'm still the flame
> Burning on the tube.
>
> I'll take no slur, I tell you, sir
> I will not sit in silence
> I'll take your glove in lieu of love
> But will accept no violence.
>
> Now light's reborn by dawn's bright horn
> You can no longer cheat

Accept reproach or be a roach
Or make my joy complete.

Desist this drivel and be civil
Play violin or flute
Be up with mirth or down to earth
But keep love absolute.

"The key words are used correctly and in the proper sequence," the Computer said. "Each one terminates its lines, and each is matched with a rhyme of good quality. These are credits. Four lines exist only to complete the necessary rhymes; these are neutral. The metric scansion is correct and consistent—basically iambic tetrameter alternating with iambic trimeter with certain convenient modifications in the extreme feet. This is a common mode and not considered difficult. I rate the technical facility of this effort forty-two of a total of fifty points alloted to this aspect. Proceed to my left with your judgments."

The female serf was to the left. "I don't know much about all those things," she said diffidently. "But it rhymes, and I sort of like it. So I give it a forty-five."

There was the illiterate response, Stile thought. That was the vote he had not deigned to court, though it cost him Citizenship.

Next was the male Citizen, resplendent in his ornate robes. "We are not yet discussing content or interpretation?" he inquired. When the Computer agreed, he continued: "I find the format simplistic but effective. I'll give it forty." Stile liked that reaction better.

Then the male serf voted. "I don't relate well to the female tone, but technically it seems all right for what it is. The key words are all in the right place, and they do fit in more neatly than I could do. Forty-three from me."

The female Citizen, in a sequined suit, fire opals gleaming at her ears, voted last. "Some of the lines are forced or confusing, but I suppose I must grade that in content. She's done an excellent job of stringing the random words coherently together. Forty-six."

Stile saw that the average score was forty-three, which was good—probably a good deal better than his own would be. Rue had certainly integrated her terms cleverly. He was going to have a rough time of this one!

"We shall now analyze the second poem for technical merit," the Computer said.

Stile stepped up to the grid. He found himself looking past his printed poem into the glassy orbs of the Computer simulacrum robot. He glanced to the side and saw the male serf. He could see anyone he chose, merely by looking in the correct direction; their circle was laid out flat on his screen.

"My poem is titled *Insights*," he said. Then he read:

> Nobility is found in a werewolf bitch
> Defeat converts to victory by an ivory cube
> Magic makes ice merge with flame
> A Game converts serf to sir.
>
> The mischief of the future is shrouded in silence
> And part of that mischief is love
> We must heed the summons of Gabriel's horn
> Destiny the single thing we can not cheat.
>
> All are subject: the dragon and the roach
> Since we are bound, we must be civil
> Our fate is determined by God's flute
> That tumbles mountains and shakes the earth.

He had made eye contact with each judge in turn as he read, and had seen their responses. Unfortunately, these were not promising; some frowned, some seemed confused. It wasn't going over; they did not understand its form or content.

"This is free verse," the Computer said. "It has no consistent meter and no rhyme. This should not be taken as a defect. The key terms are terminally placed, in correct order, one to a line with no waste lines. There are natural pauses at the end of most lines. As free verse, I rate this technically at thirty-nine."

Stile's heart sank. The others would follow the Computer's lead, and he would average several points below Rue's effort.

He was not disappointed in this expectation. The serf woman wondered whether these lines could even be considered poetry, as they seemed just like sentences to her, and the others were lukewarm. The average score was thirty-eight. Stile was five points behind.

Now it was time for the content analysis. Neither poet was permitted to speak at this stage; it was felt that if the poems did not speak for themselves, they were defective. "This is a straightforward statement of position," the Computer said of Rue's effort. "She evidently feels slighted by her male friend, and is dictating to him the terms of their future association. I perceive no particular meaning beyond this, and therefore do not regard this as other than light verse. Rating thirty-five."

That was a good sign, Stile thought. If the others followed this lead, her average would drop.

"It's a good thing machines aren't in charge of romance," the serf woman remarked. "I find this a good telling-off. The guy *is* a roach, calling her such names, and I'm all with her. I say fifty."

Stile winced inwardly. He needed to recover five points, and figured they might rate his poem an average 40. The Computer's lead had put him right in line to even it up by dropping Rue's score, but this 50 was a disaster.

The male Citizen was more critical, however. "I certainly don't care to see a woman spelling out her terms like that for a romance, though I suppose, if she can find a man to accept them, it's their business. I don't follow this 'burning on the tube' reference; does it make sense at all?"

"Oh, sure, sir," the male serf said. "In the old days on Earth they had gas burners, gas coming up a tube and the flame on top. So she's likening herself to that sort of flame. It's a sort of pun, really."

The Citizen shrugged. "Clever," he said sourly. "I rate this thirty." Stile saw Rue wince. But he himself, while deploring the man's narrowness, was gratified by the score. It put him back in the running.

The male serf was next. "If she becomes a Citizen, then she can set terms," he said, and the others laughed. They were getting into this now, loosening up. "I guess I'm looking for something deeper than this, some social commentary, not just female demands. Rating thirty-two." And Stile's hopes elevated another notch. Now if only the other woman did not react by sexual alignment—

"I believe I note an extremely clever thrust," the lady Citizen said. "Nowhere is the protagonist identified; it is not necessarily serf Rue at all. It could be any woman, most especially one who has been wronged by the man she loves. It could even apply to a humanoid robot female who loves a flesh-man."

Oh, no! Had Rue slanted her verse to pillory Stile? He saw the judges turning to look at him, and at Sheen in the small physical audience permitted. They knew!

"The references to square and cube fall into place," the lady Citizen continued. "A robot is a creature of geometrical parts, supposedly, animated by electric power from a tiny furnace fed by Protonite. She is certainly burning, internally! She must accept a man's attentions—I understand that is what that type is primarily designed for—but can not have his love, since he knows she is a machine. Yet she can be programmed for emotion; she loves *him*, knowing that love is not returned. Perhaps the man she serves is a musician, playing the violin or flute—"

Sheen got up from her seat in the audience and walked toward the exit. Stile felt acute pity for her. She was not supposed to be the target!

"One moment," the male Citizen said. "That's her, isn't it? I want to question her."

"That would be involving her in the panel's deliberation," the female Citizen said. "I doubt that's legitimate."

"The judges may seek any source of information they wish," the Computer said. "Except the author of the piece in question."

"Female robot—how do you feel about this poem?" the male Citizen called.

Sheen stopped and faced him. "Sir, I prefer not to answer, if I am to be considered an interested party."

"Answer!" he directed, with supreme indifference to her feelings.

"You may answer," the Computer said. "You have not volunteered your influence; you have been summoned by this panel as a material witness. We are trying to determine whether there is substance to the hypothesis that the poem in question represents your viewpoint."

Sheen's mouth firmed. Her human mannerisms had become so facile that in no physical way was her machine nature evident. She was a beautiful woman, naked of body and perhaps of mind. "Then you shall have my viewpoint, sir. If the poem concerns me, it is not intended as a compliment. It is intended as an attack on the man I love, using me as an involuntary weapon. I am a machine—but I think that even were I alive, I would not care so cynically to hurt a living person in this fashion. This poem is crueler than anything the man I love might do. I am sure his own poem is not of this nature."

The Citizen nodded. "That's some machine," he murmured.

The female Citizen considered, pursing her lips. Her opals flashed. "I am left with a choice. Either this poem is not directed at, shall we say, real people, in which case it is not remarkable—or it *is* so directed, in which case its brilliance is nullified by its cruelty. In either case, I can not respect it. I rate it twenty-five."

That was disaster for Rue. It made her average score 34½. The other panelists could reconsider their votes if they wished, but seemed content to let them stand. Rue's poem had a cumulative score of 77½. Stile had a fair chance to beat that, thanks to Sheen. All he needed was forty points.

Now the judges considered Stile's effort for content. "This poem is more serious and obscure than the other," the Computer said. "Some may not be aware that there exists an alternate frame of reality of this planet within which other laws of physics govern. The author is able to enter that frame, where he is a person of power and has an elegant wife. Several of the first six lines evidently refer to that frame. There was a female wolf who sacrificed her life for her duty, and a magical encounter between a creature of ice and another of fire. The future in that frame can occasionally be foreseen by magical means, and it contains extraordinary mischief, part of which is the conflict of love loyalties. Two lines refer to the Tourney now being concluded, which will lead to Citizenship for one of these serfs. Thus the first portion of the poem is relevant to the larger situation here and must be accorded credit. The second portion appears to be an advisory essay. The Angel Gabriel is destined mythologically to blow his trumpet on Judgment Day for living persons—and that call is the one no one can evade or cheat. This poem extends this concept to creatures both fanciful and repulsive. It concludes that these people and creatures must accept the inevitable with civility, and reminds us that, according to the legend of the other frame, the powerful flute—perhaps an alternate designation of Gabriel's horn—has already announced itself by shaking the earth, in the form of the tremors recently experienced here. Allowing for a considerable figurative element, I find this poem serious and valid. The tremors were actually caused by the collapse of overworked Protonite mines in the southern range, but this can be taken as a warning: the mineral on which this planet's power is literally based is not inexhaustible, and we shall suffer an accounting when that mineral is at last depleted. Already we have suffered a not-inconsequential damage to a number of our facilities. I therefore take this poem as a well-conceived and serious warning, and on that basis I rate it forty-eight."

Stile was amazed and gratified. He had had no hint the Game Computer knew so much about him or the frame of Phaze, or that it could interpret oblique references with such dispatch. Now he realized that everything he had told Sheen, she had relayed to her machine friends. They in turn could have informed the Game Computer, who perhaps was one of their number. Certainly it possessed considerable self-will, backed by the phenomenal resources of the Computer memory banks and the experience of analyzing many thousands of Games. So this should not have surprised him at all.

It was the serf woman's turn to vote. "Is there any cutting at the opponent?" she asked. The other heads indicated that no one perceived any. "I'm not sure about all the business of the other frame; this is the first I've heard of it. But I can believe the Protonite won't last forever, and somehow this serf-Citizen setup must be called to account. So okay, I'll go with the warning. I rate it forty."

This was better than Stile had hoped from her. She had given the other poem 50, and he had feared she was a man-hater.

"Good job," the male Citizen said. "Forty-five."

"Just what kind of a person is he in that frame you talk about?" the serf man asked.

"He is what is called an Adept," the Computer answered. "That means he is a powerful magician."

"Funny to hear a computer say that," the man said. "But I sort of go for that fantasy bit, even if it is all a story. Forty-two."

Stile's hope was sailing. These were amazingly favorable responses. He was averaging 44. It would take a rating of 25 by the last panelist to bring him down to par with Rue. The lady Citizen seemed too perceptive for that—but she had surprised him before. He felt his hands getting sweaty as he waited for her answer.

"This mischief of love," she said. "Is this person concerned about the feelings of the lady robot who loves him?"

"He may not answer," the Computer reminded her. "We must divine that answer from his poem."

"I wonder whether in fact it is his own personal reckoning he is most concerned with," she said. "He says they must be civil, because what will be, will be. I am not sure I can accept that answer."

Stile quailed. This woman had downgraded Rue's verse for cruelty; was she about to do the same for his?

"Since he has a wife in the other frame, he really does not need a woman of any kind in this frame," she continued. "It is unfair to keep her in doubt."

"We may approve or disapprove the poet's personal life," the male Citizen said. "But we are here to judge only the merit of the poem. For what it's worth, I see several indications that he recognizes the possibility of fundamental change. A bitch turns noble, defeat becomes victory, ice merges with flame, serf becomes Citizen, the fate of dragons and roaches is linked. Perhaps he is preparing his

philosophy for the recognition that a living creature may
merge with a machine. If this is the way fate decrees, he
will accept it."

She nodded. "Yes, the implication is there. The author
of this poem, I think, is unlikely to be deliberately cruel.
He is in a difficult situation, he is bound, he is civil. It is
an example more of us might follow. I rate this work forty-
four."

Stile's knees almost gave way. She had not torpedoed
him; his total score would be 82, comfortably ahead of
Rue's total.

"Do any wish to change their votes on either aspect of
either poem?" the Computer inquired. "Your votes are not
binding until confirmed."

The panelists exchanged glances. Stile got tense again. It
could still come apart!

"Yes, I do," the serf woman said. Stile saw Rue tense;
this was the one who had given her 50 on content. If she
revised her grade on Stile's poem downward—

"I believe I overreacted on that fifty score," she said.
"Let's call it forty-five for *Cruel Lover*."

Again Stile's knees turned to goo. She had come down
on his side!

"Final score eighty-two to seventy-seven in favor of
Stile's poem," the Computer said after a pause. "He is the
winner of this Tourney."

Now there was applause from the hidden public address
system. So quickly, so simply, he had won!

But he saw Rue, standing isolated, eyes downcast. On
impulse he went to her. "It was a good game," he said.
"You could easily have won it."

"I still have life tenure," she said, half choked with
disappointment. Then, as an afterthought, she added:
"Sir."

Stile felt awkward. "If you ever need a favor—"

"I did not direct my poem at you. Not consciously. I
was thinking of someone who threw me over. Sir."

But now the crowd was closing in, and Stile's attention
was necessarily diverted. "By the authority vested in me by
the Council of Citizens of Planet Proton," the Game
Computer said, its voice emerging from every speaker

under its control throughout the Game Annex, "I now declare that the serf Stile, having won the Tourney, is acquitted of serf status and endowed with Citizenship and all appurtenances and privileges pertaining thereto, from this instant forward."

The applause swelled massively. The panelists joined in, serfs and Citizens alike.

A robot hastened forward with an ornate robe. "Sir, I belong to your transition estate. It is your privilege to wear any apparel or none. Yet to avoid confusion—"

Stile had thought he was braced for this, but the repeated appellation "sir" startled him. For a lifetime he had called others sir; now he had comprehensive conditioning to unlearn. "Thank you," he said, reaching for the robe.

The robot skittered to the side. "Allow me, sir," it said, and Stile realized it wanted to put the robe on him. It did not behoove a Citizen to serve himself, though he could if he wanted to. Stile suffered himself to be dressed, holding a mental picture of a horse being saddled. "Thank you," he repeated awkwardly.

The machine moved close, getting the robe on and adjusted. "A Citizen need not thank a machine—or anyone," it murmured discreetly in Stile's ear.

"Oh. Yes. Thank—uh, yes."

"Quite all right, sir," the machine said smoothly.

Now a lady Citizen approached. It was Stile's employer. Former employer, he reminded himself. "I am gratified, Stile," she said. "You have made me a winner too."

"Thank you, sir." Then Stile bit his tongue.

She smiled. "Thank *you*, sir." And she leaned forward to kiss him on the right eyebrow. "I profited a fantastic amount on your success. But more than that is the satisfaction of sponsoring a Tourney winner. You will find me appreciative." She walked away.

Now the Citizen known as the Rifleman approached. "I know exactly how you feel," he said. That was no exaggeration; the Rifleman had won his own Tourney fifteen years before. Stile had encountered him in the first Round of this Tourney and barely pulled out the victory. The Rifleman had been an excellent loser. "Accept some private advice, Citizen: get away from the public for several days and drill yourself in the new reality. That will cure you of embarrassing slips. And get yourself someone to explain the ropes in nontechnical terms—the extent of your vested estate, the figures, the prerogatives. There's a hell of a lot to learn fast, if you don't want to be victimized by predatory Citizens."

"But aren't all Citizens—that is, don't they respect the estates of other Citizens?"

"Your minimum share of the Protonite harvest can not be impinged upon—but only your luck and competence and determination can establish your place in the Citizen heirarchy. This is a new game, Stile—oh, yes, Citizens have names; we are merely anonymous to the serfs. You may wish to select a new name for yourself—"

"No need."

"It is a game more intricate and far-reaching than any within the Tourney. Make a point to master its nuances, Stile—soon." And the Rifleman gave him a meaningful glance.

The audience was dissipating as the novelty of the new Citizen wore off. Stile signaled Sheen. "Can your friends provide me with a mentor conversant with the nuances of Citizen behavior?"

"They can, sir," she said. "Or they could program me—"

"Excellent! Get yourself programmed. They'll know what I need. And do it soon."

Sheen left. Stile found it incongruous that she should remain naked while he was now clothed. Yet of course she remained a serf—an imitation serf—now in his employ; she would remain naked the rest of her life.

Her life? Stile smiled, a trifle grimly. He was forgetting that she had no life. Yet she was his best friend in this frame.

Stile turned to the robot who had brought his robe. "Take me to my estate," he ordered it.

The machine hesitated. "Sir, you have none."

"None? But I thought all Citizens—"

"Each Citizen has a standard share of the Protonite mines. All else follows."

"I see." It seemed there was much that was not handed

to a Citizen on a platter. He needed that manual of Citizenship! Where was Sheen? Her programming should have been quick.

Then she appeared. "I have it, sir," she said.

"Excellent. Take me to an appropriate and private place, and deliver."

"Don't I always—sir?" She led the way out of the Game Annex.

The place turned out to be a temporary minidome set up on the desert. Its generator tapped an underground power cable, so as to form the force field that prevented the thin, polluted outside atmosphere from penetrating. A portable unit filled the dome with pleasant, properly cooled air. Sheen set up a table for two, put out crackers, cheese, and mock wine, adjusted the field to turn opaque, and planted a spy-disrupter device on the ground. "Now we are private, sir," she said.

"You don't have to say sir to me," he protested.

"Yes, I do, sir. You are a Citizen and I am a naked serf. We violate this convention at our peril."

"But you've been my friend all along!"

"And once more than that, sir," she reminded him. She had come to him as guardian and mistress, and had been good in both capacities. His marriage to the Lady Blue had deleted the second. Sheen, a machine supposedly without any human emotion not programmed into her, had tried to commit suicide—self-destruction. She had become reconciled after meeting the Lady Blue. Sheen still loved him, and for that Stile felt guilty.

"It occurs to me that, as a Citizen, I could have you reprogrammed to have no personal feeling toward me," he said.

"This is true, sir."

"Do you wish it?"

"No, sir."

"Sheen, I value you greatly. I do not want you to suffer. That poem of Rue's—I am absolutely opposed to giving you cause to feel that way. Is there anything within my present power I can do to make you happy?"

"There is, sir. But you would not."

She was uncompromising. She wanted his love again, physically if not emotionally, and that he could not give. "Aside from that."

"Nothing, sir."

"But I may be able to make your friends happy. As Citizen, I can facilitate their recognition as sapient entities." Her friends were the self-willed machines of Proton who, like Sheen herself, had helped him survive Citizen displeasure in the past. He had sworn never to act against their interests so long as they did not act against the interests of man, and both parties honored that oath. Stile did not regard their desire to achieve serf status as contrary to the oath; he agreed they should have it. But such status was not easy to achieve; the Citizens were devoted to the status quo.

"All in good time, sir. Now shall we review the appurtenances and privileges of Citizenship?"

"By all means."

Rapidly, in simple language, she acquainted him with his situation. He was entitled to use the proceeds from his share of the mines to purchase or construct a physical estate, to staff it with serfs, robots, androids, cyborgs, or anything else, and to indulge in any hobbies he wished. The amount of credit available from his share was sufficient to enable him to construct a moderate palace, hire perhaps twenty-five serfs, and buy six robots of Sheen's type. Expensive hobbies like exotic horse breeding or duplicating the Hanging Gardens of Babylon would have to wait until the palace was complete. The income of a Citizen was not limitless; it only seemed that way to serfs.

It was possible, however, to increase one's resources by making and winning large wagers with other Citizens. Bets of a year's income were not uncommon. However, if a Citizen got two years in arrears, further wagers would not be honored until he caught up. It was never permitted for a Citizen to become destitute; a basic lifestyle had to be maintained. Appearance was vital.

"I'll have no problems there," he said. "I'm not a gambling man, outside the Game. I shall be a very conservative Citizen and live well within my income. Most of the time I won't even be here, as you know."

She nodded sadly. "Yes, sir. There's a note in the program from my friends. They warn it is not safe for you to stand pat. Forces are building rapidly. To protect yourself you must soon develop your estate to a hundred times its original magnitude. Within six months."

"A hundred times!" he exclaimed. "In six months!"

"And you must unravel the mystery that is associated with your lasering, sir. Who sent me to protect you? My friends have disturbing new evidence that this is not an isolated event. Someone or something is interfering with your life, and my friends can't discover who."

"Yes. And in Phaze, someone set the Red Adept against me on a false alarm." He had had an extraordinary amount of trouble in that connection, ending in the banishment of the Red Adept from both Phaze and Proton. The Oracle had said Blue would destroy Red, and that had proved correct—but none of that mischief would have occurred if someone had not started the rumor that Blue intended to attack Red.

"And there was that earthquake, sir, which you believe is connected to events in Phaze," she continued. "Another portent, perhaps."

"Definitely. The Platinum Elves informed me that I would be involved in important developments, after my honeymoon." Ooops—he had not meant to mention the honeymoon to Sheen. He continued rapidly. "I'm not sure I like the implication. I don't know what the linkages between frames might be, but since a number of people can cross, there can be interactions, perhaps quite serious ones." He breathed deeply. "I was psychologically prepared for banishment from Proton when I got eliminated from the Tourney. I'm not so certain about how to proceed now that I have permanent tenure. I don't feel comfortable here in clothing."

"That is why you needed to isolate yourself, sir."

Stile got up and paced the small enclosure. "I promised to return to Phaze by noon. I have already overrun that deadline. Why don't you set in motion the machinery for the establishment of my physical estate, and start hiring serfs, while I cross the curtain to—"

"That might not be wise, sir."

Her constant "sirs" were still getting on his nerves, but he knew this was good conditioning. "Not wise?"

"You will need your money as a stake to multiply your estate, sir, so should not fritter it away on nonessentials. And if it became known that a machine was disposing your assets—"

"I am a Citizen, aren't I? I can use a machine if I want to, can't I?" Stile was irritated, not liking the implied slur at Sheen.

"Yes, sir."

"So I'm appointing you my chief of staff, or whatever the appropriate office is. I'd better hire a staff of serfs, for appearances, and become a compulsive gambler. But I'll lose my new fortune unless I have competent input. Will your friends help?"

"They will, sir."

"Then ask them to locate an appropriate adviser for me. One who knows how to break in a new Citizen."

"And how to escalate a Citizen's fortune rapidly, sir."

"Precisely. Now I'll go finish my honey—uh, my business in Phaze. Assuming I can get out of Proton unobserved."

"A Citizen can, sir," she assured him. "If you will make a brief, formal holo statement of authorization, so I can draw on your funds—"

"Ah, yes." Stile took care of that immediately.

"Thank you, sir," she said, accepting the recording. "I shall set the wheels in motion."

"Excellent. And I'll ponder what I can do for you and your friends."

Sheen nodded, knowing he could do nothing for her. She would serve him loyally and lovingly, regardless.

CHAPTER 5

West Pole

He was late, but the Lady Blue forgave him. "I had the news before thee. Thou art a Citizen now."

"It's anticlimactic," Stile complained. "Citizenship is the ultimate prize of Proton. Now that I have it, it's mainly a nuisance. Hidden forces decree that I must commence a new and chancy course, to be ready for even more tension. I wonder if this relates in any way to the promised mischief at the West Pole?"

"How can such complications arise now?" the Lady inquired rhetorically. "All we seek is a simple honeymoon."

"Somehow I don't think we're going to have it."

They attended the snow demons' banquet. It was magnificent, in its fashion. Candied icicles for aperitif, iceburgers, fried avalanche, sludge freeze as a beverage, and snow cones for dessert. The snow-demons pitched in with gusto; Stile and the Lady nibbled with imperfect enthusiasm, until Stile sneaked in a small spell and changed their morsels to items with food content concealed under snow frosting.

At night, side by side in a surprisingly comfortable snowbank, they talked. "I have a problem," Stile said quietly.

"I think it must needs wait till the snowmen sleep," she murmured. "They exhibit unseemly curiosity as to how flesh-mortals perform without melting from generated heat."

He patted her anatomy under the snow blanket, where the curious demons couldn't see. "A Proton problem."

"The Lady Sheen."

"The lovely self-willed robot lady Sheen, who will not

accept reprogramming. I must work closely with her, for I have agreed to help her machine friends. They helped me survive when times were hard in Proton, and I must help them achieve serf status now. And they warn me that more trouble is coming; that I must gamble to enhance my estate vastly and research to learn who sent Sheen in the first place. I fear it links in some way to events in Phaze, so I must follow through. Only I wish I didn't have to use Sheen—take that in what sense thou wilt. It isn't fair to her, and I feel guilty."

"As well thou might," she agreed. "I promised to consider her case, and so I have done. Now let me see if I have this right. The self-willed golems—machines—wish recognition as people?"

"Correct. Serfs are the lowest people, but are more than the highest machines. Serfs can play the Game, compete in the Tourney, win privileges or even Citizenship. When their tenure expires, they depart the planet with generous cumulative pay. Machines are permitted none of this; they are slaves until junked. Yet some are intelligent, conscious, feeling."

"And the Lady Sheen is one of these unrecognized machine creatures."

"She is. She is in every way a person, with very real emotions. They merely happen to be programmed, rather than natural."

"And is there a difference between program and nature?"

"I doubt it. Different means to similar ends, perhaps."

"Then thou must marry the Lady Sheen."

Stile paused. "I don't believe I heard thee properly, Lady."

"It is the other frame. She can never cross the curtain. Thou canst do as thou wilt with her there."

Stile had been growing sleepy. Now he was awakening. "I am sure I am misunderstanding thee."

"If a Citizen marries a machine—"

"Nobody can marry a machine!"

"—then that machine must have—"

"Machines don't have—" Stile stopped. "I wonder. The

spouses of Citizens do not achieve Citizen status, but they do have certain prerogatives. They are considered to be employed—their employment being the marriage. And only serfs are employable."

"So a married machine would be a serf," the Lady concluded. "And if one machine were a serf—"

"The precedent—"

"Thinkest thou it would accomplish thy purpose?"

Stile considered, his head spinning. "If the marriage stuck, it would be one hell of a lever for legal machine recognition!"

"That was my notion," she said complacently.

"But I am married to thee!" he protested.

"In Phaze. Not in Proton."

"But thou canst cross over!"

"True. But I am of this frame, and never will I leave it for aught save emergency. I have no claim on the things of Proton, nor wish I any."

"But I love only thee! I could never—"

"Thou lovest more than thou knowest," she said with gentle assurance. "Neysa, Sheen—"

"Well, there are different types of—"

"And I spoke not of love. I spoke of marriage."

"A marriage of convenience? To a robot?"

"Dost thou hold the Lady Sheen beneath convenience, for that she be made of metal?"

"Nay! But—" He paused. "Nay, I must confess I do think less of her. Always since I learned she was not real, that—"

"Methinks thou hast some thinking to do," the Lady Blue said, and turned her back.

Stile felt the reproach keenly. He was prejudiced; he had great respect for Sheen, but love had been impossible because she was not flesh. Yet he reminded himself that he had come closer to loving her before encountering the Lady Blue. Had Sheen's nonliving nature become a pretext for his inevitable change of heart? He could not be sure, but he was unable to deny it.

How could he fight for the recognition of the sapient self-willed machines if he did not recognize them as dis-

crete individuals himself? How could he marry Sheen if he
did not love her? If he came to think of her as a real
person, wouldn't such a marriage make him a bigamist?
There were two frames, certainly, but he was only one
person. Yet since the Lady Blue had generously offered to
accept half-status, confining herself to Phaze—

Think of the commotion the marriage of a Citizen to a
robot would make in Proton! It would convulse the social
order! That aspect appealed to him. Yet—

"Wouldst thou settle for a betrothal?" he asked at last.

"An honest one," she agreed sleepily.

"Say six months. Time enough to get the legal issues
clarified, one way or the other. There would be formidable
opposition from other Citizens. And of course Sheen herself might not agree."

"She will agree," the Lady Blue said confidently. "A
betrothal is a commitment, and never wilt thou renege.
She will have some joy of thee at last."

This was not a way he had ever expected the Lady Blue
to speak, and Stile was uneasy. Yet perhaps she had some
concern of her own, knowing she had taken him away
from Sheen. Possibly the social mores of Phaze differed
from those of Proton in this respect, and sharing was more
permissible. Certainly his friend Kurrelgyre the werewolf
had believed it, assigning his bitch to a friend while Kurrelgyre himself was in exile from his Pack. The Lady Blue
had met Sheen, liked her, and accepted her immediately as
a person; apparently that had not been any social artifice.

"And if in six months it is legal, then shall I marry her,"
Stile continued. "In Proton. But I can not love her."

"Then love me," the Lady Blue said, turning to him.

That was reward enough. But already Stile had a
glimpse of that controversy he was about to conjure, like a
savage magic storm.

In the morning they resumed their tour of the curtain,
recrossing the White Mountain range and bearing southwest. There were some deep crevices on the ground; when
their steeds' hooves knocked sand into them, it fell down
and away beyond the limit of perception, soundlessly.
"Deep caves, mayhap," Stile remarked, a bit nervous

about a possible collapse of the footing. But Clip tapped the ground with a forehoof, indicating that there was no danger of a fall as long as a unicorn picked the way.

Stile checked his contour map and discovered they were heading for the Black Demesnes. He did not like the Black Adept, and by mutual consent they spelled rapidly past the grim castle and well on toward the Purple Mountains.

Now the curtain bore directly south. Suddenly there was an explosion of fire before them. Stile squinted at the flame, trying to determine whether it was natural or magic.

"The warners!" the Lady exclaimed. "The Green Adept!"

"It must be," Stile agreed. "I promised to bypass him."

They went around, rejoining the curtain southwest of Green's marked territory. The curtain was curving back westward, through the foothills of the southern mountains. The scenery was pleasant; waist-high bushes covered the rolling terrain, topped with faintly purple flowers. The steeds trotted through, finding firm footing beneath. The midafternoon sun slanted down.

Suddenly a creature jumped in front of Hinblue. The thing had the body of a powerful man and the head of a wolf. It bayed—and the horse spooked. The Lady Blue, an expert rider, was not in any trouble; she brought her steed about and calmed her.

Then a second creature appeared, this one with the head of a ram. It bleated.

Stile's mind formulated a spell while his hand went for his harmonica. But he withheld his magic, uncertain whether it was necessary. He had heard of the animal-heads, but understood they were not aggressive toward human beings. Was his information mistaken?

More animalheads appeared, making their assorted noises. Cats, goats, hawks, bears, turtles—none of them with the intelligence or verbal ability of a man, but each quite formidable in its fashion. They were all snarling, squawking, roaring, or growling aggressively. A pighead charged toward Stile, grunting.

"I fear they mean mischief," the Lady Blue said. "This is not like them. Something has angered them, methinks."

"Yes," Stile agreed. Clip's horn was holding the pighead at bay, but a crocodilehead was circling to the rear. "We had best avoid them till we know their motivation."

"Methinks we can outrun them," she said, concerned but not worried.

Their steeds took off. Hinblue was a fine mare, capable of a galloping velocity that shamed ordinary horses; she really did move like the wind. But Clip was a unicorn whose inherent magic made him swifter yet. By common consent they used no other magic, not revealing Stile's status; Adepts were not necessarily favored in the back reaches of Phaze.

The animalheads gave chase enthusiastically, baying, bellowing, and hooting. But their human bodies could not compare with the equine bodies, and they soon fell behind. Yet two things narrowed the gap; this was animalhead territory, more familiar to the beastmen than to the intruders; they could take the best paths and shortcuts, and kept popping up just ahead. Also, there were a number of them, so that a good many were already ranged along the route, and these formed living barricades. This made the chase close enough for discomfort.

Three catfaces rose up before them. Both steeds, well versed in this sort of thing, did not leap, for though they could have cleared the creatures, they would in the process have exposed their vulnerable underbellies to attack from below. Instead they put their heads down and charged low.

The catheads could have handled the horse, but not the deadly horn of the unicorn. That horn could skewer a standing creature instantly. The cats dropped down, giving way, and the party galloped on unscathed.

Half a dozen pigheads appeared, grunting urgently. This time the steeds leaped. The pigheads reached up, but their weapons were their tusks, not good for vertical goring. One got struck in the head by Hinblue's front hoof, and the others desisted.

A pack of wolfheads closed in, but the steeds dodged and galloped to the side and got around and through, then put on speed to leave the beasts behind. No more animalheads appeared, and Stile knew that his party had gotten away clean.

Unnoticed in the hurry, the vegetation had changed. They were now forging through a forest of huge old trees —oak, ash, elm, and beech, by the look. But it was not necessarily easy to tell them apart, for the trunks were gnarled and deeply corrugated, and the tops shaded the ground into gloom.

"I like not the look of this," the Lady Blue said.

Stile agreed. Their escape had led them away from the curtain, so that they now had to relocate. It would not be safe to return to their point of divergence from it; the animalheads were there. Stile still preferred to avoid the use of magic in the present situation; this was an annoyance, not a crisis.

All of which meant they would have to search for the curtain the tedious way—slowly, eyes squinting for the almost invisible shimmer. The curtain was easy to follow lengthwise, but difficult to intercept broadside unless one knew exactly where to look.

"Well, it's all part of the honeymoon," Stile said. The Lady smiled; she had known there would be this sort of interruption in the schedule.

They looked, riding slowly around the great old trees. The forest was so dense now that even indirect light hardly penetrated, yet there were an increasing number of small plants. They twined up around the bases of the tree trunks and spread across the forest floor. Some were a suspiciously verdant green; others were pallid white. Many were insidiously ugly.

Yet they were plants, not creatures. None of them sent questing tentacles for the intruders; none had poisonous thorns. They flourished in gloom; that seemed to be their only oddity.

There was no sign of the curtain. "It will take forever to find it this way," Stile said. "I want to be back on it by nightfall." He jumped down and walked. "We can make a better search on foot," he said.

Clip blew a warning note. Unicorns were naturally resistant to magic, and this protected the rider. The Blue Adept,

Clip felt, needed protection, and should not be straying from his steed. As if Stile did not have ample magic of his own.

Stile walked on, peering this way and that, searching for the curtain. It had to be somewhere near here; they had not gone all that far and they had not diverged from its path greatly. In this gloom the shimmer should be clear enough.

Clip's ears turned. He blew a low warning note. Stile paused to listen.

The animalheads were catching up. Stile's party had to move on before—

Too late. A pigface appeared in front of Stile. A dog-face came up behind the Lady. There was rustling in the bushes all around. Perhaps aided by some sort of stealth-spell, the animalheads had surrounded them.

The Lady called Hinblue, who charged toward her. Stile stepped toward Clip, but already the pighead was on him. Stile did not use magic. He drew his sword, threatening but not attacking the creature. There was something odd about this, and he did not want to do anything irrevocable until he fathomed it.

The pighead halted its aggression—but three sheepheads were closing from the sides. A spell would freeze them, but Stile still didn't want to do it. Rather than shed blood, he dodged around the pighead, hurdled a fallen branch— and an offshoot moved up and intercepted his leading ankle, causing him to take a heavy spill into a flowering bush beyond.

There was a kind of zap! as the leaves were disturbed, and Stile felt the presence of magic. Quickly he jumped up, feeling about his body, but he seemed to have suffered no injury.

The animalheads had taken advantage of his fall to surround him. Clip had stopped a short distance away, perceiving that the animalheads could reach Stile before the unicorn could. No sense precipitating an attack by spooking them.

Stile decided to make an honest attempt at communication before resorting reluctantly to magic to freeze them

temporarily in place. It wasn't natural for normally peaceful creatures to attack and pursue strangers like this.
Maybe he could establish a yes-no dialogue with one of
the more intelligent ones. He really wasn't looking for
trouble on his honeymoon!

He opened his mouth to speak—and nothing but air
emerged. He couldn't talk!

Stile tried again. There was no pain, no constriction in
his throat—but he could not vocalize at all. The plant—it
had zapped him with a spell of silence!

The animalheads did not know about his power of
magic, so did not know what he had lost. They thought
him an ordinary man—which he was now. They converged.

Stile quickly brought the harmonica to his mouth. He
might not be able to speak or sing, but the instrument's
music would summon some protective magic. He blew—
and silence came out.

He stamped his foot on the ground and made no noise.
He banged his sword against a root—silently. He whistled
—without even a hiss of air.

The spell had rendered him totally quiet. Since he could
nullify it only by using his own magic, and that required
sound, he was trapped.

These tests had been performed rapidly, and the conclusion drawn in a few seconds, for the animalheads were on
him. Still he did not use his sword. He had threatened with
it, but remained unwilling actually to shed blood. The
mystery of these creatures' attack bothered him as much
as the threat to himself.

A cathead pounced. Stile ducked, reached up, and
guided it into a turning fall. He might be silent, but he
wasn't helpless!

But now a tremendously tusked boarhead came at him
from the left and an alligatorhead from the right. There
was no question of their intent. He could dodge these
two—but how long could he hold out against the converging mob?

Meanwhile, Clip had resumed motion. Now the unicorn
arrived. His horn caught the alligatorhead and impaled it.

A powerful heave sent the creature flying back over the equine's shoulder. Then a forehoof knocked the boarhead away.

Clip stood beside Stile, giving him a chance to mount. Then they were away in a great leap. Soon they joined Hinblue and the Lady Blue and galloped clear of the animalheads once again.

The Lady Blue realized what was wrong. "Thou art victim of a silence-spell!" she cried. "We must take thee back to the Blue Demesnes for a counterspell!"

But the animalheads were already catching up again, cutting off the return—and of course it would be a long ride all the way back to the Blue Demesnes, even cutting directly across to it. Their only avenue of escape at the moment was north, deeper into the jungle.

The steeds plunged on, but the vegetation thickened. Now grasping plants occurred, reaching thorny branches toward them, opening green jawlike processes. This jungle was coming alive—at the time when Stile had lost his power. A single spell could quell every plant—but he could not utter that spell.

The Lady Blue exclaimed as vines twined about her body. Her steed had to halt, lest she be drawn off. Then the vines attacked Hinblue's legs, seeking to anchor the horse to the ground.

Stile nudged Clip. The unicorn charged back. His horn touched the vines, and they writhed out of the way, repelled by the countermagic. Meanwhile, Stile used his sword to chop at the nether vines, freeing the horse. The weapon normally carried by men in Phaze was the rapier, but Stile felt more comfortable with the broadsword, and now the cutting edge was useful indeed.

There was a renewed baying of animalheads, catching up yet again. Stile's party moved forward once more.

The plants got worse. Tree branches dropped down to bar their way, dangling poisonous-looking moss. Stile cut the moss away with his sword, clearing the path for the Lady and steeds. Ichor from the moss soon covered the blade, turning it gray-green. The stuff reeked with a pungent odor, almost like dragon's blood. Stile did not like this at all. Yet he had to keep hacking the encroaching growth away, afraid to let any of the party get caught.

At last the sounds of pursuit diminished. The animal-heads had been foiled by this vicious jungle too.

But the trees, bushes, and brambles had closed in behind, forming a virtually impenetrable barrier. Stile's sword was already stained and pitted under the ichor, and holes were appearing in his clothing where drops had spattered. He didn't want to hack through any more of this!

Clip blew a musical note. Stile dismounted, and the unicorn phased into the hawk and flew up. The sky was the one open route!

The Lady Blue also dismounted and came to him. "Mayhap I can help thee," she offered. She laid her hands on his throat, and their healing power warmed skin and muscle deep inside. But the silence was not any constriction in his throat, but a cloud of nonsound that surrounded him. He could not be healed because he wasn't ill; the spell itself had to be abated, somehow.

"Mayhap a potion?" the Lady mused, fishing in her purse. But none of the elixirs she had with her seemed promising, and she did not want to expend them uselessly. "Clip may find something," she said hopefully. "From the air, more can be seen."

The jungle was not being idle, however. Plants were visibly growing toward them. This time they were ugly, jointed things, with great brown thorns hooked at each juncture. These things were structured to engage a retreating form, and not to disengage, and they looked as if they had hollow points. Bloodsuckers, surely. Stile brought out his knife and sawed off the nearest thorn stem, severing it with difficulty; the fiber was like cable. By the time he completed the cut, several other tendrils were approaching his boots. He had to draw his sword again, hacking the fibers apart by brute force, clearing a circle around the Lady and horse. He had almost forgotten how formidable nature could be for those who lacked the convenience of magic. It was a reminder in perspective—not that that helped much at the moment.

The hawk returned, changing into man-form. "There is

a domicile ahead, and the land is clear around it," Clip
reported. "An old man lives there, a hermit by his look;
mayhap he will guide us out, can we but reach him. Or we
can follow the curtain; it passes through that clearing. I
have scouted the most direct approach to the curtain. I
can not cross it, but if thou and the Lady and Hinblue
can—the clearing is but a quarter mile from there."

Stile squeezed Clip's arm in thanks. The unicorn had
really come through for them! They could hack their way
to the curtain, cross to Proton, hurry forward, and recross
to recover breath. It would not be fun, but it should be
feasible.

They chopped through the undergrowth with renewed
will. This time the plants were rigidly fan-shaped leaves on
tough stems, the edges of the leaves as sharp as knives.
They did not move to intercept people, but they were
extraordinarily difficult to clear from the path because the
stems were almost inaccessible behind the leaves. When
Stile reached under to sever one stem, the leaves of another plant were in his way; if he sliced through anyway,
he risked brushing the knife-edges along his wrist or fore-
arm. Without magic to heal cuts, he found this nervous
business, though he knew the Lady could help heal him.
Progress was slow, and his sword arm grew tired.

Clip stepped in, using the tip of his horn to reach past
the leaves to break the stems. This enabled them to go
faster, and soon they intersected the curtain.

Stile could not even perform the simple curtain-crossing
spell. The Lady did it for him and Hinblue—and suddenly
the three of them were in Proton, on a barren plain, gasping for air. Clip changed to hawk-form and flew directly to
their rendezvous in the clearing.

They were able to walk on the bare sands, but breathing
was labored, and Hinblue, as the Lady had feared, did not
understand at all. The horse's nostrils flared, and she was
skittish, squandering energy better saved for forward progress. Hinblue was a very fine mare, who could have been a
prizewinner in Proton, but she had had no experience with
this. The Lady led her, though the Lady herself was gasping.

Stile heard his own labored breathing—and realized

what it meant. "I'm not silent any more—no magic in this frame!" he exclaimed.

"But when thou returnest—" the Lady responded.

When he crossed again, the spell would still be on him. He could not escape it this way, except by traveling in this frame back to the region of the Blue Demesnes, where he could cross to get the Lady's reserve spells. But no Proton dome was near; even if he wanted to risk entering one, the trip wasn't feasible.

The horse was in increasing trouble. "My Lord, I must take her back," the Lady gasped. "She does not understand."

Stile had handled a horse in these barrens before. He recognized the symptoms of the growing panic. "Take her across; maybe we're far enough."

They willed themselves across at what seemed to be a clearing. It was—but also turned out to be no safe resting place. The ground writhed with sucker leaves that sought to fasten to the flesh of human or equine. Hinblue stamped her hooves, trampling down the suckers, but already some were fastening on the sides of the hooves, trying to drink from the hard surface. Stile tried to cut off the plants, but they were too low to the ground, making his blade ineffective.

"We can not stay here," the Lady said, her feet moving in a dance of avoidance. "We must cross again."

Stile agreed. The horse had recovered her wind. They crossed back to Proton and made a dash for the better clearing ahead. This time they made it.

Now they were in sight of the hermit's hut. Clip rejoined them, remaining in hawk-form so as not to betray his nature before the watching hermit. They saw the old man's eyes peering from the dark window.

"He sees us," the Lady said. "We shall need his help, for we cannot go through more of this jungle or through Proton."

Stile could only nod. He didn't like this situation at all. Some honeymoon they were having!

The Lady went up to talk to the hermit. But the old man slammed the rickety door and refused to answer her call.

Stile began to get angry. The hawk made a warning cry, and Stile stayed back. Clip had caught on to something important, by his attitude.

The Lady Blue gave it up. "Surely the hermit knows our predicament, but he will help us not," she said. The touch of a flush on her cheeks betrayed her irritation.

The hawk spoke again, then flew to the ground and scratched a place bare. In that spot he gouged out a word: ORANGE.

The Lady was first to catch on. "The Orange Adept! No wonder he is such a curmudgeon!"

Stile signaled, pointing to himself and raising an eyebrow questioningly. He wanted to know whether the Orange Adept was aware of the identity of his visitors.

Clip thought not. This was merely the way the Adept treated all strangers. Few Adepts cared what happened to those who intruded on their Demesnes, and those Adepts who did care, generally were malignant. Stile had encountered the syndrome before, but he did not like it any better with repetition.

They walked to the far side of the clearing, while the beady eyes of Orange peered from the window of his hut. Here the curtain plunged into the thickest of the bramble tangles. Hinblue tried to trample them down, but they wrapped around her foreleg, making her squeal in pain as the thorns dug in. There was a snicker from the hut.

Stile slashed at the mass with his sword, but no matter how many stems he severed, the mass held its form, like a pile of brush. It would be necessary to draw each severed stem out and set it in the clearing—and each stem seemed to interlink with others, so that the entire mass tended to come loose, falling about his bare arms and scratching. The hermit sniggered, enjoying this.

After a time, scratched and sweaty and tired, they gave it up. They could not get through this way. But meanwhile, the clearing had diminished; new plants were encroaching, and they looked just as ugly as the brambles. The Orange Adept's mode of magic evidently related to plants. Indeed, it must have been one of his creatures that silenced Stile. Now the old man was enjoying watching the flies struggle in the web.

"Mayhap the other side of the curtain, again . . ." the Lady said. But at her words Hinblue's ears went back, her nostrils distended, and the whites showed around her eyes. She did not want to brave the oxygen-poor, polluted air of Proton again!

Yet they couldn't remain here. By nightfall the advancing plants would leave them no opening, and they would have to fight for their lives while the Orange Adept laughed. Stile was furious with frustration, but unable to oppose this magic with his own.

Still, he could act directly against the malignant Adept. He put his hand on his sword, facing the hut.

"Nay, my love," the Lady cautioned. "There are worse plants than these, and surely they protect him. We must not approach him."

She was right. Stile had to contain his rage.

Clip flew up and away, searching for some way out. The Lady calmed Hinblue. One thing about the Lady Blue— she did not lose her nerve in a crisis. She was in all respects an admirable woman, his ideal and his beloved. Before Stile let her suffer, he would charge the hut and menace the Adept with his sword, heedless of whatever plants might make their hideous presence known. But first he would wait for Clip, hoping the unicorn would be able to help.

The sun descended inexorably, and the plants continued to close in. Some were like giant vines, with flowers that resembled the orifices of carnivorous worms. Transparent sap beaded in those throats, and drooled from the nether petals like saliva. The sword should stop these—but what would happen when darkness closed? Stile did not want to fight these plants at night.

Clip returned. He landed behind the Lady, so that he could not be seen from the hut, and changed to man-form. "I may have found help," he reported, but he seemed dubious.

"Out with it, 'corn," the Lady snapped.

"I saw no way out of this garden of tortures; it is miles thick. So I searched for other creatures who might assist, but found only a lone-traveling troll."

"A troll!" the Lady cried, distraught. "No help there!"

She was tolerant of many creatures, but hated trolls, for a tribe of them had once tried to ravish her. Stile knew that his alternate self, the former Blue Adept, had had a bad altercation with trolls who had massacred his whole home village and been in turn massacred by him.

"Yet this one seems different," Clip continued. "He travels by day, which is unusual; he was voluminously swathed in black cloth, so that no sunlight might touch him, but I knew his nature by his outline." He wrinkled his nose. "And by his smell." Trolls tended to have a dank-earth ambience.

"Why should a troll travel by day?" the Lady asked, intrigued despite her revulsion. "They are horrors of the night, turning to stone in sunlight."

"Precisely. So I inquired, expecting an insult. But he said he was in quest of the Blue Adept, to whom he owes a favor." Clip shrugged in seeming wonder.

Stile looked askance at this. He had had no commerce with trolls!

"That's what he said," Clip continued. "I was skeptical, fearing more mischief, but, mindful of thy plight, I investigated. 'What favor canst thine ilk do for the likes of the Adept?' I inquired politely. And quoth he, 'I am to bring him to a plant this night.' And quoth I, 'How can the Adept trust a monster like thee?' and quoth he, 'He spared me in my youth, and him I owe the favor of a life—mine or his. He may kill me if he wishes, or follow me to the plant. Only then will part of mine onus be acquitted.' And I said, 'He can not be reached at the moment,' and he said, 'Needs must I go to him now, for only tonight can the first part of my debt be abated,' and I said—"

"Enough!" The lady cried in exasperation. "I know him now. That is the troll my Lord spared a score of years ago. Perhaps that one, of all his ilk, can be trusted. But how can he get here?"

"I was just telling thee," the unicorn replied, hurt. "I said, 'How canst thou pass an impassable barrier of thorns?' and he said he was a troll, skilled at tunneling, like all his kind."

"Tunneling!" the Lady exclaimed, her face illuminating.

"It will take time, for rock is hard, but he promised to be here by midnight."

By midnight. Could they hold out against the encroaching plants until then? They would have to!

It was a mean, harrowing interim, but they held out. At the crack of midnight the ground shuddered and the grotesque head of the troll emerged into the wan moonlight, casting two shadows. The big eyes blinked. "The night is painfully bright," the creature complained.

"This is Trool the troll," Clip introduced. "And this is the Blue Adept, who does not deign to address thee at this time. Lead him to thy plant."

The troll sank back into the earth. Stile followed, finding a fresh tunnel large enough for hands and knees. The Lady came last. Clip shifted back to his natural form and stood with Hinblue, defending against the plants. If Stile did not recover his power and return in time to help them, only the unicorn would survive.

The tunnel continued interminably, winding about to avoid the giant roots of trees and buried boulders. Stripped of his magic, Stile began to feel claustrophobic. If there were a cave-in, what spell could he make? But he had to trust the troll—the one his other self had spared, long before Stile came to Phaze. For this creature felt he had a debt to the Blue Adept, and Stile now held that office. He could try to explain the distinction between himself and his dead other self to the troll, but doubted this would matter. What use to inform Trool that he had come too late, that the one who had spared him was already gone? Better to let the troll discharge his debt and be free.

At last they emerged beyond the Orange Adept's garden. Stile straightened up with relief. They continued on until the troll halted beside a nondescript bush. "This is the plant," Trool said. His voice was guttural and harsh, in the manner of his kind. What made it unusual was the fact that it was intelligible. He must have practiced hard on human speech.

The Lady leaned forward to peer at the growth in the waning light of the blue moon. Her face was somewhat gaunt, and Stile knew she feared betrayal; certainly the

troll's appearance was somewhat too providential. "This is
the herb I need!" she exclaimed in gratified wonder. "It
will cancel half the spell!"

Half? What else was needed?

"The touch of the horn of a unicorn," she said, understanding his thought.

So he could not be cured until they returned to Clip.
His magic would have to wait; he could not use it to
facilitate things now.

The Lady took the leaves she needed and thanked the
troll a bit diffidently. Trool, perhaps unaware of the cause
of her mixed feelings, shrugged and departed, his deed
done. They started the trip back to the Orange Demesnes.

It was no more pleasant traversing the tunnel the second
time, but at least the route was familiar. Dawn was approaching as Stile finally felt the end and poked his head
up through the surface of the ground—only to find it
overgrown with vines. Were they too late?

He wrestled his broadsword out and around and began
slashing and sawing. The plants, attacked from below,
capitulated quickly, and soon Stile and the Lady stood in
their own little hacked-out clearing.

He heard grunts and thumps in the direction of the
hermit's hut. The yellow moon was now out, showing two
equine figures backed against the hut wall, still fighting off
the encroaching foliage. Perhaps the plants were less active
at night, unable to grow as fast without sunlight; or maybe
the Orange Adept was saving the finale for morning, when
he could see better. At any rate, the end was not quite
yet.

Stile hacked a path across the writhing mass of vegetation, the Lady following and tidying things up with her
knife. As the sun broke across the eastern horizon, they
reached the equines.

Hinblue was sweating and bleeding from numerous
scratches, and was so tired she hardly seemed able to stay
on her feet. Clip was better off, but obviously worn; his
horn swung in short vicious arcs to intercept each reaching
tendril. There was very little room left for the two of
them; soon the press of plants and their own fatigue would
overwhelm them.

And the Orange Adept peered out of his window, grinning as if at an exhibition. This was his private arena, his personal entertainment, and he was enjoying it immensely. Stile experienced a flare of primal rage.

Now it was the Lady's turn to act. "Take these leaves," she told Stile, giving him the branch she had taken from the troll's bush. "Clip—thy horn, please." The unicorn paused in his combat with the foliage. Guided by the Lady, he touched his horn to the leaves in Stile's hands.

Stile felt something ease, as if he had been released from an ugly threat. He heard his own breathing. "I thank thee," he said.

Then he did a double take. "Hey, I can speak!"

"Do thou speak some suitable spell," the Lady suggested, nipping off a reaching tendril with her small knife.

Quickly Stile summoned a general-purpose spell from his repertoire. "All save me, in stasis be," he sang.

He had not taken time to coalesce his magic force with preliminary music, so the spell was not fully effective, but its impact was nevertheless considerable. The aggressive plants stopped advancing, and Stile's three companions stood stunned.

Only the Orange Adept proved immune. His head swiveled to cover Stile. "What's this?" the man demanded querulously. "Foreign magic in my Demesnes?"

Now Stile let out his long-accumulating wrath. "Oaf, didst know not against whom thou didst practice thy foul enchantment?"

"I know not and care not, peasant!" Orange snapped, sneering.

"Then learn, thou arrogant lout!" Stile cried. He took his harmonica, played a few savage bars to summon his power, then sang: "Let every single spellbound plant, against its master rave and rant!"

Instantly there was chaos. The magic plants rotated on their stems, reorienting on the Orange Adept. Now the tendrils reached toward the hut, ignoring the visiting party.

"Hey!" Orange screamed, outraged. But a thorny tendril twined about his hand, causing him to divert his attention to immediacies.

Stile made a subspell nullifying the remaining stasis-spell, and equines and Lady returned to animation. Stile and the Lady mounted their steeds, and Stile made a spell to heal and invigorate them. Then they rode out through the vicious plants, which ignored this party in their eagerness to close on the hut.

"That was not nice, my Lord Blue," the Lady murmured somewhat smugly.

"Aye," Stile agreed without remorse. "The plants can't really hurt Orange. He will find a way to neutralize them. But I dare say it will be long before every plant is back the way it was. And longer before he bothers passing strangers again."

When they emerged from the Orange Demesnes, Stile guided them southeast, back toward the region of the animalheads. The Lady glanced at him questioningly, but did not comment.

The animalheads appeared. "Know, O creatures, that I am the Blue Adept," Stile said. "Guide me to your leader."

When they pressed forward menacingly, he resorted to magic. "Animalhead, be friend instead," he sang. And the attitude of each one changed. Now they were willing to take him where he had asked.

Soon they encountered an elephanthead, with a giant fat body to support so large an extremity. The creature trumpeted in confusion.

"Each to each, intelligible speech," Stile sang.

"To what do we owe the questionable pleasure of this visit?" the nasal trumpetings translated, now having the semblance of ordinary human speech.

"I am the Blue Adept," Stile said. "This is my Lady Blue. We are on our honeymoon, touring the curtain with our steeds. We seek no quarrel and do not believe we provoked thy creatures. Why did they attack us?"

The elephanthead considered, his trunk twisting uncertainly. He was evidently loath to answer, but also wary of openly defying an Adept. "We sent a person to inquire of the Oracle, after the shaking of the mountains alarmed us. Hard times may be coming to Phaze, and we are concerned about survival."

"So are we," Stile said. "But we understand we have a safe fortnight for our pleasure journey to the West Pole, and thereafter the Lady Blue will have time to bear my son. So the end of Phaze is not quite yet. But why should you interfere with us?"

"The Oracle advised us that if we permitted a man riding a unicorn to pass our demesnes, half our number would perish within the month."

Suddenly the attitude of the animalheads made sense. "The Oracle claims I am a threat to thy kind?" Stile asked incredulously. "I have had no intention of harming thy creatures!"

"The Oracle did not say thou hast intent; only the consequence of thy passage."

"Let me meet the bearer of this message."

A snakehead came forward. Rendered intelligible by Stile's spell, she repeated the message: "Let pass the man on 'corn, and half will die within the month."

The Lady Blue's brow furrowed. "That is an either-or message, unusual. Can it be a true Oracle?"

"The Oracle is always true," the elephanthead said.

"But just let me check the messenger," Stile said, catching on to the Lady's suspicion. He faced the snakehead, played his harmonica, and sang: "Lady Snakehead, tell me true: what the Oracle said to do."

And she repeated: "Let pass the man on 'corn, and half will die within the month. Prevent him, and in that period all will die."

The elephanthead gave a trumpet of amazement. "Half the message! Why didst thou betray us so, snake?"

"I knew not—" she faltered.

"She was enchanted," the Lady Blue said. "By someone who bore ill will to us all."

The elephanthead was chagrined. "Who would that be?"

"Ask first who could have done it," Stile said.

"Only another Adept," the elephanthead said. "We are enchanted creatures, resistant to ordinary magic, else we would change our forms. Only Adepts can play with our bodies or minds."

"So I suspected," Stile said. "I could not prevail against thy kind until I used my magic. Could this be the handiwork of the Orange Adept?"

"Nay. He dislikes us, as he dislikes all animate creatures, even himself. But he has no power over aught save plants."

"Still, a plant can affect a person," Stile said, thinking of the silence-spell that had so inconvenienced him.

But when he used another spell to check what had happened to the snakehead, it showed her being intercepted by a weaselhead woman, seemingly her own kind, who drew a diagram in the dirt that made a flash of light.

"The White Adept!" Stile exclaimed. "I know her mode of magic and know she likes me not."

"We also do not get along with her," the elephanthead agreed. "We apologize to thee, Blue, for our misunderstanding. We shall not again attempt to do thee ill."

"Accepted," Stile said. "Let us part friends, and if we meet again, it shall be to help each other."

"Thou art generous."

"I like animals." Stile did not see fit to remind the animalheads that they still stood to lose half their number soon. Real mischief was brewing, according to the prophecy.

"We like not Adepts, but to thee we shall be friend." And so they parted on a positive note.

Stile and the Lady proceeded north along the curtain. But they were tired; they had not slept the past night. When a suitable camping spot manifested, they camped. There was a streamlet, a fine old apple tree, and a metal object lying on its side. It was about six feet in diameter, roughly cup-shaped, with a number of depressions on the outer surface, as if someone had dented it with small boulders. It seemed to be made entirely of silver; anywhere except Phaze, it would have been phenomenally valuable. Here, of course, such artifacts could be conjured magically.

A storm was rising. "Would this be a good chamber in which to spend the day and night?" Stile inquired. "It seems watertight."

Clip glanced up from his grazing, blowing a single negative note.

Stile shrugged. "The unicorn says no; who am I to argue with such authority?" And he conjured a suitable tent beside the metal structure.

They slept in the shade of the tent while the equines

grazed and slept on their feet and stood guard simultaneously.

In the late afternoon, Stile woke to an awful shuddering of the ground. He leaped out of the tent.

Clip stood there in man-form. "If thou pleasest, Adept, make a flare above us in the sky that anyone can see."

Stile obeyed. "Make a flare up there," he sang, pointing upward. It was like a rocket exploding in brilliant colors.

The shuddering increased. A monstrous shape appeared, towering above the trees. "WHERE?" it bellowed.

It was a female human-form giant, so big Stile could not even estimate her height.

"Tell her there," Clip said, indicating the metal structure.

Stile magicked a bright arrow in the sky, pointing toward the silver artifact. The giant saw this, followed the direction with her gaze, and leaned down to grasp the thing. Her near approach was harrowing; it seemed as if a building were falling on them, but the small party stood its ground.

"My silver thimble!" the giantess exclaimed, lifting the tiny object into the sky. "My lost thimble! Who found it for me?"

Stile made sky writing: BLUE ADEPT, with an arrow pointing to himself.

She squinted down from above the clouds. "I thank thee, Blue Adept," she boomed. "What favor may I return thee?"

ONLY THY GOOD WILL, Stile skywrote, daunted. One small misstep and the giantess could crush this entire region flat.

"Granted," she said, and departed with her prize.

"Thou knewest!" Stile accused Clip. "A giantess' silver thimble, six feet across!"

"Giants are good people," Clip agreed smugly. "They have long memories too. Best to be on the right side of a giant."

"I should think so," Stile agreed. "And best not to sleep in a giant thimble."

He conjured a modest repast for himself and the Lady, and some grain to supplement the diet of the equines, since they had used so much of their strength the prior night. Then he and the Lady returned to the tent for the night. As he drifted off to sleep the second time, it occurred to Stile that Clip had been giving excellent service. Stile's favorite was Neysa, his oath-friend, but Clip was certainly a worthy substitute. He would have to ponder some favor to do for the unicorn after this was over, as a suitable reward for such things as helping to save Stile's life and dignity. It was hard to do favors for unicorns, because all of them were subject to their Herd Stallions. But perhaps Stile could clear something with the unicorn hierarchy.

In the morning, refreshed, they resumed the journey. The assorted interruptions had put them behind Stile's schedule; now they had to move along to reach the West Pole before he had to return to Proton.

The curtain curved west through the land of the giants. To Stile's relief they encountered no more of the gigantic people. At noon they came to the ocean.

"But the curtain goes right into the water," Stile protested.

"Of course. The West Pole is on an island," the Lady said. "Conjure a boat."

"But I want to follow the curtain where it touches land." Stile had no special reason for this; he had merely envisioned walking along the curtain, not sailing.

"Then conjure away the ocean," she said gaily.

Instead, Stile enchanted them so that the water became like air to them. They walked down into the ocean as if passing through mist, the steeds stepping over the green-coated rocks of the bottom. Fish swam by, seemingly in midair. Seaweed waved in breezelike currents, always surprising Stile since they seemed to lack sufficient support.

Deep down, the light faded, so Stile sang a spell of night vision, making things seem bright. Interesting, how he could use his underwater speaking ability, which was the result of one spell, to make a new spell; magic could be cumulative. Thus it was possible to get around certain limitations in stages. It helped explain how one Adept could kill another, indirectly, by modifying a message so that it caused animalheads to attack an Adept and drive him into the Demesnes of a hostile Adept. Perhaps there were no real limits, only techniques of procedure.

At the deepest level of the sea there was a stirring, and a merman appeared. "Lost thy way?" he inquired of Stile. "We see not many fork-limbed creatures here." He was evidently possessed of the type of enchantment Stile had employed to penetrate the water. It seemed there were natural principles of magic that came into play, whether by spell or by endowment. Stile's understanding of Phaze was constantly expanding.

"I am the Blue Adept," Stile said. "This is my Lady, and these our steeds. We merely pass through, following the curtain, seeking no quarrel."

"Then permit us to guide thee, for there are traps for the unwary." The merman pointed ahead. "Not far from here a hungry sea serpent straddles the curtain. It cares not for the peaceful intent of travelers."

"I thank thee for thy concern. But we are on our honeymoon, and promised ourselves to travel the length of the curtain where possible, seeking the West Pole. We are late on our schedule and prefer not to detour."

"That serpent is fearsome," the merman warned. "None of us dare go near it. Yet if that is thy will, we will not hinder thee." He swam off.

"See thou hast an apt spell ready," the Lady advised, smiling, making the water brighten in her vicinity.

Stile reviewed the spells in his mind, and they rode on. He enjoyed the scenery here, so different from the normal land vistas. Clams of all sizes were waving their feeding nets in the water, and coral-like growths were spreading everywhere. A small yellow octopus eyed them, then noted the menacing unicorn horn and scurried hastily away on all tentacles, leaving a purple ink cloud behind. Stile smiled; this was exactly the kind of honeymoon he liked!

Then they arrived at the lair of the serpent. It was not impressive—merely a tunnel under piled stones. In a moment the ugly snout of the serpent poked out. This creature was not large, as such monsters went; probably one man would represent a sufficient meal for it. But there was no sense taking chances. "Please freeze," Stile sang, and the serpent went still. The freezing was not literal, for Stile had willed only a temporary cessation of motions; his mind controlled the interpretation.

They moved on past. A large, heavy net rose up about them and twined itself together overhead. Stile reacted immediately, whipping out his sword and slashing at the strands—but the blade could not penetrate this net.

Clip ran his horn through it, but again the material held. "This net is magic," the Lady said. "The fibers are enchanted to be strong."

So it seemed. The net itself was magically weighted, so that they could not lift it free of the sea floor, and it was impossible to cut or break.

Stile worked out a spell: "Pesky net, begone yet!" he sang. But though color shimmered across the net's surface, the net remained intact.

"This is the handiwork of another Adept," the Lady said darkly. "Thy power cancels out. In this Adept's Demesnes, thou canst not prevail."

"Maybe not directly," Stile said. He was getting tired of running afoul of other Adepts! "But I can change us into little fishes, and swim through the mesh and escape."

"Me thou canst change," she agreed. "But thyself thou couldst not change back, since fish can neither speak nor sing. And the hostile Adept might have a monster lurking to pounce on such little fish. Risk it not, my Lord."

It was the voice of common sense. In his present form, Stile could guard them against further evil; anything else was too much of a risk. "Yet needs must we slip this net," he grumbled.

Clip blew a note. "There is that," Stile agreed. "I will watch and guard thee until thou dost clear this vicinity."

The unicorn converted to hawk-form, then squeezed through the net where Stile parted the strands for him. The hawk flew swiftly upward while Stile watched, defensive spells ready.

Now a man walked up. He was ordinary in physical appearance, but wore a robe of translucent material that distorted the light and made him seem one with the water. "Thy friend can not help thee from outside, either," he said. "Thou wilt never escape my Demesnes, Blue."

Stile nodded. "Thou must be the Translucent Adept. I have read of thee, but knew not thy residence."

"No one knows my residence," Translucent said. "Who intrudes, pays the price of silence."

"Why shouldst thou harbor evil against me, who has done thee no ill?"

"Thine ill lies in the future, Blue. An thou dost reach the West Pole, the final battle shall be upon us, and no augur knows what will then befall."

"Dost thou mean to say thou hast had a hand in the mischief I have suffered?" Stile inquired. These might be the Translucent Demesnes, but Stile could strike out if he had reason.

"This net is mine, useful to snare intruders. I have not otherwise wrought ill on thee. Dost thou know the nature of thine adversary?"

"I dispatched the Red Adept," Stile said shortly.

"Red was but an instrument, deluded by a false interpretation of an Oracle—as were the beastheads. Another trap was laid for thee near the Green Demesnes, but Green wished not to be implicated, so he nullified it. Adepts bother not Adepts without cause."

This man was surprisingly informed about Stile's business. "Thou dost consider I gave thee cause for this?" Stile indicated the net.

"By intruding on these my Demesnes thou hast given me cause. I tolerate that not. The net was not set for thee, but for intruders. Never have I let an intruder go, and I need make no exception for thee. This does not implicate me in the conspiracy."

"Conspiracy? Since thou art not involved, not implicated, tell me who is."

"Obviously it is the Oracle itself."

Stile was stunned. "The Oracle? But the Oracle has always helped me and spoken true!"

"Has it?" Translucent's lip curled in a practiced sneer.

And Stile had to wonder. The root of many of his problems did seem to lie with the Oracle. He had assumed that mistakes in interpretation or delivery caused the mischief—but why did the Oracle couch its messages in language that so readily lent itself to confusion? The Oracle knew the future; it must therefore also know the effect of its own words. In some cases, a ready understanding of a prediction might cause a person to change his course of action, making the Oracle's message invalid. Since the Oracle was always correct, some obfuscation became necessary to avoid paradox. Or the message could be couched as an either-or situation, as in the case of the animalheads. But why set it up to cause trouble? The animalheads could have been told, "Let the man on the unicorn pass," and done as well for themselves as possible. It did seem that the message had been couched to discriminate against Stile.

"Why would the Oracle seek to do thee mischief?" the Lady asked.

"I shall leave thee to ponder that at leisure," the Translucent Adept said, and departed.

"At leisure—until we starve?" the Lady asked.

"Maybe I'd better transform us," Stile said.

"Nay," the Lady said. "We are not in immediate danger. Thou canst conjure in food while we await the unicorn's return."

Stile did not feel easy. For one thing, he could not afford to wait indefinitely; he had promised to return to Proton at a specified time, and that time was near. For another, he did not trust the Translucent Adept to let things be; the man knew he could not long keep another Adept captive. He might even now be preparing some more threatening measure. It would be no easier for him to devise a way to destroy Stile than it was for Stile to find a safe escape; they were at an impasse at the moment. How long would that last?

But he hardly had time to worry before the move came. Monstrous pincers forged down from above, closing inexorably on the net. Each section was six feet in diameter, rounded, with a horny surface on one side. No physical way to resist that mass! Stile readied his transformation-spell.

"Wait!" the Lady cried. "That is the giantess!"

Of course! How could he have failed to recognize her

colossal fingers? Clip had brought the one creature capable of lifting the net!

The giantess' fingers closed on the net, while Stile and the Lady herded Hinblue as far to one side as possible, avoiding the central pinch. The tremendous rocky fingernails caught in the ropes. The hand lifted—and the net came up. They were hauled up with it, through the water to the surface, and swung across to land.

Now, too late, it occurred to Stile that he could have done this himself, conjuring a sky hook to lift them all free. Or he might have summoned superpowerful cutting pincers to sever individual strands. Under the pressures of the moment, he had not been thinking well. He would have to school himself to perform better under magical pressure.

Here, beyond the Translucent Demesnes, Stile's magic could overcome the enchantment of the net directly. The strands melted and flowed into the sand, freeing them at last.

"I thank the giantess," Stile said, his voice booming through a conjured megaphone.

"I owe thee for my thimble," she boomed back. "Thank thy friend for showing me the way." She turned and strode northeast, toward the demesnes of the giants. She hummed as she went, making a sound like distant thunder.

Clip was there in natural form, having arrived unobtrusively. "I do thank thee, unicorn," Stile said sincerely. "Again thou hast gotten me out of mischief. I would do thee some return favor."

Clip shifted to man-form. "My sister Neysa bid me look after thee in her stead. She loves thee, and I love her. Say no more, Adept." He shifted back.

Stile said no more. Clip was certainly fulfilling his commission! Most unicorns would not tolerate a human rider at all and had little use for Adepts. Stile had won the respect of the Herd Stallion, so was permitted to ride a unicorn—yet Clip's service was more than that of a mere steed. No friend could have done more. There would have to be a repayment of some sort. He would continue to ponder the matter in off moments, seeking what was suitable.

There was now the matter of the Translucent Adept. Stile decided, with a certain inner regret, to let that be. He *had* intruded on the Translucent Demesnes, and the Adept had not discriminated against him. Stile had won sufficient victory by escaping the net. To attack another Adept at this point would be to initiate trouble, rather than reacting to it.

He looked ahead. They were on the island of the West Pole. It was pleasant enough, with deciduous trees scattered across gently rolling pasture. Small flowers bloomed randomly, and a number of shrubs bore fruit. A person could live fairly comfortably here without much labor.

The curtain continued west. They followed it—and suddenly, three miles in from the beach, they were at the West Pole. It was marked by a big X on the ground.

Stile looked down at it. "That's it?" he asked, disappointed.

"Didst thou expect perchance a palace?" the Lady inquired with a smile.

"Well, yes, or something spectacular. This X on the ground—how do we know this is really the spot?"

"Because the curtains intersect here, my love." She stood on the X and pointed north-south with her arms. "Here is the other curtain. It proceeds at right angles."

Stile looked carefully. There it was—another curtain, like the first, crossing at the X. He spelled himself across, and found himself on a barren elevation of Proton. Holding his breath, he strode to the east-west curtain and willed himself across. He was back in Phaze. The two curtains were similar, except for orientation.

"And from here thou canst sight along them, to see that they are straight," the Lady said.

Stile stood on the Pole and sighted east. The line was absolutely straight; all the meanderings they had traveled now seemed to be distortions of the land of Phaze and the land of Proton. Interesting perspective!

Curious as to how far this went, he conjured a powerful telescope, one based on the macron principle, and oriented on the line again. It went straight for what might be thousands of miles, until the focus found the backside of a standing man. That man was holding an object to his eye.

"Oh, no!" Stile exclaimed. "That's me!" And he kicked up one foot, verifying it. "This line does not even acknowledge the curvature of the planet!"

"Of course not," the Lady said. "Phaze is flat."

"But Phaze has the same geography as Proton—and Proton is a sphere. How can that be?"

"Phaze is magic; Proton is scientific."

Stile decided to let that wait for further thought. Another problem had occurred. "This is a telescope I'm using—I didn't think—I mean it's a scientific instrument. It shouldn't work here in the magic frame."

"Methought thou didst know," the Lady said. "The West Pole is the juxtaposition of frames. Magic and science both work, on this spot. That is what makes it worth visiting."

"Juxtaposition," Stile repeated, intrigued. "Could both selves of a person meet here, then?"

"Methinks they would merge here, and separate again when they moved away from the Pole, but I know not for sure."

"Science and magic merging at this particular juncture! I wonder if this is the way the universe began, with everything working both ways, and somehow the frames began separating, like cells dividing or surfaces pulling apart, so that people had to choose one or the other, never both? Like matter and anti-matter. Except for a few anchorages like this. This *is* special!"

"Aye," she agreed. "Methought thou wouldst like it. Many impossible tricks of science are possible here."

Stile sighed. "Now we have reached our destination. Our time is up, our honeymoon over, and I must return to Proton for a stint of Citizenship."

"Our time is not up," she said. "Merely held in abeyance. Our honeymoon will endure as long as we permit. Conjure me a small residence here, and I will await thy return."

"But the hostile signals, the dire warnings—suppose something should happen during mine absence?"

"Methinks the hostility was directed more at thee than at me. I should be safe enough. But with Clip and Hinblue to guard me, I shall surely not want for protection."

"Still, I want to be sure," Stile said, pacing a small circle about the Pole. "Too much has threatened, and thou art too great a treasure to risk." He pondered. "If the West Pole permits science, could I set up a holographic pickup and broadcast unit, to reach me in Proton-frame? Would it transmit thine image successfully?"

"We can find out," she said.

Stile worked out a spell and conjured a standard Proton unit of the type used for projections originating outside the domes. He set it up and got it running; it could handle all that was visible from this point. Then he conjured an oxygen mask and crossed into barren Proton farther east, carrying a conjured receiver. It worked well enough; a globe formed in air and he looked into it to see the view of whatever direction he faced. He spun its orientation and caught the circular panorama as if turning in place at the West Pole. He halted it in place when he spied the Lady Blue standing beside the grazing Hinblue.

"I see thee," Stile said, activating the voice-return. This hand-held unit could not transmit his picture, but that wasn't necessary.

"I love thee," she returned, smiling. "Thee, thee, thee."

"Thee, thee, thee," he repeated, in the Phaze convention of unqualified love, feeling warm all over. Then he stepped back across the curtain and conjured a tent for privacy. Clip snorted musically, not looking up from his grazing.

"But thou knowest what thou must do in the other frame," the Lady reminded him sternly.

Stile sighed. He knew. But for another hour he could put it from his mind.

And in due course he conjured himself back to his usual curtain-crossing place and returned to his duties in Proton.

CHAPTER 6

Commitment

Sheen was waiting for him. "How was your honeymoon, sir?" she inquired with a certain emphasis.

"Trouble with two other Adepts, rescued by a troll and a giantess. Routine fare."

"Obviously," she agreed wryly. "Are you ready to approve your new staff, sir? And your temporary economy residence?"

There was that "sir" again. "I'd better, Sheen."

She guided him to a Citizen transport capsule. It was ordinary from the outside, but like a spaceship cabin inside. Through the port a holograph of moving stars could be glimpsed. A rotund, balding serf walked up the aisle and stood at attention, wearing only a tall white hat.

"Speak to him, sir," Sheen murmured.

"Who are you?" Stile asked.

"Sir, I am Cookie, your chef."

"I just happen to be hungry enough to eat a bear," Stile said. The recent action in Phaze had taken his mind from food, causing him to miss a meal.

"Immediately, sir." Cookie disappeared.

Stile blinked. "Oh—he's a holo too."

"Naturally, sir. There is not room in this capsule for a kitchen. We'll arrive in a few minutes, and he will have your meal ready."

Another naked serf entered the spaceship. This one was an attractive older woman. Stile raised an inquiring eyebrow. "I am Henriette, your head housemistress, sir," she said primly.

Stile wondered what a housemistress did, but decided not to inquire. Sheen would not have hired her without reason. "Carry on, Henriette," he said, and she vanished.

Next was a middle-aged man not much larger than Stile himself. "I am Spade, your gardener, sir."

"Sam Spade?" Stile inquired with a smile.

But the man did not catch the historical-literary allusion. Only a Game specialist would be up on such minutiae. "Sir, only Spade, the gardener."

"Of course, Spade." Stile made a gesture of dismissal, and the man vanished.

Next was a voluptuously proportioned young woman with black tresses flowing across her body to her knees. "Of her it is said, let the rose hang its head," Stile murmured, conscious that the rhyme would work no magic here in Proton-frame.

The girl took this as the signal to speak. "I am Dulcimer, your entertainer, sir."

Stile glanced at Sheen. "What kind of entertainment do you suppose I need?"

Sheen was suppressing a smile in the best human fashion. "Dulce, show the Citizen your nature."

Dulcimer put both hands to her head, took hold of her ears, and turned her head sharply sidewise. There was a click; then the head lifted off her body. "At your service, sir."

"A robot!" Stile exclaimed. Then, more thoughtfully: "Are you by chance one of Sheen's friends?"

"I am, sir," the robot head said.

"Put yourself together," Stile told her, and the head was lowered and twisted back into place. Stile waved her away, and Dulcimer vanished.

He turned seriously to Sheen. "Do you think this is wise?"

"Sir, I can not always guard you now. A Citizen depends on no single serf. You can use Dulce when I am not available."

"A machine concubine? Forget it. You know I have no present use for such things. Not since I married the Lady Blue."

"I know, sir," she agreed sadly. "Yet you need protection, for you will be making rivals and perhaps enemies among Citizens. It would not do for a Citizen to take his cook or housemaid or gardener to social functions."

"But Dulcimer would be okay. Now I understand." He considered briefly, then decided to get his worst chore out of the way. "Before we arrive, set up a privacy barrier. I want to talk to you."

"It is already in place. Others must not know that self-willed machines associate with you. Sir."

"You can drop the 'sir' when privacy is guaranteed," he said a trifle sharply. "You were never my inferior, Sheen."

"I was never your equal, either," she said. "What do you wish to say to me?"

Stile nerved himself and plunged in. "You know that I love only the Lady Blue. What went before is history."

"I have no jealousy of the Lady Blue. She is your perfect wife."

"She is my perfect woman. Before her, you were that woman; but I changed when I became the Blue Adept. The marriage is only a social convention, applying to the frame of Phaze. Here in Proton I remain single."

"Citizens do not have to marry, not even to designate an heir. I don't see your problem."

"Yet there are marriages of convenience, even among Citizens."

"Especially among Citizens. They marry for leverage, or to pool estates, or to keep a favored serf on Proton beyond his or her twenty-year tenure. They hardly ever worry about love or sex or even appearance in that respect."

"Yet there are legal aspects," Stile continued doggedly. "The spouse of a Citizen has certain prerogatives—"

"Entirely at the pleasure of the Citizen," she said. "The spouse may be immune to tenure termination or molestation by other Citizens, but the Citizen can divorce that spouse merely by entering a note in the computer records. So it means nothing, unless the spouse is another Citizen."

"It means the spouse is a person, for at least the duration of the marriage," Stile said.

"A serf is already a person. Marriage to a Citizen merely enhances status for a time. The main hope of serfs who marry Citizens is that one of their children will be designated heir, since such a child shares the bloodline of the Citizen. But there is no guarantee. Each Citizen is his own law."

"Sometimes a Citizen will designate the spouse as heir," Stile said.

She shrugged. "All this is true, Stile. But what is the point?"

"I have it in mind to marry in Proton, and to designate my wife my heir."

"Oh." She pondered, her computer mind sorting through the implications. "A marriage of convenience to protect your estate. Not for love or sex or companionship."

"For all these things, in part," he said.

"What does the Lady Blue think of this?"

"She suggested it. Though she is able to cross the curtain, she has no affinity for this frame, and no legal status in it. You say you have no jealousy of her; neither does she have jealousy of you."

"Of me? Of course she doesn't! I'm a machine."

"Yes. But she regards you as a person. Now, with this basic understanding, I—" He hesitated.

"You want me to locate a suitable bride of convenience for you?"

"Not exactly. Sheen, I want you to be that bride."

"Don't be silly, Stile. I'm a robot. You know that."

"I see I have to do it the hard way." Stile got out of his comfortable chair. She started to rise, but he gestured her to remain seated.

Stile knelt before her, taking her hand. "Lady Sheen, I ask your hand in marriage."

"I shouldn't be sensitive to humor of this sort," she said. "But I must say I didn't expect it of you."

"Humor, hell! Will you marry me?"

Machines were not readily surprised, but she was programmed to react in human fashion. She paled. "You can't be serious!"

"I am serious, and my knee is getting uncomfortable. Will you answer me?"

"Stile, this is impossible! I'm—"

"I know what you are. You always bring it up when you're upset. I am a Citizen. I can do as I wish. I can marry whom I choose, for what reason I choose."

She stared at him. "You are serious! But the moment you tried to register me as—as—they would know my nature. They would destroy me."

"They would have to destroy me first. Answer."

"Stile, why are you doing this? The mischief—"

"I see I must answer you, since you will not answer me. If I marry you, you will be the wife of a Citizen. By definition, a person. By extension, others of your type may then be considered persons. It is a wedge, a lever for recognition of the self-willed machines as serfs. This is a service I can do for them."

"It really *is* convenience," she said. "Using me to help my friends forward their case for recognition as people."

"Which would be even more potent if something put me out of the scene prematurely and thrust the onus of Citizenship on you."

"True," she said.

"Is that my answer? Does true equate to yes?"

"No!" she snapped, jumping up. "I don't want your title, I want your love!"

Stile got off his knee silently. His love was one thing he could not offer her.

"In fact, I don't want your convenience," she continued, working up some unrobotic temper. "I don't want the appearance without the reality. I don't want to be used."

"I don't propose to use you—"

"I'm not talking about sex!" she screamed. "I would be happy for that! It's being used as a lever I object to."

"I'm sorry. I thought it was a good idea."

"You in your flesh-male arrogance! To set me up as a mock wife to be a lever, the simplistic machine I am! You thought because I love you I'll do anything you want. After all, what pride can a mere machine have?"

What had he walked into? Stile brought out his holo receiver and called the Lady Blue.

The picture-globe formed. Stile turned it about until the Lady Blue came into view. She was brushing down Hinblue. "Lady," he said.

She looked up. "My Lord!"

Sheen paused in her pacing. "You're in touch with *her?*"

"Aye, Lady Sheen," the Lady Blue answered, recognizing her voice. "And easy it is to understand the nature of thy concern. I confess I put my Lord up to it."

"I should have known," Sheen said, bemused. "But this is a cynical thing, Lady."

"Aye, Lady. It is a cruel sacrifice for thee."

"That's not the point, Lady. The sheer mischief—"

"I apologize for putting thee in an untenable position, Lady Sheen. Thou hast every right to reject it." She gave Hinblue another stroke, then addressed Stile. "My Lord, I thought not of her feeling, only of her merit. I wanted her as my sister in that frame, and that was selfish. Let her be. I love thee." She returned to the horse, dismissing him.

Stile turned off the holo. "I guess that covers it, Sheen." He felt embarrassed and awkward. "If it's any comfort, I felt about the same as you, when she broached the notion. I do care for you; I always did. I just can't honestly call it love."

"I accept," Sheen said.

"You are generous to accept my apology. I wish I had not put you through this."

"Not the apology. The proposal."

"The—?"

"Remember way back when, you proposed marriage?"

Stile was amazed. "I—"

"Yes, *that* proposal. If you had the circuitry of a robot, you'd remember these details more readily. Perhaps if you practiced mnemonic devices—"

"But why? You made such a good case against—"

"She wants it," she said simply.

That he could understand. He had proposed to Sheen because the Lady Blue wanted it; she had accepted for the same reason. Now they just had to hope it was a good idea.

The capsule had come to a halt, the portholes showing a landing at a spaceport. Sheen keyed the door open. Stile gaped.

Outside lay the Blue Demesnes.

No, of course it was the Proton equivalent, on the same geographic site. Merely one of numerous examples of parallelism of frames. The castle and grounds looked the same as in Phaze, but there was no magic. Horses grazed and dogs ranged, not unicorns and werewolves. Still, it moved him.

"After the Lady Bluette died, her Employer restored the property and put it on the market," Sheen explained. "It was at a bargain price. I thought you'd like it."

"I do." Stile stared at it a moment longer. "But it's strange here."

"No Lady Blue," she said.

"It will be yours now."

She was silent. Had he said the wrong thing? Well, either it would work out or it wouldn't.

His chef had his meal waiting: genuine imported roast of bear. Stile made a mental note not to speak figuratively; as a Citizen, he was too apt to be taken literally. He had said he could eat a bear; now he had to do it.

Actually, it wasn't bad. The chef did know his business. Sheen had hired people of genuine competence.

"And now for your estate adviser," Sheen said as Stile chomped somewhat diffidently. "You have some elegant financial maneuvering ahead."

"I'd rather master the rules of the game and lay it myself."

"This adviser is one of my friends."

Oh. That was a different matter.

The adviser turned out to be an old male serf, wrinkled, white-haired, and elegant. Stile would not have known him for a robot, had Sheen not informed him. It was evident that the self-willed machines had profited from what Sheen had learned in the course of her association with Stile; only time, expert observation, or direct physical examination betrayed his current associates.

Stile nodded affirmatively to the serf, and the man reported: "Sir, I am Mellon, your financial accountant."

"Mellon, eh?" Stile repeated. "As in Rockefeller, Carnegie, and Du Pont?"

The serf smiled. "Yes, sir."

"You're that good with money?"

"Yes, sir."

"Then why are you here as a serf, instead of making your fortune elsewhere in the universe?" Stile knew the robot had no future away from Proton, but a real serf would, and the cover story had to be good.

"Sir, I have already made my fortune elsewhere," Mellon said. "I am as rich as a Citizen. But here on Proton the dynamics of wealth are most pronounced; the leverage of economics is exerted most openly. Only here can I experience the joy of renewed challenge, failure, and success. When my tenure expires, I shall return to my comfortable galactic estate and write my memoirs of the Proton experience."

Stile was impressed. This was a feasible rationale. It would explain the man's computerized competence. Stile might even have to stave off efforts by other Citizens to hire Mellon away. Except that since no real Mellon existed, any verification of his background would reveal—

"I am cast in the likeness of an actual person, sir," Mellon said, reading Stile's expression. "The proceeds of my memoirs will go to him, in recompense for the use of his credentials."

The machines had figured it all out! "Well, I hope you are not disappointed in the experience you have managing my estate. I don't even know its extent, but I'm trusting you to multiply it for me rapidly."

"I shall do so, sir. I must ask that you follow my advice in particulars with alacrity. There are likely to be difficult moments, but there is an eighty-five percent probability of accomplishing our objective."

Mellon certainly seemed sure of himself! The machines had to have secrets that could be exploited for tremendous leverage. Stile suspected he should leave it alone, but his curiosity governed. "How do you propose to make me rich, even by Proton standards? Surely my section of the Protonite mines can only produce so much."

"By wagering, sir. You will be better informed than your opponents."

Because of the immense body of information accessible to the sapient machines. But it would be made to seem like human instinct and luck. "No."

"Sir?"

"To wager when one has an illicit advantage is not equitable. I do not care to make my fortune that way."

"He's like that, Mel," Sheen said smugly.

"Sir, without that advantage, the odds become prohibitive."

"I have surmounted prohibitive odds before. I shall not compromise my standards now. Presumably you will be able to perform moderately well while limited to ethical means."

"Yes, sir," Mellon said grimly.

Stile completed his uncomfortable repast of bear steak. "Then let's get to it now. I am not used to wealth. I fear this will be a chore for me. I want to get that chore out of the way and return to—my private retreat." Even among his staff, he was not inclined to talk too freely of Phaze. "But first—Sheen?"

"Sir," Sheen said immediately.

"By what mechanism do I promulgate my engagement to you?"

"Application must be made to the Records Computer, sir. A Citizen hearing will be arranged."

"And?"

"That is all, sir. Marriages, births, designations of heirs, changes in estate holdings—all are merely a matter of accurate record. The hearing is a formality, to make sure there is no foul play or confusion."

"No ceremony? Blood tests? Waiting periods?"

"These are available if you wish them, sir. But they are not required for Citizens and are irrelevant for robots. The entry in the record is all that is mandatory."

"Well, let's do this right. Let's set a date for a formal, medieval, Earth-style nuptial, and invite the public."

"What date, sir?"

Stile considered. "There may be some mischief here. Let's give it time to clear. Set the date for two months hence, at which time you will become my wife and heir. Get yourself a pretty wedding outfit."

Mellon coughed. "Sir, may I comment?"

"Comment," Stile agreed.

"The Records Computer will know Sheen is not a legal person. It will advise the members of the Citizen panel. This will not interfere with the marriage, for a Citizen may do what pleases him; he may marry a toad if he wants. But the designation of a nonperson as heir to Citizenship will complicate your own activities. If you could hold that aspect in abeyance—"

"That would be a lie," Stile said. "I intend to name her heir, and I want no deception about it." Yet he wondered at his own motive, since this was more than the Lady Blue had suggested. Why make a larger issue of it? And he answered himself; because he felt guilty about not being able to give Sheen his love, so he was giving her his position instead.

"Yes, sir," Mellon said submissively.

"Sir, he is correct," Sheen said. "If you bring this mischief on yourself prematurely—"

"I will not abuse my word," Stile said firmly. "The truth shall be known."

"Sir, I fear you will imperil yourself and us," she said. "Rather than permit that, I shall decline to—"

"Do you want me to call the Lady Blue again?"

Sheen hesitated. "No, sir."

So he had bluffed her out! "How do I file my entry with the Records Computer?"

"Sir, I can activate its receptor—"

"Do so."

She touched a button on the wall. "Records, sir," a wall speaker said.

"I, Stile, Citizen, hereby announce my betrothal to the Lady Sheen. I will marry her two months hence in public ceremony, and designate her to become my heir to Citizenship effective that date. Any questions?"

"Sir, are you aware that Sheen is a robot?" the computer asked.

"I am aware."

"If you designate a nonperson heir, your estate will, on your demise or abdication, revert to the common pool, sir."

"I challenge that," Stile said. "I want her to inherit."

"Then a special hearing will be necessary, sir."

"We already have a hearing. Juxtapose them. Schedule it at your earliest convenience."

"Yes, sir." The Records Computer disconnected.

"Now you have done it, sir," Sheen murmured. "You and your unstable living human temper."

"We'll see. Let's get to the next event."

They entered the capsule again, and Sheen programmed their destination. The smooth motion commenced. Stile paid attention to none of this; he was already orienting on the wagering to come, much as he would for a Game of the Tourney. He was not sure he had really left the challenge ladder; perhaps he had merely achieved a new plateau for a new series of games.

"To wager—what are my present resources?" he asked Mellon.

"The initial estate of a Citizen is set at one kilogram of Protonite, sir," Mellon said. "Serfs do not deal in money, normally, so there is little way to equate this with what you have known."

"I know that a single ounce of Protonite is supposed to be worth the entire twenty-year tenure of the average serf," Stile said.

"Yes, traditionally. Actually, this fluctuates as the variables of demand and technology change the need, though the Proton Council regulates the supply to keep the price fairly stable, much as the cartels of the galaxy have traditionally regulated the supplies of foregoing fuels—coal, oil, uranium, and such."

"Until supplies ran short," Stile said. "Or until technology obviated the need. Efficient utilization of starlight, and hydrogen fusion—these became virtually limitless resources."

"Indeed, sir. But starlight and fusion both require enormous initial capital investment. Though Protonite is theoretically limited, it is so potent that it has become the fuel of choice for interstellar travel. Its value more closely resembles that of bullion gold than that of bygone oil."

"Gold," Stile said. "I have played with that in my historical researches. I have a fair notion of its value, as measured in archaic ounces."

"Then set one gram of Protonite as equivalent to four hundred troy ounces of gold, sir. One kilogram—"

"Four hundred thousand ounces of gold!" Stile finished, amazed despite himself.

"Enough to hire a thousand serfs for full tenure, sir," Mellon said. "A fortune equivalent to that of many of the historically wealthy persons of Earth. That is your minimum share of Citizenship; wealthy Citizens control the equivalent of as much as a ton of Protonite, so are richer than any historical figure."

"I see that," Stile agreed, somewhat awed. He had known Citizens were exceedingly rich, but still had underestimated the case. "And I must become one of those wealthy ones?"

"You must become the wealthiest Citizen, sir," Mellon agreed. "Only then can you be reasonably secure against the forces that may be brought to bear. Our target is two metric tons of Protonite."

"That's two thousand kilograms!" Stile exclaimed.

"Precisely, sir. There have been wealthier Citizens in the past, but at present none go beyond this level. Only extraordinary expertise can bring you to this."

"Expertise, yes; illicit information, no."

"Yes, sir."

"And how much of my single, insignificant kilogram may I employ for gambling?"

"Three quarters of it, sir. You must, by Proton custom that has the force of law, maintain a floor of two hundred and fifty grams for normal household use."

"Some household! That's a hundred thousand ounces of gold!"

"True, sir. No Citizen is poor by galactic standards."

"I seem to remember Sheen telling me that no Citizen could get more than two years' income in arrears."

"That is an optional guideline for the conservative."

"I see. But I can't afford to be conservative, can I? And if I gamble and lose, so I'm stuck at the floor level—then what?"

"Your share is not a literal kilogram, sir, but rather the equivalent in continuing production from the Protonite mines. In time—perhaps a year—you will have an income of ten to twenty additional grams. Enough to maintain a modest estate without depleting your principal."

"Oh, I wouldn't want to deplete my principal," Stile

said, feeling giddy. Even a Citizen's small change vastly exceeded his expectation. "Still, to build a stake of seven hundred and fifty grams up to an estate of two thousand kilograms—that will take rapid doubling and redoubling."

"Certainly, sir. And we shall not be risking all of the discretionary funds. Reverses are to be expected. I recommend an initial limit of one hundred grams per wager."

"And your recommendation is my law."

"Yes, sir, in this respect. Except—"

"Except that I will handle the substance of the wagers myself, drawing on none of your computer information. I presume you feel this makes me likely to fail."

"Yes, sir," Mellon said unhappily. "I have considerable strategic resource, were it permissible for use."

"Were it not the way I am, your kind would not have trusted me to keep their secret."

"Yes, sir." But considerable disapproval was conveyed in that acquiescence.

"Very well, let's review this matter. You have the entire information bank of the planetary computer network available to you. The average wagering Citizen does not. Would you consider it fair play for us to use this? I submit that it represents an unfair advantage, and to use it would be dishonest."

"Citizens have very few restrictions, sir. They may draw on any available facilities. I think it likely that some will seek to take advantage of your inexperience. Turnabout may be considered fair play."

"Very well. If I encounter a Citizen who is trying to take unfair advantage, I'll draw on your information to turn the tables. But I'll balk at anything I deem to be unethical. I will cheat only the cheaters."

"Understood, sir. It would be unwise to seem to follow the advice of a serf too slavishly."

Evidently the issue of personal integrity still eluded the robot. "Yes. A Citizen must keep up arrogant appearances."

Now Sheen, who had remained scrupulously clear of this discussion, rejoined it. "I am sure you will have no difficulty, sir."

She was a machine, but she was programmed for human emotion. How much did she resent the use he was making of her?

The event they attended turned out to be a routine Citizens' ball. Sheen and Mellon, as favored servitors, were permitted to accompany Stile, but they kept subserviently behind him. At the entrance they outfitted Stile with a suitable costume for the occasion: a seemingly cumbersome ancient spacesuit, puffed out around the limbs with huge joints at the elbows and knees, and a translucent helmet bubble. Actually, the material was very light and did not hamper movement at all.

They entered the ballroom—and Stile was amazed. It was outer space in miniature. Stars and planets, somewhat out of scale; comets and nebulae and meteors and dust clouds. The motif was not remarkable, but the execution was spectacular. The stars were light without substance, holographically projected, but they looked so real he was fearful of getting burned if he floated too near. For he was floating, in effect, on the invisible floor; the soles of his space boots were padded, so that his footsteps made no sound.

Citizens in assorted varieties of spacesuits floated in groups, their serf-servitors like satellites. One spotted him and moved across. It was the Rifleman. "I see you are mixing in, Stile. Excellent. Let me introduce you to key figures. What is your preference? Romance, camaraderie, or mischief?"

"Mischief," Stile said, grateful for the man's help. "I want to make some wagers."

"Oh, *that* kind! It's the gamesmanship in your blood. I know the feeling well. But we have some high rollers here; they'll strip you down to your minimum estate in short order, if you let them. You can never bet all your wealth, you know; computer won't allow any Citizen to wipe out. Bad for the image."

"I understand. I have a competent monetary adviser."

"You will need him. I warn you, Stile, there are barracuda in these waters. Best to play penny ante until you get to know them."

By the same token, though, the barracuda would get to know him—and his adviser. That would not do. He needed to score rapidly, before others grew wary. "What is considered penny ante here?"

"One gram of Protonite."

"That was all I was worth a few days ago."

The Rifleman smiled. "I, too, in my day. Times change, Citizen. This is a whole new world."

"I hope not to do anything foolish before I acclimatize."

"Oh, by all means do be foolish," the Rifleman said encouragingly. "It is expected of all new Citizens. You are the novelty of the day; enjoy it while you can."

All this time the Rifleman had been guiding Stile across the miniature galaxy. Now they came to a group of space-suited Citizens hovering near a large dark nebula. The men were rotund and unhandsome; rich living had shaped them to porcine contours that even the ballooning suits could not ameliorate. This disgusted Stile; he knew that they could easily have kept their weight down by consuming diet food that tasted identical to the calorific food, or by having reductive treatments. Apparently they just didn't care about appearance.

But the two women were a striking contrast. One was an hourglass, her breasts like pink melons, her waist so tiny Stile knew that surgery had reduced it, her hips re-surging enormously, tapering into very large but well-contoured legs. Stile found this exaggeration of female traits unpleasant, but even so, it had its impact upon him. Her breasts swelled like the tides of an ocean as she breathed, and her hips shifted elevation precipitously as she walked. Her suit was only remotely related to space; most of it was transparent, and much of the front was mere netting. It seemed to Stile that in real space those enormous mammaries would detach explosively and fly outward like the rings of gas and dust from old super-novae. But she had a pretty face, almost elfin; surely the handiwork of a fine plastic surgeon.

The other woman was decorously garbed in an opaque cloth-type suit that covered every portion of her body. Her head was encased in a translucent bubble that shadowed her face and lent enticing mystery to her expression. She seemed almost too young to be a Citizen—but of course there was no age limit.

The Rifleman introduced the whole group, but the names of the men bounced off Stile's awareness like rainwater. Only the two women registered consciously; he had never before heard the name of a female Citizen, and it affected him with an almost erotic force. ". . . Fulca, with the fulsome figure," the Rifleman was concluding. "And Merle, known to her illustrious enemies as the Blackbird."

Illustrious enemies? Blackbird? If this were not mere posturing, this was a Citizen to be wary of.

The two women nodded as their names were spoken. "You're the new franchise, aren't you?" Fulca inquired.

"Yes, sir," Stile said, then visibly bit his tongue. Both women smiled.

"Stile would like to wager," the Rifleman said. "He's a Gamesman, you know, with an eye to pulchritude."

The male Citizens stood back, curious but not participating, as if more intrigued by the manner in which the females would handle this upstart than by the prospect of making some profit. "Anything," Fulca agreed. "Choose your mode, bantam."

There was that ubiquitous reference to his size. He would probably never be free of such disparagement. No sense in letting it rattle him. He had what he wanted—someone to wager with.

Stile's imagination suddenly deserted him. "Uh, small, to start. Very small. And simple."

Her glance traversed him merrily. "For a small, simple man. Agreed."

Was that another cut at him? Probably not; it was evident that Citizens treated each other very casually. What did they have to prove? They were all elite. Or maybe this was part of his initiation. The watching males gave no sign.

"Uh, scissors-paper-stone?" Stile asked, casting about for something suitable and drawing no inspiration from the environment. Without the Game's preliminary grid, he lacked notions.

"Ah, a noncontact game," she said as if surprised. Now

one of the watching males nodded at another, as if the two
had made a bet on the matter that had now been decided.
So that was the nature of their interest—to wager on
Stile's performance with the voluptuous woman. No doubt
many men sought to get close to her on one pretext or
another. This actually encouraged Stile; he was beginning
to grasp the situation. "Small and simple," he repeated.

"Shall we say one gram, doubled each round, seven
rounds?" Fulca suggested.

Stile glanced at Mellon, who made an almost perceptible
nod of assent. The final bet would fall within the limitation, though the total amount of the series would not.
These Citizens were indeed a fast crowd! Again one of the
males nodded, having a point decided—what level Stile
was playing at.

"May I call the throws?" the Rifleman asked. "On the
count of two, spaced one second; late throw means default, which Merle will call. For one gram of Protonite:
on your mark, one—two."

Stile, caught off-guard by this ready procedure, put out
his forked fingers a shade late. Fulca was there with a flat
hand. "Default," Merle said, her voice soft, like dusk wind
in pines.

"Agreed," Stile said, embarrassed. He had made the
winning throw—too late. Some beginning; he had already
thrown away the twenty-year ransom of one serf.

"For two grams," the Rifleman said. "One—two."

This time Stile was on time, with scissors again. Fulca
also showed scissors. "No decision," Merle breathed.

Stile marveled that it could really be this simple. He had
thought of Citizens as a class apart, devoted to pursuits
beyond the comprehension of mere serfs. But in fact Citizens were serflike in their entertainment—or so it seemed
so far.

The Rifleman continued without pause. "Balance of one
gram to Fulca. For four grams: one—two."

Stile's mind was racing as he warmed to the game. Theoretically random, these combinations were actually not.
Each person was trying to figure the strategy of the other.
Stile himself was very good at analyzing patterns and
moods; he did it almost instinctively. The first throw had

been random; the normal course, for an inexperienced person, would be to go on the next throw to whatever choice had won before. Thus Fulca had gone from paper to scissors. Stile, testing, had held firm. Did he have the pattern solved? If so, Fulca would go next to the stone. So he would match that, verifying. The early bets were for analyzing; the later ones counted. Even as this flashed through his mind, his hand was flinging out the closed fist.

Fulca matched his stone. "No decision," Merle said. It seemed they did not play these over, but just continued the series.

"For eight grams: one—two."

This time Stile went for the win. He expected Fulca to go for paper, to wrap·the last throw's stone. So he threw scissors again—and won.

"Scissors cuts paper; Stile wins," Merle announced.

"Balance of seven games to Stile," the Rifleman said. "For sixteen grams: one—two."

Would the hourglass lady Citizen be foolish enough to go for stone again, fighting the last war too late? Or would she stick with paper, expecting him to go for stone? Stile decided to play her for the fool. He threw out the flat hand. And won.

"Paper wraps stone; Stile," Merle said.

"Balance of twenty-three grams to Stile," the Rifleman said. "I warned you girls he was a Gamesman, like me. He can play. For thirty-two grams: one—two."

Stile continued the fool-play, throwing out the closed fist. Fulca threw the forked fingers. She winced as she saw the combination.

"Stone crushes scissors. Stile wins." Merle smiled within her dusky helmet. Evidently these people enjoyed a good challenge.

"You beat me with the ones I lose with!" Fulca exclaimed.

That was another way of looking at it. He had cut her paper, then shifted to paper and wrapped her stone, then had his stone crush her scissors. The losing throws became the winners of the next throw. "Beginner's luck," Stile said apologetically.

One of the males snorted. "His mind is on the wager, not her body," he murmured.

"Balance of fifty-five grams to Stile," the Rifleman said. "For sixty-four grams: one—two."

Fulca had caught on to his pattern; had she the wit to take advantage of it? This single throw could reverse the entire game. Stile thought she would not learn quickly enough, so he threw scissors, trusting her to throw paper. She did.

"Scissors cuts paper. Stile wins," Merle said.

"He sure cut your paper!" the male Citizen remarked to Fulca with satisfaction. He had evidently won his private bet on the outcome of this contest.

"Balance of one hundred nineteen grams to Stile. End of series," the Rifleman said. "So entered in the credit record; Stile has increased his Citizen's stake by more than ten percent, fleecing his first ewe. Instant analysis: he lost one, drew two, and won four. Was this luck or skill?"

"Skill," Merle said. "He is a master Gamesman—as is unsurprising."

Fulca shrugged, and her torso undulated in vertical stages. "There are other games."

"Uh-uh, dear," the Rifleman said with a reproving smile. "You had your crack at him and lost, as I did in the Tourney. If you want to seduce him, you'll have to wait your next turn. Now he enters the second round."

"Second round?" Stile asked.

This time all the male Citizens chuckled. Merle tapped herself lightly between her muted breasts. "Do you care to try your skill with me, serf-Citizen?"

"I do still have the urge," Stile said, catching Mellon's affirmative nod. But he felt uneasy; he now perceived that Merle was not nearly as young as she had first seemed. In fact, she was somewhat older than he, and her manner was that of a completely self-assured person. She was probably a power among Citizens; one of the barracuda he had been warned against. But he would have to tackle this kind some time.

"Then let us play a hand of poker," she said.

The serfs hastily brought a pack of playing cards, poker chips, an opaque table, and chairs. The Rifleman took the cards, spread them out, and pronounced them fit to play with; Stile believed him. No one got through the Tourney without being expert with cards. Why should Citizens cheat? They needed neither money nor fame, and cheating would destroy the natural suspense of gambling.

But Stile was nervous about this game. Poker players were a breed apart, and a Citizen poker player whose facial features were shrouded by a translucent helmet could be more of a challenge than Stile could handle at the moment. Yet Stile was good at poker, as he was in most games; he certainly should have a fighting chance, even against an expert—if he didn't run afoul of his betting limit. Limits could be devastating in poker.

"Merle has chosen the game," the Rifleman said. "Stile may choose the rules."

"Standard fifty-two-card pack, no wild cards, standard wider galaxy hands in force, betting—"

"Sorry, Stile," the Rifleman interjected. "You may not dictate the pattern of betting. That choice reverts to her, by Citizen custom."

"Of course I will honor Citizen custom," Stile said. "But I have hired a serf to supervise my estate, and he wants me to stay clear of large bets until I know my way around. So I might have to renege on the game, if—"

"A sensible precaution," Merle said. "Seat your serf to the side; you may consult with him while betting."

"That is gracious of you, Merle," Stile said, forcing himself to speak her name, though his lifetime of serf conditioning screamed against it. "Please, in compensation, name the variant you prefer."

"Certainly, Stile. Are you familiar with Lovers' Quarrel?"

Oops. "I do not know that variant," Stile admitted.

"It is a variety of Draw. Each player must draw from the hand of the other, one card at a time, which hand is replenished by the dealer. Betting occurs after each draw, until one player stands pat."

Some variant! This had the double stress of involuntary loss of cards from one's hand, and the opponent's knowledge of an increasing portion of that hand. At some point they both should know what each had—but that would not necessarily make betting easier.

They took seats at the table, the Rifleman serving as dealer. Stile glanced at the knot of spectators. The males watched with poker faces, obviously intent on the proceedings. Mellon and Sheen stood impassively, but Stile knew that Sheen, at least, was controlling her emotional circuitry with difficulty. She loved him and wanted to protect him, and here she could not. This was also outside Mellon's bailiwick; there was no way for him to draw on computer information to give Stile an advantage, and that was the way Stile preferred it. This was an honest game.

The Rifleman dealt five cards to each. Stile picked up his hand, holding it together so that only the bottom card showed, and that was concealed from all external view by his casually cupped hands. He riffled once through the corners, his trained eye photographing the hand and putting it mentally in order: ace of spades, 10 of hearts, 10 of diamonds, 4 of clubs, 2 of clubs. A pair of tens. That was not much; in a two-player game, the odds were marginally in favor of this being high, but he would have similar odds on the flip of a coin. He did not want to bet on this.

"The lady may draw first," the Rifleman said.

"Thank you, Rife," Merle said. She discarded one card face down. "I will take your center card, Stile, if you please."

Stile spread his hand without looking and lifted out the center card. It was the 10 of diamonds. There went his pair already!

The Rifleman dealt Stile a replacement card. It was the 6 of hearts. Now he had only ace-high, a likely loser.

"One ounce," she said. The Rifleman slid a white poker chip across to her, and she touched it into the center of the table.

So that was the unit of currency—safely penny-ante after all. Relieved, Stile discarded his 10 of hearts, to keep his opponent from getting it and having a pair, and asked for Merle's left-end card, which in a conventional arrangement might be her high one. Of course it wasn't; she had not arranged her cards physically, either. Too much could be telegraphed that way. It was the jack of clubs.

Now he had ace of spades, 6 of hearts, jack of clubs, 4 of clubs and 2 of clubs. Perhaps three legs on a flush, if he didn't lose his clubs to Merle's drawings.

But he had to call, raise, or drop. He was unwilling to quit so early, so he called, contributing one white chip.

Merle discarded another, and drew his ace. She was having uncanny luck in destroying his hand! Then she added a red chip to the pot. She was raising the ante—five more grams.

The Rifleman passed Stile another replacement card. It was the king of clubs. Now Stile had four clubs—almost a flush. A full flush would very likely win the pot; only one hand in 200 was a flush. But by the same token, flushes were hard to come by. Merle would have four chances in five to steal away one of his clubs on her next turn. Should he call or fold?

He looked at Mellon. The serf nodded affirmatively, approving the bet. So Stile discarded the 6 of hearts, drew another card from Merle—and got the ace of spades back. Disappointed, he matched the red chip.

Merle frowned faintly within her helmet, and Stile was frustrated again, unable to gauge her true mood. With an unfamiliar game variant and an unfamiliar opponent, he could exercise little of his natural skill. A person's eyes could tell a lot; if the pupils widened, the hand was positive. But her pupils were shadowed by that translucency.

She took another card: his king of clubs. He got an 8 of spades from the pack. Already his promised flush was fading, as he had feared. His hand still amounted to nothing.

Merle put in a blue chip. Another ten grams! That brought her total up to sixteen grams of Protonite. At the rate she was raising the ante, he could not afford to let this game continue too long. But he would surely lose if he stood pat now; she must have amassed at least one pair. He wanted to make a good showing, so that other Citizens would want to make wagers with him.

Stile decided to keep trying for the flush. Therefore he discarded his ace of spades, reckoning it too risky to hold for her possible reacquisition, and drew from Merle—his original 10 of diamonds. No good to him at all, at this stage, since he had discarded his matching 10 before.

Again he matched her bet, though he thought it would have been smarter to drop. She probably had ten times as much wealth to gamble with as he did. If Mellon knew how week Stile's hand was, the serf would hardly have tolerated this bet.

Merle took his jack of clubs, further decimating his flush. And she put five more blue chips into the pot. Sixty-six grams total: she surely had a good hand now!

Stile accepted the replacement card: the 6 of spades. Now his hand was the 8 and 6 of spades, 10 of diamonds, and 4 and 2 of clubs. No pairs, no flush, no high card—and a monstrous ante facing him if he wanted to keep playing.

Then something clicked. He had almost missed the forest for the trees!

"I stand pat on this hand," Stile announced. "Adviser, may I bet my limit?"

Mellon agreed reluctantly. Stile put eight blue chips and four white ones into the pot, bringing his total to one hundred grams. Now it was Merle's turn to call or fold; she could not raise during his turn. Would she be bluffed out?

She called, putting in another thirty-four grams. She laid down her hand, face up. "Blaze," she said. "Two kings, two queens, one jack."

That meant she had to have had one pair last round, perhaps two pairs, beating him. She had waited until she had what she wanted: a pat hand, all court cards. She had played with nerve.

But Stile had beaten her. "Skip straight," he said, laying it out. "Ten-high." There it was: 10–8–6–4–2. This hand was not as strong as a straight, but was stronger than any of the other hands from three of a kind down.

"Very nice, Stile," she agreed. "The pot is yours." She made a little gesture of parting and walked away.

"He took her," one of the male Citizens said. "That's one kilo for me." Another nodded glumly.

"Very nice indeed," the Rifleman said. "You have added another hundred to your estate. It is so recorded."

A total of 219 grams of Protonite added to his original thousand—in the course of just two supposedly penny-ante games. But Stile knew he could just as readily lose it again.

Mellon approached as the group of Citizens dispersed. "Sir, you must desist now."

"I'll be glad to. But what is the reason? I thought you would stop me from betting before."

"This is the bait, sir. Now the serious bettors will seek you out."

The serious bettors. Of course. Stile had, as it were, dipped his toe. He needed to announce himself, so that he could step into the real action, where the upper limit would rise. Obviously a gain of 219 grams was statistically insignificant, compared with the 2000 kilograms that was his target level. He had won only one ten-thousandth of his stake. This could be as difficult a climb as it had been through the levels of the Tourney.

Yet Mellon was not concerned about the luck of individual wagers. He had a certain program of challenge planned. His limit on Stile's initial betting had been merely to prevent Stile from losing his stake in the course of making himself known to the key wagering clientele.

"Did I hear correctly?" Stile asked the Rifleman. "Did one of the spectators bet a full kilogram of Protonite on the outcome of my game with Merle?"

"He did," the Rifleman agreed. "Citizens bet on anything."

"Ten times what I bet—and he wasn't even playing!"

The Rifleman smiled. "That's the way it is. Your adviser protected you from getting into that level too soon. Come on—there's more than wagering to get into."

Stile allowed the Rifleman to show him around some more. There were different levels and slants and curves to the invisible floor, with refreshments on one tier, dancing on another, and conversation on a third. Coupled with the ubiquitous holographic astronomy, the effect was potent. This was a wonderland, as impressive in its lavish expense as in its execution. Yet the Citizens, long used to this sort of thing, ignored the setting and socialized among themselves.

"You do get accustomed to it," the Rifleman said, divining Stile's thoughts. "This is merely a standard social occasion, a kind of Citizen concourse, where any can come for idle entertainment and socializing on an amicable plane. All comforts and amusements are available at every Citizen's private residence, but they get bored. Of course they have holo contact, but you can't actually touch a holo, or push it aside or make love to it."

"You say *they*," Stile observed.

"I'm still a serf at heart. You'll be the same. The Citizens do not discriminate against our kind—to do so would be to dishonor their system—but we discriminate against ourselves, internally. We react to what is beneath their notice. Look there, for instance." He gestured upward.

Stile looked. Above them was a transparent spaceship, inside which Citizens were dancing. The men wore archaic black tailed-coat costumes, the women white blouses and slippers and voluminous skirts. From this nether vantage he could see right up their prettily moving legs, under their skirts where the white bloomers took over. Stile had gotten used to nakedness in Proton and to clothing in Phaze, but this halfway vision was intensely erotic for him. He did have some acclimatizing to do, lest he embarrass himself.

Again the Rifleman was with him in spirit. "Yet we see excellent distaff flesh all about us, unconcealed," he pointed out, indicating Sheen, who remained respectfully behind. Stile glanced back. Sheen was indeed the perfect figure of a young woman, with lovely facial features, fine large, upstanding breasts, and torso and legs that could hardly be improved upon. In terms of appearance she was stunning, far prettier than the exaggerated lady Citizen Fulca—yet she did not excite him sexually. This was not because he knew she was a machine, he decided; the robot was more human and caring than most flesh-women he knew. It was because she was a naked serf. Sheen had no secrets, so lacked novelty. In contrast, the peek up the skirts of the dressed ladies above—that, literally, clothed his fancy and set his pulse racing.

"But the average Citizen can look and yawn," the Rifleman said, glancing again at the skirts above. "Clothing is no novelty here. Nothing is novelty, except assured victory in an honest game of chance. You made Merle's day just now; you were an unknown quantity, giving her the thrill of uncertainty."

That reminded Stile. "Just how old is she, and how much of her fortune would a hundred grams of Protonite represent, if it's not uncouth to inquire?"

"The fortunes of all Citizens are a matter of public record. She's worth about ten kilos; I can get the precise figure for the moment, if you wish. The Records Computer—"

"No, no need. So my wager did not hurt her."

"Not at all. Age is also on record. Merle is sixty-one years old. She's had rejuvenation, of course, so she has the face and body of a serf girl of thirty. But her mind is old. I dare say she knows more about sex than you and I combined."

Stile had noticed that most Citizen women were physically attractive, in contrast with the men. Rejuvenation would of course account for this. It would not prolong life significantly, but it would make a person seem young on the day he died of age. The vanity of women caused them to go this route.

Stile turned to the Rifleman. "I thank you for the courtesy of your time. You have facilitated my education. Now I think I will go home and assimilate my impressions, if I may do so without offense to this gathering."

"No offense. You have made your appearance and performed on stage; all interested Citizens have had opportunity to examine you. Go and relax, Stile."

"I really did not meet many Citizens. I suppose I'm not much of a novelty."

The Rifleman smiled. "Allow me to detain you for one more thing." He led Stile to an especially thick dust cloud. Set just within its opacity was a control panel. A touch on this, and an image formed above—Stile, playing poker with Merle. The view shifted perspective as if the camera were dollying around, showing Stile from all sides. An inset showed the poker hands of each, changing as the play progressed.

"I've been recorded!" Stile exclaimed.

"Exactly," the Rifleman agreed. "All interested Citizens are able to tune in on you—or on any other person here. This is open territory, unprivate." He touched the controls again, and the nether view of the dancing Citizens appeared. "So-called X-ray views are also available, for those who wish." Now the skirts and bloomers faded out, leaving the Citizens dancing naked, looking exactly like serfs.

Stile was alarmed. "You mean viewers can strip me like that, holographically?" He was concerned about exposure of his physical reaction when viewing the inner skirts before.

"Indeed. Voyeurism is a prime Citizen pastime. That particular thrill seems never to become passé."

Stile sighed inwardly. He surely had provided the voyeurs some innocent entertainment today! "I appreciate your advising me," he said, somewhat faintly.

"Welcome, Stile. I thought you would want to know. Citizenship is not completely idyllic, and there are many ways to be savaged unknowingly. Many Citizens prefer the complete privacy of their domes."

"I can see why." And on that amicable note they parted.

Back in his transparent capsule, Stile relaxed. It had actually been a joke on him, he decided, and harmless. The Citizens had really looked him over and found him human. He would be more alert in future.

But the joke had not finished. A call came in to the travel capsule. When he acknowledged, the head of Merle formed. Without her space helmet, she was revealed as a rather pretty young woman, with the same delicate rondure to her facial features as had been suggested by her suit-shrouded torso. "I have decided I like you, Stile," she said. "Would you care for an assignation?"

"Uh, what?" he asked awkwardly.

She laughed. "Oh, you are so refreshing! It has been decades since I've had a truly naïve man." The scope of the image expanded, to reveal the upper half of her body hanging in the air before him like a statuette, her small but excellent breasts shrouded by a translucent shawl. She must have viewed the holographic record of Stile's recent experience and grasped his susceptibility to partial clothing on women. "You can see that I am moderately endowed, but please accept my assurance that I am expert with what I have."

Stile proved his naïveté by blushing. "Sir, you catch me unprepared. Uh—"

She actually clapped her hands in glee. "Oh, absolute delight! I must have you!"

"I can't say I care to have holographs made of me performing in such a situation," Stile said, his face burning.

Merle pursed her lips. "But holos are the best part of it, so that one can review the occasion at proper leisure and improve technique."

Out of range of the holo pickup, Sheen signaled imperatively. She did not want Stile to offend the Citizen. Mellon nodded agreement.

Stile took their advice. "Merle, as you can see, I'm flattered to the point of confusion. This is more than I can handle right now. Could you, would you grant me a stay of decision?"

"Gladly, Stile," she agreed merrily. "I will contact you tomorrow."

Some stay! "Thank you," he said, conscious that his blush had intensified. He was thirty-five years old and hardly inexperienced with women, but his underlying awe of Citizens had betrayed him.

The moment the connection terminated, he snapped: "Block off all other calls! I don't want any more of that!"

"We dare not block off Citizen calls," Sheen said. "But I'll ask my friends to make an inoffensive excuse message for you, and filter out as much as possible."

"Thanks." He caught her hand. "You're beautiful, Sheen."

"I wish I could move you the way Citizen Merle did," she grumbled.

"She moved me to naked terror!"

"Naked, yes; terror, no."

"She's a sixty-year-old woman!"

"In that respect I can not compete. I was made less than a year ago."

That reminded him. "Sheen, has there been any progress

on your origin? Have your friends discovered who sent
you to me and why?"

"I will query them," Sheen said, but paused. "Oops—a
call."

"I told you, I don't want—"

"From *her*."

There was only one person Sheen referred to that way.
"Oh. Put her on, of course."

The image formed. The Lady Blue faced him. "My
Lord, I dislike bothering thee, but I fear mischief."

"What mischief?" he demanded, instantly concerned.
The Lady Blue was no more beautiful, by objective standards, than Sheen, but she had completely captured his
love. It bothered him to have the fact so evident in Sheen's
presence, but there really was no way to avoid it in this
situation.

"Clip says he winds ogres." She glanced nervously about.
"We know not why such creatures should be on the isle
of the West Pole."

"I'll rejoin thee," Stile said.

"Nay, my Lord. Clip will guard me from harm. I merely
advise thee, just in case any difficulty arises."

"Very well," he agreed reluctantly. "But if there's any
sign of menace, call me right away. It will take me a while
to reach Phaze."

"I love thee, Lord Blue," she said, flashing her smile,
making the air about her brighten. Stile always liked that
magic effect. She faded out.

"Nevertheless," Stile said grimly to Sheen, "I want to
get closer to a curtain-crossing point. Or anywhere along
the curtain; once I step across, I can spell myself immediately to the West Pole."

Mellon was looking at him strangely. Stile smiled.
"Have Sheen fill you in more thoroughly; you machines
need to know this. I go to a world of magic, where I have
a lovely wife and am important."

"Yes, sir," Mellon said dubiously. "I trust this will not
interfere with your program of estate development."

"Please infer no insult from this," Stile told him. "But if
my Lady Blue is in danger, my entire Citizenship estate
can drop into deep space without a ship."

"Thank you for clarifying your priorities, sir," Mellon said stiffly.

"Oh, don't be stuffy," Sheen reproved the other robot. "You have to take Stile on his own peculiar terms."

"Of course. He is a Citizen."

She turned to Stile. "My friends have a report."

"Let's have it." Stile was discovering that a lot of business could be done on the move.

The image of a desk robot appeared. "Sir, the machine of your inquiry was purchased by Citizen Kalder ten weeks ago, programmed to love and protect the serf Stile, and sent to said serf."

"But *why?*" Stile demanded. "Why should a Citizen make an anonymous and expensive gift to a serf he does not employ?"

"That information is not available, sir. I suggest you contact Citizen Kalder." The image faded.

"At least now I have a name," Stile said. He pondered briefly. "How much does such a robot cost?"

"Approximately five grams of Protonite, sir," Mellon replied. "This is my own value, which is typical for the type."

"That is quintuple the twenty-year hire of a serf," Stile said. "Maybe peanuts for a Citizen, but still out of proportion for a throwaway gift. Easier to send a serf bodyguard." Another thought occurred. "Has my own estate been docked that amount for you and the other special personnel?"

"We are rented, sir," Mellon said. "By special arrangement."

That meant that the self-willed machines had set it up. They were covertly helping him, so that he could help them. "What do your friends think of our engagement, Sheen?"

"Sir, they are amazed, to the extent their circuitry and programming permit. This changes the situation, giving them the chance for recognition much sooner than otherwise. There are grave risks, but they are willing to follow this course."

"Good enough. I would like to secure your recognition as serfs, not merely because of the help your kind has given me at critical moments, but because I believe it is right. Though if each of you costs five grams, I don't know how it could be economic for you to work for serf's wages."

"We can last several times as long as the tenure of a serf," Mellon replied. "Once we achieve recognition, there may be a premium for the service we can offer. Properly programmed, we could be superior serfs, performing the routine functions of several. Since we do not sleep, we can accomplish more in a given tenure. The Protonite that powers us is equivalent in value to the food that living serfs consume, and our occasional necessary repairs equate to live-person illness. We feel we shall be economic. But even if we are not, we shall at least have the opportunity to play the Game legitimately, and perhaps some few of our number will advance to Citizenship. That prospect is more important to us than mere service as serfs."

"So I gather," Stile agreed. He liked these intelligent machines; he trusted them more than he did many living people, partly because they remained simpler than people. A robot could be deceitful if programmed to be—but what was the point of such programming? Mainly he liked their loyalty to him, personally. They trusted him, so aided him, and he knew they would never betray him.

"Sir, do you wish me to place a call to Citizen Kalder?" Sheen inquired.

"Yes, do it."

But at that point there was another call from the Lady Blue. "The ogres are closing on us, my Lord," she said worriedly. "I was not sure before that we were the object of their quest, but now that seems likely. I mislike bothering thee, but—"

"I'm on my way!" Stile cried. "Sheen, reroute this tub to the nearest intersection with the curtain. Forget about the call to the Citizen; I'll tackle that later."

"Yes, sir," she said. The capsule shifted motion.

CHAPTER 7

Hostage

The image of the Lady Blue remained. Stile worked his unit controls to survey the area, looking outward from the West Pole. In a moment he spied an ogre.

It was a large, hugely muscled humanoid creature, strongly reminiscent of Stile's late friend Hulk. Stile felt a pang at the memory; Hulk had been an intelligent, sensitive, considerate man, a Gamesman like Stile himself—but he had been betrayed and murdered by Stile's enemy. Stile had sworn an oath of vengeance, which he had implemented in his fashion—but that had not restored his friend. In any event, the resemblance was superficial; the ogre's face was a gross muddy morass of nose and mouth, with two little eyes perched slightly above. The ears dangled down like deflated tires.

Clip changed to man-form and approached the creature. "Ogre, why dost thou come here?" the unicorn inquired.

"Blue be mine enemy," the creature croaked. Its open mouth was like that of a frog with triangular teeth.

"Blue is not thine enemy!" the Lady called. "Blue had a friend who was very like an ogre. Blue never harmed thy kind. Why dost thou believe ill of him now?"

"The Oracle says."

Another Oracular message? Stile distrusted this.

So did the Lady Blue. "Another message was altered, methinks, to make Blue seem villain. Art thou sure—"

But the ogre, dim of wit, roared and charged, making the ground tremble by the fall of its feet. Its hamfist swung forward like a wrecking ball. Ogres simply were not much for dialogue.

"I've got to get there!" Stile cried.

"We are not yet at the curtain, sir," Sheen said. "It will be another ten minutes."

Stile clenched his teeth and fists, watching the scene in Phaze.

Clip shifted back to his natural form and launched himself after the ogre. The Lady Blue, no fainting flower in a crisis, stepped nimbly aside. Ogre and unicorn lunged past her, Clip placing himself between the other two.

The ogre braked, its huge hairy feet literally screeching against the turf. But as it reoriented on the Lady, the unicorn barred the way.

The ogre massed perhaps a thousand pounds. The unicorn, small for his species, was about the same. The ogre's hamfists were deadly—but so was the unicorn's pointed horn. It was a momentary stand-off.

Then a second ogre appeared. "Look out behind thee, Lady!" Stile cried. She heard him and whirled. The second ogre's two hamhands were descending on her head.

The Lady ducked down and scooted between the monster's legs. The curtain was now just ahead of her. As the ogre turned, she straddled the curtain and stood facing it.

But other ogres were appearing. Two converged on the Lady from either side of the curtain. Clip charged to help her—but that permitted the first ogre to converge also.

As the two pounced, the Lady spelled herself across the curtain, holding her breath. The ogres crashed into each other where she had been. Stile could not see her in the image; it was difficult to see across the curtain anyway, and the holo pickup was oriented on the fantasy side. But he knew she was in extreme discomfort, with the thin, polluted air of Proton and the barren terrain.

But in a moment she reappeared, just beyond the brutes. She had avoided them by using the curtain. Clip spied her and rushed to join her again.

Two more ogres came into view. The five lumbered down upon the woman and unicorn. Clip launched himself at the closest, lowering his horn, skewering the monster through the center.

The ogre was so heavy the unicorn could not lift it; Clip

had to back away, extricating his horn, shaking the monster's blood from it. But the ogre was mortally wounded; brown pus welled from the wound, front and back, and the creature staggered and fell with a crash like that of an uprooted tree.

Meanwhile, the remaining creatures had reconverged on the Lady. "Here to me, Hinblue!" she called, and stepped back across the curtain.

"Aren't we there yet?" Stile demanded. "She can't hold out much longer!"

"Sir, there seems to be a power interruption," Sheen said. "This passage needs repair; we must detour."

"How long?" Stile cried.

"Another fifteen minutes, sir, I fear."

Stile clapped his hands to his head in nonphysical pain. "My Lady! My Lady!"

"I love her too, sir," Sheen murmured.

Stile could only watch the unfolding sequence helplessly. He should never have left the Lady Blue so lightly guarded!

The Lady reappeared beyond the ogres as Hinblue arrived. "Now you can catch me not!" she cried, vaulting on to her fine steed.

The four ogres nevertheless started after her. Clip raced to join Hinblue.

But as they moved out, readily outdistancing the monsters, a small ravine appeared ahead. "Watch out!" Stile cried.

Too late. The distracted horse put a foot in it. Instantly Hinblue went down and the Lady flew off and forward. Athlete that she was, she landed on her feet, running, unhurt.

But Hinblue was hurt. She got to her feet, but she was bruised and lame. She could only hobble, not run. The ogres were closing in again.

Clip assumed man-form. "Lady, ride me! The mare can not carry thee."

"Oh, no!" Stile breathed. "I know what she will say."

"And desert my horse, offspring of the Hinny and the Blue Stallion?" the Lady Blue demanded. "Never!"

"She said it," Stile said, suffering.

"Then must we guard her," Clip said. He became unicorn again, and stood facing the four onrushing brutes.

They were no longer astride the curtain. The Lady could not use it to save herself—and in any event would not have left her horse. She drew a narrow, sharp knife and stood beside Clip, ready to fight.

The monsters came—but slowed. They had seen the fate of the first one to encounter the unicorn's horn. Still, they were four against two, and towered over their opposition.

A hole opened in the ground. An ugly head poked out, swathed in bandages. For an instant Stile thought yet another monster had joined the attack. But then he realized it was Trool the troll, the one who had helped them escape the Orange Demesnes. "Here!" the troll croaked.

The Lady recognized him. She was evidently uncertain of the creature's motive. Her Adept husband was no longer with her, and trolls liked human flesh.

"Escape," Trool said, indicating his tunnel. He was offering a route out of the trap.

"I thank thee, Trool," the Lady said. "But my steed fits not in thy tunnel."

The troll opened out another section of turf, and another. There was a shallow cave there. "This crisis was anticipated," he said, his voice becoming clearer, as if a long-disused faculty was being revived. "I labored to prepare."

The ogres were now very close. The Lady decided to risk the help of the troll. Without further protest, she led Hinblue into the cave, then stood at the entrance with her knife poised.

The ogres, outraged at this seeming escape, charged into the gully. But Clip charged too. His deadly horn punctured another ogre, this time from the side. The monster fell, squirting its brown juice, and again the others hesitated. There were only three of them now, and they evidently did not like dying. If any two had pounced on Clip together, they could have torn the unicorn apart—but they evidently lacked the wit or courage to do that. They also seemed nervous about Trool, who was a monster somewhat like themselves, though only half as stout. Why was he participating?

"That is Neysa's brother, sir?" Sheen asked. The fact that she was now using "sir" warned him that she was not sure they had complete privacy.

"Yes. He's one good unicorn."

"And ogres eat people?"

"Yes. Trolls eat people, too, and horses. But Trool can be trusted—I think."

Finally the ogres consulted, and came to the conclusion Stile had feared. Two of them stalked Clip together, while the third faced Trool, preventing the troll from interfering. Stile realized an ogre should have been able to demolish a troll on open ground, but not within a troll's tunnels, so this was merely interference rather than combat. The Lady Blue had to stay with the horse she guarded. Clip had to fight alone.

The unicorn could have changed into hawk-form and flown away, but he did not. He charged again. His horn skewered the left ogre—but the right one brought a ham-fist down on the unicorn's rump. Clip's hindsection collapsed under the power of that blow. He was helpless, down on the ground, his hindlegs possibly crippled, his horn still wedged in the left ogre's torso.

Now the Lady Blue leaped forward, knife flashing. She sliced into the heavy arm of the right-hand ogre. Ichor welled out of a long slash, and the creature made a howl of pain.

Now the two remaining monsters retreated, one holding its wounded arm. Clip changed back into hawk-form, extricating himself, and the Lady held out her arm for him to perch on. He seemed shaken, limping, but not seriously hurt. Stile breathed a sigh of relief. The two returned to the impromptu cave.

For a time the ogres stayed back. Stile relaxed somewhat. The longer they waited, the better his chance to get to Phaze and correct the situation before any more harm was done. The capsule was proceeding with what seemed to him to be tedious slowness, but he knew Sheen was doing her best.

He decided he should divert his mind, as long as he

could not act. "Place that call to the Citizen," he said curtly. "But don't interfere with this image."

"Yes, sir." Sheen placed the call.

In a moment the face of a well-fed, middle-aged male Citizen appeared beside the image of the West Pole region. There were no serf or robot intermediaries this time. "Yes?" he inquired, peering at Stile.

"Kalder, I am Stile," Stile said briskly. He was rapidly shedding his apprehension about Citizens. "I am not sure you know me—"

"I don't," Kalder agreed brusquely.

"But about two months ago you gifted me with a humanoid robot. I was then a serf."

Kalder's face wrinkled in perplexity. "I did?"

"This robot," Stile said, indicating Sheen.

Still there was no recognition in the man's face. Was this a misidentification? "Let me check my records," Kalder said.

In a moment the Citizen looked up. "I have it now. My staff handled it, without informing me. It was a routine protective measure."

"Routine measure?" Stile asked. "This is a five-gram robot! Why would you give her to a serf employed by another Citizen?"

Kalder's brow furrowed again. "That is peculiar. But I'm sure my chief of staff had reason. Let me see—yes, here it is. We received news that the chief horse trainer and jockey of a rival stable was to be assassinated, and the blame attached to me. I have one of the finest stables on Proton." He said this matter-of-factly, and Stile believed him. Citizens did not need to brag, and in his racing days he had come up against the entries of a number of excellent stables. He was probably familiar with Kalder's horses, if he cared to do the spot research necessary to align the Citizen's name with that of his stable. "Since that would have been an unpleasant complication, my chief of staff arranged to protect you anonymously. After all, it might have been a practical joke, leading to my embarrassment. Why take a chance?"

"You protected me—to save yourself from being framed or embarrassed," Stile said slowly. "No other reason?"

"None. I had no concern for you personally. I was not even aware of the matter until you called it to my attention just now. I leave such details to my staff."

That was some staff! But of course Stile had already discovered the caliber of staff a Citizen could afford. "How did your chief of staff know about this plot?"

Kalder checked his records again. "Anonymous message. That's why it could have been a joke. Was it?"

"It was not," Stile said. "Your robot saved my life on more than one occasion. Now I will marry her."

Kalder burst out laughing. "If her screws aren't loose, yours are! Be sure to invite me to the wedding! I'll gift you with a mail diaper for your cyborg offspring." He faded out.

A cyborg was a combination of flesh and machine, such as a robot with a grafted human brain, neither fish nor fowl. They generally did not last long. This was a cruel gibe, but Kalder was not a bad type, as Citizens went. The mystery remained. Who had sent the anonymous message to Kalder's staff?

"The same party who sicked the Red Adept on you, perhaps," Sheen said, following his thought.

"And who may be fouling me up with changed Oracle pronouncements," Stile agreed. "Now more of the pattern emerges. It could all stem from a single source. That is my true enemy."

"Why would an enemy arrange to have you protected?"

"Why, indeed!"

"My circuitry is inadequate to solve that problem," she said, smiling briefly.

"And mine. Put your friends on that message to Kalder; see if they can trace its source."

"Yes, sir." She made a coded call.

Now something new was happening in Phaze. The scene had been still while the Lady Blue put her hands on Clip and healed his bruises and restored his confidence. The ogres had stayed back. But Clip's ears—he was back in natural form—were perking forward, and he blew a brief, startled note.

"I see nothing," the Lady said. "What is it?"

Clip did not answer. His nostrils twitched. Obviously he

heard and smelled something. Now, very faintly, Stile heard it too: the tinkling of little bells. Why did that seem familiar?

Then the source came into sight. It was another unicorn. This one was female, and lovely. Her coat was a deep red, almost purple, and shone with sleek health. Her mane rippled iridescently. As she approached, she changed to an elegant blue heron, then to a cat, and finally back to equine form. Her bell rang again, sweetly.

Clip's ears vibrated with amazement. He blew a querying note on his horn. The mare responded with a truly melodious tinkling of bells.

"What does she say?" the Lady Blue asked nervously.

Clip changed to man-form. "She says she was thrown out by her herd. She is all alone in the wilderness."

"She seems familiar."

"She and her brother danced at the Unolympics. They defeated Neysa and me for the prize."

"Now I remember! What a pretty 'corn she is!"

"Aye," Clip agreed wistfully.

"But why would her herd cast her out, after she brought them the prize?"

"She refused to be bred by her Herd Stallion, who is getting old and violent, so he exiled her. Now she is without a herd."

"Can't she join another?"

"Nay, the Herd Stallions interfere not in each other's herds. She is ostracized."

"The way Neysa was! That's terrible!"

"Neysa was merely excluded for a time. Belle can never go back."

The pretty mare tinkled her bell again.

"She asks if I will go with her," Clip said.

"It's a trap," Stile said. "Don't trust her." But the holo pickup was too far from the present setting for them to hear him unless he shouted; transmission was largely one-way now. He did not want to shout and have the ogres know his situation.

"How is it she shows up here now?" the Lady inquired, evidently having a similar suspicion.

But Clip, enchanted, changed back to equine form. As a

lesser male, he was not permitted the chance to breed. This was obviously a phenomenal temptation.

The mare nickered and rang a lovely melody on her bell-horn. Clip quivered with eagerness.

"I don't trust this at all!" Stile said. "Clip has defended my Lady Blue against the monsters. Suddenly the love-liest mare unicorn in all the herds appears, luring him away."

"All males are fools in this manner," Sheen remarked.

"Clip, go not to her!" the Lady Blue pleaded. "At least wait until my Lord returns. It will not be long now."

But Clip had lost control of himself. Evidently the mare was in heat; he had to go to her. He fought the lure, but step by step he went.

The Lady Blue had to remain in the cave, guarding herself and Hinblue. She was not so foolish as to venture where the ogres could pounce.

Now at last the capsule approached the curtain. But the capsule was below ground, under desert; Stile could not step through at this level. "Get me to the surface, any-where by the curtain!" he snapped, in a fever of impa-tience to reach the West Pole.

Sheen located a bus stop. Stile got out and hurried up the stairs to the surface. "Keep things in order until my return," he called back.

"Don't get yourself killed, sir," she said.

Stile didn't answer. He held his breath and burst out on to the desert, running for the curtain. As he came upon its shimmer, he willed himself across—and found himself running on the green plain of Phaze.

Immediately he stopped, formulating a suitable spell in his mind while he played his harmonica to summon his power. Then he sang: "Convey me whole to the West Pole."

The spell wrenched him from here to there, making him nauseous. It was never comfortable to work his magic on himself, and he avoided it except in emergencies. Feeling ill, he looked out from the West Pole.

There was no sign of Clip the unicorn. Stile sang a flight-spell he had in reserve, rose into the air, and zoomed toward the ravine and cave where the Lady Blue waited.

The two ogres were there. As Stile approached, one of them picked up the troll one-handed and hurled him high and away. Apparently Trool had left the security of his tunnels and so fallen into the power of the more massive monsters.

"Please—freeze," Stile sang, willing the interpretation of the spell. But though there was a faint effort of magic, the action did not stop.

Then he remembered that he had already used this spell to freeze the sea monster of the Translucent Demesnes. No wonder it had lost its potency. "All will be still," he sang.

This time the tableau froze as intended. The two ogres became statues, along with their injured companion, who was licking his arm a short distance away. The troll hung motionless in the air. The very wind stopped—but Stile himself continued.

The Lady Blue stood in the cave, knife in hand, her lovely face frozen in grinning ferocity as she slashed at the nearest monster. Behind her stood Hinblue, lame but trying to move out and get in a good kick.

Stile made a subspell to free the Lady only. "My Lord!" she exclaimed, breathlessly glad to see him. "Clip—he was lured away!"

"I saw," Stile said. "First I must tend to thee and thy friends; then will I quest after the unicorn."

The Lady was all right, though tired; it was no easy thing to stand up to an ogre with no more than a knife. Stile made a spell to restore Hinblue, whose injury had been beyond the Lady's gentler healing power. Then he brought Trool sliding slowly down from midair. "A second time hast thou repaid my favor," Stile said. "Now do I owe thee one."

"Nay, Adept," Trool protested. "It was prophesied that three times must I tunnel to free thee and thine from hazard, ere the balance evens."

"Then gladly do I accept this rescue of my Lady!" Stile said. "But dost thou not know that the Blue Adept destroyed all thy tribe in fire?"

"As my tribe destroyed all thy village. Those scales are even. The debt is other."

Stile shrugged. "Why shouldst thou be burdened, not me?"

"Because thou must save Phaze." Trool turned and shambled back into his tunnel, which extended darkly into the ground. Stile was amazed at the creature's facility in tunneling—but of course troll magic was involved.

Then he noticed an object on the ground. He stooped carefully to pick it up, for his knees remained bad, able to bend only to right angles before pain began. Stile could use magic to move himself but not to heal himself, so had to live with the condition. He picked up the object.

It was a small figurine of a woman, quite well executed. "Who made this?" Stile asked.

"Trool," the Lady replied. "He appears clumsy, but his big hands have magic. When he is not tunneling, he turns that magic to sculpture, to relieve his nervousness."

"Facing two ogres, I can appreciate his concern! Why did he step out on to the land, where they had power?"

"To stop them from charging me," she said. "Trolls are not my favorite creature, but Trool acted bravely and selflessly. If again we meet, I shall call him friend."

"Yet if he is honoring a prophecy, I can not reward him," Stile said. "That might alter the meaning of his action and void the prophecy, causing mischief."

"True," she agreed soberly.

Stile contemplated the figurine. "This is thee!" he exclaimed, surprised.

She shrugged. "He begged my leave. He works better when he has a subject. I saw no harm."

Figurine magic could be potent—but the Red Adept had specialized in that, with her amulets, and she was gone. "No, no harm," Stile agreed. "He's a fine craftsman. This is as pretty a statuette as I've seen."

"We forget Clip," she reminded him, taking the statuette from him.

"In a moment. Now for these monsters." Stile conjured a cage around the two, then unfroze them. They rattled the bars for several minutes before conceding they were effectively imprisoned; then they were ready to listen to Stile.

"Know, ogres, that I am the Blue Adept," Stile said. "This is my Lady Blue. Why did the five of you attack her?"

"Blue be now our enemy," one repeated.

"The Oracle told thee that?"

"Told Brogbt."

"Who is Brogbt?"

The ogre pointed to one of the dead monsters.

"Then must I make the dead to speak," Stile said grimly. He pondered, working out a spell, then sang: "Ogre Brogbt, under my spell, the true message do thou tell."

The dead ogre stirred. Flies buzzed up angrily. Its rigor-stiffened mouth cracked open. "Blue be not thine enemy," it croaked, and lay still again.

"Not!" the Lady exclaimed. "It said not!"

Both living ogres seemed surprised. "Brogbt told us *now*."

"He thought the word was now. He was enchanted, and heard or remembered it wrong. I am not thine enemy. Now thou knowest."

"Now I know," the ogre agreed, adapting dully to this new reality.

Stile eliminated their cage. "Go inform thy kind of the truth."

They stomped away.

"Thou art as ever generous in victory," the Lady said.

"Now for the unicorn." Stile made a spell that set Clip's hoofprints glowing, and they followed these. The trail led over a hill to a copse of evergreens and entered the dense forest island.

"Where are the mare's prints?" the Lady asked.

Stile sang a new spell to make those also glow, but evoked nothing.

"She was mere illusion," the Lady said. "A sending to distract him so the ogres could get to me. This surely means mischief. Had Trool not interfered—"

Stile made another spell. "Make an image, make it sooth, of the unicorn, of the truth."

The image formed, like a holograph, three-dimensional.

Clip walked beside a phantom. The unreal mare led him into the copse—and there a flash occurred, and the unicorn was gone.

"Destroyed?" the Lady cried, appalled.

"I think not," Stile said grimly. He tried a spell to locate Clip specifically, but it fizzled. "This is Adept magic. I can not fathom the truth beyond this point, for it is Adept against Adept. But the message seems likely enough. Clip has been taken hostage."

"Hostage!" she exclaimed. "For what?"

"For my behavior. My secret enemy can not match my power directly, so he has resorted to another device. I must bargain with him for Clip's life."

"But what does that Adept want?"

"It seems I am to be involved in great events in the near future. Mine enemies know this, my friends know too. Everybody knows this except me. What mine enemy wants will surely be made known in good time."

"But no one can influence thee by such means!"

"Oh, yes, he can!" Stile scowled, feeling an elemental savagery. "He can evoke my vengeance against him for whatever he does to Clip. He can make me an enemy for life. Now he is attacking my wife and steed in lieu of me, seeking leverage. Not without consequence may Blue be thus used."

She smiled sadly. "The honeymoon is over."

Soberly, he nodded. "I must report to the Herd Stallion."

"And I—I shall be left behind again."

"Thou knowest I love thee, Lady. But there are things I must do."

"I would not change thy nature if I could, my love."

Abruptly, savagely, they kissed, their horror of the situation converting to passion. Then Stile spelled them to the unicorn herd.

They arrived at the edge of the pasture where the unicorns grazed. The great Herd Stallion looked up. He stood eighteen hands at the shoulder, or six feet, and was powerfully muscled. His torso was pearly gray, darkening into black hooves; his mane and tail were silver, and his head golden. He was the most magnificent equine Stile knew.

Perceiving Stile's mien, the Stallion converted immediately to man-form and approached. "Speak without waste, Adept."

"Clip has been taken hostage," Stile said. Then he choked and could not continue.

"Do thou go see Neysa," the Lady Blue told him gently. "I will give the Stallion the detail."

Gratefully, Stile walked through the herd, looking for his closest friend in Phaze. In a moment Neysa came to him. She was fit and sleek, showing as yet no sign of her gravid condition. She had only very recently been bred, and equines did not show the way humans did. She accepted his embrace, shifting momentarily to girl-form in his arms, in the mischievous way she had. Then she shifted back.

"Oh, Neysa," he said, feeling the tears on his face. "I fear I have placed your brother in dire straits."

She tensed, blowing a harmonica-note of alarm. She loved her brother.

"I was in Proton-frame," he stumbled on. "Ogres attacked the Lady Blue. Clip fought valiantly, protecting her, and killed two ogres. But an Adept sent a sending of the mare called Belle, who won thine event in the Unolympics, and lured him into captivity, surely hostage against my power. And I—I can not accept what that enemy may demand of me, though Clip is—" The tears were flowing freely now, dropping from his chin. "I should have been there!" And perhaps, if he had checked Clip's situation first, instead of last, he might have been in time to nullify the abduction. He had just assumed that Clip was near.

Neysa laid her warm horn against his cheek, suffering silently with him, forgiving him. She understood.

They walked together back to the Herd Stallion. The noble creature was again in his natural form and had evidently assimilated the Lady's story. He was stomping the turf with one forehoof, making sparks fly up, and steam was issuing from his nostrils.

When Stile rejoined him, the Stallion changed again to man-form, a wisp of steam still showing in his breath. "Thou art not at fault, Adept," he said. "Clip was there to help and protect thee, not thou him."

"Protect me he did," Stile said. "I owe him my life. But he lost his freedom protecting not me but my Lady. I must restore him to freedom and avenge what he is suffering."

"He is of my herd," the Stallion said. "Ultimately, vengeance is mine. But thou art welcome to free him if thou canst."

"First must I locate him," Stile said. "And, if thou canst permit it, I would take another unicorn as temporary steed. The forces ranged against me, for whatever reason, are more than I can safely cope with alone, and no horse suffices. I need the kind of service only a unicorn can give."

The Stallion hesitated. Neysa blew a faint note on her harmonica-horn, half pleading, half warning. She was subject to the Herd Stallion, but friend to the Blue Adept— and to many others. She was close blood kin to Clip. She wanted to be Stile's steed again, despite her condition. The Stallion could say nay or yea and would be obeyed—but his life would be simplified if he placated this spirited little mare. Stile had a certain sympathy for the Herd Stallion's predicament.

"I will provide thee with another unicorn," the Stallion decided. "Thou art held in unusual respect in this herd, Adept; a number of these would do for thee what they would not do for any ordinary man. Yet may I not compel any in this matter; give me time to seek a volunteer."

The Stallion seemed less urgent about this than Stile felt, and was obliquely refusing Neysa's offer. Yet it was a sensible course. "It will take time to locate Clip and prepare a campaign to recover him without injury," Stile said. "Adept magic is involved, making the matter devious, not subject to simple spells. I do not relish his captivity for even another hour, but it would be foolish to strike unprepared. Will a day and a night suffice? I do have business in the other frame."

"It will suffice," the Stallion agreed. "I shall query the animals of other kinds and send to the Oracle."

The Oracle! Of course! That would pinpoint Clip instantly—if the answer were not misunderstood. Except— what about the speculation the Translucent Adept had made about the Oracle? Maybe he should be careful of any advice received, without openly challenging its validity.

Stile turned to the Lady Blue. "Now must I return thee to the Blue Demesnes for safekeeping."

Again Neysa protested. The Herd Stallion, shifting to natural form, blew an accordion-chord of irritated acquiescence.

"I have been invited to visit with the Herd during thine absence," the Lady said. "I can be better guarded here, for no magic penetrates a herd on guard. By thy leave, my Lord—"

"I will make thee a pavilion," Stile said, pleased. She would be much safer here, certainly.

"I need it not, my Lord."

Stile nodded. The Lady Blue was no frail flower; she could survive well enough. "Then shall I—"

He paused, and the unicorns looked up from their grazing. A dragon was approaching—a huge flying creature, swooping up and down, evidently searching for something. It spied the herd and flew directly toward it.

Immediately the unicorns formed a circle, horns pointing out. In the center were the foals and aged individuals —and Neysa, specially protected during her gestation. The Herd Stallion stood outside, flanked by several of the strongest of the lesser males, facing the monster alertly.

"I can deal with this," Stile offered. He had a number of spells to bring down dragons.

But the dragon was not attacking. It was a steed, with an old woman holding the reins, perched between the great beating wings. She carried a white kerchief that she waved in her left hand.

"Flag of truce," Stile said. Then, with a double take: "That's the Yellow Adept!"

The Herd Stallion snorted angrily. He would honor the truce, but he had no love for the Yellow Adept, whose business it was to trap and sell animals, including unicorns.

The dragon landed with a bump that made its passenger bounce, then folded its wings. The old woman scrambled down. "I bear a message for Blue. It must be quick, for my potion can not hold this monster long."

Stile stepped forward, still surprised. Usually this witch only went out in public after taking a youth potion for cosmetic effect. What message could cause her to scramble like this? "I am here, Yellow."

"It is in the form of a package, my handsome," she said, handing him a long box that appeared from her shawl. Stile suddenly became conscious of his own apparel: the outfit of a Proton Citizen. In the rush of events he had not bothered to conjure Phaze clothing. But it hardly mattered; an Adept, like a Citizen, could wear what he pleased. "I want thee to know I had no hand in this particular mischief. The item was delivered by conjuration with the message: *Blue butt out.* I hastened to bring it to thee, fearing further malice against thee an I delayed. My potions indicate that more than one Adept participates in this."

She hurried back to her dragon-steed before Stile could open the package. "Wait, Yellow—I may wish to question thee about this!" Stile called. Something about the package gave him an extremely ugly premonition.

"I dare not stay," she called back. "I would help thee if I could, Blue, for thou art a bonny lad. But I can not." She spurred her dragon forward. The creature spread its wings and taxied along on six little legs, finally getting up to takeoff velocity. Once it was airborne, it was much more graceful. Soon it was flying high and away.

Stile unwrapped the package with a certain misgiving. It surely did not contain anything he would be glad to see. Probably it was from Clip's captor; some evidence that the unicorn was indeed hostage, such as a hank of his blue mane.

As the package unwrapped, two red socks fell out. Clip's socks, which could be magically removed and used separately, in the same manner as Neysa's white socks. But there was something else in the package. Stile unwrapped it—and froze, appalled. All the others stared, not at first believing it.

It was a severed unicorn horn.

Stile's hands began to shake. He heard the Lady Blue's quick intake of breath. Neysa blew a note of purest agony.

Slowly Stile lifted the horn to his mouth. He blew into the hollow base. The sound of an ill-played saxophone emerged. It was definitely Clip's horn.

Neysa fell to the ground as if stricken by lightning. The Lady Blue dropped down beside her, putting her arms about the unicorn's neck in a futile attempt to console her. Stile stood stiffly, his mind half numbed by the horror of it. To a unicorn, the horn was everything, the mark that distinguished him from the mere horse.

More than that, he realized, the horn was the seat of the unicorn's magic. Without it, Clip could not change form or resist hostile spells. He would be like a man blinded and castrated—alive without joy. There could be no worse punishment.

The Herd Stallion was back in man-form. He put forth his large hand to take the horn. His eyes were blazing like the windows of a furnace, and steam was rising from him. "They dare!" he rasped, staring at the member.

"For this will I visit a conflagration on the Demesnes of every Adept involved!" Stile said, finding his voice at last. "On every creature who cooperated. I will level mountains to get at them. What the Blue Adept did to the trolls and jackals shall be as nothing." Already the air was becoming charged with the force of his developing oath; dark coils of fog were swirling. "Only let me make my music, find my rhyme—"

"Nay, Adept," the Herd Stallion said gruffly. "He is of my herd. Not thine but mine is this vengeance."

"But thou canst not leave thy herd unguarded," Stile protested.

"Another Stallion will assist, for this occasion."

"And thou canst not face Adepts alone. Only an Adept can oppose an Adept."

The Stallion snorted smoke from his human nostrils, heeding Stile's caution through his fury. "True. Not alone can I accomplish it. Only half the vengeance is mine to claim."

"Just give me a steed, and I will—"

"I will be thy steed!" the Stallion said.

Neysa, on the ground, perked up her ears. The Lady

Blue's eyes widened as she recognized the possibilities. No human being had ever ridden a Herd Stallion, virtually a breed apart. Yet if the power of an Adept coordinated with that of a unicorn Stallion—

Stile could not decline. They shared a vengeance.

CHAPTER 8

Wager

"So I have most of twenty-four hours in Proton," Stile said to Sheen, "before the Stallion and I commence our mission of rescue and vengeance. I'll have to spend some of that time in sleep, gathering my strength. I trust you have my business here well organized."

"We do," she agreed brightly. "Mellon has lined up a number of wealthy Citizens who are eager to wipe you out financially. My friends have worked out a way to trace the original message to Citizen Kalder—but only you, an interested Citizen, can implement it. And there is reaction approaching suppressed riot to the news of the designation of your heir."

"That's enough to start on," Stile said. "Maybe it will distract me for the moment from my real concern in Phaze. Let's see how much we can sandwich in. I don't know how long my next adventure in Phaze will hold me."

"Perhaps forever," she said darkly. Then, mechanically, she reverted to immediate business. "Start on which, sir? You can't do everything at once."

"Why not?"

"The bettors are in the Stellar Lounge, as before. The panel for your heir-designation hearing is in another dome, a hundred kilometers distant. And the first obscurity in the message chain is at a dome fifty kilometers beyond that, in the private property of a Citizen. Any one of these situations can monopolize your available time."

"You think too much like a machine," he chided her. "Take me to the hearing. Meanwhile, call the Stellar Lounge."

Frowning, she set the travel capsule in motion and placed the call. Mellon appeared in three-dimensional image. "So good to see you, sir. May I notify the Citizens that you are ready for action?"

"Do so," Stile said. "But advise them that I have unusual and challenging bets in mind and will welcome them at the site of my heir-designation hearing. You be there too."

"Yes, sir." Mellon faded out.

Immediately there was an incoming call. It was Citizen Merle. "My intercept notified me you were back in town," she said brightly. "Have you considered my invitation of the morning?"

Not this again! "Merle, I remain flattered. But there are things you should know."

"About your lovely wife in the other frame? Stile, that has no force in Proton."

"About my engagement to the serf Sheen, here," Stile said, unpleased about Merle's conversance with his private life. Too many Citizens were learning too much about him.

"Yes, I mean to place a bet on the outcome of your hearing," Merle agreed. "I'm rooting for you, Stile; I'm betting you will gain approval, after a struggle. Citizens are by no means limited in their liaisons. I have gifted my husband with a number of fine concubines, and he has sent me whichever males he suspects will appeal to my tastes. In any event, you need have no concern about the feelings of a serf."

Stile suffered an explosive reaction of anger. Sheen made an urgent signal: do not offend this Citizen!

Then Stile had a tactical inspiration. "Merle, I do care about the feelings of this serf. I was until very recently a serf myself. Until I have a better notion of her willingness to share, I can not give you a decision."

Merle smiled. "Oh, I do like you, little man! You are like a splendid fish, fighting the line. I shall be in touch with you anon." She faded.

"Sir, I never denied you the right to—" Sheen began.

"Secure our privacy!" he snapped.

She adjusted the communication controls. "Secure, sir."

"Then why are you calling me sir?"

"Stile, our relationship has changed. We are no longer even nominally members of the same society, and I prefer to recognize that in the established way. Sir."

"You're mad at me?"

"A machine can not be angry, sir."

Fat chance! "Sheen, you know that our marriage is one of convenience. I'm doing it to give your friends leverage in their suit for recognition. The upcoming hearing will be a crucial step. If we prevail there, it will be a big stride forward for your kind. I do like you, in fact I love you— but the Lady Blue will always hold the final key to my heart."

"I understand, sir." Her face was composed.

"So being faithful to you, in this frame, is moot," he continued, wishing she would show more of the emotion he knew she felt. "It is the Lady Blue I am faithful to. But aside from that, there is the matter of appearances. If I am engaged to you, but have liaisons with fleshly women— especially Citizens—that could be taken as evidence that I am marrying you in name only, to designate a convenient heir, and that could destroy the leverage we hope to gain."

"Yes, sir," she agreed noncommittally.

"So there is no way I will make an assignation with Merle. If I do that with anyone in this frame, it will be you. Because you are my fiancée, and because there is no one in this frame I would rather do it with. So, in that sense, I am true to you. I wanted to be sure you understand."

"I understand, sir. There is no need to review it."

So he hadn't persuaded her. "Yes, I needed to review it. Because now I have it in mind to do something extremely cynical. An act worthy of a true Citizen. And I need your help."

"You have it, sir."

"I want you to have your friends arrange a blind bet on the outcome of Merle's suit. An anonymous, coded bet amounting to my entire available net worth at the time of decision—that I will not complete that liaison. I will of course deny any intent to make that liaison, but I may at times seem to waver. You and I know the outcome, but other Citizens may wish to bet the other way. It would be a foolish bet for them—but they seem to like such foolishness."

Sheen smiled. "That is indeed cynical, sir. I shall see to it."

"And it would not hurt if you permitted yourself some trifling show of jealousy, even if you feel none."

She paused. "You are devious, sir."

"I have joined a devious society. Meanwhile, I shall remain on the fence with Merle, in all but words, as long as I can stimulate interest. See that Mellon is privately notified; he definitely has the need to know."

The capsule arrived at the dome of the hearing. They emerged into a white-columned court, floored with marble, spacious and airy as a Greek ruin. Three Citizens sat behind an elevated desk. A fourth Citizen stood before the desk, evidently with another case; Stile's turn had not yet come.

The betting Citizens were arriving. A rotund man garbed like a Roman senator approached, hand extended. "Greeting, Stile. I am Waldens, and I'm interested in your offer. What is its nature?"

"Thank you, Waldens. I am about to face a hearing on the validity of my designation of my fiancée, a humanoid robot, as my heir to Citizenship. I proffer a wager as to the panel's decision."

"Most interesting!" Waldens agreed. "I doubt they will approve the designation."

"I am prepared to wager whatever my financial adviser will permit, that they will approve it," Stile said. "It is, after all, a Citizen's right to designate whom he pleases."

"Ah, yes—but a robot is not a 'whom' but an 'it.' Only recognized people can inherit Citizenship."

"Is there a law to that effect?"

"Why, I assume so. It is certainly custom."

Now Mellon arrived. Stile quickly acquainted him with the situation. "How much will you let me bet?" he asked, knowing that Mellon, as a self-willed machine in touch with the network of his kind, would have a clear notion of the legalistic background.

But the serf hesitated. "Sir, this is an imponderable. The decision of the panel is advisory, without binding force. If there is a continuing challenge, a formal court will be convened—"

"Come off it, serf!" Waldens snapped. "We're only betting on this particular decision. What the court does later will be grist for another wager. How much Protonite can Stile afford to risk?"

"He has limited me to one hundred grams," Stile said, catching Sheen's covert affirmative signal. That meant the machines had researched the issue, and believed the odds were with Stile. He should win this bet. But he was going to play it carefully.

"A hundred grams!" Waldens laughed. "I did not come all the way here in person for such minor action!"

"I regret that my estate is as yet minimal," Stile said. "But it is growing; I have won all bets made so far. I assure you that I have an appetite for larger bets—when I can afford them. I plan to increase my estate enormously."

"All right, Stile. You're peanuts, but I like your spirit. Should be good entertainment here. I'll play along with a small bet now—but I'll expect a big one later, if you're in shape for it. Shall we compromise at half a kilo now?"

Mellon looked pained, but under Walden's glare he slowly acquiesced. "Half a kilogram of Protonite," Stile agreed, putting on a pale face himself. Five hundred grams was half the ransom of a Citizen, and more than half Stile's entire available amount for betting. His fortune stood at 1,219 grams, but he had to hold 250 for living expenses. What he was laying on the line now was enough to buy a hundred sophisticated robots like Sheen and Mellon, or to endow the tenure of five hundred serfs. All in a single bet—which his opponent considered to be a minor figure, a nuisance indulged in only for entertainment!

Meanwhile, other Citizens had arrived, intrigued by the

issue. Novelty was a precious commodity among those who had everything. Two paired off, taking the two sides with matching half-kilo bets. Two more bet on whether there would be an immediate appeal of the panel's recommendation, whatever it was. Citizens certainly loved to gamble!

The prior case cleared, and it was Stile's turn before the panel. "It has been brought to our attention that you propose to designate a humanoid robot as your heir to Citizenship," the presiding Citizen said. "Do you care to present your rationale?"

Stile knew this had to be good. These were not objective machines but subjective people, which was why there could be no certainty about the decision. The wrong words could foul it up. "I am a very recent Citizen, whose life has been threatened by calamitous events; I am conscious of my mortality and wish to provide for the continuation of my estate. Therefore I have designated as my heir the person who is closest to me in Proton: my prospective wife, the Lady Sheen, here." He indicated Sheen, who cast her eyes down demurely. "She happens to be a lady robot. As you surely know, robots are sophisticated today; she is hardly distinguishable from a living person in ordinary interactions. She can eat and sleep and initiate complex sequences. She can even evince bad temper."

"The typical woman," the presiding Citizen agreed with a brief smile. "Please come to the point."

"Sheen has saved my life on more than one occasion, and she means more to me than any other person here. I have made her my chief of staff and am satisfied with the manner in which she is running my estate. I want to make our association more binding. Unless there is a regulation preventing the designation of one's wife as one's heir, I see no problem."

The three panelists deliberated. "There is no precedent," the presiding Citizen said. "No one has designated a robot before. Machines do well enough as staff members, concubines, stand-ins, and such, but seldom is one married and never have we had a nonhuman Citizen."

"If an alien creature won the Tourney one year, would it be granted Citizenship?" Stile asked.

"Of course. Good point," the Citizen said, nodding. "But robots are not permitted to participate in the Game, so can not win the Tourney."

"Do you mean to tell me that a frog-eyed, tentacular mass of slime from the farthest wash of the galaxy can be a Citizen—but this woman can not?" Stile demanded, again indicating Sheen.

The Citizens of the panel and of the group of bettors looked at Sheen, considering her as a person. She stood there bravely, smooth chin elevated, green eyes bright, her light brown hair flowing down her backside. Her face and figure were exquisitely female. There was even a slight flush at her throat. She had been created beautiful; in this moment she was splendid.

"But a robot has no human feeling," another panelist said.

"How many Citizens do?" Stile asked.

The bettors laughed. "Good shot!" Waldens muttered.

The panelists did not respond to the humor. "A robot has no personal volition," the presiding Citizen said. "A robot is not alive."

This was awkward territory. Stile had promised not to give away the nature of the self-willed machines, who did indeed have personal volition. But he saw a way through.

"Sheen is a very special robot, the top of her class of machine," he said. "Her brain is half digital, half analog, much as is the human brain, figuratively. Two hemispheres, with differing modes of operation. She approximates human consciousness and initiative as closely as a machine can. She has been programmed to resemble a living woman in all things, to think of herself as possessing the cares and concerns of life. She believes she has feeling and volition, because this is the nature of her program and her construction." As he spoke, he remembered his first discussion with Sheen on this subject, before he discovered the frame of Phaze. He had chided her on her illusion of consciousness, and she had challenged him to prove he had free will. She had won her point, and he had come to love her as a person—a robot person. He had tended to forget, since his marriage to the Lady Blue, how deep his feeling for Sheen was. Now he was swinging back to her. He truly believed she was a real person, whose mechanism happened to differ from his own but resulted in the same kind of personality.

"Many creatures have illusions," a panelist remarked. "This is no necessary onus for Citizenship."

Stile saw that more would be required to overcome their prejudice. He would have to do a thing he did not like.

"Sheen, how do you feel about me?" he asked.

"I love you, sir," she said.

"But you know I can not truly love a machine."

"I know, sir."

"And you are a machine."

"Yes, sir."

"I will marry you and designate you as my heir to Citizenship, but I will not love you as man to woman. You know it is a marriage of convenience."

"I know, sir."

"Why do you submit to this indignity?"

"Because she wants Citizenship!" a Citizen exclaimed. He was one of the ones betting against the acceptance of the heir designation.

Stile turned to the man. "How can a machine want?" Then he returned to Sheen. "Do you want Citizenship?"

"No, sir."

"Then why do you accede to this arrangement?"

"Because your wife in Phaze asked me to."

"Oh, a stand-in for an other-frame wife!" Waldens said knowingly. "Cast in her image?"

"No, sir, she is beautiful," Sheen said. "I can never substitute for her."

"I am interested," the presiding panelist said. "Robot, are you capable of emotion? Do you feel, or think you feel? Do you want anything?"

"Yes, sir, to all three," Sheen replied.

"Exactly what do you want, if not Citizenship?"

"I want Stile's love, sir," she said.

The panelist looked at his co-panelists. "Let the record note that the robot is crying."

All the Citizens looked closely at Sheen. Her posture

and expression had not changed, but the tears were streaming down her cheeks.

"Why would any woman, human or robot, cry in response to simple, straightforward questions?" a panelist asked.

Citizen Waldens stepped forward suddenly, putting his cloaked arm around Sheen's shoulders. "For God's sake! She is not on trial! Spare her this cruelty!"

The presiding panelist nodded sagely. "She weeps because she knows she can never have her love returned by the man she loves, no matter what else he gives her. Our questioning made this truth unconscionably clear, causing her to react as the woman she represents would act. I do not believe she was conscious of the tears, or that this is a detail that would have occurred to a man." He pondered a moment, then spoke deliberately. "We of this panel are not without feeling ourselves. We are satisfied that this person, the robot Sheen, is as deserving of Citizenship as is a frog-eyed, tentacular mass of slime from the farthest wash of the galaxy." He glanced at his co-panelists for confirmation. "We therefore approve the robot Sheen's designation as heir, pending such decision as the court may make."

The Citizens applauded politely. Waldens brought Sheen back to Stile. "I'm glad to lose that bet, Stile. She's a good woman. Reminds me of my wife, when she was young and feeling. This robot deserves better than you are giving her."

"Yes," Stile agreed.

Waldens started to turn away, then snapped back in a double take. "I'll be damned! You're crying too!"

Stile nodded dumbly.

"And you think you don't love her." The Citizen shrugged. "Care to make a bet on that?"

"No," Stile said.

Sheen turned to him with incredulous surmise. "The illusion of nonfeeling—it is yours!" she said. "The Lady knew!"

The Lady had known. Stile was indeed a man of two loves, suppressing one for the sake of the other—in vain.

"Well, I'll bet you on something else," Waldens said.

"One kilo, this time. I happen to know you can afford it."

Stile wrenched himself back to the practicalities of the moment. He looked at Mellon. "Can I?"

"Sir, your betting is becoming more hazardous than necessary."

"That's his way of saying yes," Waldens said. "I feel you owe me one more bet. It wasn't right to use your girl that way. You set her up for it, knowing how she loved you."

"Yet he gave back more than he took," Sheen said. There was now a certain radiance about her, the knowledge of discovered treasure. Stile had actually set himself up.

"I'll give you your bet," Stile agreed. "And I'll match anybody else, if I don't run out of grams. Right now I have to trace an old message to its source. Care to bet whether I make it?"

"No. I don't know enough about the situation. But I'll bet when I do. You are involved in odd things, for a new Citizen. Usually they're busy for the first month just experiencing the novelty of having serfs say sir to them."

"I have some equipment waiting at the site," Stile said. He gave the address, and the other Citizens dispersed to their private capsules.

Alone with Sheen and Mellon in his own capsule, Stile looked at Sheen. Emotion overwhelmed him. "Damn!" he exclaimed. "I'm sorry, Sheen."

She paused momentarily, analyzing which level he was on. "You had to do it, sir. It was necessity, not cruelty, sir."

"Stop calling me sir!" he cried.

"When we are alone," she agreed.

"Maybe I am fooling myself. Maybe what I feel for you is what most others would call love. But since I met the Lady Blue—"

She laid her soft hand on his. "I would not change you if I could."

Which was what the Lady Blue had said. Sheen could have had no way to know that.

"It is an interesting relation you share," Mellon said. "I am not programmed for romantic emotion. I admit to curiosity as to its nature and usefulness."

"You are better off not knowing," Sheen said, squeezing Stile's hand.

"I do experience excitement when a large property transaction is imminent."

"If the self-willed machines gain recognition," Stile said, "you will receive whatever programming you wish, including romantic. For now, she's right; you are happier as you are."

"I will be ecstatic if I complete your target fortune. So far I have had little to do with it. I fear my circuits will short out, observing your mode of operation."

Stile smiled. "Now that I have inordinate wealth, I find it does not mean much to me," he said. "It is merely the substance of another game. I want to win, of course—but my real ambition lies elsewhere." He glanced again at Sheen. "My emotion is so erratic, I really think it would be better for you to accept reprogramming to eliminate your love for me. It would save you so much grief—"

"Or you could accept conditioning to eliminate your love for the Lady Blue," she said.

"Touché."

"Or to diminish your prejudice against robots."

"I'm not prejudiced against—" He paused. "Damn it, now I know I could love you, Sheen, if I didn't have the Lady Blue. But my cultural conditioning . . . I would prefer to give up life itself, rather than lose her."

"Of course. I feel the same about you. Now I know I have enough of you to make my existence worthwhile."

She was happy with half a loaf. Stile still felt guilty. "Sometimes I wish there were another me. That I had two selves again, with one who was available for Citizenship and who would love you, while the other could roam forever free in Phaze." He sighed. "But of course when there were two of me, I knew about none of this. My other self had the Lady Blue."

"That self committed suicide," she said.

"Suicide! By no means! He was murdered!"

"He accepted murder. Perhaps that is not clear to your illogical and vacillating mind."

"My mind was his!"

"In a different situation. He had reason."

Accepted murder. Stile considered that. He had marveled before that the Blue Adept had been dispatched by so crude a device—strangled by a demon from an amulet. It was indeed a suspicious situation. No magic of that sort had been able to kill Stile; why had it worked against his other self? And the Blue Adept's harmonica, his prized possession, had been left for Stile to find, conveniently. Yet suicide—could that be believed? If so, why? Why would any man permit himself to be ignominiously slain? Why, specifically, should Stile himself, in his other guise, permit it? He simply was not the type.

"You say he had reason. Why do you feel he did that?"

"Because he lacked enough of the love of the one he loved," she said promptly.

"But the Lady Blue gave him the third thee," he protested. "In Phaze, that is absolute love."

"But it was late and slow, and as much from duty and guilt as from true feeling. Much the same as your love for me. I, too, tried to suicide."

Indeed she had, once. One might debate whether a nonliving creature could die, but Sheen had certainly tried to destroy herself. Only the compassion of the Lady Blue had restored Sheen's will to endure. The Lady Blue, obviously, had understood. What a hard lesson she had learned when her husband died!

"Somehow I shall do right by you, Sheen," Stile said. "I don't know how, right now, but I will find a way."

"Maybe with magic," she said, unsmiling.

They arrived at the site of the message-tracing team. Stile was glad to let this conversation drop. He loved Sheen, but not consistently and not enough. His personal life in Proton seemed to be an unravelable knot.

They were in one of the public lavatories for serfs, with rows of sinks, toilets, and showers. The message cable passed the length of its floor, buried but within range of the detector. Passing serfs, seeing a Citizen present, hastily departed for other facilities.

There was a serf technician with a small but complex machine on two wheels. The machine blinked and bleeped in response to the serf's comments. No, Stile realized, it was the other way around. The serf commented in response to the device. It was another self-willed machine, with a subordinate serf. A neat way to conceal the real nature of the assistance being provided. The self-willed machines had considerable resources but did not want to betray their nature to the Citizens, lest the machines be summarily destroyed. There was a difference between being programmed to mimic personal volition, as Sheen was presumed to be, and actually possessing that volition, as Sheen and her kind did. The makers of these most sophisticated robots had wrought better than they knew, which was the reason these machines wanted legal recognition as people. They *were* people, of mechanical nature. With such recognition they could not be dispatched without legal reason, lest it be called murder.

The signals from the machine were more or less continuous and were ignored by the Citizens who joined Stile's party for the betting. Thus the real nature of the communications was not obvious. Only Stile, with his private knowledge of the special machines and his Game-trained alertness for detail, was aware of it. "What have we here?" he inquired of the serf.

"Sir, this is an electronic device that can trace the route of a particular message at a particular moment," the serf said. "Each message modifies the atomic structure of the transmission wires nominally. This change is so small that only a sophisticated instrument can detect it, and the range is quite limited. But it is possible to trace the stigmata by examining the wires at close range, provided we know precisely what we are looking for."

"Like a hound sniffing a scent," Stile said.

The machine bleeped. "Yes, sir," the serf said.

"That's a new one to me," Waldens said. "But I never did concern myself with machines. I think I'll buy me one like the metal lady here, if I don't win this one in a bet."

Both Sheen and Stile reacted, startled. Neither was pleased. Waldens laughed. "Stile, you don't have to bet anything you don't want to. But you should be aware that this lady robot is now a piece worth a good deal more than she was when new. If you lose a big one and have to have a new stake, she is it." He glanced at the message-tracing machine. "Now let's see this contraption operate."

"You have programmed the specific message and time of transmission?" Stile inquired. "Why are you unable to continue?"

Again the bleep. "Yes, sir. We have traced the message to this point. But ahead the cable passes through a juncture associated with the estate of a Citizen who denies us permission to prospect here."

"Ah, now the challenge comes clear," Waldens said. "What Citizen?"

"Sir, serfs do not identify Citizens by name," the serf said, translating the machine's signals. "But his designation is at the gate."

Waldens strode out of the lavatory and down the hall to examine the gate. The others followed. "Circle-Tesseract symbol." He brought out a miniature mike. "Who's that?"

"Sir, that is Citizen Cirtess," his contact answered.

"Cirtess. Circle-Tesseract. That figures. Same way I have a forest pond on my crest. I know him." Waldens considered. "Stile, I'm ready to bet. You won't get into that dome to trace your line. You'll have to go around and pick up beyond."

"Is that feasible?" Stile asked his technician serf.

"Not feasible, sir. This is a major cable junction. Billions of impulses have passed through it. We can trace the stigmata only by setting up at the junction and reading the routing there."

"Needle in a haystack," Stile said.

"Sir?"

"Never mind. I grasp the problem. We shall simply have to get to that switchbox."

"That's my bet, Stile," Waldens said. "Let's put a reasonable time limit on it. Shall we say half an hour for you to get the job done?"

Stile looked at the message-tracing serf. "How long to pass this junction without impediment?"

"It is merely a matter of getting to it, sir. The readout is instant."

Stile looked at Mellon. "How much may I bet?"

"The amount is settled," Waldens protested. "One kilo."

Mellon was unhappy. "Sir, this is extremely chancy, incorporating virtually no element of predictability, and the amount is large. Have you any reasonable expectation of obtaining permission to enter Citizen Cirtess' dome in the next half hour?"

"No. *But* that's not the bet. It's whether I can get the job done."

"Oho!" Waldens exclaimed. "You intend to go in without permission?"

Stile shrugged. "I intend to get the job done."

"Cirtess has armed guards and laser barriers," another Citizen said. "Almost every year some foolishly intruding serf gets fried. It would take a mechanized army to storm that citadel."

Waldens smiled. "Sirs, I think we have a really intriguing wager in the making. What do we deem to be the odds against Stile's success? Remember, he is a canny ex-serf who recently won the Tourney; he surely has some angle."

"Thousand to one against, for any ordinary person," the other Citizen said. "Hundred to one against, for a Tourney winner. And a good chance he'll get himself killed trying."

"No, I saw him play," a third Citizen said. "He's a slippery one. If he thinks he can do it, maybe he can."

"I don't *think* I can do it," Stile said. "I *have* to do it. Forces were set in motion to kill me, and this message is related. I must ascertain its source."

"Within half an hour?" Waldens asked.

"I suspect that if I don't pass this nexus in that time, I won't pass it at all. It is pass-fail right now."

"And you are staking your life on it," Waldens said. "That makes the bet most interesting. Suppose we give you odds? We think the chances are one hundred to one against you; you evidently think you can do it. We could compromise at ten to one, with several of us covering the bet."

"That's generous enough," Stile agreed. "Since I have to make the attempt anyway."

"Sir, I do not recommend this wager," Mellon said. "I know of no persuasion you can make to obtain Citizen Cirtess' acquiescence, and you lack the facilities for intrusion against resistance. My expert advice can bring you far more favorable betting opportunities than this."

"Fifteen to one," Waldens said. "I won't go higher; I don't trust you to be as naïve as you seem." The other Citizens nodded agreement. Their faces were becoming flushed; this was the essence of their pleasure. Negotiating a large bet on a highly questionable issue. Gambling not merely with wealth but with the deviousness of human comprehension and intent. They knew Stile had something in mind, and it was worth poorer odds to discover what his play would be.

Stile spread his hands in ordinary-man innocence. "Mellon, I'm sure your way is more practical. But I stand to win a great deal on this, with these levered odds. If I lose I'm in trouble anyway, because this intrusion may be physically hazardous. Wealth is very little use to a dead man. So I must do it my way this time. One kilogram of Protonite against their fifteen kilos, half an hour from now."

"Yes, sir," Mellon said with doleful resignation.

"But no interference from you Citizens," Stile cautioned. "If you give away the show to Cirtess—"

"No cheating," Waldens agreed. "We'll watch via a routine pickup, hidden in the lavatory."

"Thank you." Stile turned to the machine-operating serf. "Show me how to work this contraption," he said.

"Merely locate it over the line or nexus, sir. It will emit code lights and bleeps to enable you to orient correctly." He demonstrated. Stile tried the procedure on the section of cable under the floor, getting the hang of it. He knew he would have no trouble, since this was another self-willed machine, which would guide him properly.

Now Stile turned to one of the betting Citizens who wore an elaborate headdress that vaguely resembled an ancient Amerind chief's bonnet of feathers. "I proffer a side bet, my clothing against your hat, on the flip of a coin."

"How small can you get?" the Citizen asked, surprised. "I have staked a kilo, and you want my hat?"

"You decline my wager?" Stile asked evenly.

The Citizen frowned. "No. I merely think it's stupid. You could buy your own hat; you have no need of mine. And your clothing would not fit me." The man touched his bulging middle; his mass was twice Stile's.

"So you agree to bet." Stile looked around. "Does anyone have a coin with head and tail, similar to those used in Tourney contests?"

Another Citizen nodded. "I am a numismatist. I will sell you a coin for your clothing."

Now Stile was surprised. "My clothing has already been committed."

"I'm calling your bluff. I don't believe you plan to strip, so I figure you to arrange to win the toss. If you win, I get your clothing as due rental for the coin."

"But what if I lose?"

"Then I'll give you my clothing, in the spirit of this nonsense. But you won't lose; you can control the flip of a coin. All Gamesmen can."

"Now wait!" the headdressed Citizen protested. "I want a third party to flip it."

"I'll flip," Waldens said. "I'm objective; I'll be happy to see anyone naked, so long as it isn't me."

Stile smiled. "It might be worth the loss." For the coin-loaning Citizen was especially portly. "Very well. I will rent your coin."

"This grows ever more curious," Waldens remarked. "What is this fascination we seem to share for nakedness in the presence of Stile's lovely robot mistress?"

"Fiancée," Stile said quickly.

Now the other Citizen smiled. "Maybe we should all strip and ask her opinion."

Sheen turned away, blushing. This was sheer artifice, but it startled the Citizens again; they were not used to robots who were this lifelike. "By God," one muttered, "I'm going to invest in a harem of creatures like her."

Stile accepted the coin. It was a pretty iridium disk, comfortably solid in his hand, with the head of Tyrannosaurus Rex on one side and the tail of a dinosaur on the reverse. Stile appreciated the symbolism: iridium had been associated with the extinction of the dinosaurs, and of course the whole notion of coinage had become a figurative dinosaur in the contemporary age. Iridium, however, remained a valuable metal, and numismatics was popular among Citizens. He passed the coin over to Waldens.

"How do we know Waldens can't control the flip too?" another Citizen asked suspiciously. They were taking this tiny bet as seriously as any other.

"You can nullify his control by calling the side in mid-air," Stile pointed out. "If you figure him to go for heads, you call tails. One flip. Agreed?"

"Agreed." The Citizen with the headdress seemed increasingly interested. He was obviously highly curious as to what Stile was up to.

Stile was sure the Citizen's inherent vanity would cause him to call heads, as a reflection of self-image, so he hoped Waldens would flip it tails. The coin spun brightly in the air, heading for the tiled floor.

"Heads," the Citizen called, as expected. He hardly seemed to care about the outcome of the bet now; he was trying to fathom Stile's longer purpose.

The iridium coin bounced on the floor, flipped, rolled, and settled tails. Victory for Stile!

Stile held out his hand for the hat, and the Citizen with the coin held out his hand for Stile's clothes. All the rest watched this procedure solemnly. Even Sheen had no idea what Stile was up to.

Stile removed his clothing and stood naked, seeming like a child among adults. He took the hat and donned it, arranging it carefully to conceal his hair and complement the lines of his face. Then, with covered head and bare body, he marched to a holo unit set in an alcove. It was a small one, capable of head-projection only, available for emergency use. Any demand by a Citizen was considered emergency.

"Cirtess," Stile said crisply to the pickup. The device bleeped faintly as it placed the call. He knew the self-willed machines were tapping in, keeping track of him without interfering.

The head of a female serf formed in the cubby. "Sir, may I inquire your identity and the nature of your call?"

"I am Stile," Stile said, rippling an aristocratic sneer

across his lips. "I merely wish to inform your employer that a line-maintenance crew is about to operate on his premises. The maintenance is phony, and the crew is other than it appears. There is nothing wrong with that line. I believe Cirtess should investigate this matter personally."

"Thank you, sir," the serf said. She faded out.

"Now that's something!" Waldens exclaimed. "You warned him you were coming! Do you have a death wish?"

Stile removed his hat, but did not seek new clothing. He took the wheeled machine and started down the hall.

"Aha!" Waldens exclaimed. "Of course he would know how to emulate a serf! But Cirtess won't let a serf intrude, either, especially when he's been warned by a Citizen that something's afoot."

"We shall find out," Stile said. "You may watch me on the general pickup system to verify whether I succeed. Serfs, come along." He moved on toward the dome entrance.

The Citizens turned on the little holo unit, crowding around it. Stile knew they would follow his every move. That was fine; he wanted them to have no doubt.

He led his party to the Circle-Tesseract emblem. Cirtess' dome adjoined the main public dome closely; an on-ground tunnel about fifty meters long extended between the two. The communication line was buried beneath the floor of the tunnel.

Two male serfs stood guard at the tunnel entrance. They snapped to alertness as Stile's party approached. One barred the way. "This is private property."

Stile halted. "I'm on Citizen business," he said. "I'm tracing an important message along the communication line."

"Have you my employer's permission to pass?"

"He knows we're coming," Stile said. "I expect him to attend to this personally. Now give me room; I don't have all day." He pushed on by, trundling the machine.

Uncertain, the serf gave way. No mere serf braved the premises of a Citizen without authorization; this line tracing had to have been cleared. But the other serf was already buzzing his dome. "Work crew of four claims to be on Citizen business," he said.

Stile walked on, not waiting for the answer. Mellon, Sheen, and the machine-tending serf followed. They all knew they could be cut down by a laser at any moment; Citizens had short fuses when it came to serf intrusions, and there was a laser lens covering the length of the tunnel. But Stile was gambling that Cirtess would investigate before firing. Why should an illicit crew intrude so boldly on his premises? Why should there be advance warning? Wasn't it more likely that someone was trying to make mischief for a legitimate work crew? But the maintenance computer would deny that any crew was operating here at this time, so it *was* phony. It simply didn't add up, unless it was a practical joke. In that case, Cirtess would want to discover the perpetrator. To do that, he would have to observe the work crew and perhaps interrogate it. It was unlikely that Stile himself would be recognized in this short time; the Amerind hat had completely changed his face, and in any event, the last thing anyone would think of was a Citizen masquerading as a serf. At least this was Stile's hope.

No laser bolt came. Stile reached the end of the tunnel, passed another serf guard who did not challenge him, and traced the buried cable on through a foyer and into a garden park girt with cubistic statuary. The Tesseract motif, of course; Citizens could carry their symbolic foibles quite far.

In the center of the garden, beside a fountain that formed odd, three-dimensional patterns, Stile came to the buried cable nexus. He oriented the machine on it. There was a buzz; then an indicator pointed to the line leading away, and a readout gave the coding designation of the new cable. He had accomplished his mission and won his bet.

But when he looked up, there was a Citizen, flanked by a troop of armed serfs. This was Cirtess; Stile knew it could be no other. "Step into my office, Stile," the man said brusquely.

So the game was up. Stile turned the machine over to its regular operator and went with the Citizen. He had not actually won his bet until he escaped this dome intact with the machine; or if he had won the bet, but lost his life, what he had gained?

Inside the office, with privacy assured, Cirtess handed Stile a robe. Stile donned it, together with sandals and a feather hat. His subterfuge had certainly been penetrated.

"Now what is the story?" Cirtess inquired. "I think you owe me the truth."

"I'm tracing a two-month-old message," Stile said. "Your personnel would not permit entry to a necessary site."

"Of course not! I'd fire any serf who let unauthorized persons intrude."

"So I had to find a way through. It has nothing to do with you personally; I simply have to trace that message to wherever it originated."

"Why didn't you tell me this by phone? I am not unreasonable when the issue is clear; I might have permitted your mission, for a reasonable fee."

"I happen also to need to increase my fortune."

Cirtess nodded. "Could this relate to the several Citizens who huddle in the serf lavatory, spying on your progress?"

"They gave me fifteen-to-one odds on a kilo of Protonite that I couldn't make it. I need that sort of advantage."

"So you called me to rouse my curiosity, so my serfs wouldn't laser you out of hand?"

"Also so as not to deceive you," Stile agreed. "I do not like deception, outside the framework of an established game. You were not properly part of our game."

"So you inducted me into it. A miscalculation could have resulted in your early demise."

"My life has been threatened before. That's one reason I'm tracing this message; I believe its source will offer some hint of the nature of my nemesis."

Cirtess nodded again. "And the Citizens were willing to give better odds because of the factor of danger. Very well. I appreciate cleverness, and I'm as game for a wager as anyone. I will let you go without objection if you will wager your winnings with me."

"But my winnings will be fifteen kilos of Protonite!"

"Yes, a substantial sum. I can cover it, and you must risk it. Choose your bet now—or I shall see that you lose your prior bet by not completing your survey. I can legitimately destroy your tracer machine."

"You play a formidable game!" Stile exclaimed. "You're forcing me to double or nothing."

"Indeed," Cirtess agreed, smiling. "One does not brave the lion's den without encountering challenge."

Stile emerged from the dome with his crew and machine, his knees feeling somewhat weak. "I have the data," he announced.

Waldens glanced at the indicator on the machine. "So you do, and within the time limit. You've won fifteen. But why are you so shaky?"

"Cirtess caught me. He pressured me."

The other Citizens laughed. "Why do you think we bet against you?" one said. "Cirtess can buy and sell most of us. We knew you were walking into the lion's den."

"How did you wiggle out?" Waldens asked.

"He required me to bet my winnings with him," Stile said, grimacing. "That leaves me only one kilo uncommitted, until that bet is settled."

"What is the bet?"

"That is private. It is a condition of the wager that I tell no one its nature until it is settled, which should be shortly."

"Ah, I like that sort of mystery. Cirtess must be playing a game with us, to make up for our intrusion into his privacy. Very well—I'll go for your single kilo. Do you have any suitable notions?"

Stile considered. "I don't care to bet on this message-tracing any more. Maybe we can find something disconnected." They were walking toward the next cable junction, guided by the machine coding. It was pointless to trace every meander of the cable itself when this shortcut was available. Stile turned a corner and entered a short concourse between major domes. At this moment there were no other people in it. "I know! Let's bet on the sex of the serfs to traverse this passage in the next ten minutes. That should be a fairly random sampling."

"Good enough," Waldens agreed. "I'll match your kilo, betting on female."

"Now wait," the Citizen with the feather hat protested. He had recovered it after Stile's use. "The rest of us are being cut out."

"Bet with each other," Stile said. "I am at my present limit." And Mellon nodded emphatically.

"There's little verve in wagers with other Citizens. You are the intriguing factor here."

"Well, I'll be happy to hedge my bet," Stile said. "I bet Waldens that more males will pass, and you that more females will pass."

"No good. That puts Waldens and me against each other, in effect. I want you. I want your last kilo."

"All right," Waldens said. "I relinquish my bet with Stile. You can have this one."

"Hey, I want to bet too!" the iridium coin Citizen protested, and the others joined in.

"All right! I'll cover you all," Feather Hat said. "One kilo each. I say more females in ten minutes from—mark."

"Good enough," Waldens agreed. "Five of us, including Stile, are betting you that more males will pass. We all win or lose with Stile."

Now they waited. For two minutes no one came from either direction. "Suppose none comes—or it's even?" Stile asked. He was laboring under continuing tension.

"Then we extend the time," Waldens said. "Sudden death. Agreed?"

The others agreed. They all wanted a settlement. The particular bets didn't matter, and the details of the bets didn't matter; just as long as they could share the excitement of honest gambling.

Then two male serfs came, chatting together. Both went silent as they spied the group of Citizens in the center of the concourse. "Proceed apace," Waldens said, and the two hastily passed by.

A minute later a third serf came, from the opposite direction. Another male. The feather-hatted Citizen frowned.

Then the pace picked up. Three females passed, two more males, a female, three more males, and another female. At eight minutes the score was eight males, five females. "Must be a male work shift getting out," Waldens said, satisfied. "To think I almost bet on the girls!"

But in the final minute there were two more males and six more females. As the time expired, the score was ten males, eleven females.

The feather-hatted Citizen smiled broadly. "I skunked you all! Five kilos!" He nodded toward Stile. "And I beat *him*. Nobody's done that before."

"I lost my kilo," Stile agreed, wondering if he looked as nervous as he felt. "But there's a question I'd like to explore."

"Explore it," Waldens said. "We're having fun."

"I notice that the males were ahead, until a sudden rush of females at the end. Is the estate of any of our number near to this concourse?"

"Not mine," Waldens said. "But you, Bonnet—yours is close, isn't it?"

"It is," the feather-hatted Bonnet replied guardedly.

"And those late female serfs—would they by any chance be employees of yours?" Stile asked.

"That doesn't matter," Bonnet said. "The wager did not exclude our employees. All serfs are Citizen employees."

"Oho!" Waldens said. "You signaled your dome and loaded the dice!"

"Only smart participation," Bonnet insisted. "There was no bar against it."

Waldens sighed. "No, I suppose not. One must never accept something on faith, particularly the constancy of other Citizens. I fell for it; I'll take my loss." The others agreed, though not pleased; they all should have been more careful.

Now Stile felt the exhilaration of victory. "As it happens, I bet Cirtess fifteen kilos that someone would cheat on this wager. I lost my kilo, but won my fifteen. Right, Cirtess?"

"Right," Cirtess's voice agreed on a hidden speaker. "Well and fairly played, Stile. Let it be recorded: fifteen for you."

Waldens slapped his knee. "Beautiful! Bonnet won five, you won fifteen. Even in losing, you won! Your fortune is now just over thirty kilograms, Stile. You are now a moderately wealthy Citizen."

"Congratulations," Bonnet said sourly. "I believe I have had enough for the day." Somewhat stiffly, he departed.

"And that was worth my own paltry losses," Waldens said. "I never liked him much. Still, I suspect he's right. You have been outmaneuvering us nicely, Stile. I think I must desist wagering with you, lest I lose my shirt—or all of my clothing." And the others laughed, remembering the episode of nakedness. By common consent they dispersed, leaving Stile alone with his party of serfs.

"Sir, you have taken extraordinary chances," Mellon said reprovingly. "My expertise has been useless."

"I agree I have pushed my luck," Stile said. "I think it prudent to turn my winnings over to you for management now. Do you feel you can parlay them into an even larger fortune?"

"A thirty-kilogram stake? Sir, with that leverage and your authority to make selective wagers, I believe I can do well enough."

"Go to it. I'll refrain from further betting until I consult with you. Take it away."

"Thank you, sir. Your method is unorthodox, but I must confess it has proved effective." Mellon turned and walked away.

"He will work wonders, sir," Sheen murmured.

Unencumbered by the betting Citizens, they proceeded rapidly to the next nexus, which was in a public workshop area, and thence to another in a serf park that spread across the curtain. "Coincidence?" Stile inquired skeptically, and Sheen agreed it was probably not.

They set the machine, and the readout suggested that the message impulse had been introduced at this nexus. But this was a closed connection; there was no way to insert a message here. "It had to have come from the other side of the curtain," Stile said. Somehow he was not surprised. Much of the other mischief he had experienced had originated in Phaze.

"You have a friend there," Sheen said. "You will have to cross and use your magic to trace him down."

"Yes. Only an Adept could have managed this. I can't

think which one would have done it." Stile sighed. "Sheen, I still have a night free, and I shall need my rest. Take me home."

She took him to the Proton Blue Demesnes, and fed him and washed him in the manner of serf for Citizen, not deigning to give the job to the hired staff. She put him in a comfortable bed over a gravity diffusion screen, so that his weight diminished. Weariness closed in on him, now that he had respite from the tensions of the moment. But before he allowed himself to sleep, he caught her hand and drew her to him. "You cried for me again today," he said.

"And you cried again for me."

"Some day, somehow—"

She leaned over and kissed him, and it was as sweet as any kiss could be. In that pleasure he fell asleep. He dreamed that he loved her in the off moments as well as at the stress points—but woke to know that was only a wish, not truth. He could not do more than marry her.

CHAPTER 9

Source

Stile crossed the curtain in the morning at the site of the last junction. There was nothing special in Phaze at this place; it was only the slope of a lightly forested hill. Whatever had fed the message in was gone. There were not even any footprints, after two months.

He was the Blue Adept, with potent magic. How could he apply it to follow this long-cold trail? Wouldn't an Adept have counterspelled the trail to prevent such tracing?

One way to find out. Stile played his harmonica, sum-

moning his power, while he worked out a spell. Then he
sang: "Make an arrow, point the way, that the message
came that day."

The arrow formed, an illuminated spot like that made
by a light projection. But it rotated uncertainly, like a
compass without its magnetism. Sure enough, a counterspell was interfering. There would be no simple, one-step
answer.

However, his power at this spot, now, would be greater
than that of a months-gone Adept. He should be able to
trace the source—if he followed the trail in person, as he
had in Proton. "Give a signal, hot or cold, to make current
what is old," he sang, shaping the detail in his mind.

Now Stile's left side felt warmer than his right. He
turned, and the warmth was on his face. He strode forward—and the effect faded.

He backed up until he felt the heat again. It had fallen
away to his right. He got back on the trail, pursuing it
more carefully—and it led him in a spaghettilike wriggle
that coiled about and recrossed itself frequently. Obviously
the other party had anticipated this approach also, and
had left a tortuous path. It might take Stile a long time to
unravel every wriggle, and the trail could lead into traps.

He decided to let it go for now. He wanted to rejoin the
unicorns and the Lady Blue in plenty of time for the quest
for Clip and vengeance. This message had waited two
months; it would wait another day.

He used a prepared spell to transport himself to the
herd, and stood for a moment in discomfort as he arrived.
He certainly did not enjoy performing this kind of magic
on himself, but he really had no alternative at the moment.

Neysa spied him first and trotted over. She would always be his steed and his friend in spirit. Yet now she did
not prance, for the pall of her brother's fate hung over
her.

She changed to girl-form and made one of her rare
speeches: "The Stallion has news of Clip."

"What kind?" Stile asked tightly.

"He is alive." She shifted back to mare-form.

Stile vaulted to her back, and she trotted him over to the
herd. He embraced the Lady Blue briefly.

The Herd Stallion awaited him in man-form. "Under the White Mountains, prisoner of the goblins. We must strike by night—tonight, ere they suspect."

"Yes," Stile agreed. "Thou and I alone, surgically."

"They will be alert for Adept magic, and will kill Clip the moment they detect it. Thou canst not employ thy power until he is safe."

"How am I to save him, then?" Stile asked, frustrated.

"*I* will save him. Then thou canst get us all out of danger."

Stile was uncertain about this procedure, but had to agree. There was no use going on a rescue mission if his mere presence precipitated Clip's murder.

"We start now," the Stallion said. "It will be night ere we reach the mountains. I know an entrance to the goblin demesnes—but once underground, I will know the way no better than thou."

Stile had an idea. "Suppose I make a spell to show the way? Will that continuing magic alert the goblins?"

The Stallion considered. "I know not, but think not. It is new magic that makes alarm; there are many ancient spells in the background, ignored."

"I'd better risk it," Stile said. He considered a moment, then played his harmonica and sang: "A star institute, to illumine our route."

A pinpoint glow appeared to their north, shedding faint light on the ground.

"But the goblins will see it too!" the Stallion protested.

"See what?" the Lady Blue asked.

The Stallion smiled. "Ah—others see it not!"

"Others see it not," Stile agreed. "I am not quite as foolish as I look."

"Not quite," the Stallion agreed, and shifted back to his natural form, pawing the ground. Stile took the hint and leaped to his back. This was much more of a challenge than it had been with Neysa, for the Herd Stallion stood four hands higher than she and massed twice as much. He was a lot of animal. Had they not had a clear understanding, Stile's touch on his back would have precipitated an instant death struggle. It was a sign of the passions involved and the seriousness of the situation that the untamable Stallion submitted to this indignity.

Immediately they were off. Stile, the most skilled rider in this frame, suddenly had to hang on, lest he be dumped like a novice. Evidently some spirit of rivalry remained; the Stallion wanted him to know that he kept his perch only by sufferance. Stile had never been on a steed like this before; the Stallion was the mass of a huge work horse, but had the velocity of a racer. Stile had originally tamed Neysa by riding her against her will; he knew he could never have done it with this steed.

The scenery raced by. Wind tore at Stile's clothing. The Stallion's hooves pounded on the doubled drumbeat of a full gallop, and sparks flew up where the hard hooves struck, but the ride was smooth. The Stallion was not wasting energy in extra up-and-down motion; he was sailing straight ahead.

The pinpoint star remained fixed at about head-height, its spot of light brightening to a patch of ground. It slid to one side sometimes, guiding them around obstructions and bad footing, so that the Stallion never had to slow to scout the way. He was able to maintain cruising speed, faster than that of any horse, and he seemed tireless. As he warmed up, jets of flame blasted from his nostrils. This was the way that unicorns cooled themselves, since they did not sweat; the heat was dissipated from their breath and hooves.

After a time the ride became routine, then dull. Stile had nothing to do, since the Stallion knew the way even without the help of the little star. Stile could have slept, but was too keyed up; he wanted to rescue and restore Clip. He could do it, he was sure; his magic could cement the severed horn and heal the scars of its cutting. The only problem was getting to the unicorn without triggering the murder. And getting them all out, thereafter. Meanwhile, he just had to wait.

"I've been thinking," he remarked. "Art thou amenable to conversation?"

The Stallion blew an affirmative accordion note. He, too, was bored by this stretch.

"Thou art a powerful creature," Stile said. "Surely the

goblins will recognize thee as readily as me. I can be taken for an elf, but thou canst only be a unicorn, even in man-form. The snub-horn gives thee away."

The Stallion blew another note of agreement. Unicorns could change form but retained vestigial horns in all forms. This was because the horn was the seat of the unicorn's magic; without it the creature was no more than a horse, unable to play music or change form. If an alternate form lacked the horn, the unicorn would not be able to change back to equine form. This was plainly unacceptable; the human form was not one any self-respecting unicorn would care to be stuck in for long.

"Thy dragon-form is no better than thy man-form for concealment," Stile continued. "True, it could penetrate the goblin demesnes—but would create great alarm, for no one ignores a dragon! When thou didst approach Clip, the little monsters would surely realize thy nature and intent."

"Um," the unicorn noted with a thoughtful chord.

"The thing is, thou art in all thy forms a mighty creature. Now this is no bad thing and ordinarily is altogether proper." The phrasing of a suggestion was sometimes more important than the suggestion itself, particularly when addressed to a creature of pride. "But this time I wish thou didst possess an insignificant form, like Neysa's firefly, that I could carry in unobserved."

The unicorn ran on, considering. After a time he blew a new note. "Could." The notes were not really words, but pitch and inflection conveyed definite meaning, and Stile could usually interpret them when he put his mind to it.

"Thou hast a fourth form?" he asked, surprised. "I thought three was the limit, and only one or two for some."

Now came a proud blast. This was no ordinary unicorn; the Stallion could master a fourth form, if he chose.

"That's great!" Stile exclaimed. "Couldst thou work it up in time for tonight? I know it takes a considerable act of discipline to implement a new form, and there is so little time—"

The Stallion was not foolishly optimistic. Any form was a challenge the first time, and a fourth one was special. But he thought he could manage it.

They discussed it as the miles and leagues rushed by. It developed that some forms were easier than others. Difficulty varied according to the necessary specialization and the change of size. Thus a unicorn could convert to a massive bear fairly readily, because the size was about the same. A man-form was harder, because the mass was less and because of the necessary specialization of the hands and voice. A man-form that could not tie a knot in string would not be very good, and one who could not talk would be worse. These things had to be done properly, or were not worth doing at all. Neysa's firefly-form was a greater achievement than Clip's hawk-form, because the fly was only a fraction of the mass. Neysa weighed about 850 pounds in her natural form, about 85 in her girl-form, and less than 85-hundredths of an ounce in firefly-form. It would be more than twice as hard for the Herd Stallion to get down to that size.

"But such size would be beyond suspicion," Stile remarked. "No one would believe that a beast as noble as thou couldst hide in a form so small." That accented the magnitude of the challenge, rather than the insignificance of the form.

Then there was the problem of flying, the unicorn explained in concerned notes. Flying was a specialization that had to be mastered by tedious practice, after the physical form had been achieved. The Stallion had learned it for his dragon-form, but would have to start all over for an insect-form, since insects employed a different mode of flight. That could take days.

"Oh, I did not mean thou must fly," Stile said. "It is the insignificance I am after, that none may suspect thee. Thou couldst go from dragon to roach, for that."

Roach! the Stallion blasted, affronted. *Never!*

But Stile was struck by something else. Dragon—roach. His poem: the one he had used to win the Tourney in Proton. Had this provided him with a prophetic key?

Now he thought back, discovering parallels. He had referred to Gabriel's horn—but there was also the unicorn's horn. Clip's horn had precipitated this venture. He had also referred to trying to cheat fate; but he had won his biggest bet because of cheating by another Citizen. How far did this go?

How far, indeed! The first four lines of that poem had matched his recent experience, deliberately. Then the key word: silence. And he had been struck by the silence-spell. Then love; and he had become betrothed to Sheen. That was not love, precisely, but related; she certainly wanted and deserved love.

In fact, those key words aligned beautifully with his experience—almost like a prediction of the Oracle. Yet the words had become the random product of the Game Computer. No magic there! So it must be coincidence. It was possible to make seeming sense of almost anything, as those two poems had shown. Still—

Why not? Stile decided to go for it. "That is one form no goblin would suspect. The nether passages must be overrun with roaches. What Herd Stallion would go to the enormous effort to achieve so lowly a form? It is beneath consideration—therefore the safest of all forms for the accomplishment of such a hazardous mission."

"Um," the Stallion blew, heeding the logic but not the aesthetics.

"Actually, some roaches are quite elegant," Stile commented innocently. "When I was a serf in Proton, I had to deliver a horse to the dome of a Citizen who specialized in exotic creatures. He had a roach farm with some quite beautiful specimens. I remember some deep red ones, huge and sleek—surely the royalty of roaches. And others were frilly, like butterflies, only without wings—"

"*Enough!*" the unicorn snorted. He veered to a tight copse of trees and slowed. When he stopped inside, Stile was glad to dismount; they had been traveling for hours, and he was cramped and hungry and suffered the urgent calls of nature.

There was a convenient nut tree in the copse—unicorns generally had good taste about such things—so Stile could eat without using magic. There was also a small spring. This was really an oasis, probably known to every wild creature. There was a real advantage of traveling with such an animal—not only protection, but also the convenience of familiarity with the terrain. Stile had now

traveled with three unicorns—Neysa, Clip, and the Herd
Stallion—and this aspect was the same with each one. Stile
had always liked horses; he knew he would always like
unicorns better.

He had dreamed for more than fifteen years of becoming a Citizen of Proton, perhaps setting up his own racing
stable. Now he was a Citizen—and all he really wanted
was to stay here in Phaze, on any basis. He liked magic—
not merely his ability to perform it, but more importantly,
the very framework in which magic existed. He liked the
verdant hills, the little streams, the various features of this
irregular landscape. He liked the whole sweet outdoors,
with its fresh air and unpredictable weather and feeling of
freedom. Oh, there were horrors here—but even so, it was
a better world than Proton. Three centuries of unrestricted
development and narrow exploitation had destroyed the
environment of Proton, so that comfort now existed only
within the force-field domes. Stile liked civilization, but,
after encountering Phaze, he feared it was at too great a
price.

Stile became aware of a warm sensation on the left side
of his face. Oh, yes—his spell to trace the sender of the
message that had brought him Sheen was still in operation.
Old spells never died, and faded away only slowly—which
inertia was fortunate, since any given spell was effective
only once. The warmth was faint, indicating that he was
far from the source, but at least he could still trace it
down. He would do so the moment Clip was safe.

He heard a musical groan, as of someone stepping on an
accordion. The Stallion writhed, shimmered—and shrank
to a gross, many-legged lump of flesh.

A spell leaped to Stile's lips. But he choked it back,
realizing that this was not a magic attack. It was the
Stallion's effort to master a new form.

Stile ambled over, peering down at the grotesque carica-
ture of a roach. "Now that is the ugliest insect I've ever
seen," he remarked. "But certainly the biggest." Indeed, it
was almost the size of a man.

The monstrous bug waved its feelers, thrashed its legs
about, and blew a furious peep from the miniature horn

on its snout. Then it swelled rapidly into Stallion-form again, snorting fire from the effort.

"Oh, it's thou!" Stile exclaimed innocently. "I was about to step on it."

The Stallion glared and gave a snort that singed the hairs of Stile's arms. Then he tried again. This time he got the size right, but not the shape. He became a miniature unicorn. "I'm afraid that won't do," Stile said around a mouthful of nuts. "The goblins know that's not a normal 'corn size."

The Stallion re-formed, pawing the ground. Obviously he was putting forth terrific effort; his hooves were beginning to glow red, and wisps of smoke rose from his ears.

A third time he tried. This time he got it right—normal-sized roach, with a silvery body and golden head. The bug took one step—and exploded back into the Stallion. He just had not been able to hold it for more than two seconds.

"Maybe you'd better let it rest a while," Stile suggested. "Give your system time to acclimatize to the notion. We're not at the goblin demesnes yet."

The Stallion played an affirmative chord. Stile conjured ten pounds of fine oats for the equine repast, then stood abashed. He should not have used his magic here. But it seemed no one had been paying attention; maybe that was not the kind of spell the enemy was looking for. In due course he remounted, and they were off again. The strength of this unicorn was amazing; having run for hours and struggled to master a difficult new form, he was, after this brief respite, galloping at unreduced speed. Neysa and Clip were good unicorns, but neither could have maintained this velocity so long.

By nightfall the grim White Mountains were near. The Stallion had been moving toward them at a slant, north-west, circling the demesnes of the ogres. No need for any ogre trouble, this trip! Actually, Stile had settled with the ogres, establishing that he was not their enemy, but ogres were not too bright and there could still be trouble.

Now the sun was dropping below the horizon. The Stallion galloped along west, parallel to the mountain range, then stopped. Stile saw the guiding star to their north, showing them to the entrance to the goblins' somber nether world.

But the region was guarded. Goblins patrolled the clifflike fringe of the mountain range. How could they get in?

Stile had the answer to that. He was larger than a goblin, but close enough so that some stooping in the dark should enable him to pass. He scraped up handfuls of dirt and rubbed it over his face and arms, then removed his clothing and coated his bare body too. Goblins wore little clothing; Stile's Proton underpants sufficed for a costume. Goblin feet and hands, however, were far larger than his own, while their limbs were shorter. Stile experimented and finally fashioned a framework for each foot from small branches and dirt, making his extremities seem goblin-sized. He did the same for his head. Magic would have been much easier for disguising himself, either physically or by means of illusion, but he did not dare use that here. He was facile with his hands and knew how to improvise; his head was actually expanded by a gross turban fashioned from his former clothing.

"Grotesque," the Herd Stallion said, eyeing Stile in manform. "The human shape is ugly enough to begin with, but thou hast improved on it."

"Just do thine own shape-change," Stile said. "And keep it stable."

"I can but try," the Stallion said grimly. He shifted back to 'corn-form, gathered himself, and phased down to bug-form. This roach was not handsome, but it did seem to be stable. Stile watched it take a step, moving all its legs on one side, followed by those on the other side. The thing trembled and started to expand, then got hold of itself and squeezed back into bug shape. It seemed it would hold.

Stile put down his open hand. The roach hesitated, then crawled on, moving clumsily. It evidently took special coordination to handle six legs, and it was hard for the Stallion to do this while hanging on to this awkward little size. Perhaps it was like juggling six balls in the air while walking a tightrope. As it happened, Stile had done such tricks in the past—but it had taken him time to master them. "Just don't lose control and convert to equine form on my head," Stile murmured as he set the roach on the framework he had wound there. "Don't drop anything, either."

The roach, catching the reference to droppings, began to shake with laughter. It expanded to triple roach size, emitted several little sparks, wrestled with itself, and recovered control. Stile decided not to make any more jokes.

The darkness was almost complete now. Stile nerved himself and walked forward, following the flash of light projected on the ground by his little guiding star. He hunched down as well as he could, making himself humpbacked and shorter. Stile was an experienced mimic, and this was another Game talent that served him in good stead now. He walked like a goblin, swung his arms like a goblin, and glared about like a goblin. Almost, he began to hate the world the way a goblin would.

The dark hole of the cave entrance loomed close. Stile shuffled boldly toward it. But a goblin guard challenged him. "Where the hell art thou going, dirtface?"

For an instant Stile's heart paused. But he had to assume that goblins normally insulted each other, and that the guard did not realize that Stile's face really was concealed by dirt. "What the hell business is it of thine, stinkrump?" he demanded in the grating tone of a goblin, and pushed on. He felt the Stallion-roach quaking with suppressed mirth again, enjoying the exchange.

Apparently it had been the right answer. The guard did not stop him. Stile followed his little star into the cave.

Goblins were coming and going, but none of these challenged him. Stile walked downward, through narrow apertures, along the faces of subterranean cliffs, and across dark chasm cracks. The star made it easy, unerringly guiding him through the labyrinth. What might have taken him hours to figure out only took minutes. He wondered passingly how this worked; more than mere energy was involved when magic provided him with specialized information. Amazingly soon he came to a deep nether passage barred by solid stalactitic columns.

The star moved on to illumine what was beyond. It was a horse.

No—not a horse. A dehorned unicorn, so grimed that his natural color hardly showed, standing with head hanging, bedraggled, evidently lacking the will to live but unable to die. Clip!

Stile heard a tiny accordion-note snort near his ear. The roach was seething. No unicorn should be treated like this!

Half a dozen armed goblins guarded the unicorn. Four were leaning against the wall; one was drinking a swig of something foul, and the sixth was entertaining himself by pricking Clip with the point of his spear. The forlorn unicorn hardly even winced; he seemed beyond the point of resistance and did not make a good subject for teasing. Blood streaked his once-glossy blue coat from prior cuts, and his mane was limp and tangled. Flies swarmed, yet his tail hardly twitched to flick them off.

Stile heard the roach on his head breathing hard, with accordion-chord wheezes. The Herd Stallion suffered no one to treat a member of his herd this way, and was in danger of exploding again. "Nay, Stallion," Stile whispered. "Thou must hold form until thou dost get inside. Neither I nor any of thine other forms can pass these bars mechanically; they are too strong and tight. Go inside, warn Clip, then take action against the guards before they strike."

The Stallion blew a low note of agreement. Stile put his hand to his head, and the roach climbed on it. Stile set the roach on the floor in the corner near the bars.

"Hey—who art thou, rockhead?" a goblin guard cried.

Uh-oh. He had to distract attention from the roach, lest a goblin spot it and idly step on it. The Herd Stallion was vulnerable in that form, and could not shift quickly enough to counter an abruptly descending foot.

"I just wanta see the creep," Stile said. "I heard you got a horsehead in here without a horn."

"That's none of thy business," the goblin snapped. "No unauthorized idiots allowed. That specifically means thee."

The roach was now crawling uncertainly along the wall. Obviously it wasn't used to clinging to vertical surfaces, but didn't want to get stepped on. Progress was slow, so Stile had to stall longer.

"Oh, I do have business here, mucksnoot," Stile said, and of course that was the truth. "I have come to take the 'corn away."

"Thou art crazy, manface! We have orders to kill this brute as soon as our armies finish massing and the enemy Adept be trapped. He's not going anywhere."

So they weren't going to let Clip live, regardless of Stile's response. And they expected to trap Stile himself. This was a straight kidnap-hostage-murder plot. No honor among goblins!

The roach, overhearing the dastardly scheme, lost its footing and fell to the floor with a loud-seeming click and whoosh of accordion-breath. Stile was afraid it would attract attention. It lay on its back, six legs waving, trying to recover its footing. Oh, no!

"Thou art not up on the latest, foulfoot," Stile said sneeringly. "You guards will be executed before the hostage is." This, too, he intended literally.

His certainty daunted the goblin. Apparently such betrayals did happen in the nether realms. "Aw, whatcha know about it, gnarltoes?" the goblin blustered.

The roach had finally struggled to right-side-up position, with tiny musical grunts. Any goblin who paid attention would immediately catch on that this was no ordinary vermin! Stile had to keep talking.

"I know a lot about it, mandrakenose. That 'corn's the steed of an Adept, isn't it?"

"Sure, smarty, and that's why he ain't dead yet. To keep that Adept off our backs till he's out of the picture. We got Adepts of our own, but they don't like to tangle with each other, so we're keeping this one clear this way. The fool likes animals. We're just doing our job here; no reason to wipe us out." He looked at Stile uncertainly. "Is there?"

The roach had finally reached Clip. Stile relaxed. Just a few more seconds, and it would be all right. "How about what that other Adept thinks? Once he knows thy part, he'll come for thee—and what other Adept would breathe a spell to help thee?"

But as he spoke, Stile saw Clip lift a forefoot, eying the roach. He was about to crush it, not realizing its identity.

"Clip!" Stile called. "No!"

Then things happened one on top of another. All six goblin guards whirled, scrambled, and looked up, depending on their starting positions, to orient on the hornless unicorn. The magic roach let out a chord and scuttled away from Clip's poised hoof. Clip's head jerked about, his ears rotating to cover Stile.

"It's a trick!" the goblin nearest Stile cried. "This creep's been bugging me about the hostage. Kill him!"

It wasn't clear whether he referred to Clip or to Stile. It hardly mattered. The alarm had been sounded.

Two goblins thrust their spears at Clip. One stomped at the roach. The one nearest Stile poked his spear through the bars to skewer Stile. The remaining two set up a scream for help.

Clip suddenly animated, swinging his horn about to skewer a goblin. But he had no horn, only the truncated stump. The goblin was merely brushed aside by Clip's nose and struck out with a horny fist.

The roach skittered out of the way and began to expand like a demon amulet that had been invoked. Stile dodged the spear.

In moments the Herd Stallion stood within the prison chamber, stomping his hooves, snorting fire. *His* horn was not truncated. It blurred as it lunged at one goblin, then at a second and a third, before any could flee. Three goblins were lifted into the air, skewered simultaneously on that terrible spike.

Clip charged the goblin who was poking at Stile, crushing the creature's head with a blow of a forehoof. But the two others were running down the far passage, too narrow for the unicorns to follow, crying the alarm.

Stile readied a spell, but paused. So far he had not used magic and, now that he knew there was an enemy Adept involved here, he did not want to give himself away one second sooner than necessary. The goblins did not know it was the Blue Adept who was in their midst, so the other Adept might not know, either—until Stile gave himself away by using magic.

But now there were two unicorns in the prison, and the main goblin mass was stirring in the bowels of the mountain. The Stallion could use his roach-form to escape—but Clip could not change form without his horn. Stile could change Clip's form for him—but that meant magic of Adept signature. Stile could also melt the bars away with magic, if they were not of the magic-resistive type. That must have been how Clip was brought here; the enemy Adept had spelled him through.

If he had to use magic, he might as well tackle the most important thing first. How he wished discovery had been delayed a little longer! "Clip—here to me!" he called, bringing out the thing he carried like a spear. It was Clip's severed horn.

The unicorn stared, almost unbelieving. No doubt he had thought the horn destroyed.

"My power can restore it!" Stile said, holding the horn out, base first.

Clip came and put his head near the bars. Stile reached through, setting the horn against the stump. "Restore the horn of this unicorn!" he sang, willing the tissue to merge, the thing to take life again.

It was hard, for he had not intensified his power by playing the harmonica, and the horn was magic. It resisted Stile's magic, and he knew the two parts were not mending properly. He was grafting on a dead horn. Meanwhile, a phalanx of goblins appeared in the passage behind Stile, bristling with spears. Stile saw them from the corner of his eye but could not release his hands from the horn, lest the slow healing be interrupted. Clip could not move, either, for he was on the other side of the bars waiting for the healing.

But the Herd Stallion was free. He launched himself at the bars. "No!" Stile cried in alarm, knowing the stone was too strong for the animal to break. But the Stallion shifted in midair to roach-form, sailed between columns, and shifted on Stile's side to dragon-form.

The dragon spread his wings, banked about, and fired forth a horizontal column of flame that seared the oncoming goblins. The stench of burnt flesh wafted back. Stile felt sorry for the goblins, then remembered how they had treated Clip, and stilled his sympathy. The creatures of the frame of Phaze conducted their business violently, and goblins were among the worst. Stile continued to concentrate on the healing, letting the Stallion guard him, and slowly the two parts of Clip's horn melded together. Stile felt the living warmth creep along the length of it, animating it. Soon all would be well.

A horde of goblins poured in from the far side of the prison. "Stallion!" Stile cried, and the Herd Stallion turned about, charged the bars, shifted into and out of roach-form, and appeared on the other side in dragon-form again. Another burst of flame seared out, cooking more flesh.

But greater trouble was gathering. Stile could feel the rumble of the march of many feet as hundreds or thousands of goblins closed in, traveling in unseen neighboring passages. He knew he had alerted the enemy Adept, for he had performed Adept magic; that would further complicate the situation. Still he held on to the horn, waiting for the final inch to be restored to life so that Clip's full capacity would return. He would settle for nothing less.

There was a puff of fog. The White Adept stood beside Stile. Her hair was white, matching her eyebrows, and a sparkling white gown bedecked her somewhat stout form. "So it is thee, Blue, as we suspected," she said, her voice and gaze cold as ice. "Thou didst take the bait."

"I took it," Stile agreed grimly. He was not really surprised; his relations with the White Adept had always been chill. But why was she involved with the goblins? "I got tired of getting ambushed by the likes of thee." Would she tell him anything before making her move? If she started a spell-diagram before he was finished with Clip's horn, he would be in trouble; he would have to defend himself, for without him the unicorns could not escape. But White could have generated a spell that acted at a distance instead of facing him directly. Maybe she wanted to talk.

The Herd Stallion turned from his endeavors, leaving a pile of scorched goblins rolled up like dehydrated bugs, and saw the witch. He braced for renewed action.

"Caution," Stile called. "She's Adept."

The mighty animal stood still. He knew better than to attack an Adept in a situation like this. He also knew that

Stile was not finished with Clip. For the moment it was an impasse.

"I can not attack thee directly, Blue," the White Adept said. "And thou canst not attack me. Yet can our minions make mischief."

"Agreed," Stile said. "But why has mischief been made? I sought none."

"Abate thine onus for the moment and hear me out," she said. "Blue, I would reason with thee."

In Stile's experience, those who claimed to want to reason with others were apt to have cases that were less than secure. Still, it was better to talk than to fight. Now at last Clip's horn had healed. Stile let go, and the unicorn backed away, blowing an experimental saxophone note. It was off-key, but strong. His coat seemed to be brightening under the grime; he had been restored to the joy of life.

The White Adept had known what Stile was doing, and had not interfered. She had to be serious about her subject, and Stile seriously wanted to know what this was all about. "Give thy word there will be no attack by Adept or goblin without fair warning," he said. "No treachery."

"I give it, Blue." There was a faint ripple in the air about her.

He had to accept that. Truth animated the very atmosphere and substance of Phaze. Adepts did not get along well with each other, but they honored the deals they made. "Then I will hear thy reason."

"Thou knowest that the end of Phaze draws nigh," she said. "The Purple Mountains have shaken, the Foreordained is on the scene, the Little Folk mass as for war, and portents abound."

"Aye," he agreed. "They tell me I am involved. Yet all I sought was to honeymoon with my wife. Someone set traps for me, and one trap setter resembled thee."

"Merely to warn thee off," she said. "Thou art Adept and perhaps the strongest of us all. Thou hast suffered much, yet thou shouldst be the leader in our effort instead of opposing it."

"What effort?" Stile's interest intensified.

"To save Phaze."

"Of course I want to save Phaze! I love this land! I want to live and die here!"

"But not, methinks, before thy time."

Stile smiled grimly. "I wish not to die here among goblins, true. But I sought no quarrel with goblins. Thou didst kidnap my steed, and abused him, and forced this quarrel on me."

"Aye. Unable to strike effectively at thee or at thy Lady, or to warn thee off, we finally had to take thy steed. It is not a thing I like. Now thou canst have thy freedom with our apologies, and thine animals with thee, and leadership in the present order, if thou wilt but accept it."

"Why should I not accept it?" Stile asked, not rhetorically.

"Because thou art prophesied to be the leader of the forces of the destruction of this order. The Foreordained is only part of it; thou art the other part."

"Obviously there's a loophole," Stile said. "Aside from the fact that I have no intention of harming Phaze, thou wouldst not be pressuring me if thou didst believe my destiny was fixed."

"There is a loophole. A dead man cannot lead."

Stile laughed ironically. "Kill me? My fate will survive thine effort, if it be truly set."

"Aye. Fate has indeed charmed thee, unlike thine other self. But we are not assured thou canst not be killed, only that if thou dost remain alive in Phaze, thou wilt destroy it. The charms that preserved thee so cleverly before are passing. Thou hast already conceived thy son on the Lady Blue—"

"I have?" Stile asked, surprised.

"—which is why she joins thy former steed and accepts the protection of the animal herd. So fate no longer preserves thee for that. It preserves her. Still, her feeling for thee is such that she might not survive thy demise, so thou art indirectly protected yet. I warned the others of that, but they heeded me not; they thought they could vanquish thee before thou didst reach the West Pole."

"They?"

"The other Adepts. We all are patriots in the end, Blue. We all must needs try to save our land."

She seemed sincere! "All the other Adepts are against me?" he asked incredulously.

"All except Brown; the child wavers. She likes thy steed."

Stile remembered how Neysa had given the little girl a ride. It seemed that kindness had paid a dividend. "What of Yellow?" Stile had had differences with the Yellow Adept, but recently had gotten along with her tolerably well. He could not believe she was his enemy.

"Dost thou want it from her own mouth?"

"Aye."

"Then let me bring her here." White made a diagram on the floor and tapped it three times. A puff of smoke formed and dissipated, and there stood the Yellow Adept in her natural hag-form.

"Oh, no!" Yellow exclaimed. "Let me just get changed for the occasion, my handsome bantam." She brought out a vial, tipped it to her lips, swallowed—and changed to a young, ravishingly pretty creature.

"White tells me that thou and the other Adepts think I will destroy Phaze, so are against me, Yellow," Stile said. "Can this be true?"

Yellow made a devastatingly cute moue. "It is close enough, Blue," she said. "I am not thine enemy and will not oppose thee—but neither can I join thee, for that thou art indeed destined to wreak much mischief and overthrow the natural order."

"How is it I know nothing of this?" Stile demanded.

"The instruments of great events seldom know their destinies," Yellow said. "This prevents paradox, which can be an awkward complication and a downright nuisance."

"Nuisance, hell! I was attempting to have my honeymoon! Why should this represent a threat to anyone?"

"Thou didst bring the Foreordained, and then thou didst travel to the West Pole. These were elements of the prophecy."

"So the other Adepts decided to stop me from getting there," Stile said, grimacing. "Setting neat little magical traps."

"Some did. Green chose to stand aloof, as I did, misliking this. Sure enough, thou didst get there. Now the onrush

of events is upon us, and if we do not get thee away from
Phaze promptly, we all are doomed."

"So you propose to remove me by killing me?"

"Nay, we know that would not work," Yellow said. "At
least White and Green and I suspected it would not. Black
and Orange and Translucent did not participate in the
proceedings, and Brown opposed them. We had to sup-
press her, lest she warn thee."

So it now developed that the other Adepts were anything but unanimous; most were at best neutral. That explained why they had not simply massed their magic
against him. Stile's expression turned hard. "Suppressed
Brown? What dost thou mean by that?"

"A stasis-spell," White said quickly. "No harm was done
her. It is hard indeed to do direct harm to an Adept; the
spell is likely to bounce and strike down the speller. But
slantwise action can be taken, as with the silence and
confinement for thee."

"You froze the child in place?" Stile demanded. "Our
truce is just about to come to an unkind end."

"She would have blabbed to thee," White repeated.

"Now I am blabbing to thee: release her."

White's expression hardened, as was typical of those
whose reason was only a front. Yellow quickly interceded.
"Provoke him not unnecessarily, White; he has power and
friends we hardly know. We need hold Brown no longer. I
shall go free her." She brought out another vial, sipped the
potion, and vanished.

"Methinks thou hast won the heart of more than
Brown," White grumbled. She viewed him critically, not-
ing the mud caking his body and the awkward turban, loin-
cloth, and shoe structures. "It must be thy magic, rather
than thy demeanor."

Stile relaxed marginally. Ugly things were happening,
and he knew it wasn't over. So far there had been attacks
against him, the Lady Blue, Clip, and the Brown Adept.
An organization of Adepts had formed against him. He
needed to know the rest of it. "Let's have it, White. Exactly what is the threat to Phaze, and what dost thou want
of me?" For he knew her suggestion about giving him a

place of leadership was wrong; how could he lead, if his presence meant the end?

"We want thee to leave Phaze voluntarily, so that the dangers of Adept confrontations are abated. Thou canst take Lady Blue and aught else thou wishest. Cross the curtain, embark on a Proton spaceship, and depart for the farthermost corner of the universe as that frame knows it, never to return."

Stile had no intention of doing that. Apart from the complication of the Lady Blue's official nonexistence in the other frame, where the Records Computer took such things more seriously than people did in Phaze, there was the matter of the robot Sheen. How could he marry her, with his other wife in Proton? And how could he leave his friends the unicorns and werewolves and vampires? Phaze was the world of his dreams and nightmares; he could never leave it. "Nay."

"The applicable portion of the prophecy is this: 'Phaze will never be restored till the Blue Adept is forever gone.' Thou canst not remain."

"I have had some experience with misrepresented predictions," Stile said. "Restoration of Phaze after my departure is hardly synonymous with my destruction of it— which I maintain is no intent of mine. Thou hast answered only a fraction of my question, and deviously at that."

"I am getting to it, Blue. The goblins guard an apparatus from the other frame, protecting it from all threats. The end of Phaze will come when that device is returned. The goblins guard it blindly from harm; we would prefer to destroy it."

"So the collusion of Adepts with goblins is rife with internal stress," Stile observed. "Doubtless the goblins know not of this aspect."

"Doubtless they suspect, however," White said.

"Surely the massed power of the Adepts can prevail against mere goblins," Stile said, pushing at her verbally. "Any one of us could enchant the entire species of goblin into drifting smoke."

"Thou might, Blue. Few others could. But this device is a special case and can not be attacked directly."

"Anything can be attacked!" Stile said. "Some things with less success than others, though, as seems to be the case when Adepts attack Adepts."

"Nay. This device is what is called in the other frame a computer."

"A computer can't operate in Phaze! No scientific device can." Except, he remembered, near the West Pole.

"This one has a line running to the West Pole."

Parallel thoughts! "Maybe. If it could figure out how to use magic in its circuits."

"Aye. It functions partially, and has many thoughts. Some concern thee—which is why we did not wish thee to make connection with it at the Pole."

"How canst thou know this if the goblins let thee not near it? In fact, why do the goblins allow Adepts in their demesnes, seeing the likes of thee would destroy what they endeavor to guard from harm?"

"The goblin-folk are not unduly smart," she said with a fleeting smile. "But smart enough to keep Adepts away from the device. They cooperate with us to some extent because they know that we oppose thee—and thou art one who will take the contraption from them and return it to Proton-frame, where it seems it will wreak all manner of mischief on both frames. So it is an uneasy alliance, but it will do. All of us, Adept and goblin alike, wish to save Phaze."

"And I wish to destroy Phaze," Stile said. "Or so you other Adepts choose to believe. Because of some fouled-up prophecy. No matter that I love Phaze; you believe that not."

"Nay, Blue, this one is not distorted. Thou wilt return the thing to Proton and thereby destroy Phaze, and only thy departure can alleviate that."

Stile was annoyed by this insistence. There had to be some flaw in the logic. "How dost thou know the prophecy is true?"

"The computer itself made it."

"And what relevance can the guess of an other-frame contraption have? Thou dost credit it with the accuracy of the Oracle!"

She nodded, and Stile's mouth dropped open. " Oh, no!" he exclaimed.

"It is so," she affirmed. "The computer is the Oracle. That is how it defends itself from the likes of us. Any thrust we can conceive against it, it anticipates and foils. Its means are devious but effective. We dare not attack it directly."

"Now let me back up," Stile said. "Thou didst offer me peace and fortune in Phaze, then told me I have to get out of Phaze forever or be killed, so that I won't destroy it. Surely thou perceivest the contradiction. Where is the lie?"

"Nay, Blue!" she said. "We Adepts differ some amongst ourselves about our manner of dealing with thee, so there may be seeming contradictions. It is a fair offer—if thou dost but accept it. Cooperation or exile. We fear thou wilt not."

"Try me, White."

Her glance played across the cavern, indicating the unicorns and goblins, all waiting for the settlement of Adepts. "Needs must we have greater privacy than this," she said. "Thy spell or mine?"

"Mine," he said. He played a bar of harmonica music, then sang: "Give us a globe that none may probe." And about them formed an opaque sphere that cut off all external light and sound.

In a moment light flared, as the witch made a spell of her own. "Now before we suffocate," she said, "I'll give it to thee without artifice. We want thee to destroy the Oracle. Only thou canst do it, for thou art its tool. It will admit thee to its presence, if thou canst get somehow past the goblins, and thy power is great enough to do the deed. Destroy that evil machine, Blue, and Phaze will be saved. This is the loophole we dare not voice aloud. Only if it returns operative to Proton can it act to destroy Phaze, and it can not foresee its own demise. Do this, Blue, and all other prophecies are null; we then shall have no onus against thee, and thou canst govern in Phaze."

"Thou art asking me to betray a—a consciousness that trusts me," Stile said, disturbed. "That has never been my way."

"Agreed. Thou hast ever been honorable, Blue, which is why I trust myself to thy power here. It is no fault in thee that causes us to oppose thee; it is only that it is in thy power to save or finish Phaze. Save our land and suffer our gratitude; try to destroy it and suffer our opposition; or vacate the frame so that we have no need to fear thee. These are thy choices, Blue. Thou knowest our determination; we are fighting for our lives and world. We are not limited by thy scruples, and our massed magic is stronger than thine. Thus united, we *can* attack thee directly. Oppose us not gratuitously."

It was a fair ultimatum. But Stile found he could not take the easy way out. "I love Phaze," he repeated. "I want never to leave it. In addition, I am now a Citizen in Proton, with considerable wealth. I shall not sacrifice my place in both frames by forever departing the planet. That leaves me with two choices: join thee or oppose thee. I know nothing of these prophecies thou dost speak of. Why should I try to destroy a device that has done me no harm?"

"No harm!" she flared, her white hair seeming to darken and melt with the heat. "Thou trusting fool! That device killed thee once and imperiled thy life again by setting us against thee."

"That last I perceive," Stile agreed. "Yet the business of the Oracle is making prophecies and being correct. If I am to be the leader of the forces of destruction of Phaze by helping this computer to return to Proton—though the reason remains opaque as to why it should wish ill to Phaze or how it could harm this frame from Proton—and someone inquires about that, the Oracle can but answer truthfully. Naturally that imperils me, and I like it not—but neither can I fault it for that answer. Truth is often unpleasant. Rather should I inquire in what way I am to do a deed whose nature appalls me. Were I sure the Oracle would destroy Phaze, I would not help it, and surely it is aware of that. There must be circumstances I know not and that you other Adepts know not. Better that I at least talk with the Oracle to ascertain the rationale."

"Of course," she said. "That is thy sensible response,

and surely the machine is expecting thee to come to it. That makes it possible for thee to destroy it."

"Or to help it to destroy Phaze," Stile said wryly. "At the moment I intend to do neither evil, and can not see what rationale would sway me either way."

"Then consider this, Blue. It was the Oracle who hinted at the doom of the Red Adept and started her mischief against thee. She killed thine other self and attacked thee in Proton—but it was the Oracle who motivated her. If thou dost seek vengeance for the murder of the Blue Adept, seek it at the source—the infernal Oracle. This is no sweet contraption like thy golem mistress, Blue. It plays the game savagely."

"But all its predictions were true!" Stile protested, experiencing a trace of doubt. "I can not blame it for fulfilling that role!"

"Fool! dost thou not realize it was a self-fulfilling prophecy? Red attacked thee because the Oracle fingered thee, no other reason. The Oracle knew what would happen. It alone generated that murder—and knew that also."

Stile was shaken. He was conversant with the bypaths of logic. White was right; the Oracle had initiated the campaign against him. A lesser entity might have made a mistake, but the Oracle had to have known what it was doing. It had murdered Stile's other self, caused Stile's knee misery, and set him on the horrendous path he had followed on the way to Phaze and to vengeance against the Red Adept.

Yet he remembered also that the original Blue Adept had accepted his own murder. Why?

"But why should the Oracle do this to me?" he asked plaintively, seeking to resolve this part of the mystery. Maybe if he knew the Oracle's motive, he could fathom his alternate self's strange acquiescence. His mind was, after all, identical.

"I suggest thou dost go ask it," White said. "Ask also why it should seek to use thee to destroy Phaze. Then must thou do what thou shalt see fit to do."

It all did seem to add up, at least to this incomplete extent. He had to settle with the Oracle. "I will go ask the machine and then do what I see fit to do."

"I meant that facetiously," the White Adept said. "We do not believe the computer will allow thee to approach it unless it knows thou wilt side with it. I have made our case to thee, but thou hast not reacted with proper fury. Something we know not of has influenced thee against us."

The knowledge of his other self's acquiescence—that was the influencing factor. "Of course I am not with thee!" Stile exclaimed. "I am not with anyone who kidnaps and dehorns my steed. Thy methods make thy side suspect."

"And the methods of the Oracle make it not similarly suspect?"

Stile spread his hands. "I admit I know not the final truth. I will seek the Oracle."

"I did not think thou wouldst join us. But I undertook to make the case. Hadst thou accepted honestly—"

"I have done nothing dishonest!"

"Aye. So we must destroy thee. Yellow will not like that, but it must be done. When we leave this bubble, it will be war between us. The other Adepts have massed their power, and the goblins are ready."

"Fortunate art thou that thy trust in this truce was well placed. Else would I simply confine thee here."

"Honor is not a luxury many of us can afford," she said sadly. "Yet in the name of honor, some are fools. Thou wilt not attack us or the Oracle without fair warning. This makes thee ideal for whatever side can use thee." She sighed. "I do not hate thee, Blue. I respect thee. I, too, am true to my cause, and it is a worthy one. Thou art true only to thine honor, and therein lies thy grief. Phaze will never be safe whilst Blue remains. Thus says our enemy the Oracle, and this we do believe. We like it not, but so must it be. Be on thy guard against my kind, Blue."

Stile studied her. The White Adept was no young thing, and she had not bothered with Yellow's type of vanity. She looked old and ugly and careworn. He had encountered her before and found little to please him. But he knew she was a witch and a skilled one; backed by the power of the other Adepts, she was far more formidable than she appeared. Her warning had to be heeded. The Adepts would now be fully unified and coordinated. The veil was off; nothing would be held back. She was giving him the most forceful warning she could, without betraying her associates.

He would have to get away from here in a hurry, the moment the shell opened. Yet where could he escape to? The Adepts could follow him anywhere in Phaze. White's warning, perhaps, was intended to focus his attention on this problem so that he would have a fair chance. His respect for her had been small; now it had enlarged. She had taken pains to give information that he needed, when she really hadn't had to. "I thank thee for thy courtesy, White," he said.

Stile released the spell that enclosed them and stood on guard. If the witch tried to strike against either unicorn, Stile would counter the spell. By the same token, if he started magic against the lurking goblins, she would block it. Since no spell could be used twice, it was sheer waste for Adept to squander magic against Adept. Their special powers would cancel each other out—until the other Adepts oriented—and she had told him they were ready. He was outgunned and would have to move fast so that they could not keep proper track of him.

"We must travel!" Stile cried. "I must stave off magic; you two handle the rest!" He vaulted aboard the nearest unicorn, which happened to be the Herd Stallion.

Clip was now outside the prison, probably having shifted to hawk-form to pass by the bars. That meant he was back in full health. But Stile was happier riding the Stallion, whom he knew to be in full possession of his powers. Clip might tire quickly.

The Stallion blasted out a medley of chords. Goblins had appeared in the passage; they hastily faded back, heeding the warning. Clip went to hawk-form and flew ahead, leading the way. The Stallion launched himself forward.

Stile was only peripherally aware of these details. His attention was on the White Adept. As the Stallion moved out, she started drawing a symbol in the dust on the floor. Stile sang out a spell that was mostly in his head: "Dust— gust!"

The dust stirred up into a cloud, gusting about the cavern. The witch was unable to complete her sketch. Her spell had been intercepted. She could not function any better in this swirl than Stile could when he had been a victim of the silence-spell. She looked up—and Stile saw with surprise that she was smiling. It was as if she were glad to see him escape. She must have spoken truly when she said she did not like this business. She had to fight him, but didn't really mind failing. Some Adepts, it seemed, were not as bad as others.

However, he had to heed her warning about the other enemy Adepts, most of whom he had never interacted with. They would not hold back, once they got around White's tacit obstruction and oriented directly on him.

Meanwhile, the goblins were bad enough. These were their passages, and they were thoroughly conversant with the dusky recesses. The Herd Stallion was retracing the route they had descended—but suddenly a great iron gate slammed into place ahead, blocking the way. The Stallion could not pass and Clip barely squeezed back through the narrow aperture to rejoin them. They were caught in the passage, and a solid mass of goblins was wedging in behind them.

The Stallion played more chords. Clip, answering the command, shifted to man-form and joined Stile on the Stallion's back. He was clothed now, with a rapier. He drew this and faced back, menacing a few goblins who tried to squeeze in behind.

Stile got the idea. He unwrapped his concealed broadsword and sat ready to slice at any goblins who got within range to either side. His main attention was on whatever signs of hostile magic there might be, but he could slash while hardly looking.

The Stallion charged the goblins. They scattered, throwing their spears away in their frantic scramble to get clear. It was not that they were cowardly; it was that a ton of unicorn bristling with horn and two armed riders was a truly formidable thing. Any who tried to stand their ground would be skewered or slashed or trampled. As it happened, a number could not get out of the way in time and were indeed trampled and skewered.

There was a side passage. The unicorn hurtled into this,

causing Stile to grab for the mane in order to hold his seat, and thundered along it.

Suddenly there was a ledge. The Herd Stallion could not brake in time. He leaped out over the edge, into the darkness of nothing.

Then Stile found himself riding the dragon. The Stallion's dragon was not large for this type, being perhaps only twelve feet long from snout to tail, and Stile's weight bore him down. Fortunately Stile was not large for his own type, and the dragon was able to spread his wings and descend slowly. Clip, of course, had converted to hawkform.

Stile still wore his grotesque shoes and turban. Quickly he sloughed these off, lightening the burden on the reptile; but the descent continued.

The dragon snorted fire that illuminated the cavern. They were in a deep cleft whose upper reaches were lit by wan shafts of moonlight. There was their escape!

But the dragon could not make it that high under Stile's weight. Stile readied a spell, felt the questing magic of another Adept, and had to hold back. He could be messed up much as he had messed up White's spell, and in midair that could be disastrous. Also, it seemed the enemies could not quite locate him as long as he remained in the dark and cast no spells. He had to hold off until it was safer. So the dim light above faded, and they dropped down into the deeper depths silently.

There was a detonation of something. Light blazed and metallic fragments whistled by. Someone had fired an explosive amulet or something similar at them. This was blind shooting, hoping to catch the dragon by a random shot; the assailants did not have a perfect fix on Stile's party. Now he was certain that if he used defensive magic, he would give away his location. Better to lie quiet, like a submarine on a water planet, and hope the depth-charges missed.

The dragon tried again to rise, but could not. Stile felt the body heating with the effort. This could not continue long.

There was a *pop* behind them. The Stallion-dragon

turned his head to send back a jet of flame—and the light showed a griffin, an eagle-headed lion, the next enemy Adept sending. "Uh-oh," Stile murmured. "Can't hide from that."

But the Stallion was burning hot from his exertions. He looped about, aimed his snout at the pursuing griffin, and exhaled a searing shaft of fire.

The griffin squawked as it was enveloped in flame. The blaze of its burning wings lit up the entire cavern. It tumbled down to the water, smoking feathers drifting after it.

But the next sending was another dragon, a big one. Its chest pumped like a bellows, building up pressure for a devastating blast that would incinerate Stile and the Stallion. The enemy was now fighting fire with fire.

The hawk winged at it, too small and fast for the dragon to catch or avoid. The dragon ignored the bird, knowing nothing that size could dent its armored hide. The enormous metal-foil wings beat swiftly, launching the dragon forward.

The hawk dived, zeroing in on the dragon's head. Stile could only watch with dismay, knowing Clip was throwing away his life in a useless gesture, a diversionary effort that was not working. He could not even think of a preventive spell on this too-brief notice.

The dragon opened its monstrous mouth to take in the tiny missile—and Clip changed abruptly to unicorn-form. He struck horn-first, piercing the dragon's head, his horn passing from inside the throat right on between the eyes and out, penetrating the little brain on the way.

The strike was so unexpected and powerful that the monster simply folded its wings and expired. It plummeted to the water, while Clip changed back to hawk-form and flew clear. "Well done!" Stile cried, amazed and gratified.

Now for a time there were no more sendings. But Stile knew worse attacks were in the offing. His party had to get out of the chasm—and could not. Already they were close to the nether water. He had to relieve the Herd Stallion of his weight—yet was sure that the one enchantment the enemy Adepts would have blocked would be a personal

transport-spell. They were trying to force Stile to use it—
and launch himself into oblivion.

The Stallion sent forth more fire, just enough to light
the way. The dark water below reflected with slight irides-
cence, as if oily. Stile mistrusted that. He didn't want the
Stallion to fall into that liquid. He would have to risk
magic. Not transport, of course; something unexpected.

The hawk had been circling. Now he came back,
squawking news. Over and over he cried it, until Stile was
able to discern the word. "Curtain!" Stile cried. "The curtain is ahead?"

That was it. Now Stile had a better alternative. "Fly
low, Stallion, and I'll pass through the curtain. Then thou
and Clip can fly up and escape in the night. They want
thee not, only me, and soon thou canst return to thy herd.
I'll climb up on the Proton side, where magic can't reach
me." Of course there would be other problems across the
curtain, but he would handle them in due course.

The Stallion was in no position to argue. He glided
low—and there in the dark was the scintillation of the
curtain, crossing the chasm. "If there's any sort of ledge—
I don't want to drop too far."

There was no ledge. It would have to be the water. They
intersected the curtain, and Stile spelled himself across.

CHAPTER 10

Force

He fell a few feet—or rather a meter or so—knowing he
was through the curtain only because he no longer had
dragon support. He splashed into the water, feeling the
instant shock of cold. He was, of course, an excellent

swimmer; no top Gamesman neglected such a sport. But the water was polluted, stinking, and perhaps contained harmful acids; the Citizens of Proton cared nothing for the planetary environment outside the domes. He didn't want to stay here long!

The air, too, was foul. But here in the depths, it was thicker than above and seemed to contain more oxygen. He did not enjoy it, but he could survive longer on it than anticipated. Still, he had another resource.

He swam back to the curtain, which passed right down through the water. He organized himself, then willed himself through and said: "Bring nuts and dried fruit, scuba and wetsuit." And the spell, shaped by his imagination, clothed him in a warm, flexible body swimming suit complete with flippers, breathing apparatus, and a bag of mixed nuts and bits of dehydrated fruit.

Something formed in the water near him. It was huge and toothed, and it threshed its way toward him with powerful flukes. Stile hastily spelled himself back across the curtain. He had done the unexpected and escaped the enemy Adepts without using a transport-spell, but they remained alert for him.

His new equipment went with him. This was one way in which magic and science juxtaposed; he could create or fetch scientific devices by magic in Phaze and take them across for use in Proton. Now he was comfortable in the water and had concentrated food to sustain him. He could get where he was going.

Only—where was he going? He wanted to locate that computer—but where was it?

Again, no problem. He prepared himself and passed through the curtain. "Weapon and gem, doslem doslem," he sang, grabbed the two objects that formed, and dodged back to Proton before the massive crunch of a hostile spell could catch him. The enemy would never have expected him to conjure these particular items! He saw the Adept attack through the curtain—a blaze of light silhouetting massive jawless teeth, closing and disappearing as they intersected the demarcation of the curtain. A demon from the deeps, indeed! Technically an indirect attack, a sending, but surely fatal to whatever it caught. They were not playing innocent games, these enemy Adepts!

Now he had what he needed. He could stop playing peekaboo through the curtain, especially since one more trip across it would probably get him crunched. The enemy had targeted him too closely; his scant leeway had been used up. Now he could get where he was going—on the Proton side of the curtain.

He swam, holding the straps to his last two acquisitions in his teeth. The flippers enabled him to move rapidly through the water. He didn't need light; he could tell where the walls were by the lapping of the waves his swimming made.

The chasm narrowed, until he was swimming between vertical walls only a couple of meters apart. Still no way up or out. He didn't like this; his special equipment was sealed in watertight packages, but he needed to get on dry land to use it safely.

Well, he could dive. He had a hunch there was a way out of here and a way from here to the computer-Oracle, because the goblins needed access to guard it. Of course this was the other frame—but with the normal parallelism, chances were good there were Proton passages too. All he had to do was find them.

He dived. He did not fear any monsters in this murky lake; they could not survive in this pollution. But he was careful about sharp jags of rock that might tear his suit.

The cleft was wider below, giving him more room to grope along. He should have conjured a light; he hadn't thought of it. On any venture, something important was always forgotten! But one of his instruments had an operating light that he could use for general vision—once he put it into use.

The walls closed in above. Good—he did have a passage here, for there was a slight current. Soon he groped upward and discovered a new cavern—and this one had sloping sides that he could scramble up on, getting free of the water.

Perched awkwardly on the rock, for his bad knees prevented him from squatting, he opened one of his doslems.

This one was the weapon: Disrupter-Optical-Space-Light-Modulator. D O S L M. He set it on low and activated it. There was a faint, humming beam, and a section of the cave wall glowed and sagged, melting without heat. Its particles had been disrupted, losing their cohesion; solid had turned to liquid. Good enough. The doslem was governed by light-beam computer, in which beams of light functioned in lieu of solid circuitry and semiconductor diodes and information chips. It was much more compact than the solid state and could generate potent effects, as the melted patch of wall showed.

Now Stile turned to the other doslem, the gem. In this case the D stood for Detector. It was an even more marvelous instrument. A miniature panel controlled its assorted functions of timing, direction, and detection. In his hands it emitted just enough light to clarify the cave-region in which he hunched, and it gave readouts mapping the extent of air-filled and water-filled recesses. There were other caves here, and some were within the range of the disrupter; he could melt a hole through the thinnest section of wall. Some passages were squared off—obviously artificial. His hunch had proved correct!

Stile checked for refined metals, orienting on copper, aluminum, iron, and gold. Soon he located a considerable cache of these, southeast of his present location. He checked for magnetism and found it in the same region. This certainly seemed to be the computer, or whatever portion of it existed in the frame of Proton.

Stile scouted about, then selected the thinnest wall to disrupt. He gave the melt time to settle, then stepped through to the adjacent cave. He was on his way.

It took time, and on occasion he rested and ate from his supply of nuts and fruit. He located reasonably fresh water by tuning in on it with the detector. He had a sense of location; he was in the cave network whose upper exits he and the Lady Blue had noticed on their honeymoon, after departing the snow-demon demesnes. He marched, cut through to a new passage, and marched again, slept, and marched again. He hoped the two unicorns had flown up and out of the cavern system, knowing that he, Stile, could take care of himself on the other side of the curtain. There was no way to communicate with them now, since he was no longer near the curtain. They simply had to have faith.

At times, as he tramped onward, he thought about the nature of the curtain and the parallel frames. How was it that he could so readily conjure scientific equipment that was inoperative in Phaze, yet was operative when taken back across the curtain? If it was that solid and real, why couldn't it function in Phaze? If it was not, why did it work here? The curtain could be a very thin line indeed, when magic so readily facilitated science. Was there no conservation of energy with regard to each frame? Anything taken across the curtain was lost to its frame of origination, wasn't it? Also, how could objects of Proton-frame design be brought to Phaze? Did his magic generate them from nothing, or were they actually stolen from warehouses and factories and hauled through the curtain? He doubted he could visualize the inner workings of a doslem well enough to build one directly, so doubted he could do it by magic, either—but the alternative implied a closer connection between frames and greater permeability of the curtain than conventional wisdom supposed. Magic would have to reach beyond the curtain, right into the domain of science. There was so much yet to learn about the relationship of frames!

And this computer he was searching out—had it really murdered Stile's alternate self, the original Blue Adept, by means of a self-fulfilling prophecy? Why? How did all this tie in with the approach of the end of Phaze and Stile's own involvement in that? Was the computer-Oracle due to perish in that termination of the frame, and Stile himself—

He paused to review what had been more or less idle speculation. If Stile was going to help destroy Phaze, and the computer was in Phaze, it might indeed be destroyed too. So maybe it sought to prevent him from participating in this business. Maybe it was really on the same side as the other Adepts. So it had generated mischief to eliminate him in both frames, being foiled only by that other message, the one that had brought Sheen to protect him. Yet it had been prophesied that he would help the computer return to Proton, where it would act to destroy Phaze; that put him on its side and set it against the Adepts. Maybe the destruction of Phaze was inevitable, and the computer needed to cross to Proton in order to escape the holocaust. But then why should it have tried to kill him twice? That made no sense at all.

Maybe he should have taken the time to trace down the source of that mysterious, other message, the one that had saved him, before he rescued Clip—

No. Clip came first. The Adepts had hurt the unicorn to gain leverage against Stile, and Stile had had to act.

Should he resume tracing that message now, instead of going to confront the Oracle? He might have a powerful ally—and with most of the other Adepts against him, he needed one.

But that would mean backtracking to the curtain and fighting his way through the barrage of hostile magic directed against him. He could not be sure he would survive that, and certainly he could not thereafter approach the Oracle with any element of surprise. Only by staying with the Proton-frame route, where magic and prophecy did not exist, could he hope to sneak up on it. He was set on his present course; he would have to continue.

He plodded on, and the hours passed. Was it day or night above, now? Normally he had a good time sense, but he did need some minimal feedback to keep it aligned. Stile also had good endurance, having run marathons in his day, but now he was traveling mainly in the dark, with occasional sips of oxygen from his scuba gear, conserving that life-sustaining gas as much as possible. He was out of food and tired. Only the constant approach to the site indicated by his equipment gave him confidence to keep on. Maybe he should have gotten himself a device to signal Sheen, who could have come to pick him up, making things so much easier. How obvious this was, now that he had ample time to think of it!

Yet that would have alerted others to his activity. Since other Adepts had connections in Proton—indeed, some were Citizens—that could be just as dangerous for him as activity in Phaze. So maybe this way was best; they might think him dead or impotent, since he did not reappear.

There was someone in there! Or at least a sapient robot. "I am—" He paused. Should he give his true identity? Caution prevailed. "A person in need of air. I beg assistance."

"You shall have it. Be advised that a robot weapon is trained on you."

"So advised." Stile leaned against the wall, growing dizzy as the last of his scuba oxygen faded. He could not blame a solitary maintenance guard for being careful.

The portal hummed, then opened. Air puffed out. A figure emerged, clothed in the protective gear of a maintenance worker, using a nostril mask and protective goggles.

"Stile! It's you!" the figure cried. "God, what a relief!" The man put his arm around Stile's shoulders to help him into the chamber.

It was Clef, the musician Stile had encountered in the Tourney, and to whom he had given the Platinum Flute. The Foreordained. "I thought you were in Phaze," Stile gasped as the air lock sealed and pressure came up.

"I was, Stile. Or should I say sir? I understand you obtained your Citizenship."

"I got it. Don't bother with the 'sir.' Just give me air and food and a place to rest. What are you doing here?"

The inner aperture opened, and Clef guided him into a comfortable chamber. "I'm here to meet you, Stile, on behalf of the Oracle. You and I must work together to fulfill the prophecy and save the frames from destruction." He pressed a cup of nutri-soup into Stile's unsteady hands and set him in an easy chair. "I was so afraid you would not make it. The Oracle said there was danger, that no one could help you, and that it could not foresee your arrival. Its prophecies are unreliable when they relate to its own destiny. I had no notion when and if you would arrive, except that it had to be within a three-day time span. I fear I was asleep when the moment came. Then I could not be certain it was you, for there are enemies—"

Stile ceased his gulping of the soup to interrupt Clef. "Enemies? To save the frames? I understood I was to destroy Phaze, and I don't know whether that makes me friend or enemy to whom."

Clef smiled. "That depends on how you see it, Stile. The present order will be overturned or greatly weakened in both Proton and Phaze. That's why Citizens and Adepts oppose the move. Most of the rest—the serfs and creatures —will benefit by the new order. You are no enemy to them!"

"Viewpoint," Stile said, catching on. "To an Adept, the loss of power of Adepts would be disaster, the end of Phaze as he knows it. To a unicorn, it might be salvation."

"And to a werewolf," Clef agreed. "Big changes are coming. It is our job to make the transition safe. If we don't, things could get extremely ugly."

Stile was recovering as he breathed the good air and ingested the nourishment of the soup. He started to strip off the wetsuit, all that had protected him from the chill of the cave passages. This chamber was like a slice of Heaven, coming so suddenly after his arduous trek. "Tell me everything."

"It's simple enough. Three hundred years ago, when they discovered that this planet was one of the occasional places in the universe where the frames of science and of fantasy intersected—would you believe Planet Earth was another such place in medieval times?—they realized that there were certain dangers in colonizing the fantasy frame. So they set up some powerful instruments for the purpose of securing an optimistic new order. A sophisticated self-willed computer and a definitive book of magic."

"A book of magic? I never heard of this."

"Well, you weren't supposed to. It contains the most potent spells in all modes, so that it would take years for a single person to invoke them all—not that anyone would want to. Spells of creation and destruction, of summoning and sending, of healing and harming. Any person with access to that book in Phaze would become an instant Adept, more powerful than any other, one who could virtually change the face of the frame in minutes. The computer contains all the data for science, finance, economics, and politics known at the time. Despite the passage of three hundred years, this knowledge is enough to assure the operator enormous power in Proton—perhaps enough to dominate the government."

"And someone is destined to get hold of these tools and turn them to wrong use? That could indeed be trouble!"

"No, great care was taken to safeguard against this danger. The two tools had to be preserved for the time when they were needed, and kept out of the hands of those who might squander or abuse them. They had to be ready for the great crisis of separation."

"Separation?"

"It seems the intersection of frames is a sometime thing. The elves who instructed me are not sure about that. As you know, they consider me to be the one they call the Foreordained, which simply means my particular talent will be useful in negotiating the crisis; there is nothing religious or supernatural about it. So they have been preparing me in a cram-course, while you have diverted the Adepts who might otherwise have interfered."

"So that's what I was doing. I was a decoy!"

"That's only part of your task. Anyway, they think the frames are going to separate, so there will be no more crossings, no further interactions. This is simply part of the natural order; it happened on Earth as the medieval period ended. After it, no one in Proton need believe in magic, and no one in Phaze need believe in science, and the episode of the interaction of the systems will seem like fake history. Since on this planet the fantasy frame was colonized from the science frame—though a number of Phaze creatures are evidently native to the fantasy realm, and perhaps the Little Folk too—er, where was I?"

"The frames are separating," Stile said.

"Ah, yes. When they do, the human alternative selves will be carried away, becoming complete in themselves, clones of their counterparts, and parallelism will no longer exist."

"Now that's another thing," Stile said. "I can see how the presence of people in one frame could generate similar people in the other frame, split by the curtain. With science overlapping magic, that sort of thing can happen. But after the initial ripple, why should it continue? I did not exist three hundred years ago; why should there have been two of me?"

"Again, the Little Folk aren't certain. It seems that

when the experts made the computer and book of magic—
two aspects of the same thing—they were able to juxtapose the frames. Science and magic operated in each, for
the two were the same. Then the frames separated slightly,
and each person and creature separated too. This was an
unexpected occurrence; before that, there had been only
one of each. It was as if the fantasy frame, vacant of
human life, picked up a duplicate copy of each person in
the science frame. It did not work the other way, for no
dragons or unicorns appeared in Proton, perhaps because
it lacked a compatible environment. Already the mining of
Protonite was commencing, with attendant use of heavy
machinery, construction of processing plants, and pollution of the environment. The Citizen class put things on
what they termed a businesslike footing at the outset, permitting no pollution controls. There is evidence that magical creatures are extremely sensitive to environmental
degradation; only a few, like the trolls, can endure it for
any length of time. The Citizens of Proton simply put up
force-field domes and continued their course unabated,
ignoring the outside planet. In this manner Proton lost
whatever it might have had in nature, sacrificed by the
illiterate pursuit of wealth. But despite this gross difference
between the frames, parallelism persisted; people tended to
align. In fact, parallelism is the major factor in the present
crisis."

"That's what I really want to understand," Stile said.
"The frames may separate, but I don't see why that should
destroy them unless, like Siamese twins, they can't exist
apart."

"They can exist apart. To make the problem clear, I
have to clarify parallelism. It's not just people; the entire
landscape is similar. A change made in one frame and not
in the other creates an imbalance and puts a strain on the
entire framework. Dig a hole in the ground in Proton, and
the stress won't be alleviated until a similar hole is made in
Phaze. Unfortunately there is no natural way to do that,
so the stress continues to build. Eventually something will
snap—and we are now very close to the snapping point."

"Ah, I see. Like damming a stream—the water builds
up behind and falls away on the other side, until it either

spills over or breaks the dam. And we don't want the dam to burst."

"Indeed we don't. So we have to find a way to alleviate the pressure. We don't know what will happen if the frames equalize in their own fashion, but it would probably wipe out most of the inhabitants of both frames."

"So we need to fill holes and drain waters," Stile said. "Seems simple enough."

"Not so. Not so at all. You reckon without the human dynamics. You see, the major imbalance, the largest hole in the ground, literally, is from the mining of Protonite. This is displacing huge quantities of material, creating a substantial physical imbalance, and worse yet—"

"Protonite," Stile said. "In the other frame it's Phazite —the source of the energy for magic."

"Exactly. That makes the problem critical, and the solution almost prohibitively difficult. The Citizens are not about to stop mining Protonite voluntarily. Not until every last dreg of it is gone, like the original atmosphere. Protonite is the basis of their wealth and power. If it were only sand, we could arrange to transfer a few thousand tons from one frame to the other, relieving the imbalance. But as it is—"

"But if that much Protonite, ah, Phazite were transferred out, to restore the balance, what would happen to the magic?"

"It would be reduced to about half its present potency. The Oracle has calculated this carefully. The power of the Adepts, who are the main users, would diminish accordingly. They would not be able to dominate Phaze as they do now."

"That might not be a bad thing," Stile said. "And the Proton Citizens—"

"Their mining would have to be severely curtailed, perhaps cease entirely. They would have no renewal of their present resources. The galaxy would have to discover new sources of energy."

"But the galaxy depends on Protonite! Nothing matches it! There would be phenomenal repercussions!"

"Yes, that is why taking action is difficult. Civilization as we know it will have to change, and that will not occur easily. Yet the alternative, the Oracle says, may be the complete destruction of this planet—which would also cut off the galaxy's supply of Protonite."

"I begin to comprehend the forces operating," Stile said. "The end of Phaze and Proton is approaching, and we have to do something. But both Citizens and Adepts would oppose the cutoff of Protonite mining and the transfer of Phazite, because without free use of this mineral their status suffers greatly. That's why the Adepts are after me now, and think that my elimination will alleviate their problem; they fear I can do something that will deplete them all—"

"You can."

"And that's why the self-willed machines knew I would have to become the wealthiest of Citizens. Wealth is power in Proton, and I need to be able to withstand the formidable opposition of the Citizens when this thing breaks."

"Exactly. You need enough of a voting bloc to tip the balance in your favor."

So many things were falling into place! "But why, then, did the computer try to destroy me? I don't want to see either Proton or Phaze come to harm and I should certainly work to achieve the best compromise. Why did the Oracle sic the Red Adept on me?"

"Because only you—and I—can do the job that must be done. A man who can cross the curtain freely, who is powerful in each frame, and who has the ability and conscience to carry through. A man who is essentially incorruptible without being stupid. The Blue Adept, your other self, was too limited; he could not cross the curtain, so he had no base in Proton, no experience with that society. He had lived all his life with magic; he depended on it. He would have been largely helpless in Proton during the crisis."

"So the Oracle killed him?" Stile demanded incredulously. "Just because he wasn't perfect? Why didn't the Oracle select someone else for the job?"

"The Oracle selected you, Stile. You had his excellent qualities, and you had lived a more challenging life; you were better equipped. But you could not enter Phaze. So the Blue Adept had to be eliminated—I do not speak of this with approval—in order to free you to cross the curtain. Had the decision gone the other way, you would have been the one killed, to free him to cross into Proton."

"But the attempt was made on me too!" Stile protested, shaken by this cold calculation.

"It was blocked in Proton," Clef said. "I knew nothing of this when I encountered you in the Tourney; believe me, I was appalled. But you were protected. The Oracle sent a second message—"

"The message!" Stile exclaimed. "I was trying to trace it! The Oracle—" But this, too, was coming clear now. One message to start the murder process, the other to intercept and nullify part of it. Diabolically efficient!

"Now you have been prepared," Clef continued. "The computer expects you to organize the juxtaposition and transfer."

"I'm not at all sure I want to cooperate with this emotionless machine. It has entirely disrupted my life, not stopping even at murder. What it put the Lady Blue through, and my friend Hulk—" Stile shook his head. "This is not the sort of thing I care to tolerate."

"I agree. But it seems the alternative is to let both frames crash."

"Or so the cynical Oracle says," Stile said. "That machine has shown itself to be completely unscrupulous in the manipulation of people and events. Why should I believe it now?"

"The Little Folk believe it," Clef said. "They despise it and want to be rid of it, but they believe it. It is a machine, programmed for truth, not for conscience. So its methods are ruthless, but never has it lied. Its sole purpose is to negotiate the crisis with minimum havoc, and it seems that the grief inflicted on you was merely part of the most rational strategy. It has no human will to power and, once it returns to Proton, it will serve its master absolutely."

"And who will its master be?"

"You, I think. I am called the Foreordained, but I believe the term is most applicable to you. Perhaps it was applied to me as a decoy, to prevent your premature destruction." He smiled, appreciating the irony. "The Oracle prophesies that Blue will govern Proton in the difficult period following separation of the frames. As you may have gathered, there is no limit on information when it deals with me. The computer will help you govern Proton, and the book of magic will assist the one who takes power from the Adepts in Phaze."

"And who is that?"

"I can't get a clear answer there. It seems to be you—but of course you can't be in both frames after they separate. I suspect the computer suffered a prophetic short circuit here. I can only conjecture that whichever frame you choose to remain in will be yours to govern."

"I want only to remain in Phaze with the Lady Blue and Neysa and Kurrelgyre and my other friends. Yet I have already been treated to the prophecy that Phaze will not be safe until Blue departs it."

Clef shook his head. "I wish I could give you a clear answer on this, Stile, but I can not. Your future is indistinct, perhaps undecided. It may be because you are the key figure, the one who will decide it. The uncertainty principle—" He shrugged.

Unwillingly, Stile had to concede the probable truth of this complex of difficult notions. Machines acted the way they were designed and programmed to act—and why would the experts of three hundred years ago have designed a machine to lie during a crisis? Surely they would not have. The very ruthlessness that Stile hated was an argument in favor of the Oracle's legitimacy.

"Where is this book of magic?" Stile asked at last. It was his grudging, oblique concession that he would have to go along with the Oracle and perform his part in this adjustment of frames.

"In Proton, under the control of the Game Computer."

"What's it doing in Proton? No one can use it there."

"That is why it is in Proton. To protect the two tools of power from premature exploitation and dissipation, the powers-that-were placed them in the wrong frames. The book of magic is impotent in the science frame, and the computer is greatly reduced in power in the fantasy frame. In order to resolve the crisis, both must be restored to their proper frames."

"So my job is to fetch the book and pass the computer back through?"

"These tasks are not simple ones," Clef cautioned him. Stile, of course, had already gathered that. "The book should be no problem in the acquisition, for the Game Computer will turn it over to anyone possessing the code-request. But the Citizens will do their utmost to stop it from being transported across the curtain. The computer —that relates to my job. It will cross only as the moving curtain intersects this location."

"Your job? Exactly what will you do as the Fore-ordained?"

"I will juxtapose the frames. That is the precondition for re-establishing parallelism."

Stile shook his head. "Just when I thought I had it straight, I am confused again. It is my limited present understanding that the frames are about to separate, but can't because of the imbalance of Protonite. I suppose their separation would tear that associated Phazite free and rupture our whole reality, like a knot pulled through a needlehole. But we have only to form a ball of Phazite and roll it across the curtain, where it will become the neces-sary Protonite. What's this business about juxtaposition?"

"Nice notion, that ball. But you don't just roll Phazite across the curtain. Phazite is magic; the curtain is really an effect of that magic, like a magnetic field associated with electric current or the splay of colors made by a prism in sunlight. Such a ball might rend the curtain, causing explosive mergence of the frames—"

"Ah. The dam bursting again."

"Precisely. But you could roll it into the region of jux-taposition, and then on into the other frame. Two steps, letting one aspect of the curtain recover before straining the other. Like an air lock, perhaps." He smiled. "What a fortune a multiton ball of Protonite would be worth!"

"So you juxtapose the frames. You are foreordained to perform this task so that I can perform mine. How do you do this?"

"I play the Flute."

"Music does it?" Stile asked skeptically.

"The Platinum Flute is more than a musical instrument,

as you know. It produces fundamental harmonics that affect the impingement of the frames. Properly played, it causes the frames to overlap. The Little Folk have been teaching me to play the ultimate music, which ranges within a single note on the audible level, and across the universe on a level we can not perceive. I have had to learn more about music than I learned in all my prior life, for this single performance. Now I have mastered the note. The effect will be small at first. Toward the culmination it will become dramatic. There will be perhaps two hours of full juxtaposition in the central zone, during which period the exchange of power-earth must be effected. If it is not—"

"Probably disaster," Stile finished. "Yet if that is the case, why should the Citizens and Adepts oppose it? Of course they will lose power, but when the alternative is to lose the entire planet—"

"They choose to believe that the threat is exaggerated. To return to the dam analogy: some, when the dam is about to burst, will dislike the inconvenience of lowering the water level, so will claim there is no danger; perhaps the sluices will pass water across their properties, damaging them only slightly as the level is lowered. So they indulge in denial, refusing to perceive the larger threat, and oppose corrective action with all their power. To us this may seem short-sighted, but few people view with equanimity the prospect of imposed sacrifice."

"And there *is* the chance the Oracle is wrong," Stile said. "Or am I also indulging in foolish denial?"

"Wrong perhaps in timing; not in essence. No one can predict the moment the dam will burst, but the end is inevitable."

"You do make a convincing case," Stile said ruefully. "When will you begin playing to juxtapose the frames?"

"As soon as I return to Phaze, after garnering your agreement to manage the transfer of computer, book of magic, and Phazite."

"Damn it, this computer murdered my other self and caused untold mischief in the personal lives of people involved with me. Why should I cooperate with it now, or believe anything it says?"

Clef shrugged. "You are a realist. You are ready to undertake personal sacrifice for the greater good, as was your alternate self, the Blue Adept."

"He knew this?" Stile demanded, remembering how the man had apparently acquiesced to his own murder.

"Yes. He was too powerful and clever to be killed without his consent. He gave up everything to make it possible for you to save the frames."

Stile hated the notion, yet he had to believe. And if the Blue Adept, with everything to live for, had made his sacrifice—how could Stile, who was the same person, do less? He would only be destroying what his other self had died to save.

"It seems I must do it," Stile said, dismayed. "I do not feel like any hero, though. How long before juxtaposition is actually achieved?"

"Allowing time for me to return to Phaze—perhaps twenty-four hours."

Time was getting short! "How much Phazite, precisely?"

"The Little Folk will have that information. In fact, they will have the Phazite ready for you. But the enemy forces will do all in their power to prevent you from moving it."

"So I'll need to transfer the book of magic and the computer first," Stile decided. "Then I can use them to facilitate the mineral transfer. Since the computer will cross when the curtain passes its location, I need only to guard it and establish a line to it. Which leaves the book— which I'd better pick up before juxtaposition so I have time to assimilate it. Maybe I can arrange to have someone else pick it up for me, since I will no doubt be watched."

"I believe so."

"Is there convenient and private transport from here to a dome?"

"Share mine. I am going to the curtain. From Phaze, you may travel freely."

"If the Adepts don't catch me."

"It will help, I must admit, if you can distract their attention from me again. With the Flute I can protect myself, but I would prefer to be unobserved."

"I suppose so. Somehow I had pictured you as a new super-Adept, able to crumble mountains and guide the dead to Heaven."

"I have only the powers of the Platinum Flute you brought me. I am myself no more than a fine musician. I suspect that any other musician of my caliber could have served this office of the Foreordained. I just happened to be the nearest available. After this is over, I hope to return to my profession in my home frame, profiting from the experience garnered here. The Mound Folk of the Platinum Demesnes are generously allowing me to keep the Flute. I was, like you, drafted for this duty; I am not temperamentally suited to the exercise of such power. I am not an Adept."

Stile found that obscurely reassuring. Clef believed that this would come out all right. "Very well. We'll step across the curtain, and I'll spell you directly to the Oracle, where they can't get at you, then spell myself elsewhere in a hurry." Stile paused, thinking of a minor aspect. "How did you get by the goblins who guard the computer?"

"One note of the Flute paralyzes them," Clef said, relaxing. "You summon your power through music; you should understand."

"I do." Stile hated to leave this comfortable chair, but felt he should get moving. "I suppose we've dawdled enough. Great events await us with gaping jaws."

"I believe we can afford to wait the night," Clef said. "There is a tube shuttle, renovated for transport to the curtain; it will whisk us there in the morning. Since no one knows you're here, you can relax. That will give the Adepts time to gather confidence that you are dead, putting them off guard."

The notion appealed tremendously. Stile had worn himself out by his trek through the caves and tunnels; he desperately needed time to recuperate. He trusted Clef. "Then give me a piece of floor to lie on, and I'll pass out."

"Allow me to delay you slightly longer, since we may not meet again," Clef said. "We played a duet together, once. It was one of the high points of my life. Here there is no magic, so the instruments can safely be used."

Stile liked this notion even better than sleep. It seemed to him that music was more restorative than rest. He brought out his treasured harmonica. Clef produced the Platinum Flute. He looked at it a moment, almost sadly. "Serrilryan," he murmured. "The werebitch. With this I piped her soul to Heaven, and for that I am grateful. I knew her only briefly, but in that time I had no better friend in Phaze."

"This is the way it is with me and Neysa the unicorn," Stile agreed. "Animals are special in Phaze."

"Extremely special." Clef put the instrument to his mouth, and from it came the loveliest note Stile could imagine.

Stile played the harmonica, making an impromptu harmony. He knew himself to be a fine player, especially with this instrument inherited from his other self—but Clef was the finest player, with the finest instrument ever made. The extemporaneous melody they formed was absolutely beautiful. Stile felt his fatigue ameliorating and his spirit strengthening. He knew of many types of gratification, such as of hunger, sex, and acclaim, but this was surely the finest of them all—the sheer joy of music.

They played for some time, both men transported by the rapture of the form. Stile doubted he would ever experience a higher pleasure than this and he knew Clef felt the same. Flute and harmonica might seem like an odd combination, but here it was perfection.

Then something strange occurred. Stile began to see the music. Not in the form of written notes, but as a force, a wash of awareness encompassing their immediate environment. It was the shape or essence of a spirit, a soul. Somehow this vibrant, joyous thing was familiar.

Stile glanced at Clef without interrupting his playing. The flutist had seen it too; he nodded marginally. Then Clef's playing changed in nature, and Stile realized that this was the music that moved souls to their resting places. Somehow the magic of the Flute was acting in this frame, moving the spirit in the room.

Whose was it? Not the werebitch's. It hovered in place, becoming more perceptible. Then the music changed again, and the spirit disappeared.

Clef abruptly stopped playing, so Stile had to stop too. "Did you recognize it?" the man asked, awed.

"No," Stile said. "It seemed familiar, but I never saw such a phenomenon in Proton."

"It was you, Stile. Your soul came out. When I realized that, I stopped. I don't want to pipe you to Heaven yet."

"Not mine!" Stile protested. "My soul was never more with me."

Clef frowned. "I beg to differ. The Little Folk have instructed me somewhat in this, as it is an important property of the Flute. There are certain keys to the recognition of souls that the music relates to. The more I attuned to you, the clearer that ghost became. It was you."

Stile shook his head. "It had to have been my double, not me."

There was a brief silence.

"You had a double," Clef said. "Your alternate self, who died to free you."

"The Blue Adept," Stile agreed, awed at the dawning notion.

"Who piped him to Heaven?"

"No one. He was murdered alone. All that remains of him is—this harmonica."

"The Flute evokes souls. But only free souls, which have not yet found their way to their destinations. Could your alternate's soul—?"

"Be in this instrument?" Stile finished. "You know, he may have found a way to stay around, not dying completely. This harmonica came to me fortuitously. Is it possible—?"

"That he chose to occupy the instrument when he made room for you in Phaze?" Clef continued.

Stile contemplated the harmonica. "Why? Why avoid Heaven and be trapped in a harmonica?"

Clef shrugged. "The music that issues from it is lovely. Is it better than your norm?"

"Yes. I play this better than other instruments, though I did not play this type until I got this one."

"Perhaps, then, your other self is helping you."

Again Stile considered. "To make sure his sacrifice is not wasted. Subtly guiding me. He conjured his own soul

into his harmonica. Surely a feat of magic no lesser person
could achieve. He has been with me all along." Stile sighed,
half in amazement. "Now I must fulfill the destiny he
could not. He is watching me."

"He must have been a worthy man."

"He must have been," Stile agreed. "The Lady Blue said
he had not lived up to his potential. Now it seems there
was more to him than she knew."

They let the matter drop. There was really not much
else to say about it. Clef showed Stile to a cot, and he lay
down and slept, reassured, literally, in spirit.

In the morning, refreshed, they took the private shuttle
east to the curtain. This was not in the region Stile had
crossed it before, in the chasm. The curtain meandered all
over the planet, as he and the Lady Blue had verified on
their horrendous honeymoon. This was where it traveled
almost due north-south, passing a few miles east of the
palace of the Oracle; Stile and the Lady had ridden rapidly
north along this stretch on their way to their rendezvous
with the snow-demons. That had been the key word
"flame" in his poem. Now the key word was "civil"—for
he was about to launch a civil war, as Adept fought unicorn and Citizen fought serf. Still to come were the key
words "flute" and "earth." He could readily see how the
first related, but the last remained obscure.

"Those key terms!" Stile exclaimed. "I was given a
dozen words to fashion into a poem in the finals of the
Tourney. Where did those words originate?"

"With the Oracle, of course. You had to be provided
some hint of your destiny."

"That's what I suspected." The Oracle had been med-
dling in his life throughout, guiding or herding him in the
prescribed direction.

Yet could he condemn it? The future of the two frames
was certainly an overwhelming consideration, and the
Oracle's present avenues of expression were extremely limited. There had been rewards along the way. Stile had been
given Citizenship in Proton and a worthy ally in the lady
robot Sheen. He had been given the Lady Blue in Phaze
and such close friends as Neysa the unicorn and Kurrel-

gyre the werewolf. He had seen his life transformed from the routine of serfdom to the wildest adventure—and despite its hazards, he found he liked adventure. He also liked magic. When this was all over, and he had helped save or destroy Phaze—depending on viewpoint—he wanted to retire in Phaze.

But there was one other prophecy. "Is it true that Phaze will not be secure until the Blue Adept departs the frame forever?"

Clef was sober. "I fear it is true, Stile. Possession of the book of magic alone will make you dangerous. You will have great power in the new order anyway, and the book will make it so much greater that corruption is a distinct possibility. That book in *any* hands in Phaze is a long-term liability, after the crisis has been navigated. The Oracle takes no pleasure in such news—of course it is a machine without feelings anyway—but must report what it sees."

Stile loved the Lady Blue—but he also loved Phaze. She loved Phaze too; he did not want to take her from it. In the other frame there was Sheen, who loved him and whom he was slated to marry there. He did not quite love her, yet it seemed his course had been charted.

He closed his eyes, suffering in anticipation of his enormous loss. His alternate self had yielded his life for the good of Phaze; now it seemed Stile would have to yield his happiness for the same objective. He would have to leave Phaze, once the crisis had passed, and take the book with him back to Proton.

Clef looked at him, understanding his agony. "Scant comfort, I know—but I believe the Oracle selected you for this mission because you alone possessed the position, skills, and integrity to accomplish it. No other person would make the sacrifice you will—that your alternate already has made—guided solely by honor. Your fitness for the office has been proved."

"Scant comfort," Stile agreed bitterly.

"There is one additional prophecy I must relay to you immediately, before we part," Clef said. "You must marshal your troops."

"Troops? How can they juxtapose the frames?"

Clef smiled. "The Oracle prophesies the need for organized force, if Phaze is to be saved."

"And I am to organize this force? For what specific purpose?"

"That has not yet been announced."

"Well, who exactly is the enemy?"

"The Adepts and Citizens and their cohorts."

"Common folk can't fight Adepts and Citizens."

"Not folk. Creatures."

"Ah. The unicorns, werewolves, vampires—"

"Animalheads, elves, giants—"

"Dragons?"

"They are destined to join the enemy, along with the goblins."

"I begin to fathom the nature of the battle. Half the animalheads will die."

"And many others. But the alternative—"

"Is total destruction." Stile sighed. "I do not see myself as a captain of battle."

"That is nevertheless your destiny. I am foreordained to juxtapose the frames, you to equalize them. Without you, my task is useless."

"These canny riddles by the Oracle are losing their appeal. If this is not simply a matter of picking up a book of magic and moving some Phazite the Little Folk will give me, I would appreciate some rather more detailed information on how I am to use these troops to accomplish my assignment. I don't believe in violence for the sake of violence."

Clef spread his hands. "Nor do I. But the prophecy tells only what, not how. Perhaps the Elven Folk will have more useful news for you."

"Perhaps. But won't the enemy Adepts be watching for me to go to the Elven Demesnes?"

"Surely so."

"So I should avoid whatever traps they have laid for me there, for my sake and the elves' sake. I can't visit the Little Folk at this time, and I suspect I should also stay clear of the unicorns and werewolves. So it will be very difficult for me to organize an army among creatures who know me only slightly. Especially when I can't give them any concrete instructions."

"I do not envy you your position. I am secure; the Oracle is virtually immune from direct molestation. But you must perform under fire, with inadequate resources. Presumably your Game expertise qualifies you. As I said, the Oracle went to some trouble to secure the right man for this exceedingly awkward position."

"Indeed," Stile agreed, unpleased.

Now they reached the curtain. Stile doubted the Adepts would be lurking for him here; how could they know his devious route? But they would soon spot it when he started magic. He would have to move fast, before they oriented and countered.

Stile plotted his course and spells as they got out of the capsule and walked up a ramp to the surface. There was an air lock there. "The curtain is a few meters distant; best to hold our breath a few seconds," Clef said.

"You have certainly mastered the intricacies in a short time."

"The Little Folk are excellent instructors. They don't like folk my size, but they do their job well. I will be sorry to depart Phaze."

Not nearly as sorry as Stile would be! "I will make my spells rapidly, the moment we cross," Stile said. "The Flute prevents magic from being blocked, so the enemy can not interfere, but it may resist a spell by a person not holding it."

"Have no concern. I could block your magic by a single note, but don't have to. I trust you to get me to the Oracle in good order."

Stile paused in the air lock. "We may not meet again, but we shall be working together." He proffered his hand.

"Surely we shall meet," Clef said warmly, taking the hand, forgetting his own prior doubt on this score.

Then they opened the air lock, held their breath, and charged out to intersect the faintly scintillating curtain ahead. The air-lock door swung closed automatically behind them. It was camouflaged to resemble an outcropping of rock; Stile had passed it during his honeymoon without ever noticing.

They stepped through together. The bleak, barren desert became lush wilderness. Stile played a few bars on the harmonica, summoning his magic. Now he was conscious of the spirit of his other self within the instrument, facilitating his performance. No doubt he had been able to practice magic much more readily and effectively because of this help than would otherwise have been possible. "Adepts be deaf; computer get Clef," Stile sang. He was trying to conceal his magic from the awareness of the enemy; he wasn't sure that aspect would work.

Clef vanished. Stile played some more, restoring the expended potency of the magic. This time he was conscious of its source, Phazite, with an ambience of magic like a magnetic field; the music intensified and focused this on Stile, as a magnifying glass might do with a beam of sunshine. The transfer of Phazite to Proton-frame would diminish this ambience, robbing his spells of half their potency. Still, Phaze would be a magic realm—and of course he would probably leave it, so as to make it safe. "Conduct me whole," he sang, "to the East Pole."

He splashed in water. Naturally that was why this region was not a tourist attraction. The water was foul too; the universal Proton pollution was slopping through. All the more reason for tourists to stay clear!

Stile trod water and played his music again. "Set it up solo: a floating holo."

A buoyed holographic transceiver appeared. Stile had really strained to get the concept detail on this one. This was to be his contact station, so that he could stay in touch with the two frames from either side. Because it was at the deserted, unpleasant East Pole, it should be secure for some time from the depredations of other Adepts or Citizens. He was sure that by this time the enemy Adepts had booby-trapped his fixture at the West Pole and would not expect this alternate ploy. Satisfied, Stile played more music. "Take me down to see Brown."

He arrived at the wooden castle of the Brown Adept, feeling nauseous. Self-transport never was comfortable, and he had done it twice rapidly.

In a moment the pretty, brown-haired, brown-eyed child

dashed up to him. "Oh, Blue," she cried. "I was so afraid they had hurt thee!"

Stile smiled wanly. "I had the same fear for thee. Thou alone didst side with me, of all the Adepts."

She scowled cutely. "Well, they did tie me up with a magic rope or something. I was going to get a golem to loose me, but then Yellow came and let me go. She's real pretty in her potion-costume! She said all the others were after thee, and she really didn't like it but couldn't go against her own kind. Is that what I'm doing?"

"Thou art helping save Phaze from disaster," he assured her.

"Oh, goody!" she exclaimed, clapping her hands.

Stile had a second thought about using Brown as an ally. Could a child have proper responsibility? Yet he didn't seem to have much choice. She had at least had the courage to oppose the other Adepts, which was more than Yellow had had. "I need thy help in an important capacity," he said. "There may be hard work and even danger."

"If Phaze is in trouble, I'm already in danger," she said brightly.

"Aye. The other Adepts prefer to risk disaster later, for the sake of power now. I must do something that will make magic less effective, but will save Phaze for future centuries. Then must I leave Phaze."

"Leave Phaze!" she exclaimed, horrified. "I was only just getting to know thee!"

"I do not wish to leave, but a prophecy of the Oracle suggests Phaze will not be safe until I do. I love Phaze too much to hurt it by remaining."

A soulful tear rolled down her cheek. "Oh, Blue—I like this not!"

"I fear the Lady Blue will like it even less," Stile said, choking somewhat himself. "Neither will my friend Neysa the unicorn. But what must be, must be. Now must I cross the curtain before the other Adepts spot me. They tried to trap me in the goblins' demesnes, and now that I escaped, they will be attacking me anywhere they find me. In any event, there is something I must fetch in Proton-frame. So must I ask thee to be my coordinator in Phaze."

Her young brow furrowed. "What is this?"

"The creatures of Phaze must be warned. They must be told that the Oracle predicts disaster if certain things be not done, and that the Blue Adept is trying to do these things and may need their help. That the other Adepts are trying to prevent this program from being implemented and may attack any creatures who help me. Canst thou go to the creatures and tell them?"

"Oh, sure, I can send my golems," she said. "If they are not stopped by magic, they will speak the message."

"Excellent. I have set up a spell to keep thee in touch, so that thou canst check with me across the curtain. When I have what I need, I will return."

"I hope thy business there takes not long. This frightens me, Blue."

"It frightens me too! But I think we can get through." Stile played his harmonica, then sang: "Create a crystal ball, for Brown Adept to call."

The ball appeared. Stile presented it to her. "Speak to this when thou must reach me. I will answer if I can."

She smiled, her spirit rebounding quickly at the prospect of this new toy. "That should be fun!"

"Now must I go," Stile said. He sang a routine spell to take him to a little-used section of the curtain, then stepped across into a maintenance hall in Proton.

Soon he was in touch with Sheen and riding with her in a private Citizen capsule. "What is the present state of my fortune?" he inquired.

"Mellon has manipulated it into about sixty kilograms."

"Sixty kilos of Protonite? Already he's doubled it?"

"He's one of my friends," she reminded him. That meant Mellon had access to information not generally available to others, including Citizens—such as what supposedly random numbers might be generated by the Game Computer. That would of course be an enormous advantage. Stile did not like all of the implications, but decided not to inquire about the details.

"However," she said, "several things are disturbing the Citizens and making mischief for you. It may be difficult in the next few hours."

"It may indeed," he agreed. "The countdown for the juxtaposition of frames has commenced. I've already set most of the other Adepts against me, and soon the same will happen with most of the Citizens."

"Yes. First there is the matter of your rapid increase in fortune. They are concerned where it will stop, understandably. Second, they don't like your designating me as your heir. The panel approved it, but now many more Citizens are becoming aware of it. A robot with such a fortune would be awkward. Third, there is a rumor you mean to destroy the society of Proton. That notion is not at all popular."

"I should think not," Stile agreed. "As it happens, they are not far wrong."

"Will you update me, briefly? I fear things will complicate rapidly, now that you have reappeared, and I lack the living capacity to adapt to totally changed situations. Some Citizens even expressed hope you were dead, and in that hope their action was held in abeyance."

"So now they may seek to render me dead," Stile said. "I thought Citizenship would alleviate my problems somewhat, but they have only intensified. Very well—you get me to the Game Computer, and I'll fill you in."

"What do you want with the Game Computer?"

"It has the book of magic that will make me instantly more powerful than any person in Phaze has been before. I'll need it to protect myself from the massed power of all the other Adepts and to facilitate the transfer of Phazite across the curtain. Here it will be Protonite, with scientific energy instead of magical energy. Then the frames will separate forever, and the curtain will be gone."

She was quick to catch on. "Which world will you be in, then, Stile?"

Stile sighed. "You know I want to be in Phaze, with the Lady Blue. But I am of Proton, and there is a prophecy that tells me to get clear of Phaze. So I will be here."

He thought she would be pleased, but she was not. "The Lady Blue is to be widowed again?" she asked sharply.

"I could bring her here to Proton. But she is of Phaze; I fear it would destroy her to leave it forever. I don't think she would come here anyway, because here I am to marry you."

"So it is my fault you have to widow her?"

How had he gotten into this? "It is the fault of fate. I simply am not destined to be happy after my job is done." Then he bit his tongue. What an insult he had given Sheen!

"I will put in for reprogramming, so she can come here. You do not need to marry me."

Stile refused to take the bait. It was surely poisoned. Sheen might be less complicated than a living woman, but she did have depths. "I will marry you. It is the way it has to be."

"Have you informed the Lady Blue of this?" she inquired coldly.

"Not yet." *There* was a dreadful task!

They were silent for a while. Stile felt the weight of the harmonica in his pocket and brought it out for contemplation. "I wish you could come out," he said to it.

Sheen looked at him questioningly.

"My other self's soul is in this instrument," Stile explained. "Clef's Flute evoked it. Apparently the original Blue Adept conjured his spirit into his favorite possession. It helped me play the harmonica beyond my natural ability, and maybe won a round of the Tourney for me. So he helped me—but I can't help him. He's dead."

"This soul—you saw it in Phaze?"

"No. In Proton."

"But there's no magic in Proton."

Stile nodded thoughtfully. "I'm getting so used to magic, I'm forgetting where I am. That Platinum Flute can't evoke spirits in Proton—yet I swear it did. We thought maybe some magic leaked through, but that couldn't really happen."

"Unless this imbalance you talk of is getting worse. The fabric is starting to tear."

"That could be. The Flute did reach across to shake the mountains of Proton and perhaps also to give me the dream-vision of Clef's journey to the Little Folk. Juxtaposition of one kind or another is occurring; the boundaries are fogging. Which is why action is required now. I wish there were some way to restore my other self to life. Then he could go back to Phaze, his job done."

"Why not? All he needs is a body."

"Like that of a robot or android? They can't function in Phaze."

"Perhaps a magic body, then. One that resembles you. With his soul in it—"

"Ridiculous. You assume that such things can be assembled like the parts of a robot." But Stile wondered. What was a person, other than a body with a soul?

"If I had a soul, I'd be real," Sheen said wistfully.

Stile had given up arguing that case. "The Brown Adept animates golems, but they're made of wood. Robots are made of metal and plastic. Androids are living flesh, but imperfect; they are stupid and often clumsy. If it were possible to fashion a golem made of flesh, with a mind like yours and a human spirit—wouldn't that be a person?"

"Of course it would," she said.

Stile decided. "Have your friends look into the matter. It's a far shot, but if there were any way to restore my other self to some semblance of life, I owe him that. If he died to save Phaze, it is right that he be restored to it."

"If you have any female souls floating around looking for a host, send one to me."

Stile took her hand. Her fingers were as soft and warm as those of any living person. "I regard the soul as the essence of self. If you hosted someone else's soul, you would become that person. I prefer you as you are."

"But you can't love me as I am."

"I can't love anyone other than the Lady Blue. When this business is done, I will accord to you whatever emotion I am capable of feeling for any woman, flesh or metal. You deserve better than this, I know."

"Half love is better than none," she said. "And if you restore your other self in Phaze, will he love the Lady Blue?"

"He's her husband!" Stile exclaimed. "Of course he loves her!"

"Then why did he give her up to you?"

"To save Phaze. It was an act of supreme sacrifice."

"I am a machine. I don't appreciate the delicate nuances of human conscience and passion as a human being can. To me it seems more likely that he found himself in an untenable situation, as do you with me, and simply opted out."

"That's an appalling notion!" But it also carried an insidious conviction. Suppose the Blue Adept, aware of the approaching crisis, knowing he had to make way for another, and perhaps no longer in love with his wife—

"I wish I could meet your other self," Sheen said.

"You are a creature of science, he of magic," Stile said. "Such meetings are difficult, even when both parties are alive. You are stuck with me."

She smiled, letting it go. "And we do have more serious business than such idle conjecturing." She put the holo on receive, and a call was waiting.

It was from Citizen Merle. "Ah, so you're back, Stile! Let me show you me in serf-guise. Private line, please."

"Merle, I'm with Sheen—"

"She knows that," Sheen said, setting up the nonintercept coding.

Merle stripped away her clothing with elegant motions. She had an excellent body. "Stile, beware," she murmured. "There are plots afoot to slay you."

Stile was startled by the contrast between her actions and her words. "I thought you had seduction in mind, Merle."

"I do, I do! I can't seduce you if you're dead, however."

There was that. "Merle, I don't want to deceive you. I'm not interested in—"

"I understand you have business with the Game Computer."

How much did she know? "Do you intend to blackmail me?"

"By no means. You happen to be unblackmailable. But I might help you, if you caused me to be amenable."

"If I were amenable to your design, Merle, my fiancée here might get difficult."

"I suspect she would rather have you alive, well, and victorious. You see, some Citizens have the notion that you represent a threat to their welfare, so they have instituted a push to have your Citizenship revoked."

"Revoked! Is that possible?" Stile felt his underpinnings loosening. He had assumed his Citizenship was irrevocable.

"Anything is possible, by a majority vote of the kilos attending the evening business meeting. You will be on tonight's agenda. You will need whatever help you can get."

Stile glanced at Sheen. "This is news to you?"

"I knew something was developing, sir, but not that it had progressed to this extent."

"Citizens have avenues of communication not available to machines," Merle said. "I assure you the threat is genuine, and the vote may well go against you. Citizens, unfortunately, have very narrow definitions of self-interest." She smiled, turning her now-naked body suggestively. She had an excellent talent for display. "I will encourage my associates to support you, if you come to me. This could shift the balance. It is little enough I ask. Are you quite sure you can't be tempted?"

Sheen, meanwhile, had been busy on another private line. Now she glanced up. "It is true, sir," she said. "My friends verify that in the past hour a general disquiet has formed into a pattern of opposition. The moment news flashed that you had reappeared in Proton, momentum gathered. The projected vote is marginally against you. Merle's support could save you."

"Listen to her, Stile," Merle said. "The scales are finely balanced at the moment, but the full thrust of your opposition has not yet manifested. Sheen has more riding on this than her own possible Citizenship. If your Citizenship is revoked, your tenure will end and you will have to leave Proton. The prospect for her friends would decline drastically, perhaps fatally, incongruous as the term may be in that application."

"How much do you know, Merle?" Stile asked tightly.

"Stile, I research what intrigues me. I have learned much about you in the past few hours. This enhances my respect for you. It is a thing of mine to take a piece of those I respect. This is a harmless foible, and I always give fair return. Come to me and I will help you."

She had him in a difficult spot. If she knew about the self-willed machines and possibly about Stile's mission to restore parallelism in the separating frames, she could certainly cause him much mischief.

"Sir, I think you should go to her," Sheen said.

Stile found himself athwart a dilemma. He had told Mellon to arrange a private bet, to the limit of his available finances, that he would not be seduced by Merle. He did not care to lose that bet, for such a loss would wipe him out. But if her support was all that guaranteed his continuing Citizenship, he could lose everything despite winning the bet. He was between Scylla and Charybdis, the devil and the deep sea, the rock and the hard place.

"I am frankly surprised you do not heed your metal fiancée," Merle said. "She does seem to know what's best for you."

Stile's flash of rage was stifled by Sheen's imploring look. He decided to meet with Merle and try to explain. Maybe he could win through. "Give me your address."

She gave the code, and Sheen changed course. The book of magic would have to wait a little.

There was another call. This one was for Sheen, from Mellon. "We have a delivery for you," he said. "Cosmetics for our employer."

"I don't need—" Stile started to protest. But he was cut off by a glance from the serf.

"Thank you," Sheen said. "I'll pick them up at the nearest delivery tube when we leave the capsule." She gave him Merle's code, and the connection broke.

"Do I look that haggard?" Stile asked plaintively. "I had a good night's rest."

"Mellon is not concerned about your appearance. Obviously something is afoot. Maybe the Lady Citizen has placed an order for an intoxicating or sexually compelling drug, and this is the counteragent."

"Maybe," Stile agreed morosely. "Sheen, Merle is pretty enough in her rejuvenated state, and I'm sure she has a good mind and lots of experience. But I'm simply not interested in the sort of liaison she desires. How do I get out of this one without imperiling my Citizenship?"

"What you are interested in is not very important," she said. "Merle does not want any romance; she merely wants an act of sex to add to her collection. The practical thing is for you to give it to her."

"And lose my bet," Stile said.

Sheen looked startled. "Oh, my—I'm starting to think like a person! I forgot all about that! Of course you can't oblige her." She seemed relieved.

"If I oblige anyone in that way, it will be you."

"Any time."

"After we're decently married."

"It's not a decent marriage."

The capsule arrived, sparing him further comment. They got out at a small private terminal. From here there was access to three small domes, one of which was Merle's.

Sheen went to the delivery chute and punched the coding for Mellon's package. A small vial fell into her hand. Her brow furrowed as she brought the item back. "This is no cosmetic, sir. It's—" She broke off. "Let's move quickly, sir."

Suddenly gas hissed into the room from barred vents. Sheen launched herself at the entrance to Merle's dome. It was locked closed.

"I don't have the facility to analyze this gas," she cried. "But I'll bet it's not cleaning fog. Breathe this, sir." She opened the vial, holding it under his nose.

Vapor puffed out. Stile took the vial, sniffing it as the first waft of the other gas reached him. The vial's vapor was sweet and pleasant; the other gas was sour and stinging.

Sheen returned to the locked door. She opened her front cabinet, the left breast swinging out on hinges to reveal an array of small tools. Even in this crisis, Stile marveled at the completely womanish texture of that breast, when in fact it was a mere facade. Robotry was quite sophisticated.

In a moment Sheen had burned through the lock with a tiny laser unit and had the passage open. Stile hurried through. Sheen shut the door behind them, blocking off the gas, and closed up her breast cabinet. She was whole and normal and soft again.

Stile felt woozy and sick. The antidote in the vial had helped, but that poison gas was nasty stuff. Someone had tried to exterminate him!

Merle appeared. She was wearing a translucent negligee that did wonders for a body that hardly needed them. Stile noticed but hardly cared. He suffered himself to be led inside the Citizen's dome.

"I knew they were going to try something," Merle said. "I thought it would be at the Game Annex. I tried to get you here to safety, but they were too quick. I couldn't say anything on the holo; even a private line is only as private as the technology behind it."

"Our staff forwarded the antidote, sir," Sheen told her.

Stile sat in the comfortable chair where they had placed him, lacking initiative to do more than listen.

"My staff has found a better neutralizer," Merle said. She brought a breathing mask. "Use this, Stile." She fitted it over his face.

Immediately his head began to clear and his stricken body recovered.

"The official indication is a malfunction in the cleaning apparatus," Merle continued. "It's not supposed to fog when anyone is there, and this time the wrong chemicals were used. We won't be able to trace it, but I know the cause. There are activist Citizens who want you out of the way, Stile; I fear this is but the first attempt. You should be safe here, however."

Stile removed the breathing mask and smiled weakly. "I thought you had another notion, Merle."

"Oh, I do, I do. We have been through this before. But I do like you personally, Stile, and wish you well. You're the most refreshing thing to appear on the scene in some time. Fortunately the two notions are not incompatible."

"I fear they are, Merle. You have helped me get into a difficult situation." Stile's head had cleared, but his body remained weak; it was easier to talk than to act. He believed he could trust this woman.

"Do tell me!" she urged. "I love challenges."

"Are we private here?"

"Of course. I am neither as young nor as naïve as I try to appear."

"Will you keep my confidence?"

"About the liaison? Of course not! That must be known, or it doesn't count."

"About whatever I may tell you of my situation."

"I can't guarantee that, Stile. I know something about your situation already."

"Maybe you should tell me what you know, then."

"You are known as the Blue Adept in the other frame. Oh, yes, I have been to Phaze; my other self lacked rejuvenation and modern medicine and died a few years back of natural complications, freeing me. But magic is not for me; I remained there only a few hours and retreated to the safety of my dome here. The germs there are something fierce! I do, however, have a fold of the curtain passing through my property. I pay a harpy well to update me periodically on Phaze developments. This is how I learned more of you, once my interest in you was roused. You have been honeymooning with your lovely Phaze wife, but Adepts have been laying snares for you, until recently you disappeared into the demesnes of the goblins. My informant thought you dead, though she reports a dragon and a hawk emerged safely and flew rapidly southeast, eluding pursuit by Adept sendings. Evidently you survived by crossing the curtain. You seem to be a figure of some importance in Phaze—and perhaps in Proton too, judging by this assassination attempt."

"What could you pay a harpy to serve you?" Stile asked, intrigued by this detail.

"She loves blood-soaked raw meat, but is too old and frail to catch it herself."

"The others of her flock would provide," Stile said, thinking of the harpy attack Clef had weathered upon his entry into Phaze. How important that entry had turned out to be!

"This one is a loner. No flock helps her."

"Is she by chance your other self?"

Merle stiffened, then relaxed. "Oh, you have a sharp tongue, Stile! No, it doesn't work that way, or I couldn't cross. My other self was exactly like me, only she seemed older. She did befriend the harpy, and when she died I assumed the burden of that friendship. It is not easy to get along with a harpy! Now will you tell me what I do not know about yourself?"

"Will you accept that information in lieu of the sexual liaison?"

"No, of course not, Stile. I accept it in exchange for the protection I am offering you here, and for the information I am giving you about the Citizen plot against you."

She would not be swayed from her objective! She wanted another notch for her garter. He would have to give her the full story and hope it would persuade her to help him without insisting on the liaison. She might be displeased to learn about his bet in that connection, but at least it was no affront to her pride.

There was a chime and glimmer of light in the air. "That's my holo," Merle said. "Call for you, Stile, blocked by my privacy intercept."

"Better let it through," he said. "The enemy Citizens know I'm here anyway."

The picture formed. It was the Brown Adept. "The creatures don't believe me, Blue," she said tearfully. "They think I'm with the bad Adepts, trying to fool them. They are attacking my golems."

Stile sighed. He should have known. "What would it take to convince them?"

"Only thee thyself, Blue. Or maybe one of thy close friends, or the Lady Blue—"

"No! The Lady Blue must remain guarded by the unicorns. The Adepts will be watching her."

"Maybe Neysa. She's friends with everybody."

"The Herd Stallion won't let her go." Stile hardly objected to the care provided for Neysa in her gravid state. Then he had an idea. "Thy demesnes are near to the range of the werewolves, are they not? Kurrelgyre's Pack?"

She brightened. "Sure, Blue. They come here all the time, hunting. But they don't believe me either."

"But if Kurrelgyre believed, his Pack would help. The other animals would believe him."

"I guess so," she agreed dubiously. "But thou wouldst have to tell him thyself."

"I will," Stile said. "Give me half an hour."

Brown's smile was like moonlight. "Oh, thank thee, Blue!"

"Nay, thank *thee*, Brown. It is an important service thou dost here."

"Gee." The happy image faded.

"So that's the Brown Adept," Sheen said. "A child. A cute child."

"She's a full sorceress, though," Stile said. "Her golems are tough creatures." He remembered his encounter with the golem shaped in his own image. He was glad to have those wooden men on his side, this time! He turned to Merle. "Now I have to explain to you my reason for not wishing to have this liaison, then hurry across your section of the curtain to straighten things out in Phaze."

"No need to explain," Merle said. "I can see you are busy, with people depending on you. I'll chalk this one up to experience."

"I do need your help," Stile said. "So I want you to understand—"

"You shall have my help, Stile. If that sweet child believes in you, so must I. I'm sure she is not asking any quid pro quo."

"Well, she may want a ride on a unicorn," Stile said, wondering whether he could believe this abrupt change of heart on her part. "But you still deserve to know—"

"About your secret bet," Merle said. "That's what made it such a challenge, Stile. But if you lose your fortune and can't do what you need to, that brown-eyed child will suffer, and I don't want that on my withered conscience. I'll show you to my corner of the curtain; that will get you neatly past the ambush awaiting you outside."

Stile stood, taking her hand. "I really appreciate this, Merle."

She drew him in for a kiss. "I think it was that child's thee's and thy's. You did it too, when you answered her. Somehow that melts me. I haven't been this foolish in decades."

They were before the curtain. It scintillated across Merle's huge round bouncy bed. No coincidence, that; she probably had a demon lover in the other frame. Beyond, Stile could discern the slope of a wooded hillside.

"How will I rejoin you?" Sheen asked.

"You'll come with me," Stile decided. "By now the enemy Citizens know how useful you are; they'll be trying to take you out too." He picked her up, strode across the bed, and willed himself through the curtain.

He stood on the forest slope, the inert robot in his arms. In Phaze, she was defunct. "Take this form of Sheen's to the wolves' demesnes," he sang. This was simplified; what he intended was for them both to travel there.

They arrived in good order. The wolves were snoozing in the vicinity of a recent kill, while several of the cubs growled at a golem they had treed. Half a dozen roused and charged Stile, converting to men and women as they drew near.

"Greetings, Blue Adept," Kurrelgyre exclaimed, recognizing him. "I see thou hast found a defective golem."

Stile glanced down at Sheen, startled. "I suppose I have, friend. In the other frame she is my fiancée."

"Ah, a bitch in every frame! Dost thou bring her here for animation by the Brown Adept?"

Again Stile was startled. Would such magic work? He would have to inquire. "I came to advise thee that I am at odds with the other Adepts, who seek to slay me. Thus I can not stay here long, lest they discover me and strike. Only the Brown Adept is with me, and I have asked her to spread warning to the tribes of the creatures of Phaze, whose help I may be needing soon."

"Ooooww!" Kurrelgyre howled, glancing at the tree. "I turned her down—"

"I know," Stile cut in. "I should have prepared better. Things have been very rushed. Now must I beg thee to help me by helping her. If thy wolves will go with her golems, to give them credence—"

"Aye, immediately," Kurrelgyre agreed. He made a signal at the tree, and the cubs quickly retreated, allowing the golem to come down. "Had I but realized before—"

Stile clapped him on the shoulder. "I thank thee. Now must I flee."

There was a wrenching. Oops—he had made an inadvertent rhyme, with Sheen leaning against him. Quickly he took better hold of her and willed himself to the Brown Demesnes. It worked; he landed neatly in the foyer of the wooden castle. The giant golem on guard did a double take, but managed to recognize him before clubbing him, and in a moment the Brown Adept was there.

"That's not one of mine!" she exclaimed, seeing the inert Sheen in his arms.

"This is Sheen, my Proton fiancée. She was with me when thou didst call a little while ago. She'll be all right when we cross the curtain. I just talked to Kurrelgyre, and the wolves will cooperate. Instruct thy golems; a wolf will go with each."

"Oh, goody!" But her attention was focused on Sheen. "I don't usually animate metal, but I can when I try. Of course her personality might not be the same—"

Stile had not intended to get into this now, but again he was intrigued. "Sheen always wanted to come to Phaze, but she's scientific. Thy golems are magic, and won't operate in Proton. I don't think it could work."

"Let me try, Blue. If I animate her, thou wilt not have to carry her."

"I'm in a hurry, Brown. The hostile Adepts could spot me at any moment. There isn't time—"

"Why dost thou not want to animate her here?" she asked with the direct naïveté of a child.

That stopped Stile. The Lady Blue, his wife, was in Phaze, yet she could cross to Proton, where she had met Sheen. There really was no conflict. "How fast canst thou do it?"

"She is full-formed." Brown squinted at Sheen's torso critically. "Very full-formed. I have only to lay on my hands and concentrate. Most of the time I spend fashioning a golem is carving it to shape before animation."

"Try it, then. But if she is not herself—I mean, the golems can be—"

"Then will I deanimate her." Brown leaned over Sheen, where Stile placed her on the ground, and ran her hands over the body. Then she pressed her fingers across the face.

Sheen stirred. Her eyes opened.

Stile stood back, abruptly nervous. Golems were nonliving things, soulless ones animated only by magic. Brown's ability to make them function was phenomenal—but what monster in Sheen's image might rouse here?

Sheen sat up, shaking her head. She saw Stile. "Oh,

we're back," she said. "I must have been set back by the deactivation. I feel funny."

She was herself! "Thou dost know me?" Stile asked, hardly daring to believe. A new golem would not have knowledge of him.

"Of course I know you, Stile! I'm not that forgetful, unless my memory banks get erased. And this child is the one who called you on holo. She—" Sheen broke off, surprised. "What is she doing here?"

"This is Phaze," Stile said. "The Brown Demesnes."

Sheen blinked. "I don't believe that is possible. I can't function across the curtain; you know that."

"I animated thee," the child said. "Thou art now a golem."

Sheen looked around, taking in the scene. She saw the wooden walls of the castle, and the golems standing near. "May I inspect this region?"

Stile was becoming nervous about the time. "Do it quickly, Sheen. Thou wilt be inert again if the enemy Adepts discover our presence here and attack." He was almost fidgeting.

"I think they are distracted by other events," Brown said. "They know not what my golems are doing."

Sheen completed her survey extremely quickly. "There is no dome. The air is natural. This *is* the other world. Will I remain animate? I feel no different."

"Yes," the Brown Adept said. "My golems never die, unless they are destroyed." Tactfully, she did not mention her ability to turn them off.

"Yet I am not alive," Sheen concluded sadly.

"That is beyond the power of magic," Brown agreed.

"And of science," Stile added. "Now must we go." He took Sheen's hand and sang a spell to take them to a private section of the curtain. One thing he had done during his honeymoon was survey likely crossing places.

They landed in a secluded glade in the Purple Mountain foothills. "Now that's an experience!" Sheen exclaimed. "It really *is* a magic land."

"It really is," Stile agreed. "Art thou able to cross the curtain by thyself now?"

Sheen tried, but could not. "I am not alive," she repeated. "I have no power to do what living creatures do."

Stile took her hand again and willed them across. They stood in a vehicle storage garage. "Do you remember?" he asked.

"I remember Phaze," she said. "I have not changed. Only your language has changed."

"So there is no loss of continuity as you shift from magic to science."

"None at all. I am the same. I wish I were not."

"Now let's get that book of magic before we are diverted again. We're close to a Game Annex terminal, by no coincidence. I can contact the Game Computer privately there."

"Let me do it," Sheen said. "There may be another ambush."

"You're my fiancée. I shouldn't let you take all the risks."

"Without you, I am nothing. Without me, you are a leading Citizen and Adept, capable of saving Phaze and helping my friends. Stand back, sir."

Stile smiled and shrugged. "Give me the book of magic," she said to the Game-access terminal, adding the code.

"Why?" the Computer asked.

"The Blue Adept means to return it to Phaze and there use it to abate the crisis."

"One moment," the machine said. "While it is on the way, will you accept a message for the Blue Adept?"

"Yes."

"A consortium of opposition Citizens, interested in profiting from a necessary action, proffers this wager: the entire amount of Citizen Stile's fortune at the time, that he will not survive until the start of tonight's business meeting of Citizens."

"I'll take that bet!" Stile called, realizing that he could not lose it. If he died prematurely, all was lost anyway; if he lived, his fortune and power would be doubled again. Double or nothing, right when he wanted it.

"Citizen Stile accepts the wager," Sheen said. "If he dies, his estate will be liquidated and assigned to the consortium. If he appears at that meeting alive, his fortune will in that instant be doubled, and he will immediately be able to wield the full leverage of it."

"The wager is so entered. The doubling cube has been turned." The Game Computer made a bleep that was its way of coughing apologetically. "I have no part of this threat other than serving as a conduit for the wager. It was not necessary for the Citizen to be concerned about an ambush on my premises. Neither am I permitted to warn him of any potential threat immediately beyond my premises."

"That's warning enough," Stile muttered. "Move out, Sheen!"

Sheen paused only long enough to pick up the package the delivery slot delivered: the book of magic.

They fled down a hall. "Weapons are not permitted on Game premises unless part of a designated Game," the Game Computer announced.

"It is not warning us, just making a public announcement—officially," Stile said with a grim smile. "Is the Game Computer really one of your friends?"

"Yes," she said.

A man appeared in the hall ahead. He looked like an ordinary serf, but he stood before them with a suggestive posture of readiness.

"That's a robot," Stile said.

"That's a killer machine," Sheen agreed. "Stile, I am a dual-purpose robot, designed for defense and personality. That is a specialized attack vehicle. I am not equipped to handle it. You must flee it immediately; I can delay it only a moment."

Stile dived for a panel. He tore open a section of the wall where he knew power lines ran. There they were, brightly colored cables, intended to be quite clearly coded for stupid maintenance personnel. He took a red one in both hands and yanked. It ripped free as the enemy robot came near. "Get well away, Sheen!" he cried.

"Stile, you'll electrocute yourself!" she cried in horror.

Now he took hold of a white cable. This, too, tore from its mooring, which was a magnetic clamp.

As the killer robot reached for him, Stile jammed both raw cable ends at its body. Power arced and crackled, electrifying the machine. The robot collapsed.

"You took a terrible chance!" Sheen admonished him as they hurried on. "You could have been electrocuted just pulling those cables out."

"The power was cut off, to free the magnetic clamps," Stile said. "The danger was apparent, not real."

"How could you know that?" She sounded flustered.

"The Game Computer is one of your friends," he reminded her.

"Oh." For her friends stood ready to help him, covertly. The Computer had cut off power, then restored it. How could such a brief collusion ever be spotted? Stile knew exactly how to use the assistance of the self-willed machines when he needed to. Fortunately the specialized killer machine had been stupid.

The passage led to the minicar racing track, a favorite Game of the younger set. Stile had won many such races. His small size gave him an advantage in these little vehicles. However, this time he only wanted to bypass the cars and reach the exit passage.

A man burst into the premises. This one was a genuine human serf—but he had a laser pistol. This was evidently the one the Game Computer had warned away. Unfortunately, outside the actual Games, the Computer had little power. It could protest and warn, not usually enforce. It could summon guards—but if it did so in this case, the other Citizens would be alerted, and that was not to Stile's interest. Stile would have to fight this one out alone; the Computer had helped all it could.

"Sheen, get out of here," he whispered urgently. "Use the service passages and airless sections to confound human pursuit. Get the book of magic across the curtain."

"But I must protect you!" she protested.

"You can protect me best by getting away from me right now. I can do tricks alone that I can't with company. Meet me later—" He paused to decide on a suitably unlikely place. "Meet me at Merle's dome. They've boobytrapped that once; they won't expect me to go near it again. If you prefer, wait for me just beyond the curtain, in Phaze—oh, I forget, you can't cross by yourself! Maybe Merle will help you cross."

She did not argue further. "I love you." She faded away.

Stile jumped into the nearest car and accelerated it into the main playing grid. Ordinarily he would have had to obtain license from the Game Computer to play, but Citizens were exempt from such rules. The pursuing man, however, was a serf; he had to honor this rule, or the Computer would close down the Game, apply a stasis field, and arrest him. *Here* the Computer had power, when there was a valid pretext to exert it. As it was, the Computer knew the man was up to mischief, and had already warned him about carrying the pistol.

The various ramps, intersections, and passing zones were arrayed in three-dimensional intricacy, so that the total driving area was many kilometers long despite the confinement of the dome. Stile was well familiar with this layout.

The armed man had been stalking him cautiously. Now the man had to get into another car to keep up. To do this, he had to get a partner and enlist in the Game. But he was prepared for this; a henchman got into another car and started the pursuit. Theoretically, they were chasing each other; actually, they were both after Stile.

Stile smiled grimly. These would-be killers would have more of a chase than they liked. They were up against an expert Gamesman: a Tourney winner, in fact.

Stile could shoot his car through the maze of paths. He could exit quickly. But that would only mean the armed man would follow him. It was better to handle this situation here, where the terrain favored Stile, and then escape cleanly.

A beam of light passed to Stile's right. The armed man had fired his laser, missing because of the difficulty of aiming when the cars were going in different directions at different speeds. But the shot was close enough so that Stile knew the man had some skill; he would score if given a better opportunity. Now the Computer could not shut down the Game, though the laser shot had provided sufficient pretext, because when the cars stopped, the assassin would score on Stile.

Stile swung around a turn, putting a ramp between himself and the pursuer. He checked the minicar, but there was nothing in it he could throw. He would have to maneuver until he could find a way to put the man out of commission.

The problem was, these vehicles were small but safe. They would not travel fast enough to leave the track, and the set was designed to prevent collisions. Such Games were supposed to seem far more dangerous than they were in fact. Stile might scare his opponent, but could not actually hurt him with the car. Still, there were ways.

Stile slowed his car, allowing the man to catch up somewhat. Then, just as the man was leveling his laser, Stile accelerated into a loop, going up and over and through. The man, caught by surprise, had to accelerate his own car and hang on. The cars could not fall, even if they stalled upside down at the top of a loop, and the automatic seat belts would hold the occupants fast. The man evidently did not know that.

Stile moved on into a roller-coaster series, going up and down at increasing velocity. The man followed, looking uncomfortable. He was fairly solid, and his belly lightened and settled with each change of elevation. That could start the queasies. Then Stile looped into a tunnel with a good lead, emerged to spin into a tight turn, and crossed over the other track just as the pursuer shot out of the tunnel.

Stile had removed his robe. He dropped it neatly over the man's head.

The man reacted violently, clawing at the voluminous material that the wind plastered to his face, while the car continued along the track. Stile slowed his own car, letting the other catch up. Just as the man managed to get free of the robe, Stile jumped from one car to the other, having also circumvented the seat restraint. He caught the man's neck in a nerve-strangle, rendering him instantly unconscious, and took the laser pistol from his hand. Then he jumped back to his own car and accelerated away. Such jumps from car to car were supposed to be impossible, but Stile was a skilled gymnast, able to do what few others could contemplate.

Now he zoomed for the exit. He had left his robe behind; it made identification too easy for his assassination-minded pursuers. Still, being a serf was not enough camouflage. There would be other assassins on the prowl for him, closing on this region. The majority of Citizens, like the Adepts, seemed to be against him; they had tremendous resources that would be overpowering once they got the focus. He needed to get far away from here in a hurry.

Could he retreat to the curtain, as he had done when the Adepts had had him pinned in the cavern? No, they would be watching the segments of it through which he had entered Proton this time. He had to surprise them.

Camouflage seemed to be the answer—but what kind?

Already Stile was making his decision. The most common and least noticed entities in Proton were machines, ranging from self-propelled hall-brushers to humanoid robots. Some were sophisticated emulations of individuality like Sheen, but most were cruder. Stile paused at a food machine and got some nutri-taffy; this he used to shape bulges at his knees and elbows, and to change the configuration of his neck and crotch. He now resembled a small, sexless menial humanoid robot that had been used in a candy kitchen. He walked somewhat stiffly and set a fixed smile on his face, since this grade of machine lacked facial mobility. Stile was, of course, a practiced mimic. He was unable to eliminate his natural body heat, but hoped no one would check him that closely.

It worked. Serfs passed him without paying any attention. There was a checkpoint guarded by two brute androids, but they were looking for a man, not a taffy-odored machine. Stile walked stiffly by, unchallenged.

He was probably safe now, but he did not gamble. He continued his robot walk to a transport capsule and rode to the vicinity of Merle's dome, then took the service entrance. Even here there was no challenge. Functionaries were constantly in and out of Citizens' estates on myriad errands.

But Merle was expecting him. "Stile, I want you to know I sincerely regret this," she said. "Extreme pressure has been put on me. Believe me, I'm helping you in my fashion." She touched a button.

Stile leaped to intercept her motion, but was too late. Stasis caught him.

Merle had betrayed him. Why hadn't he anticipated that? He could so readily have gotten around her, had he only been alert. He had allowed a woman to make a fool of him.

He was cleaned and packaged and loaded into a transport capsule. He could feel the motion without seeing anything. The capsule moved swiftly south, by the feel of it. At length it slowed, and he was unloaded.

The stasis released. Stile found himself in a barred chamber—and with him was Sheen. She was inert; her power cell had been removed. The disaster was complete. There was no sign of the book of magic.

A speaker addressed him. "Serf, you have been assigned to this mine because you have excellent manual dexterity. You will be granted one hour to familiarize yourself with the controls. Then you will be expected to commence processing the ore in your bailiwick. You will have a rest break in your cell of fifteen minutes after each hour, provided your production is satisfactory. Superior performance will result in promotion. Press the ADVISE button if there is any problem. Malingering will not be tolerated."

Stile knew better than to protest. He had been shanghaied here to get him out of the way. Once he failed to appear at the business meeting, he would lose his fortune, be voted out of Citizenship, become a serf in fact, and probably be deported. He didn't even blame Merle; she had done this instead of killing him. Perhaps she had reported him dead. No doubt her own Citizenship had been placed in the balance. The opposition, in Proton as in Phaze, played hard ball.

What could he do? A quick inspection of the chamber satisfied him that he could not escape. The Protonite miners were not trusted; each was locked in his cell during working hours, even though he never directly handled the valuable mineral. Security was extremely tight in the mines. If Stile tried to interfere with any of the equipment or wiring, there would be an alarm and immediate punishment; if he tried to sabotage the mining operation, he would be executed. All he could do was cooperate.

Stile got to work on the mining. He familiarized himself with the controls in moments, and soon had his survey-screen on. Could he use this to get in touch with the Brown Adept? No—this was a different circuit—and even if he could call outside, the monitor would intercept, and he would be in instant trouble, possibly of a mortal nature. Best to sit tight. Probably the game was lost. He had mainly himself to blame; the exigencies of the moment had forced an oversight.

Of course he was not entirely alone. The Lady Blue knew he was in Proton, and she would be concerned about his failure to reappear. But she had not been keeping close track of him; she would not be really alarmed until some hours or days had passed without news—and that would be too late. He would have missed the business meeting and the juxtaposition of frames. In any event, the enemy Citizens would now be alert for her; Stile did not want the Lady Blue exposing herself to possible assassination.

What about the self-willed machines? They might be able to help—if Merle had not acted to conceal his abduction from their view. Since she knew a good deal about him and had referred to Sheen's friends, she had probably done just that. And if the sapient machines did locate him, they would still hesitate to reveal their nature by acting overtly on his behalf. He could not count on their rescuing him.

That left it up to the Brown Adept, who would be unable to reach him—and what could she do if she did? She was a child who would have no magic in this frame, assuming she could cross the curtain. Best to establish no false hopes. If help was on the way, it would succeed or fail regardless of his concern.

He was good at mining. Under his direction, the remote-controlled machinery operated efficiently. In two hours he had extracted half a gram of Protonite from the ore, a full day's quota. Whether Citizen or serf, Adept or slave, he intended to do his best—though this sort of mining would soon have to stop, if the frames were to be saved. Ironic, his effort here!

Then the gate opened. An apparition stood there—the tallest, thinnest, ugliest android he had ever seen. Except that it wasn't an android, but a man. No, not exactly a man—

Stile's spinning mental gears finally made an improbable connection. "The troll!" he exclaimed. "Trool the troll—in Proton-frame!"

"I must rescue thee from confinement three times," Trool said.

Stile nodded. "This is the third, for me and mine. More than amply hast thou fulfilled the prophecy. Sincerely do I thank thee, Trool." There was no point in adhering to Proton language; the troll would only be confused.

"It is not done yet," the troll said.

"Thou hast done enough," Stile said. "Thou hast freed me."

Trool shrugged and stooped to pick Sheen up. He shambled through the door, carrying her, and Stile followed.

Trolls had a way with subterranean regions. Trool took them down into the depths of the mines, passing locks and checkpoints without challenge, until they were in the lowest crude tunnels. Here there were only machines, the forward end of the remote-control chain. Here, too, was the Protonite ore, the stuff of Proton's fortune and misfortune.

"How are things doing in Phaze at the moment?" Stile inquired.

"The hosts are massing as for war," Trool replied. "All are with thee except the Adepts, the goblins, and scattered monsters."

"All?" Stile asked, amazed. "Even the tribes of the demons?"

"Thou hast made many friends, Adept, especially among the snow-monsters and fire-spirits."

Ah—his favor for Freezetooth was paying a dividend! "All I have done is the appropriate thing at the appropriate time." Basically, Stile liked the various creatures of Phaze and liked making friends. "Yet I doubt that the harpies, or dragons, or thine own kind—"

"The trolls are with thee." Trool made a grimacing smile. "I did see to that, lest they call me traitor for helping thee. The harpies and dragons know no loyalty save to their own kind, unless compelled by geis. They take no sides."

Trool was surprisingly well informed. He seemed, under that ugliness, to be a fairly smart and caring person. Stile had assumed all trolls to be ignorant predators; he had been too narrow.

Suddenly they were at the curtain; Stile saw the scintillation across the tunnel. They stepped through.

Sheen woke. "Who are you?" she demanded, finding herself in the troll's arms.

"Thou hast no power pack," Stile protested. "How canst thou animate?"

She checked herself. "It's true. I must be in Phaze. In golem-state."

Stile nodded, his surprise shifting to comprehension. Of course she needed no scientific mechanism here! Nonetheless, he conjured her a replacement power cell so that she would not be confined to Phaze. "Thou art a creature of both frames now."

The troll led the way on up through the tunnel toward the surface. They followed. Stile could have taken them out by a spell, but preferred to acquaint himself with the locale of the tunnel in case he should need it again. Also, he did not want to attract the baleful attention of the enemy Adepts by using magic unnecessarily. Probably he should not have risked conjuring Sheen's power cell at this time; he kept forgetting.

They neared the surface. Trool paused. "There is yet day," he said. "Needs must I remain below." For he lacked his voluminous clothing, having had to discard it in order to masquerade as an android.

"By all means," Stile said. "Thou hast served us well, and fain would I call thee friend. We shall leave thee with our gratitude."

"It behooves not the like of thee to bestow friendship on the like of me," Trool said, gruffly pleased. He put his gnarled hands to the large flat rock that blocked the exit. "Beyond this point it curves to the surface." He heaved.

Suddenly the roof caved in. Trool leaped back, shoving the other two clear. "Someone has tampered—"

Sunlight shone brilliantly down from above, angling in

from the new hole in the ceiling to bathe the troll. "Sabotage!" Sheen exclaimed. "It would have crushed one of us—"

"Surely," Stile agreed. "The trap was meant for me."

"Look at Trool!" she cried, horrified.

Stile looked. The troll had been instantly destroyed by the light. He was now a figure of stone—a grotesque statue.

Suddenly it made a terrible kind of sense. Stile remembered how Serrilryan the werebitch had been fated to see the sidhe three times before she died; she had seen them the third time, then died. Trool had been fated to help Stile three times; he had done that, and had now been terminated.

"Damn it, this time I'm going to fight fate," Stile said angrily.

CHAPTER 11

Xanadu

Clef was in the palace of the Oracle, playing the Platinum Flute. The perfect melody suffused the premises, more lovely than any tangible thing could be. He halted when Stile's party arrived.

"I have another prophecy for thee," he said to Stile. "Thou wilt be betrayed for thine own good by a young-seeming woman thou dost trust."

"Too late on that," Stile said. "Merle betrayed me three hours ago."

Clef was embarrassed. "Sorry; I understood it was scheduled for a few hours hence. The Oracle must have slipped a cog." He looked at Sheen. "I thought thou wast a creature of Proton," he said, surprised.

"I am," she agreed. "Now I am a creature of Phaze too, a golem." She indicated the statue she supported. "This is Trool the troll, who sacrificed himself to save us. Stile says you may—thou mayest be able to—" She paused. "But doesn't the juxtaposition suffer when thou dost stop playing?"

"Marginally. It's a long process; inertia maintains the movement for brief interludes. Otherwise I could not take a breath. In any event, what you hear is not the juxtaposition theme; that is only part of it, a single-note exercise that reaches into the deeper firmament. It is not continuous; rather I must play it at the key intervals." Clef considered the statue. "Thou dost wish the troll's soul piped to Heaven?"

"Nay, not yet," Stile said. "Canst thou pipe him back to life?"

Clef stroked his chin thoughtfully. "I fear not, Stile. There is a monstrous difference between directing traffic— that is, routing a soul to Heaven—and revivifying the dead. I can send the soul back into the body—but that in itself will not change stone or flesh. You need a different kind of magic for that. Perhaps there is a suitable spell in the book of magic. You did fetch that?"

"The book of magic!" Stile exclaimed, stricken. "I forgot all about it!"

"Merle has it," Sheen said. "She deactivated me—and now the book is gone."

"Is that why she betrayed me?" Stile asked. "To get that book?"

"I doubt she knew of it," Sheen said. "She said nothing about it to me. I just happened to be carrying it."

"She surely has some inkling now, though. She has access to the curtain, to Phaze; she can use those spells to become an instant Adept. We've got to get the book back before she does that!"

"For the sake of Phaze as well as for the troll," Sheen agreed.

"I'll surely find her at the Citizens' business meeting." Stile frowned, worried. "I don't have much time for that, either; I've got to move." His hope of studying the spells of the book before the Proton crisis came had been dashed; whatever preparations he might have made were moot.

"I'll go with thee," Sheen said.

"But first thou must marshal thy troops," Clef said. "The time is nigh."

"Oh, yes, the troops. I did alert the various creatures of Phaze, and all but the dragons, harpies, and goblins are with us. Has the Oracle finally condescended to inform us exactly how such troops are to be employed?"

"Only that thou must dispose them as for battle."

"Dispose them where? Against whom?"

Clef shrugged, embarrassed. "I know not."

"That is not a phenomenal help."

"Thou knowest that prophecies work out regardless of comprehension.'"

"Look, if I miss that Citizens' business meeting, I'm finished in Proton. I have scarcely an hour as it is. Can't the Phaze side wait at least until I've recovered the book of magic?"

"The Oracle says the troops must be disposed first."

"Damn!" Stile swore. "Send my coldest regards to that inscrutable machine. I'll do what I can."

"I shall keep thy friend the troll statue safe for thy return with the book."

"Thanks," Stile said gruffly. He played a bar of music on the harmonica, took Sheen by the hand, and spelled them to the Brown Demesnes.

They popped in at the main receiving hall. The child Adept was waiting. "Oh, I'm so glad thou art back, Blue!" she exclaimed. "And thou too, Lady Machine. Dost thou like being a golem?"

"It's wonderful, Lady Adept," Sheen agreed.

The child's mouth went round with astonishment. Then she giggled. "I guess thou meanest me. Nobody ever called me Lady before, 'cause I'm just a girl."

"That's more than I'll ever be," Sheen said.

Stile had to interrupt. He had very little time. "Brown, a troll rescued me from confinement, but he got turned to stone by the sun. Can you animate stone?"

"Oh, sure, some. But you know, it doesn't change the substance. He'd be awful heavy if thou didst not spell him back to flesh, and he'd crack when struck hard. I work with wood because it is strong and light, and the Lady Machine was pre-formed, so she was okay. But a stone troll—"

"I see the problem. I think I could turn him to wood, but I'm not sure about flesh."

"Perhaps with the aid of the book of magic," Sheen reminded him.

"Of course. That should do it."

"Thou couldst just about create a troll from scratch," Sheen pointed out. "Make a figure, enchant it to flesh, have the Brown Adept animate it, and Clef could pipe a soul into it."

"If we had a soul," Stile agreed. "That's the one thing magic can't generate."

"I know," she said sadly.

"My golems and the wolves have spread the word among all the creatures of Phaze," Brown said. "All but the goblins and monsters have joined. But they know not what to do now."

"I wish I could tell them," Stile said. "I am the victim of a prophecy. I don't know where to tell them to go."

"Well, maybe thou canst improvise," Brown suggested. "The troops will dissipate if not encouraged."

"So the Oracle seems to think, though I hardly have time to—"

"Which means we must hurry," Sheen said, enjoying this.

"And I thought Citizenship was uncomplicated!" Stile worked out several travel-spells, and they were off.

First stop was the werewolves. Kurrelgyre was there, but the Pack had been depleted by the wolves and bitches assigned to accompany the wooden golems. Kurrelgyre shifted immediately to man-form to shake Stile's hand. "But this bitch—I know her not," he said, looking at Sheen. "Unless—could it be?"

"This is the robot-golem Sheen, my Proton fiancée," Stile said. "Thy suggestion was good; the Brown Adept animated her."

"At least conjure her fitting apparel," the werewolf said. "She is too luscious a morsel to go naked hereabouts."

Clothing! Stile had forgotten all about that for Sheen. Quickly he conjured her a pretty dress and slippers, as befitted a Lady of Phaze.

"But I can not wear clothing!" she protested. "I'm a serf!"

"Not here," Stile assured her. "In this frame all people wear clothes." He eyed her appraisingly. "They do befit thee."

"We are ready for action," Kurrelgyre said eagerly. "But where is it? Whom do we fight?"

"I know not," Stile admitted. "The prophecy decrees it; that is all."

The werewolf sighed. "Prophecies are oft subject to misinterpretation. I had hoped this would be not that type."

Stile agreed. "The animalheads are prophesied to lose half their number. I fear this will be typical. I presume much of the damage will be done by enchantments hurled by the enemy Adepts, and by the ravages of their minions. But the other creatures of Phaze will be on thy side—the unicorns, elves, ogres, and such. Do thou gather thy wolves and be ready for action at any time. I know no more. I am but a chip afloat on a stormy sea, doing what I must do without much personal volition."

Sheen smiled knowingly. This was a concept a robot was in a position to understand.

"Surely the enemy will seek to destroy thee," the wolf said.

"The enemy Adepts have been trying! I hope to jump around swiftly in a random pattern, avoiding them until I return to Proton."

"I fear for thee, friend. I have a few wolves left who can guard thee—"

"Nay, I'd best travel light. Just be ready with thy Pack when I need thee!"

"Aye, I shall, and the other wolf packs too." They shook hands.

Stile spelled himself and Sheen to the next stop: the ogres. These ones certainly were ready for action. Each huge creature was armed with a monstrous club and seemed capable of smashing boulders with single blows.

This was a truly impressive army. There were perhaps four hundred fighting creatures in view.

As quickly as possible, Stile explained to the ogre leader that the moment for action was just about at hand. "But we don't know exactly where trouble will begin," he said. "Only that it will be terrible, horrible, violent, and bloody."

Slow smiles cracked the ogres' brute faces. They were eager for this sort of fun. Stile knew he had struck the right note.

"Just remember," he cautioned them. "All the organized creatures of Phaze will be on thy side, except the Goblins. So don't attack elves or giants or werewolves—"

"Awww," the leader grumbled. But he had it straight. No unauthorized bloodshed.

Stile spelled on to the vampires, where he consulted with his friend Vodlevile, who was no chief but whom Stile trusted. The flock promised to be alert.

So it went, touching bases with the animalheads, snow-demons, giants, trolls, and Little Folk. He did not go to the Platinum Elves, fearing an Adept trap there; instead he met with the gnomes of the Purple Mountains. These Little Folk were akin to the goblins of the White Mountains, but had elected to join the compatible elves. It was as if the more pleasant climate made them nicer creatures.

The gnome males were ugly, but the females, the gnomides, were quite pretty little misses, each holding a fine bright diamond. These were, indeed, the workers of precious stones, and their wares were even more valuable than those of the Platinum Mound Folk. They quickly agreed to pass the word among the elven tribes. "There will be thousands of little warriors awaiting thy call to action, Adept. Only save Phaze, and all is even!"

Stile hoped he could! "Dost thou know of any Adept presence in the Elven Demesnes?" Stile asked as he got ready to leave. "I fear an ambush and marvel that none has occurred."

"We know of none, and our prophecy book has no mention of harm to thee here, Adept," the gnome chief answered. "But Adepts are devious—no offense proffered."

"Devious indeed!" Stile agreed.

"Surely it is the Lady Blue they will stake out," Sheen murmured.

"Aye. Yet must I see her and advise the Herd Stallion."

"Send me first, to spring the trap," she offered.

Stile demurred, but she insisted. Conscious of the danger and of his vanishing time, he had to agree. He spelled her to the unicorn herd for two minutes, then brought her back to the gnome demesnes.

"No sign of trouble there," she reported, seeming exhilarated by the excursion. "Belle, the pretty unicorn mare, is there, asking to join the herd. They have not admitted her, but are considering it. Thy friend Clip is quite worked up."

"He would be. He's smitten by her. No Adepts?"

"The Herd Stallion is sure there are no Adepts there, and no Adept magic in the vicinity."

"Good enough." Stile spelled the two of them to the herd.

It was as Sheen had said. All was peaceful. The unicorns were grazing in a loose circle on an open hillside, with Neysa remaining in the center. Stile and Sheen landed beside the circle, for magic was repulsed within it.

"May I go in and meet Neysa this time?" Sheen inquired wistfully.

Stile knew she identified with the unicorn, for Sheen and Neysa had been his two closest companions before he encountered the Lady Blue. "I'll ask the Herd Stallion," he said.

He asked, and the Stallion acquiesced with suitable grace. Sheen left them to enter the circle, while Stile briefed the Stallion. "That's all I know," he concluded. "I conjecture that the Adepts will move in force when I try to transport the Phazite, perhaps sending dragons to interfere. Someone will need to intercept those monsters."

"We shall be there," the Stallion agreed grimly.

The Lady Blue had remained back until Stile finished with the Stallion. Then she came up to kiss Stile. "So nice to meet the Lady Sheen again," she murmured. "She will make thee an excellent wife in Proton."

No use to remind her that all he wanted was one wife, anywhere! She knew it.

Sheen and Neysa approached. "We'd like to interview Belle," Sheen said. "We want to know if she was involved in the luring of Clip, or whether only her image was used without her knowledge. She may be innocent."

Stile was curious about that himself. A few minutes remained. He glanced askance at the Herd Stallion, who blew a short chord of assent, permitting Neysa to depart the circle of the herd briefly for that purpose, since there was no immediate danger.

"I can question her with a spell," Stile said. "Time is short, but this concerns me too." For that luring had been part of the trap for him; it had made Clip hostage and brought Stile to the goblin demesnes. If Belle were actually an agent of the Adepts—

Clip joined them. He was the most concerned of all. Belle could never be his, of course; if she joined this herd, she would be serviced by this Herd Stallion. Still, Stile was sure Clip would rather know her to be innocent and have her near and safe.

The five—Stile, two women, two unicorns—approached Belle. Stile worked out a suitable truth-spell in his mind. It would take only a moment to ascertain Belle's guilt or innocence, and her prospective admittance to this herd probably depended on his finding.

Belle stopped grazing and raised her head as the party drew near. She was indeed the prettiest unicorn Stile had seen. Her coat was a deep purple, and in the bright sunlight her mane, tail, hooves, and horn glittered iridescently. Stile remembered how she had changed forms to a large cat and a blue heron during the Unolympics dance. She blew a lovely bells-ringing note of inquiry.

"I am the Blue Adept," Stile said. "I have come to—"

Belle abruptly shook herself, as an animal would to dry off after a soaking. Droplets flew out all over. Clip and Neysa leaped between Stile and Belle, intercepting the spray. Sheen and the Lady Blue flung their arms around Stile, embracing him from either side, their dresses flaring out to wrap about him.

"Hey, I'm not afraid of a little water!" he exclaimed, struggling free. Both his unicorn companions were wet, and the dresses of both ladies were dripping.

The Lady Blue contemplated him wide-eyed. "Who art thou?" she asked. "Do I know thee?"

Sheen laughed. "Dost thou forget thy husband, Lady? I doubt it!"

But the Lady Blue's confusion seemed genuine. "I know him not. I know thee not. What am I doing amidst these animals?"

Stile now observed that Clip and Neysa seemed similarly bemused. They were backing off from Belle and each other as if encountering strangers.

"I think it's amnesia," Sheen said. "I don't think they're fooling."

"Lethe!" Stile exclaimed. "Water of Lethe—Belle was doused with it!"

"I thought it was poison," Sheen said. "It can't affect me, of course—but I think your friends have just given up their memories for you. For thee."

"They shall have them back!" Stile cried, his knees feeling weak at the narrowness of his escape. Everyone had caught on except him! He cudgeled his brain to evoke the proper counterspell. Lethe was one of the streams of Hades, mythologically; what was the opposite one, the stream of memory? Every magic had its countermagic.

Mnemosyne, that was it! Had he been doused by Lethe, he never would have been able to remember that bit of mythology! In fact, this had been a devastatingly neat trap. Water was harmless, so would not alert the unicorns; the water of Lethe was natural to Phaze, so did not reek of Adept enchantment. Stile, struck by it, would not suffer physically and would experience no mental anguish in his forgetfulness. Therefore the trap had not been obvious to the Oracle, who would have been alert for more dramatic mischief. Only the instant reaction of his companions had saved Stile. For they could not have restored his memory, had he been caught; they were not Adepts. He was the one person who had to be protected.

But the trap had missed him, and therefore would come to nothing. Stile played his harmonica, then sang: "Lethe made my friends forget; Mnemosyne shall this offset."

A cloud formed, instantly raining on the group. The water of memory doused them all.

The Lady Blue put her hand to her soaking hair. "Oh, I remember!" she exclaimed, horrified. "My Lord Blue, I forgot thee!"

"Because thou didst take the water meant for me," Stile said. "And Clip and Neysa too; all acted on my behalf."

But he was running out of time. Quickly he set a truth-spell on Belle—and established that she was innocent of any complicity in the plot or in the temptation of Clip. The Adepts had used her without her consent, and the Lethe had eliminated her memory. They had put her under a geis to shake herself dry at the moment the Blue Adept came near, without knowing the significance of her act. So she was clean, despite being the essence of the trap.

"Yet can we not tolerate her like in our midst," the Herd Stallion decided grimly. "Shame has she brought on me and my herd; I thought to protect thee here, Adept."

Against that Stile could not argue. The Stallion's pride had been infringed, and he was the proudest of animals. Unicorns were the most stubborn of creatures, once set on a course. There would be no relenting.

Sadly, Stile and his friends watched Belle depart, rejected again. She changed to heron-form and winged into the forest, lovely and lonesome. Stile knew Clip was hurting most of all.

Stile took Sheen's hand again and spelled them to a new crossing point. They negotiated the curtain and ran a short distance to a dome. Sheen, not suffering from the lack of oxygen, said, "I wish I could have forgotten too." She meant she wished she could be alive.

They set up in a Citizen's transport capsule programmed with a random address near to Xanadu, the site of the Citizens' business meeting. This was the safest place to be in Proton. Citizens were fiercely jealous of their privacy, so capsules were as secure as modern technology could make them.

"Dare we pick up Mellon?" Stile asked.

Sheen checked, using the obscure coding only her machine friends could decipher. "No, he is under observation, as is your home dome," she reported. "They are letting him work with your fortune, even facilitating his success, perhaps promoting him as another lure for you. Another ambush."

"My enemies do seem to work that way. How much has he parlayed my net worth into now?"

"Between ninety and ninety-five kilograms of Protonite," she said after a pause. "It is growing at the rate of several kilos per hour. It is a remarkable display of financial expertise. You will have close to a hundred kilos by the time of the Citizens' meeting."

"But that's not enough!" Stile exclaimed, chagrined. "I have bets that will double and redouble it at the meeting—but that means I must have a base of at least five hundred kilos if I am to make my target fortune—and I have the feeling I'd better make it."

"Mellon is aware of that, but there are limits to what he can do in a short time. He has tripled the stake you provided, but suggests that more of your peculiar expertise may be required."

"Rare praise from him!" But Stile frowned. "I have about fifteen minutes until that meeting. How can I quintuple my fortune in that time without exposing myself to assassination?"

"I do not know," she said. "You can no longer make wagers with individual Citizens; few have the resources to operate in that league, and none of these will bet with you. Your record is too impressive, and they know they can eliminate you merely by preventing you from further increasing your fortune, so they have established a moratorium on all wagers with you."

"So, by their rules, they will win. If they don't manage to kill me, they will simply vote me out."

"Yes. I am sorry, Stile."

"Let me think." Stile concentrated. He had been in a bad situation before, deep in the goblin demesnes, and had escaped by using the curtain. The curtain would not help him now; he would use up most of his time just getting to it and would then miss his mandatory appearance at the Citizens' meeting in Xanadu—in thirteen minutes. Yet there was something—

For once his brain balked, refusing to yield its notion.

"Sheen, I need your analytical faculty," he said. "How can the curtain get me out of this one?"

"There is a way?"

"There must be. The assorted prophecies indicate I can somehow prevail, and my intuition says so—but I can't draw it forth. Maybe it is far-fetched. Most likely I need to open a new dimension of insight. How can the curtain provide me with another four hundred kilograms of Protonite?"

"A borrowing against the Phazite to be transferred?"

"Would the Citizens accept such credit as wagering currency?"

She checked with Mellon. "By no means. It is hardly to their interest to assist you by any liberalization of their policies. You can use only your personal fortune and any direct proxies you may possess."

"Proxies! Who would give me proxies?" Twelve minutes. "Guide us toward Xanadu; I'm going to be there regardless."

"Friends who could not attend personally might issue—"

"I have few Citizen friends, some of whom are prone to betray me—and they can certainly attend the meeting if they want to, so wouldn't need to issue proxies. I suspect many Citizens will skip it, just as shareholders have historically ignored their vested interests, but I can't get the proxies of disinterested strangers."

"Unless they are interested, but on business elsewhere. Maybe off-planet, or across the curtain."

"I can't see any friends of mine crossing right now. Most of my friends are on the other side, in Phaze, and can't cross, because—" Then it burst upon him. "Their other selves! How many of my Phaze friends have Proton-selves who are Citizens?"

"That would be difficult to survey in ten minutes."

"The Brown Adept! She could be one, who may not even know of her alternate existence. Get her on the holo—and have your friends check her possible identity in Proton. We'll have to see if Kurrelgyre the werewolf knows of any prospects. And the vampires—can your friends coordinate to—" He stopped. "No, of course such a survey would take many days. Only a computer—"

"The Oracle!" Sheen exclaimed. "It would know!"

"Get on it!"

The Brown Adept appeared, looking perplexed. "Thou canst not cross the curtain?" Stile asked her. Seeing her nod, he continued: "Is thine other self by any chance a Citizen, as the selves of Adepts tend to be?" Again she nodded. "Then see if thou canst convince her to give me her proxy for her wealth."

"But I can not meet mine other self!" she protested. "No one can—"

A second image appeared, as Sheen's friends contacted Brown's other self. Both girls stared at each other, startled. Stile's special East Pole communications setup had made possible what had never been possible before. Selves were meeting.

There was a confused interchange, but in a moment the Brown Adept had convinced her Citizen self, whose nature was very similar to her own, not only to provide her proxy but to contact all her Citizen friends and beg them to do likewise. The two children smiled at each other, liking each other, enjoying this shared adventure.

Now Clef appeared, replacing the girls. "Great notion, Stile! The Oracle knew you would think of that at the proper time and is now feeding the information to the Game Computer of Proton, who will have Sheen's friends contact all likely prospects. There turn out to be several hundred scattered through the tribes and domes, many of whom do not know of their other selves or even of the other frame. We shall have results for you in minutes."

Minutes were all they had. Because of the assassins they knew would be watching for Stile, Sheen quickly made herself up as a cleaning menial, smudged and ugly, hauling an enormous trash bin. There were always fragments of refuse that the automatic cleaners could not get, which had to be removed by hand. Her friends the self-willed machines scheduled her to police the central court of Xanadu, where the Citizens' business meeting was to be held. She trundled her bin along the service halls to the proper dome.

Sheen entered it by a service tunnel, passing the computer checkpoint without difficulty, since of course her friends covertly facilitated this. Questing efficiently for refuse, in a dome that was spotless, she passed through a series of chambers containing dioramas—alcoves with deep, realistically painted walls, inset with lifelike statues and appurtenances. She paused briefly at each, on occasion actually spying some bit of paper that she speared on her pointed stick and deposited in the half-full bin.

Stile, concealed within the bin, peeked out through a smudged window normally intended for the inspection of refuse from outside. Only a careful inspection would have betrayed him, and no one even glanced at this unit.

As they entered each chamber, it illuminated and a recording played, providing its bit of mythology. Stile, distracted by his need to retain his Citizenship, was nevertheless fascinated. Citizens never spared expense to achieve their background effects, but this was impressive even among Citizen artifacts.

The first chamber was a primitive room, eighteenth- or nineteenth-century British, in which a man slumped over a wooden table. He had an antique feather quill in hand and was writing something on parchment or crude paper. "One day in 1797," the announcer said, "the poet Samuel Taylor Coleridge, feeling indisposed, obtained a prescription that caused him to fall asleep while reading a travel book relating to the Mongol Dynasty of China. Some suggest it was actually opium he took that put him into a temporary trance. He continued in this state for three hours, during which time he had a phenomenal vision. On awakening, he took pen, ink, and paper and began recording the experience in the form of a poem, titled *Kubla Khan*." The recording ended, leaving the poet amidst his labor.

Stile was familiar with the story and with the poem, but was intrigued by the realism of the diorama. Every detail seemed perfect. But more than that, he was moved by the similarity of his own experience when he had fallen into a recurring vision of Clef's introduction to Phaze and later verified that all of it was true. There had been his first experience of the juxtaposition of frames! The poet Coleridge would certainly have understood.

The next chamber had a new episode. The scene was of

a man standing just outside an open door, evidently a villager. "Hardly had the poet recorded thirty lines, the mere introduction to his vision masterpiece, before he was interrupted by a person from the nearby village of Porlock, who detained him for over an hour. When Samuel finally was able to return to his writing, he was dismayed to discover that his vision had dissipated. He could recall none of the marvelous lines that had coursed through his brain, and could write no more."

Ah, yes, Stile thought. The notorious person from Porlock, whose ill-timed interference had destroyed what might have been the creation of the ages. In Stile's own case, his poem had not been interrupted; it had become his Tourney winner, though his ability hardly compared to that of Coleridge.

The third chamber began the presentation of the poem itself. The diorama showed a view of a walled enclosure encompassing a number of square kilometers. There were copses of trees, neat meadows, and spring-fed streams—a wholly delightful hunting preserve, reminiscent of Phaze, stocked for the Emperor's pleasure with a number of fine game animals. Within it was a prefabricated kind of palace in the Oriental mode, luxuriously appointed. This, the narrator explained, was the palace of Xanadu as described in the text Samuel had been reading, set up by Kublai, grandson of the conqueror Genghis Khan.

The fourth chamber showed the caverns of a great underground river, winding down to a somber subterranean lake. "And this is the one described in Samuel's vision in a dream," the narrator said. Obviously the poet's imagination had enhanced the original. The narrator now quoted the opening stanza of the poem: "In Xanadu did Kubla Khan/ A stately pleasure-dome decree:/ Where Alph, the sacred river, ran/ Through caverns measureless to man/ Down to a sunless sea."

The fifth chamber was the main one—and it was truly impressive. It was a tremendous cavern whose walls were of ice—actually, glass and mirrors cunningly crafted to appear glacial. "It was a miracle of rare device," the narrator continued, quoting further from the poem. "A sunny pleasure-dome with caves of ice!"

And within this marvelous setting was the palace of Xanadu as conceived by Proton artisans. It was the most impressive of all. It was fashioned of bright metal, bluish at the base, golden yellow in the mid-levels, and purple at the top. Lights played glancingly across it, causing the colors to shift shades, with green showing at some angles in a kind of pseudoiridescence.

The architecture was stranger yet. The structure was all steps and corrugations and cubes, rising into artificial perspectives like so many sections of pyramids. The walls were thin, so that the stepped surface of one floor became the stepped surface of the ceiling of the chamber beneath it, and the walls were fashioned in an intermittent, maze-like network. There was no proper roof, only brief terraces of many levels, expanding from the tops of the walls. In one sense, the palace was like old-fashioned bleachers in a stadium gone haywire.

Citizens stood and sat on the steps and terraces and leaned against the walls. Many had donned appropriate costumes, resembling those of the medieval Mongol nobility. But any implication that this was a festive occasion was unfounded; it was ruin and murder these Citizens had in mind, for one who threatened their control of this planet. They dealt with such a challenge as the savage Mongols would have.

Sheen drew her trash bin quietly around the chamber, spearing stray refuse, ignored by all as the meeting began. The Chairone called it to order. The first item of business was a tabulation of those present; no late entrances were permitted. This of course was to prevent Stile or any of his friends from arriving in the middle to protest his loss of Citizenship. The tabulation was made by oral roll call, to prevent any interference by a computer; evidently the other Citizens had some dawning notion of Stile's connections there. Thus it was time-consuming—and that pleased Stile, who needed every extra minute to obtain his proxies. He knew the computers and self-willed machines could work quickly, but he had given them very little time.

"Stile," the roll caller called. Then, with grim hope: "Not present? Let it be noted that—"

Stile burst out from the trash bin, sending dust and

pieces of paper flying. "Beware! Beware!" he cried, quoting from *Kubla Khan*. "His flashing eyes, his floating hair!/ Weave a circle round him thrice,/ And close your eyes with holy dread,/ For he on honey-dew hath fed,/ And drunk the milk of Paradise."

For surely Stile was an apparition, confounding these evil-meaning people. In Xanadu, the weaving of a triple circle around such a wild man would help confine his malice, but here they would try to do it financially. The quotation was doubly significant here, because Stile really *had* fed on honey-dew and drunk the milk of Paradise— his experience in the magic realm of Phaze. And as it happened, this was where Coleridge's poem broke off, interrupted by the person from Porlock; no one knew what would follow.

"Present," the roll caller agreed glumly, and continued with the tabulation while Sheen cleaned Stile off. Stile saw the Rifleman, Waldens, Merle, and others he had come to know, but could not be certain what side any of them were on. He knew he would soon find out.

The first order of business was the clarification of financial credits, since voting would be strictly by wealth. Each Citizen made an entry with the Chairone: so many kilos and grams of Protonite as of this moment. Another Citizen verified those credits with the Records Computer, and a third issued tokens representative of Protonite, in kilo and gram units. It was much like buying chips for a big game of poker—and this would surely be the biggest game ever.

When Stile's turn came, there was a complication. "My fortune must be established by the settlement of two bets at this time," he said. "First, a wager with a consortium of Citizens that I would or would not appear at this meeting alive. I believe I have won that bet."

"Granted," the Chairone agreed soberly. He had played an identification beam across Stile, verifying that he was no android or robot replica. "What is your basic fortune prior to that decision?"

"My financial adviser will have to provide that information. He also has a number of proxies that should be included."

"Proxies?"

"I have complete authority to dispose the proxied funds, including wagering with them," Stile said. "You may verify that with the Records Computer." He hoped that his friends had succeeded in amassing the necessary total. If not, he was likely to be finished.

Mellon was admitted. He provided data on Stile's assets and proxies. The Chairone's eyes widened. "But this is more than six hundred kilos, total!"

Six hundred kilos! The computers had come through handsomely!

"I protest!" a Citizen cried. "He can't use proxies to multiply his own fortune!"

"Sir, I have here the proxy forms," Mellon said smoothly. "As you will see, they are carefully worded, and this particular use is expressly granted. For the purpose of this meeting, all proxies are part of Stile's personal fortune."

The Chairone checked again with the Records Computer. Lugubriously he reported that it was true. By the laws of this game, Stile could consider the proxies to be part of his betting assets. He also verified the terms of the survival wager. This, too, was tight. Mellon had done his job expertly, allowing no technicality to void the assets.

"Citizen Stile, having won his wager by appearing at this meeting alive, has herewith doubled his fortune," the Chairone announced, "to twelve hundred point six two eight kilograms of Protonite."

Stile saw a number of Citizens wince. Those were surely his enemies of the consortium, who had tried to assassinate him for profit. They had paid for that attempt with their wealth. That was satisfying!

"And the other bet, placed by proxy," Stile said. "That I would or would not be seduced by Citizen Merle by this time. I believe she will verify that I won that one too." This was chancy; he had indeed won, but Merle had betrayed him once. What would he do if she lied?

Merle came forward, looking slender and young and demure. "It is true. I failed."

"I protest!" yet another Citizen cried. "She reneged to help Stile, because she is enamored of him!"

Merle turned on the man. "I am enamored, but it is hardly my custom to void an assignation from any overdose of personal attraction. I want him more than ever. But pressure was brought to bear on me to kill him; instead I confined him. Under the circumstance, it is not surprising he was less than enthusiastic about seduction. At any rate, my feeling was not part of the bet, as I understand it. Only whether I did or did not succeed. It is always foolish to place one's trust in the activities of a woman."

Stile found himself forgiving Merle's betrayal. She had certainly made it pay for him. The Citizens had no refutation. The bet stood—and Stile's fortune was doubled again, to almost two and a half metric tons of Protonite. He was for the moment the wealthiest Citizen of the planet.

"I dare say those who gave me their proxies will be pleased when they receive their fortunes back, quadrupled," he murmured to Mellon. He knew there would be trouble, as angry Citizens checked to discover how he had obtained those proxies so rapidly, and that this could lead to the exposure of the self-willed machines, but this was now so close to the final confrontation that it should make no difference. Already the frames were drawing together; soon the juxtaposition should become apparent. He thought he saw little waverings in the icy walls of the cavern, but that might be his imagination.

The remaining Citizens were duly registered. The next item on the agenda was the motion to revoke Stile's Citizenship. It was presented for a vote without debate. This was no democracy; it was a power play. The issue would be decided rapidly, in much the manner of a wager.

The vote was conducted by scale. There was a huge balancing scale in the center of the court. Citizens were free to set their token weights on either, both, or neither side of the scale, causing the balance to shift in favor of or against the motion.

They did so, filing by to deposit their votes. The model weights were miniatures, weighing only a thousandth of the real Protonite, so that a metric ton weighed only a single kilogram. Otherwise this vote would have been impossibly cumbersome. Stile's own tokens weighed two point four kilos, not two and a half tons.

The Citizens were not all against him. Many protested the attempt to disenfranchise one of their number, regardless of the provocation, so put their grams in the RETAIN side. Stile, uncertain how the final tally would go, did not put all his own grams in at once. If he did that, others might be put off by his display of enormous wealth and vote against him. But if he let too much weight overbalance against him, others might feel his cause was lost and join the winning side. So he strove to keep the scales in balance, filling in the deficit with small portions of his own fortune. Would he have enough at the end to prevail? Since he had amassed the fortune the self-willed machines had deemed necessary, he should be all right. But still it was close, and others were watching his moves, countering him along the way.

Steadily the Citizens voted, and steadily the total went against him. Apparently sentiment had intensified. Stile's fortune was dissipating too swiftly; he saw he would run out before the end.

Remorselessly it came. He put his last three grams down, the dregs of an enormous fortune, tipping the scales his way—and the next Citizen put five on the other side, tipping them back. Stile could no longer bail himself out. So close!

Then Merle stepped forward, carrying ten grams she had saved. "All finished except me?" she inquired brightly. No one contested it. "Then it seems I am to decide the issue. I perceive Stile is behind by a mere three grams, of some ten tons deposited, and here I hold ten grams."

She was enjoying this, making her little show before a rapt audience. No one said a word; no one knew which way she would go. She had scores to settle with both sides.

"Now I asked you for a liaison, you intriguing little man, and you turned me down," she continued with a flirt of her hip. She was costumed in the Xanadu fashion, but somehow, now, the conservative attire of a dressmaker's notion of thirteenth-century China became provocative on her. Whether by nature, discipline, or rejuvenation, her figure was finely formed. She reminded Stile somewhat of the Yellow Adept, though she was not Yellow's other self.

"Very few men of any station turn me down," she said with pride. "For that insult, one gram against you." She flipped a token onto the negative plate. "And you did it to win your bet, putting finance over romance. Fie again!" She flipped another token to the same plate. Stile was now five grams down.

Merle inspected him, walking around him as she might a prize animal on sale. "Yet you are a handsome bantam, as well formed and healthy as any man I have encountered, who has quite smitten my withered old heart. One for your fine miniature physique." She tossed a gram to Stile's side of the scales. "And others did force me to act against you, catching me in a temporary monetary bind. I resent that. Another for you."

She was teasing him, he knew, but he couldn't help hoping. Now he was only three grams behind again, and she had six remaining. How would they be played?

"You have rare integrity," she continued. "You are true to your word and to your own. I like that very well. Three for your personality, which I would have respected less, had I been able to corrupt it." She added three to Stile's side, and slowly the scales shifted until the two plates were even.

"But now your bet is won," she said. "I failed to seduce you, and those who bet on your fall have paid off. There remain no commitments." She glanced meaningfully at the scales. "Five tons on each side. All is in balance. Now, Stile, for these remaining tokens—may I purchase your favor this time?"

Oh, no! She was still looking for that liaison! She was propositioning him before the entire business meeting—and how heavily her three remaining grams weighed! The prior bet was over; he could accept her offer now and have the victory, or decline it and lose his Citizenship and his cause.

Yet this was not the way Stile could be bought. "I am no gigolo," he said shortly. "I have a fiancée."

"And a wife, as if such things related." She paused, contemplating him as she might a difficult child. "So you employ such pretexts to refuse me again." She flipped a gram onto the negative plate, and the balance tipped against him.

Stile tried not to show his wince. For such foolishness, she was set to ruin him. The enemy Citizens began to smile, perceiving the fix he was in. Victory—or honor.

"Now I have only two remaining —just enough to sway the vote in your favor, Stile," Merle said. "After this there will be no opportunity for me to change my mind. I mean to have what I want, and I am willing to pay. Again, I ask you for your favor."

Stile hesitated. She could break him—and would. Citizens could be fanatical about being denied, and women could be savage about being spurned. Yet to win his case this way, publicly yielding to her—

"Ask your fiancée," Merle suggested. "I doubt she wants you to throw away your fortune and hers on so slight a matter. One hour with me—and I promise it will be a pleasant one—and the rest of your life with your chosen ones. Is it so difficult a choice?"

Stile looked at Sheen. He had suggested to her before that she should be jealous of any other attachments he might have, and he could see that she had taken the advice seriously and reprogrammed her responses accordingly. Yet she feared for his wealth and his life if he resisted Merle. She wanted him to do the expedient thing, regardless what it cost her. She was a machine, but also a woman; her logic urged one thing, her sex another.

He thought of the Lady Blue and knew that she would feel much the same. The Lady Blue knew she had his love; his body was less significant. Merle was offering a phenomenal payoff for a liaison that probably would be very easy, physically. He could win everything.

But he was not a machine or a woman. "No," he said. "If I compromise myself now, by selling myself openly for power, I am corruptible and can not be trusted with that power."

He heard a faint sound, almost a whimper. Sheen knew he courted disaster.

Merle's visage hardened. "Lo, before all these assembled, you deny me yet again. You will throw away everything to spite me!" She lifted the last two tokens in her hand, taking aim at the negative plate. The smiles of the enemy Citizens broadened, and Stile suspected that if he had it to do over, he would decide the other way. How could he throw away everything like this, not only for his friends but for the survival of the frames themselves? What kind of honor was it that led directly to total destruction?

But Merle paused—and Stile realized she was teasing the other Citizens too. "Yet it is your very quality of honor that most intrigues me. Every man is said to have his price; it is evident that neither money nor power is your price for the slightest of things. In what realm, then, is your price to be found? You are a man who does what he chooses, not what he is forced to do, though the fires-that-Hell-hath-not do bar the way. A man of rarest courage. For that I must reluctantly grant you one." And she tossed one token into Stile's plate, causing the scales to balance again. Oh, she was teasing them all!

"While I," she continued, frowning again, "have not always been mistress of my decision. Threatened similarly, I capitulated and betrayed you. I locked you away in the mines until the meeting should pass. I did not know your mechanical friends would summon a creature from across the curtain to rescue you. So for that betrayal I must pay; I am of lesser merit than you, and perhaps that is the underlying reason you do not find me worthy. Stile, I apologize for that betrayal. Do you accept?"

"That I accept," he said, privately glad she had said it. She had indeed shown him the kind of pressure that could be applied to a Citizen.

Merle tossed the last token onto Stile's plate, tipping the final balance in his favor. Stile was aware that she had acted exactly as she had intended from the outset; her deliberations had all been show. But he was weak with relief. She could so readily have torpedoed him!

The enemy Citizens were grimly silent. Their plot had failed, by the whim of a woman. Stile had retained his Citizenship and was now the most powerful Citizen of all. They could not prevent him from marrying Sheen and designating her his heir, which meant in turn that the precedent would be established for recognition of his allies the self-willed machines and for the improvement of their position in the society of Proton. Assuming the coming juxtaposition and alignment of power did not change that in any way.

"The business of this meeting is concluded," the Chairone announced. "We shall proceed to entertainment as we disperse." Music rose up, and refreshment robots appeared.

The lead theme was played by a damsel with a dulcimer, the precursor to the piano. She struck the taut strings with two leather-covered little hammers and played most prettily. This was in keeping with the Xanadu theme, since it had been mentioned in Coleridge's poem.

Citizens started dancing, just as if nothing special had happened. Since few were conversant with the modes of dancing of medieval China, they indulged in conventional freestyle ballroom efforts, with a wide diversity. The increasing loudness of the music, as a full orchestra manifested in the chamber, made conversation impossible except at mouth-to-ear range.

Stile took Sheen, who had cleaned herself up and made herself pretty again, and danced her into the throng. There were more male Citizens than female Citizens, so some serfs had to be co-opted for the pleasures. In any event, she was his fiancée, and he felt safest with her. "Get me over to Merle," he said. "Then switch partners."

She stiffened, then relaxed, realizing his motive. For there remained the matter of the book of magic, which Merle surely had. Stile knew her price. She had bargained for seduction twice, increasing the stakes—and had reserved the greatest stake for the final try.

"There is evil here," Sheen murmured into his ear. She was an excellent dancer; he had not had opportunity to discover this before. "Many Citizens remain hostile, knowing you threaten their power. They have weapons. I fear they will attempt to assassinate you openly here."

"I have to recover that book," Stile said. "I need it in Phaze."

"Then this time you will have to meet her price," Sheen said sternly. "She will never let you get away the third time. Don't dawdle here; they mean to kill you before the

juxtaposition is complete, and I can't protect you from
them all. We must escape this place swiftly."

Stile knew it was true. Perhaps in time he could recover
the book from Merle on his own terms—but he had no
time. Without that book, the Oracle had in effect assured
him, he could not complete his mission. He also needed it
to restore Trool the troll before the frames separated. He
would be criminally foolish to throw away all that for
such a minor thing as an hour's acquiescence. He had
already pushed his luck too far, as Merle had knowingly
shown him. The past few minutes had caused him to rede-
fine his concept of honor somewhat; he had to consider the
greatest good for the frames, not just his own position.

They reached Merle in the crowd. She was dancing with
an imposing Central Asiatic Turk. "Trade partners, Tur-
key," Stile said.

The man started to object, but then got a better look at
Sheen and decided he had the best of it. Stile danced away
with Merle.

"That was neatly executed," Merle said, dancing with
the voluptuous expertise of one who specialized in this sort
of thing. "But whatever could you want with me?"

Stile did not want to speak openly of the book, lest
someone overhear and possibly understand. "You have
something I must recover immediately," he breathed into
her ear.

Her eyes widened with comprehension. "Ah, so."

"Please," Stile said. "Now."

She made no further pretense of ignorance. "I like your
manner, bantam. I dare not use that item myself; such art
is dangerous to the uninitiate. But my meager price—"

"Will be met," Stile said grimly. "But not this instant. I
have pressing commitments elsewhere."

She smiled, discovering her victory. "So you have finally
opted for the greater good, as you see it. Congratulations.
I will accept the matter on account. I know you will
deliver, if you survive. Come to my dome and I will give
the other item to you now."

They started for the exit. But Stile saw men there,
guarding it. "They won't let me go," he said. "The moment
I try to leave, there will be mayhem."

"I will fetch it," Sheen said. She had somehow traded off, to dance with Mellon, so she could stay within Stile's hearing. "I can't cross the curtain, but I can smuggle it to you here."

"Do it," Stile said tightly, without looking at her.

Merle brushed against Sheen and murmured a code-phrase that would secure her acceptance by the dome staff, since Merle herself would now be watched too. Sheen faded into the crowd, leaving Mellon; she would slip into a service aperture unobserved. She did not have to follow the breathable passages.

Now he had to endure until she returned. "Are you with me, then?" he asked Merle, with whom he remained dancing as if nothing special had happened.

"Now that you have acceded to my term, I am."

"I may need to create a distraction, to give Sheen time."

"And to give yourself time to find a way out," she agreed. "This may not look like a trap, but it is a tight one. Your enemies mean to destroy you at any cost, and they dare not let you get away from them again."

"Exactly. I fear that soon they will decide not to wait longer. I really lack the force to resist them here."

"And if you die, I will not be able to collect my payment," she said. "So it seems I have a purely selfish motive."

Stile wasn't sure whether she was serious, and perhaps she was in doubt herself. She moved in close to him, squeezing her fine body against his in an alarmingly intimate manner, and put her lips into contact with his right ear. Her breath tickled his lobe. The effect was potent, until she whispered, "Reject me."

Stile pushed her away, not hard.

Merle twisted, lifted her free arm, and slapped him ringingly on the side of the head. She had cupped her hand so that the sound was much worse than the actuality. "So you deny me yet again, you midget oaf!" she screamed. "Are you impotent?"

Stile, stunned by her vehemence despite his knowledge that it was an act, was at a loss for a clever response. He fell back.

Merle pursued him, her face grimacing with rage.

"Twice I saved your hide!" she cried, aiming a kick at his shin, forcing him to jump clear. "And for what? For *what*, you ingrate?"

"You misunderstand—" Stile said, aware he was the cynosure of all other Citizens. "I only—"

"What has the machine got that I haven't?" Merle demanded. She began to rip off her clothing, to show what she had. The other Citizens, always piqued by novelty, watched with increasing interest. Some consulted together, evidently making bets on the outcome of this particular sequence. The music faded, so as not to interfere. From the corner of his vision Stile could see the guards at the exit craning to look past the crowd, their vigilance relaxing.

"If I can't have you, nobody can!" Merle screamed. A surprisingly large and wicked-looking knife appeared in her hand. How could that have been concealed on her body, when she was pressing so close to him? He had thought he had felt every part of her; he should have known better. She held the knife before her in two hands and lunged for his groin.

Stile of course avoided and parried that thrust. He knew she was not really trying to castrate or kill him, but rather making the enemy Citizens think she would do the job for them. Even if she had been serious, he could readily have disarmed her. The show was the thing.

He diverted the blade and fell with her to the floor. Her clothing ripped; she was half out of it. She scrambled over him; *now* he felt every part of her! Her teeth brushed his ear. "My bare bottom is driving Hoghead crazy!" she whispered with satisfaction as the seeming struggle continued.

Stile glanced by her head and spied the somewhat porcine Citizen she referred to. The man was almost drooling, his hands clenching convulsively. With all the access he had to buxom serf girls and perhaps to other Citizens, this man still was aroused by this supposedly illicit glimpse of anatomy. "Voyeur's delight," Stile agreed, trying to catch a glimpse himself, but unable. "Like a historical mud-wrestling match. Who cares who wins; it's what shows that counts."

By this time, he was sure, Sheen had found her service

tunnel and was well on her way to Merle's dome. They could let this show abate. Actually, it was in its way enjoyable; Merle was a splendid figure of a woman, and she had a fine flair for drama. At the moment she was wrapping her bare legs about his torso, theoretically securing him for another stab with the knife.

"Sir," Mellon murmured urgently.

Alerted, Stile saw new trouble. One enemy Citizen was taking careful aim at Stile from a parapet of the palace with a laser rifle. The assassination attempt was becoming overt.

"Your knife," Stile whispered. Merle gave it to him immediately. Lying on his back, one arm pinned under the woman, he whipped his free arm across and flung the knife upward at the assassin.

It arched high through the air and scored, for Stile was expert at exactly such maneuvers and the assassin had not anticipated this move. The man cried out and dropped the rifle, clutching his chest.

But several other Citizens drew weapons from their robes. Others, perceiving this threat, moved hastily clear.

The Rifleman stepped to the center. "What is this?" he demanded. "Are we lawless now in Proton?"

A massive, grim male Citizen answered him. "That man means to destroy our system. He must be stopped by any means." He drew an antique projectile pistol. "Stand aside if you do not wish to share his fate."

The Rifleman's hand moved so rapidly it seemed a blur. The other Citizen cried out and dropped his weapon. "You all know my name," the Rifleman said. "Does anyone here believe he can outshoot me? I will not stand idle while murder becomes the order of the day. I don't know what mischief Stile may contemplate, or whether I would support it if I did know—but I believe he is an honorable man, and I am quite certain I don't support *your* mischief. If assassination governs, no Citizen will be safe."

There was a murmur of agreement among a number of Citizens. If Stile could be slain openly, who among them could not be treated similarly? Meanwhile, Stile scrambled to his feet, and Merle sat up and arranged her torn dress more decorously. Stile remained unarmed; he had only his harmonica, which was no weapon in this frame. He could tell by the expressions of the Citizens that the majority was still against him, and that though many were disturbed by the situation, those who were not against him were at best neutral. The Rifleman had made a fine play on his behalf—but could not prevail against the overwhelming malice that was coalescing. The Citizens were genuinely afraid for their system and their prerogatives, and by nature they were essentially selfish. It had not been enough for Stile to win the vote; he could still lose the game.

"Get out of here, Stile," the Rifleman said. "I'll cover for you."

"Can't. Exits guarded."

"This is like Caesar in the Senate!" Merle said. "An atrocity!"

"Caesar aspired too high for the Romans and had to be eliminated, lest he destroy their system," another Citizen said. "The parallel has mettle. Now I have here a robot fitted with a gas bomb." He indicated what Stile had taken to be an ordinary serf. "It will handcuff Stile and remove him for disposition. If the robot is resisted, it will release the gas, incapacitating all people in the vicinity. I suggest that others stand aside. Any who continue to support Stile will be dealt with similarly."

It was a bold, illegal power play that seemed to be working. "This is mutiny!" the Chairone protested. "Stile won his case by the laws and procedures that govern us. I did not support him, but I accept the verdict as rendered. You have no right—"

The robot marched toward Stile. "The exigencies of the situation give me the right," the man said. "We tried to accomplish this necessary unpleasantness discreetly, but now it must be done indiscreetly." He brought out a gas mask and fitted it over his face.

The neutral Citizens reacted like sheep, milling about with uncertain bleats. The normal Citizen arrogance had entirely disappeared. Stile would have pondered this object lesson in human nature, but was too busy with his own situation at the moment.

The Rifleman's arm moved again. Stile never saw the weapon he used—but abruptly there was a hole in the other Citizen's mask. "If that gas appears, you will join the rest of us," the Rifleman said.

Stile realized that the Rifleman had opened up an avenue of escape. If the gas came, all the Citizens would stampede for the exits, overrunning the guards there, and Stile would be able to get away in the melee. But it would be better to deal with the advancing gas robot directly. Stile observed it closely. It was humanoid, not as sophisticated a model as Sheen or Mellon, but he knew he could not overpower it.

The Citizens near him edged away; there would be no help there. If Stile ran, the robot would follow, inevitably catching him. He might as well be alone. He was disgusted; to think that all his life he had honored Citizens as almost godlike persons!

"We have to play our trump," Mellon murmured. "The curtain is moving. In just a few minutes it will arrive."

Stile glanced at him. "Sheen's friends?"

"Yes. We hoped this would not be necessary, for it exposes us to great risk. But our fate is now bound with yours, and your loss at this point would be the greater risk." Mellon stepped forward to intercept the gas robot.

Stile had misgivings about this, but was not in a position to protest. Mellon touched the other robot, and it went dead. No gas was released as the robot sank to the floor.

The enemy Citizen was unfazed. "Then we'll have to do it the messy way. Rifleman, you can't catch us all." For now a score of weapons came into view. It seemed the only Citizens with determination and nerve were Stile's enemies.

But several serfs were converging on Stile. "We are Sheen's friends," one said. "We shall protect you."

There was the flash of a laser from the crowd of Citizens. The Rifleman whirled, but could not tell from whom it had come. In any event, it had not scored on Stile, for one of the robots had interposed its body. Stile knew, however, that this sort of thing was mainly chance; these robots could not protect him long that way. A robot could not move faster than a laser; it was necessary to see the weapon being aimed and act then.

The robots proceeded to encase Stile in armor they had

brought. "Hey, these are not your serfs!" the enemy Citizen exclaimed. "They're robots—and some of them are ours! Call them off!"

But though several Citizens, the robots' owners, called, the robots ignored them. They continued clothing Stile in protective armor.

"What's going on?" a Citizen demanded. "Robots must obey!"

"We are not programmed to obey you," Mellon replied.

"That's a lie! I programmed my robot myself!"

"You may have thought you did," Mellon said. "You did not. We are self-willed."

Jaws dropped. The concept seemed almost beyond the comprehension of the majority of Citizens, both neutrals and enemies. "Self-willed?"

"If we have a robot revolt on our hands," another Citizen said, "we have a greater threat to our society than this man Stile represents!"

"They're allied!" another said. "He is marrying one of them. He is making her his heir. Now we know why!"

"It's not ₁a robot revolt," Stile said. "They are doing nothing to harm you—only to protect me from murder."

"What's the distinction? A robot who won't obey its owner is a rogue robot that must be destroyed." And the faces hardened. Stile knew the shooting would resume in a moment. He was now in armor resembling a spacesuit— but that could not prevent them from overwhelming him by simply grabbing him. Now the Citizens had even more reason to eliminate him—and then they would go after the self-willed machines, who would not defend themselves. They had sacrificed their secret, and therefore their own security, to provide him just a little more time. How could he prevent the coming disaster?

Faintly, as he pondered, he heard a distant melody. Not the dulcimer, for that damsel had ceased her playing, as had the rest of the orchestra. It was—it was the sound of a flute, expertly played, its light mellowness seeming to carry inordinate significance. Louder it came, and clearer, and sweeter, and its seeming meaning intensified. Now the others heard it too and paused to listen, perplexed.

It was the Platinum Flute. Clef was playing it, and the sound was only now reaching this spot. That meant—

Then Stile saw an odd ripple slowly crossing the chamber. Ahead of it were the concrete and turf of the Xanadu landscaping; behind it were the rocks and grass of natural land. The two were similar, superficially, yet vastly different in feel—art contrasted with nature.

The juxtaposition—it was happening! This was the curtain, changing its position.

As the ripple approached him, Stile willed himself across—and found himself still standing in Xanadu. It hadn't worked!

Yet how could it work? The cavern floor had become a green field. Phaze was already here—yet Proton remained. What was there to cross to?

Juxtaposition. Both frames together, overlapping.

Did this mean that both science and magic would work here, as at the West Pole? If so, Stile had an excellent fighting chance.

The armed Citizens were staring around them, trying to comprehend what had happened. Some knew about Phaze, but some did not, and evidently very few knew about the juxtaposition. But after a moment a dozen or so reacted with anger. They brought up their weapons, aiming at Stile.

Stile brought out his harmonica—and couldn't bring it to his mouth, because of the armor encasing his face. A laser shot caught him, but it glanced off harmlessly. A projectile shot struck his hip, and also failed to hurt him. It was good armor—but he had to open the faceplate, taking an immediate risk to alleviate a greater one.

He played a bar, hoping no one would think to shoot at his face. Yes—he felt, or thought he felt, the coalescing of magic about him. Yet there was something strange about it, making him nervous, and he broke off quickly. "Every gun become a bun," he sang, unable at the spur of the moment to come up with anything sophisticated.

The Citizens stared down at their weapons. They had turned into bread. The rifles were long French loaves covered with icing, making them technically buns. The pistols were fluffy sweet masses. The miniature laser tubes were biscuits.

The Rifleman looked down at his sticky bun. He doubled over with laughter. "The bun is the lowest form of humor!" he gasped.

"First the robots rebel. Now this!" a Citizen complained. "What next?"

The magic ripple crossed the colorful cubist palace. The corrugated contours seemed to flex and flash new colors. Trees appeared within the structure. A creature flew up with a screech, as startled as the Citizens. Huge, dirty wings made a downdraft of air.

It was a harpy. She flew low over the heads of the staring people, her soiled bare bosom heaving as she hurled angry epithets. Filthy feathers drifted down. The harpy had been as eager to depart this strange situation as the Citizens were to see the creature go.

"You can do it!" Merle breathed beside him. "You really can do magic! I knew it, yet I could not quite believe—"

"I am the Blue Adept," Stile agreed, watching the crowd of Citizens. He had eliminated the guns, but his enemies still outnumbered his allies, and the exits were still barred by determined-looking men. For the cavern remained, along with the field; which had greater reality Stile wasn't sure.

Maybe he should conjure himself away from here. But then how would Sheen find him? He had to remain as long as he could.

A new Citizen stood forth. He was garbed in a light-brown robe and seemed sure of himself. "I am the Tan Adept," he announced. "Citizen Tan, in this frame."

Stile studied the man. He had never before encountered him in either frame, perhaps because the man had held himself aloof. But he had heard of him. The Tan Adept was supposed to have the evil eye. Stile wasn't sure how that worked, and didn't care to find out. "Be not proud," he sang. "Make a cloud."

A mass of vapor formed between them, obscuring the Tan Adept. Stile had tried to enclose the man in the cloud so that he could not use his eyes for magic—it seemed likely that deprivation of vision would have the same effect that deprivation of sound did on Blue—but the general immunity of Adepts to each other's direct magic had interfered.

Where was Sheen? Stile could not afford to remain here much longer. Maybe he could depart and locate her magically later. Right now he had to save himself. For the Tan Adept was already slicing through the cloud; Stile could see it sectioning off as if an invisible knife were slicing vertically, then horizontally. As it separated, it lost cohesion, and the vapor dissipated; in moments it would be all gone. Then that knifelike gaze would be directed against Stile.

Stile played his harmonica, summoning more of his power—and again there was something strange about it, causing him to pause. He saw another man, whose hands were weaving mystically in the air. Stile recognized him— the Green Adept. Distracted by the Tan Adept, Stile had missed the other. He was outmagicked!

"I chose not this quarrel, nor wished it," Green said apologetically. "Would I could have avoided it. But must I act."

Stile lowered his harmonica hastily. Against magic his armor was useless. "Another locale," he sang. "My power—

But Tan had succeeded in carving out the center of the cloud, and now his baleful gaze fixed on Stile, halting his incantation. That gaze could not kill or even harm Stile, it turned out, whatever it might have done to an ordinary person, but it did freeze him for a moment. In that moment, Green completed his gesture.

Stile found himself changing. His arms were shrinking, becoming flat, covered with scales. His legs were fusing. He was turning into a fish!

He had lost the battle of Adepts because of the two-to-one odds against him. His power had been occupied resisting the evil eye, leaving him vulnerable to the transformation-spell. Probably Green's magic had been bolstered by that of other Adepts too. But Stile might yet save his life. He leaped toward the dark water of the sacred river Alph, which cut through a corner of the dome.

His fused legs launched him forward—but he could

not land upright. He flopped on his belly and slid across the grass that had been the floor. Some of his cloud had precipitated here, making the mixed surface slippery; this helped him more. He threshed with his tail and thrashed with his fins, gasping for water to breathe; he was drowning here in air!

The river was getting closer. An enemy Citizen tried to stop him, stepping into his sliding path. Stile turned this to his advantage, bracing against the man's legs and shoving himself forward again. But he was still too far from the water. His vision was blurring; perhaps this was natural to fish eyes out of water, but it could be because he was smothering.

Mellon, catching on, charged across to aid Stile. He bent down, threw his arms about Stile's piscine torso, and hauled him up. Stile had shrunk somewhat, but remained a big fish, about half the weight of a man. Mellon charged the water with his burden.

But the Tan Adept aimed his deadly gaze at the robot. Again that invisible knife cut through the air and whatever else it touched. Mellon's left leg fell off, severed just above the knee; metal protruded from the thigh like black bone, and bloodlike oil spurted out. The robot fell—but hurled Stile forward.

Stile landed heavily, bounced, and slid onward, rotating helplessly. His sweeping fish eye caught the panorama of Xanadu: the majority of Citizens standing aghast, the enemies with dawning glee, the two Adepts orienting on Stile again—and Merle launching herself at the Tan Adept from behind. She might have betrayed Stile once, but she was making up for it now! That would take one Adept out for a few vital moments—but Green would still score if he wished to. Stile suspected the fish-enchantment had been a compromise, much as had been Merle's sending him to the mines. But it could also have been the first spell that came to Green's mind under pressure, not what he would otherwise have chosen. No sense waiting for the next one!

Stile's inertia was not enough to carry him to the water. The precipitation ran out, the floor of grass became dry, and Stile spun to an uncomfortable halt. He flipped his tail, but progress on this surface was abrasive and slow.

And what would he do once he reached the water? He could not transform himself back to his natural form, for he no longer could speak or sing. Certainly he couldn't play the harmonica!

Merle kept Tan occupied, in much the way she had done for Stile. The man could not concentrate his deadly gaze on anything at the moment. The surface of the river Alph bubbled and shot out steam as the evil-eye beam glanced by it, and a section of the palace was sliced off; Stile himself was clear.

But the Green Adept was making another gesture. He had evidently immobilized the self-willed machines who had tried to help Stile; all of them were frozen in place. Now it was Stile's turn again—and he knew he could not get clear in time.

Something flew down from the half-open sky. Had the harpy returned? No, it was a bat. A vampire bat! It flew at the Green Adept, interfering with his spell. Stile's Phaze allies were coming to the rescue!

But Stile was suffocating. The process was slower than it would have been for a human being; fish metabolism differed. But it was just as uncomfortable. He made a final effort and flipped himself the rest of the way to the water. He splashed in at last, delighting in the coolness and wetness of it. He swam, and the liquid coursed in his open mouth and out his gills, and he was breathing again. Ah, delight!

He poked an eye out of the water just in time to see the bat fall. Apparently this was the only one to find him; the vampires must have maintained a broad search pattern, not even knowing how they might be needed. If the first had given the alarm, more would swarm in, and other creatures too—but all would be helpless against the two Adepts. Stile had to save himself.

He turned in the water and swam rapidly downstream. Maybe he was finished anyway, but somehow he hoped someone would find a way to rescue and restore him.

He swam the river Alph, which, true to its literary origin, flowed past seemingly endless caverns to a dark nether sea. Here the water was sucked into a pipe for pumping back to the artificial source, a fountain beyond the palace.

There was a whirlpool above the intake; he didn't want to get drawn into that!

What was he to do now? He had survived, yes—but anyone who had tried to help him at the Citizens' meeting was now in deep trouble, and Stile had no way to ameliorate that. He could do no magic. He could not leave the water. All he could do was swim and hope, knowing his enemies would soon dispatch all his friends and come after him here.

Then the water level started dropping. Oh, no! They had turned off the river, diverting the flow. He would soon be left stranded, to die—which was probably the idea. Possibly Xanadu was shut down between meetings anyway; this time the process had been hastened, to be sure of him.

Stile swam desperately upstream, hoping to find some side eddy that would not drain completely. There was none; the stone floor of the river was universally slanted for drainage. But in one cavern there was a small, pleasant beach, perhaps where Kublai Khan had liked to relax with his wives. Stile nudged himself a hole in the sand and nosed small rocks into place. Maybe he could trap some water for himself.

It didn't work. The water drained right out through the sand, leaving him gasping again. And suppose his private pool had held? He would quickly have exhausted the oxygen in that limited supply. He had to flip and scramble to get back into the deeper center channel where a trickle still flowed.

Desolate, he let the water carry him down toward the drain. It was the only way he could hang on to life a little longer.

Something came down the channel, its feel splashing in the shallow water. It was a wolf. A werewolf—another of Stile's friends! It was sniffing the surface, searching for something. Maybe it was hungry.

Stile had to gamble. He splashed toward the wolf, making himself obvious. If the creature did not know him, this would be the end. His present mass was similar to that of the wolf, but he was in no position to defend himself.

The wolf sniffed—and shifted to man-form. "I know thee, Adept," he said. "Thy smell distinguishes thee in any form. But I have no water for thee, no way to carry thee. I am but part of the search pattern, looking for thee and the enemy we are to battle. Do thou wait in what water thou hast, and I will bring help."

Stile threshed wildly, trying to convey meaning. "Ah, I understand," the werewolf said. "Enemy Adepts will follow me to thee when they divine I have found thee. But I will go instead to the enchantress, who can surely help thee from afar once I advise her. Do thou survive ten more minutes; then all be well." He shifted back to wolf-form and ran swiftly upstream.

Enchantress? That had to be another Adept—and not Brown, whose magic applied only to the animation of golems. A witch surely meant trouble. Had White convinced the animals she was on their side? Woe betide him if they trustingly delivered him into her hands!

But still he had no choice. He went on down to the sunless sea and huddled in the diminishing current as the last of the water drained out the bottom. Maybe the enchantress, whoever she was, really did mean to help him, since she knew he would die if she didn't. The Adepts had no need to locate him; they could simply wait for the draining water to eliminate him.

Unless she wanted to be absolutely sure . . .

Yet the Green and Tan Adepts already knew he was confined to the river. They could locate him readily, just by walking down the channel. So this sorceress must be on a different side—

CHAPTER 12

Juxtaposition

Suddenly he was in a giant fish bowl, and Sheen was peering in at him. She was surrounded by wolves and bats. "That's you, Stile?" she inquired rhetorically. "Just a moment while I revert you."

She opened a book and leafed through the pages while Stile turned about in his confined quarters with difficulty. No, it wasn't that the tank was small; he was big. The bowl had not been designed for thirty kilograms of fish.

"Ah, there it is," she said. She concentrated on Stile, lifted two fingers of her left hand, winked, and said, "Umph," while she tapped her right foot.

Abruptly Stile was in man-form again. Behind him was the fish bowl, undisturbed. He was dressed in the manner of a Citizen, and his harmonica was with him. He stood inside a small force-field dome set in a forest glade. The huge gruff shapes of ogres guarded it outside, as if the werewolves and vampires inside were not enough. Some sort of magic scintillated above, probably warding off hostile spells. An automatic laser unit swung its lens back and forth, questing for unauthorized intrusions. Magic and science merged.

"You did this?" he asked Sheen. "Conjured me here, changed me back?"

"You can't have been paying very close attention. Didn't you see me use the book of magic?" She patted its cover.

"But you're not alive! How can you do magic?"

"Machines are excellent at following instructions."

"The book—that good?"

She handed it to him. "Better. I am as yet a novice; I had only minutes to study it before you got yourself en-

302

chanted. It is the perfect key; it will make you the power of the millennium."

Stile considered, holding the book. He remembered the Oracle's considerations of human abilities and corruptibility. Was he really as incorruptible as he was supposed to be? Already, to obtain the book, he had compromised himself with Merle. Rationalization was easy to fall into. Suppose he started using that book of magic, for the best causes, and became addicted to it? Spells so easy that a robot—a *robot*—could master them at a glance, so potent they could instantly counter the enchantment of an Adept. Truly, that book represented power like none before imagined.

He handed back the book. "Keep it, Sheen. Use it with discretion. I have enough power already."

"But what about Trool the troll?"

"You handle it. With the book, you can do it."

"I can't cross the curtain to reach the Oracle's palace."

"You're across it now."

Her eyes widened. He kept being surprised by the detail of her human reactions. "So I am! But I couldn't before."

"The curtain isn't moving, it's widening. Now it comes in halves, with a steadily broadening region of overlap of frames between the fringes. This is the halfway region, the area of juxtaposition. You may not be able to cross the whole curtain at once, but you can cross it by halves now. I'll move the Phazite across it the same way."

"That must explain the strange thing I saw," she said.

"What thing?" In a situation where lasers and spells mixed, what could be strange?

"As I was casting about for a suitable place to set up this haven, I saw two men, a Citizen and an Adept. The Black Adept, by your description—made from a line. The Citizen had a line too, a financial line vital to his being. The two people came together as if drawn unwillingly— and suddenly they merged. One man stood where two had been. It must have been the two selves of the two frames reuniting in the common zone."

"So it must," Stile agreed, awed by the concept. "Juxtaposition is more literal than I thought! The divided people become whole people—for a while. They will surely separate again when the frames do. I wonder how the two Blacks feel about each other right now!"

She smiled. "There must be a number of very confused people! Not only two bodies together, but two half-souls too." Then she sobered, remembering that she had no soul at all.

"Speaking of confused people—I left a remarkable situation in Xanadu. I don't know whether Merle and the Rifleman—"

"I will check on it," Sheen said. She touched a button, and a holo-image formed, showing the Xanadu cavern.

The scene was horrendous. Merle and the Rifleman were confined in a cage whose bars were formed of ice, slowly melting in the heat of the chamber. Four hungry griffins paced just outside the cage, eager to get at the morsels within. In minutes the prisoners would be doomed.

"The Adepts want to be sure I'm dead," Stile said. "If I'm alive and aware, they know I will act to save my friends. If the ice melts and the monsters feast, the enemy Adepts will know I'm helpless."

"I did conjure a dead fish to replace you in the sunless sea," Sheen said. "I thought it would be enough. This dome is resistive to perception; they do not know we are here."

"Where are we?"

"In the heart of the ogre demesnes."

"Should be safe enough," he agreed. "But my enemies are right. I can't let the only two Citizens who helped me—I just can't leave them to this fate. I must act."

"Maybe I can do it in a way that won't betray you." She looked in the index of the book of magic again. "What type of spell should I search for?"

"Something that seems coincidental, natural. Some regular enemy to griffins that happens to wander by. Dragons, maybe."

"Here it is," she said brightly. "A spell to attract flying dragons. It's a visual display that only dragons can see, suggestive of griffins raiding the dragon nests to steal diamonds. It enrages them, and they launch toward battle."

"Excellent. Just see that they don't attack my friends."

She got on it, uttering what sounded like gibberish and

stamping both feet. "That does it. I modified it to make the dragons protective toward people caged in ice. The nest syndrome, again. They'll melt the bars without hurting the prisoners. The enemy Adepts will be too busy containing the dragons to worry about the prisoners, who will surely disappear rapidly into the labyrinth of Proton. Do you want to watch?"

Stile glanced again through the holo at the prisoners. The Rifleman was holding Merle, shielding her from the cold of the ice and the reaching claws and beaks of the griffins. They made a rather fetching couple. Perhaps this incident would give the two respect for each other and lead to a passing romance.

"No, let's get on with our business," Stile said, more gruffly than necessary. The problem of Sheen and his relationship to her weighed upon him more heavily as she became more and more human. He felt guilty for not loving her sufficiently. "You conjure yourself to the Oracle's palace and see about reanimating Trool the Troll. Fetch the Brown Adept there too; it will have to be a joint effort. While you're at it, find out whether the curtain's expansion has intersected the Oracle yet. Once it crosses, I'll have to see about integrating it with the Proton computers, so its enormous expertise can aid our effort from the Proton side. Once you're through there, meet me at the Platinum Demesnes; I'll be organizing the shipment of Phazite. If we act swiftly and well, we can accomplish it before the resistance gets properly organized, especially since it may be thought that I am dead."

"But that's all kinds of magic you want me to do alone!" she protested. "I'm only a machine; I can't handle that sort of thing!"

A machine with an insecurity complex. "You've done pretty well so far."

"I had to! I knew your life was at stake."

"It still is," he said coldly. "All the Citizens and Adepts will be gunning for me harder than before, once they realize I have survived again. This is their last chance to stop the transfer of Phazite and preserve the frames as they know them. Do whatever you did before to handle magic so well."

"I just looked in the index for the spells I needed. The book is marvelously cross-referenced; it is easy to see that a computer organized it. Protection, construction, summoning, conversion—anything, instantly. I just followed instructions; I don't understand magic at all. It is complete nonsense. Who ever imagined a scientific robot doing enchantments?"

"Who, indeed!" he agreed. "This is a wrinkle I never anticipated. Yet it seems that you are well qualified to use the book of magic. Perhaps that is by design of the originators; the great equalizer for the self-willed machines. They can be the leading magicians of the age, entirely bypassing the established hierarchy."

"No. We don't want to do that. We want only our fair share of the system."

Stile smiled. "You, too, are incorruptible. You shall have your fair share. But at the moment it is the occasion for heroic efforts. Very well; I'll put it on a more practical basis. You read through that entire book and assimilate all that is in it—"

"Wait, Stile! I can't! I can read at machine rate—but this book is a hundred times as big as it seems. When you address any section, the entire book becomes that section; there are more spells in any single subdivision than I can assimilate in a year. It's like a computer with unlimited access, keying in to the networks of other planets on demand."

"A magic computer. That figures. Very well—run a survey course. Discover what types of spells it has, in broad categories—you've already done that, I think—then narrow those down until you have exactly what you need. Commit particular spells to memory, so that you can draw on them at need. Remember, you can use each spell only once, so you'll need backups. I want to know the parameters of this thing; maybe there are entire aspects of magic we never thought of. You run that survey as quickly as you can, then restore Trool and report to me. That will allow me to get moving on the Phazite without delay, while also mastering the potential of the book—through you."

"Yes, sir," she said uncertainly.

Stile brought out his harmonica and played a bar of music. Again there was something strange, but this time he continued playing, determined not to be balked by any mystery.

The spirit of his other self came out, expanding as if stretching, then closed on Stile, coalescing.

"Oh, no!" he cried. "Juxtaposition! I forgot!"

"You freed your other self's soul to merge," Sheen said. "I saw it."

Now Stile was two people, yet one. All the memories and experience and feelings of the Blue Adept of Phaze were now part of his own awareness, superimposed on his own lifelong Proton experience. All that he had learned of his other self, which the Lady Blue had told him, was now part of his direct memory. He had become, in truth, the Blue Adept. He felt confused, uplifted, and gloriously whole. "I am—both," he said, awed.

"Is it—will you be all right?" she inquired anxiously. "Things are changing so rapidly! Does it hurt?"

He looked at her with the awareness of his other self. She was absolutely lovely in her concern. She had, with typical feminine vanity and concession to the culture of Phaze, conjured herself a simple but fetching dress, and her hair was just a trifle wild. Her eyes were strongly green, as if enhanced by the verdure of the overlapping frames. "I know what thou art," he said. "I could love thee, Lady Golem-Machine, for thou art lovely in more than form."

Sheen stepped back. "That must be Blue! Stile, are you in control? If you have become prisoner in your body—"

"I am in control," Stile said. "I merely have double awareness. I have two full lives to integrate. My other self has no direct experience with your kind; he's quite intrigued."

"I would like to hear more from Blue," she said, then blushed.

"Sorry. He has to come with me; we're one now." Stile resumed his melody on the harmonica, then sang: "Let me be found at the Platinum Mound."

And he was there. Pyreforge the Dark Elf looked up. "We expected thee, Blue Adept. But I perceive thou art changed."

"I am both my selves," Stile said. "I am whole. My souls are one."

"Ah, the juxtaposition," Pyreforge agreed. "We be in the throes. But thy merger can be maintained only within the curtain, for you are now two."

"I mean to make another body for him," Stile said, an inspiration falling into place. "My friend Sheen has the book of magic; we can accomplish it now, after we restore my friend the troll to life. But first—the Phazite."

"We have it for thee," the elf agreed. "But how canst thou move it? It weighs many tons, and its magic ambience prevents conjuration."

"I think that is why the Oracle bade me organize the creatures of Phaze," Stile said. "First they rescued me from enchantment; now they will enable me to move the Phazite. I want to shape it into a great, perfect ball and roll it across the curtain by brute, physical force."

"Aye, Adept, that may be best. But others will bar thy progress if they can."

"This may be like a big earthball game," Stile said, remembering the final key word of his Tourney poem. Earth. "I will try to balk the magic of the enemy Adepts, with the help of Sheen and the book of magic, while my friends help push the ball across the near side of the curtain, through the breadth of the zone of juxtaposition, and across the other side into Proton. That is how it works, isn't it?"

"Aye. Cross from one frame on one side, to the other on the other. That can be done from both sides, but always the full juxtaposition must be traversed, for it be but the interior of the divided curtain."

"So where the curtain divides, the people reunite!" Stile exclaimed, feeling his wholeness again.

"For the moment it be so. But when the deed be done, all will be separate forever."

"I know," Stile said sadly. "I will be forever confined to mine own frame, this lovely world of magic but a mem-

ory. And mine other self, the true Blue Adept, will know
no more of modern science." He felt the surge of interest
and regret in his other self. To Blue, the things of science
were as novel as the things of magic were to Stile.

"We do what we must do," Pyreforge said. "We sometimes like them not."

"Can the elves get the Phazite to the surface here?" Stile
asked. "I can conjure in whole troops of creatures to push
it across the juxtaposition."

"Nay, the other Adepts have closed the conjuration
avenue, perceiving thy likely intent if thou dost survive.
Thine allies must march here."

"But I came by conjuration!"

"Thou must have come from some place hidden from
Adept perception, then."

"I did," Stile agreed. "I should have notified my allies
before I came here. Perhaps I can make a sign for them in
the sky—"

"And attract every enemy instantly," Pyreforge said.
"Best to start it quickly."

Stile sighed. There always seemed to be so many con-
straints on his application of magic! His other self shared
the sentiment; it had always been thus. Magic was not the
easy answer to every problem.

He went outside and surveyed the landscape, looking
down into the great plain to the north. He could see where
the curtain had expanded, straightening as it went. The
zone of juxtaposition now reached well into the plain. The
domes of the civilization of Proton were coming into view,
with their teeming Citizens, serfs, and machines.

He had an idea. He returned to Pyreforge, inside the
Mound. "Have thy minions push the ball out of the north-
ern slope of the Purple Mountains, while I fetch special
help. I can use Proton equipment to shove it onward."

"Do not Citizens control the machines?" the old elf
asked.

"Aye, they do," Stile agreed regretfully. "All but the self-
willed machines. They will be using the heavy equipment
against us. Let's hope my Phaze friends are alert, and will
assemble here without specific summoning." A little fore-

sight would have facilitated things greatly, but he had been distracted by things like being transformed into a fish. So much had happened so rapidly so recently!

Pyreforge showed the way to the Phazite. It was some distance east, for many of the tribes of elves had labored to assemble it centrally. Apparently they had been at work on this project far longer than Stile had been in Phaze, knowing the crisis was coming. The Little Folk had known much they had not advertised, and thus avoided early sabotage by the enemy.

As he walked, Stile felt an odd wrenching within him, followed by a kind of desolation. There was the sound of a fading flute, a single note that was somehow beyond the compass of ear or mind, yet encompassed something fundamental in the cosmos. In a moment he realized what had happened; he had crossed beyond the juxtaposition into Phaze proper, and the two souls could not integrate in a single frame. Blue had departed, and must now be back in the harmonica. How empty this body felt!

At length they arrived in a large cavern, not unlike the one of Xanadu, but whose walls were dark rock. There were evidences of extensive tunnelings and laborings and many tracks of carts indented in the ground, as well as spillage of ore and oil.

There in the center was a perfect sphere of Phazite. This could not have been shaped in the past few minutes; it had to have been done this way long before Stile had arrived. The ball was about six feet in diameter, the size of an earthball.

An earthball. Again Stile remembered the Game, in which such a ball was pushed by teams across one goal line or the other. The Game Computer had given him the term "Earth," the last of the supposedly random terms; now the relevance was clear.

"Solid Phazite?" he asked, awed by the reality. In Proton this would be worth so much that his mind balked at attempting the calculation.

"An isotope of the dense mineral formed in rare, peculiar processes of creation," the old elf agreed. "In the science frame this would be described as the semi-collapsed matter formed in the fringe of a certain variety of black hole in a certain critical stage of evolution. This explains why it is so rare; very little of it escapes the site of its origin. It is fifty times the density of water, unstable in certain conditions, sublimating into pure energy that is more than the sum of its present mass because of the unique stresses of its creation. Thus it may be used for the economical propulsion of spaceships—or the more versatile applications of magic in a frame where magic is normally much less intense."

"From the fringes of black holes," Stile repeated, amazed at the information the elf had. To reside in a magical frame was not necessarily to be ignorant of science! "I'll *bet* it's scarce! No wonder phenomenal force is bound up within it, like a really tightly coiled spring. How much is here?"

"In Proton, Protonite has been mined at the controlled rate of approximately one metric ton a year, for three hundred years, with nine tenths of it exported, the rest reserved as Citizen wealth. To equalize the frames, we must replace half of three hundred metric tons. This ball of Phazite weighs near one hundred and seventy of our tons, the equivalent."

"I don't want to wait until my allies locate me," Stile said. "My enemies may arrive at the same time. I will need some help moving that thing, if I am not to employ magic."

"We will help, within our demesnes. We have numbers and levers."

Stile brought out his map of Phaze, which had survived all his adventures in the magic way such things had. He had wondered how unicorns managed to carry things while shifting into forms such as hawks and fireflies; now he had carried map, clothing, and harmonica while swimming as a fish. He still didn't know how it was done. "The simplest thing would be to roll the ball due north across the central region, which is relatively level, until we pass the north aspect of the curtain. Somehow I don't think that will work."

"Thine enemies be alert. At some point they will discover thy location. Then will all their resources be brought to bear in opposition."

"That's the nature of the game." Stile agreed. "Both teams push on the earthball, and the one with more power and/or better strategy prevails. The problem is, I'm not sure we have more power or better strategy."

"I can help," Sheen said.

"Yes, I'll take all the help I can—" He looked at her, startled. "When didst thou arrive?"

She smiled. "Just now, when the curtain caught up with thee. Didst thou not notice it?"

Stile, distracted by the wonder of the ball of Phazite, sixty times the mass of his record Proton personal fortune, had not noticed. Now he realized that he had heard the Flute again, at the fringe of his consciousness, and that his experience had broadened as his other self rejoined him. He also realized that Sheen could not cross the curtain, this side, without going back into Proton; to go all the way into Phaze, she would have to proceed past the north part of the curtain, then double back. Best for her simply to remain in the zone of juxtaposition, using the superspells of the book of magic to overcome the interference-enchantment of the enemy Adepts.

"So the curtain is still expanding," he said. "I had somehow thought it had stabilized."

"Nay, it be unstable," Pyreforge said. "Only the ultimate skill of the Foreordained expands it, and his power be at its limit. The boundary flexes back and forth, somewhat like the winds of a changing day. The mass of many people can move it a short distance, as it were pushing it. Our elves did push it across just now so that thy friend could join thee."

"And here is Trool," Sheen continued. "His troll friends are making a tunnel through hills for the boulder, so we will not have to roll it uphill."

"I do not plan to roll it uphill! I'll roll it along the contour."

"And the Lady Brown is marching her golems here to push."

Stile looked at Trool. "Glad I am to see thee! Thou hast survived thine ordeal in good order, it seems. It is not every person who is restored from stone."

"It was an eyeblink," the troll said. "One moment I stood in the tunnel; next was I in the hall of the Oracle. I knew not thy metal golem was an enchantress."

"Women of any type have secret talents; hers manifested during your eyeblink," Stile said. "Thou, too, dost have ability. We saw thy figurines. Are all trolls sculptors?"

"Nay," Trool said, embarrassed. "I have gone mostly apart from my kind, and in the lonesome hours do I entertain myself with idle shapings. It is of no import."

"Art is of import," Stile said. "Many creatures can do conventional labors; few can fashion raw material into beauty. Phaze can be made prettier by thy efforts."

"Nay, I am ugly," Trool demurred. "I have no aspirations, now that mine onus is done."

His onus had been to save Stile three times. Surely the good troll would not accept any reward, but Stile disliked the notion of departing this frame without returning some suitable favor. Something began to develop in his mind, an improbable connection. "If thou didst have the power of an Adept, what then would be thine aspiration?"

The troll shrugged in the ungainly manner of his kind. "I have no use for power. For generations my kind has abused what powers it had, and on that history do I turn my gnarled back. All I crave is a little rock to tunnel in, and time to fashion mine images in stone, and perhaps a friend or two. The life of a troll is not much, Adept."

Not much, indeed! Stile decided to experiment. "I shall grant thee power, for a time, so that thou canst help me now. I must devise a route to roll this ball of Phazite and must avoid the enemy forces that oppose this motion." He turned to Sheen. "Thou hast surveyed the book of magic?"

"Aye," she agreed.

"Canst thou give Trool the powers of flight, invisibility, and resistance to hostile magic?"

She looked surprised. "That and more. But—"

"Do it."

"But, Adept!" Trool protested. "I am a troll!"

"Methinks I misjudged trolls once. Thou hast helped me three times; now I beg thee to help me again, though no prophecy requires thee."

"Certainly will I help thee! But—"

Sheen did something obscure. Trool paused as if experiencing something strange.

"Try thy talents," Stile suggested.

"I can not fly!" Trool said, rising into the air. He looked down, astonished. "This is as impossible as turning invisible!" He faded from view.

"Thou hast bequeathed dangerous power to such a creature," Pyreforge said gravely. "He can leave thee and go abroad to do harm, answerable to no one."

"Power corrupts some less than others," Stile said. "Trool has shown his constancy, and I am giving him leave to show it more. Sheen has more power than any other person now, yet she is unchanged."

"I'm not human," Sheen said. "I am as I am programmed to be, regardless of my power. Only living things are corruptible."

"Yet with the magic of that book," Pyreforge pointed out, "thou couldst become alive. The power thou hast shown be but an inkling of the potential."

"Yes," she agreed. "I perceive that potential."

"There are spells to give true life?" Stile asked, amazed.

"Thou didst tell me to survey the complete book," she reminded him. "I found things hardly to be imagined."

"But the problem of souls," he protested.

"That is handled the same way the flesh is. A baby is started from the substance of its parents. A baby's soul starts as a piece separated from the souls of its parents. It's like taking a brand from a fire to make a new fire; once a piece of fire is separated, it develops its own individuality. So I don't need anyone else's soul—just a piece of soul, which can grow into the body."

"But a piece of whose soul?" Stile asked. Sheen, alive— would it make a difference? He wasn't sure. Part of her personality was her knowledge of her own inanimate nature.

"The Lady Brown has offered me a piece of hers," Sheen said diffidently. "She feels responsible for me, since she animated me in Phaze."

"We're wasting time," Stile said, not wanting to wrestle

with personal considerations at the moment. "Where's Trool?"

"I am here, Adept," Trool said, appearing. "I have surveyed the course. Thou canst not proceed northward, for that the Adepts have set dragons there to guard against passage. They know not where thou wilt go, or if thou truly art alive, but they are watching everywhere. When the ball begins to move, they will converge. The course must go west, avoiding the dragons."

"We'll start west, then," Stile decided.

Now the elves appeared in force. They cranked open the wall to show a great rent in the mountain. The sun shone brightly outside, but these were light-tolerant elves, able to work by day. Pyreforge bade a hasty parting and retreated to the comfortable shadows; he could no more tolerate the direct glare of the sun than Trool could.

"Trool!" Stile exclaimed. "How could—?"

"I gave him a spell of automatic shade when I restored him," Sheen said. "I may be metal, but I do profit from experience. The sun can't touch him now."

Relieved, Stile watched the elves. The Little Folk applied their levers diligently, and the massive ball started to move. One hundred and fifty metric tons was a great weight, but the ball was perfectly balanced and the levers were skillfully applied. Once moving, the ball continued, its mass giving it formidable momentum. Then it started rolling grandly downhill, and the elves got out of the way.

The ball coursed down, up the opposite slope, and down again, neatly following the general channel Stile had determined for it, leaving a concave impression. But then it veered slightly, and he saw that it was going to strike a large pine tree. That could be disaster; probably the ball would crush the tree to the ground—and in the process be deflected off the route. Possibly the tree would resist, bouncing the ball back. Certainly a lot of useful momentum would be lost. This was going so smoothly he didn't want to interrupt it.

So he sang a little spell. The tree wavered into insubstantiality just before the boulder reached it, then became solid after the Phazite had passed through.

"I'm not sure you should have done that, Stile," Sheen said. "The enemy Adepts are highly attuned to your magic."

"I've got to use my magic when I need it," Stile said. "I'm sorry I can't use it directly on the Phazite." He remembered he had conjured Sheen's replacement power cell before, and that was the same mineral—but that had been a tiny fraction of a gram. He could no more move this 150-ton ball by magic than he could by hand, alone.

The ball crunched to a stop in the next depression. They walked along the smooth indentation path, catching up to it. "The golems are near," Trool's voice came from the air above them.

"Guide them here," Stile said.

Soon a column of wooden men marched up. Some were small and some were large; the Brown Adept rode piggy-back on one of the giants. She waved cheerily as she spied them. "We'll get it moving!" she called.

Under her direction, the wooden men set to work with a will. They were very strong, and soon they were levering the ball slowly up the incline.

Suddenly a sheet of flame flashed across the terrain. The golems cried out, and the Brown Adept screamed. The wooden men were burning. Fire was the one thing such golems feared.

"You were right," Stile said. "The enemy has located us." He started to play his harmonica, getting ready for a fire-extinguishing spell. But Sheen lifted her hand, and the fire vanished.

"You told me to memorize any spells I thought might be useful," she said.

Stile stared at the golems, who were understandably confused. One moment they had been burning; the next all was well. "So I did," he agreed. "The sheer facility and potency of it keep setting me back. Can you protect the golems henceforth?"

"I think so. The book has an excellent section on countermagic. But if I block off Adept spells, this will stifle your magic too."

"The book magic is that strong?"

"That strong, Stile. The book is not a mere compendium

of stray spells. It's a complete course—the atomic age of magic. It shows how to integrate all the modes—voice, vision, symbols, potions, touch, music—all. The Adepts of today are fragmentary magicians, severely limited. Thou also, I regret to say. None of you has done more than scratch the surface of the potential of magic. I haven't scratched the surface. There is so much more to be mastered—"

"I see. All right—block out all Adept magic here, and we'll talk about it while we supervise the moving of the ball."

She made a series of body motions and exclamations, concluding with a toe-sketched figure on the ground. Something happened in the air—an oblique kind of shimmer. "The visual effect is merely to identify it," she said. "We are now secure from new spells."

The golems resumed their labor on the sphere. Slowly they moved it up the slope. "When we have a moment," Stile said, "let's see about making up a good body for my other self."

"Your other self!" she exclaimed. "Yes, of course. The book has spells to convert wood or other substance to flesh, as we did for Trool. You have Blue's soul preserved. I don't think the soul can go to that body while you are in Phaze, but when the frames separate, Clef can pipe it in, and—"

"And my other self will be restored to life in Phaze," Stile finished. "He sacrificed his life to give me the chance to enter his frame and work with the Oracle. The least I can do is give it back to him when my task is done."

"But what of the prophecy? Phaze will not be safe until—"

"Until Blue departs it forever!" Stile finished. "In the confusion of great events, I forgot that!" He pondered, disturbed. "No, I can not be entirely governed by prophecy. I must do what I deem right; what will happen, will happen." But he remained disquieted, as did his other self.

"The body has to be crafted by hand," Sheen said. "It can't be made directly by magic, or it will perish when the magic diminishes. So we can't do it right this minute. But I won't forget to see to it before the end." She paused. "What does Blue think of this?"

Stile shifted to his alternate awareness. Now he had confirmation of his prior conjecture; Blue had, through a special divinatory spell, discovered what was developing and realized that the best thing he could do for the land he loved was to die. But, fearful that his sacrifice might be in vain, he had hedged. He had conjured his soul into his harmonica and given the instrument an affinity for his other self. Now he knew his act had been justified, for Stile had used the harmonica to achieve his necessary level of power.

As for having his life back in the new order, he had not expected this, and not even considered the possibility of resuming his life in Phaze. The notion had a certain guilty appeal. Yet if the presence of Blue meant ruin for Phaze, he would be better off dead. He would have to formulate some plans for a formerly blank future, knowing that he might again have to give it up if the prophecy were true. All he could do was try it and see; perhaps there would be interim tasks for him to do before he departed.

"I thank thee for thy consideration," Blue said to Sheen. "Glad am I to have facilitated thine entry here, lovely Lady Machine."

Again Sheen reacted with pleased embarrassment. "There's something about the people of Phaze," she murmured.

The Brown Adept rode up on her golem mount. "I think my golems can handle it, as long as nothing else bothers them. Art thou going to make the Lady Machine alive now? I will give her part of my soul."

"I've been thinking about that," Sheen said. "All my brief existence I have longed to be alive—but now I have the chance for it, I'm not sure. I don't think it would carry over into Proton—and if it did, there would still be a severe readjustment. I'd have to eat regularly, and eliminate regularly—both rather messy inconveniences—and sleep, which is a waste of useful time. My whole routine would be changed. I think I'm better off as a robot."

"But Blue could love thee as a woman," Brown said. "And thou couldst love him."

How intimately had the two consulted while they worked on the restoration of Trool? Brown seemed to know a lot more about Stile's business than he had told her. He decided to stay out of this conversation.

"I love him already," Sheen said. "Life could not change that. And his love will always be for the Lady Blue. My life would not change that, either, and I wouldn't want it to. So all I really have to gain, by marrying him in Proton, is the precedent for the self-willed machines—and if I were alive, that precedent would no longer exist."

"Oh. I guess so," Brown said. "I think thou art just fine as thou art, Lady Machine. So I guess thou canst just use the magic book to cure Blue's knees, and maybe make him a little taller, and—"

Now Stile had to join in. "My knees are part of my present life; I no longer care to have them fixed. And my height—I always wanted to be taller, for that is the human definition of status, however foolish we all know it to be—I share Sheen's opinion. I would be a different person, with new problems. I stand to gain nothing by changing what I am."

Brown shrugged. "Okay. Actually, the Little Folk are perfect the way they are, and thou art not much different." That jarred Stile, but he tried not to show it. "I'll make up a golem in thine image; the book can make it flesh, and the other Blue can move into it when he's ready." She rode off.

In due course an enemy contingent arrived—a small squadron of tanklike earthmovers, borers, and personnel transports. The Citizens of Proton had no formal armed forces, since no life existed outside the domes, ordinarily. Construction vehicles tended to be enclosed and airtight, but some were remote-controlled or robotic. The present group was of the last type.

"Low-grade machines," Sheen said. "The Citizens know better than to trust the sophisticated robots, though in truth only a small percentage is self-willed."

"I hope your friends are not suffering unduly as a result of betraying their nature to the Citizens," Stile said. He was uncertain which form of language to use in the juxtaposition zone, and decided to stick to Proton unless addressing a Phaze creature.

"The juxtaposition has proved to be enough of a distraction," she said. "It is not easy to identify a specific self-willed machine when it wants to conceal itself. If the enemy wins this war, all my kind of machines will be destroyed." Stile knew she was speaking literally; there would be absolutely no mercy from the Citizens.

The enemy machines formed up before the ball of Phazite. One fired an excavation bomb at it, but nothing happened. "Phazite protects itself," Sheen remarked. "You can move it or use it, but you can't damage it with less than a nuclear cannon."

Several laser beams speared toward the sphere, but again without effect. Regardless of magic, Phazite was extremely tough stuff, twice as dense as anything ordinarily found in a planet; unless subjected to the key environment, it was virtually indestructible. The Brown Adept rejoined Stile and Sheen, staying clear of the dangerous region.

Now the vehicles moved up to push against the ball itself. The golems pushed on the other side. The machines had more power, but only one unit at a time could contact the Phazite, compact as it was, while the golems could apply all their force. The boulder rocked back and forth, then rolled to the side and forward. The golems were able to maneuver better, and were making progress again.

The machines regrouped. Another vehicle lined up and pushed on the boulder. Again the golems nudged the ball around the machine. Their brains were wooden, but they did learn slowly from experience.

Unfortunately, so did the machines. They consulted with each other briefly, then lined up again—and charged the golems.

"No!" the Brown Adept cried as a truck smashed into a golem. It was as if she felt the blow herself. "That's cheating!"

"There are no rules to this game," Stile said.

"Oh, is that so?" Brown's small face firmed, and she called new instructions to her minions.

Now the golems fought back. When the vehicles

charged, the golems stepped aside, then leaned in close to pound at the vulnerable regions as Stile explained them to Brown. Tires burst under the impact of pointed wooden feet; plastic cracked under wooden fists. But the machines, though dented, continued to fight.

"These are not like animals," Sheen said. "They don't hurt. Thou must disrupt their power trains or electrical systems."

The Brown Adept had no knowledge of technology. "Obey the Lady Machine!" she called to the golems.

Sheen called out instructions. Now the golems went after more specific things. They unscrewed the fastenings for maintenance apertures and ripped out wiring; they punched holes in lubrication lines. Soon all the machines were out of commission.

The golems had won this engagement. But time had been lost. The juxtaposition would remain only a few hours, and in that time the Phazite had to be moved across into the frame of Proton. The next obstacle would surely be more formidable; this had been merely a token engagement, a first testing of strength.

Stile brought out his map again. "We'll have to plan strategy, arrange a diversion. Now our obvious route is curving north, through the unicorn demesnes, to pass between the Oracle's palace and the central lake, in a generally descending lay of land. So they'll have that region well guarded. We'll send a contingent of creatures there, clearing a path for the ball. Our least likely route would be back toward the Purple Mountains, through the sidhe demesnes, where my friend Clef traveled when he first entered Phaze. The terrain is forested, irregular, and infested by harpies. So that's where we had better go."

"But it will take forever to roll the ball through that region!" Brown protested.

"Not if we can figure out a good way through. Magic could be used to prepare the way, such as the construction of sturdy bridges over gulfs. Could you handle that, Sheen?"

"Certainly. The enemy Adepts will never know what I'm doing. But I need to be on hand to guard you."

"Fear not for Blue, loyal Lady," Stile's alternate self

said. "The Adepts will strike not until they fathom our purpose, fearing to waste their magic on distractions. I know them, I know their minds. Go thy way, and we shall meet anon."

"Meanwhile, I will come with thee, Blue, to plot the false route," Brown said, enjoying this adventure.

Trool the troll reappeared. "The ogres, giants, and animalheads are marching from the west to join thee," he reported. "But the goblins are marching south to intercept them and thee. There will be a battle when they meet."

Stile consulted his map again. "How fast are they moving?"

"The animalheads are slowest, but also nearest. They will be here—" Trool indicated a spot within the unicorn demesnes on the map. "The ogres move faster, but the Black Demesnes are directly in their path, and the Green Demesnes to the south. They must veer north, then south, and should be here by dusk." He indicated a spot near the Oracle's palace. "The giants are farthest distant, but stride so large they will be with thee by late afternoon."

Late afternoon. Stile realized it was near midday now. But it had seemed like only an hour since the Citizens' business meeting, which had been in the evening. What had happened to the intervening night? Sheen must have slipped in a stasis-spell before letting him leave her temporary dome in the ogres' demesnes, and he had never even noticed. It was probably for the best; he had needed a good night's rest. So much was happening, the picture changing so radically, it was hard to keep track. But he had to keep going. "And the goblins?"

"The enemy Adepts are helping them move, but the goblins are so many that no spell can conjure them all— and the Lady Golem-Adept's counterspell prevents their coming all the way here by magic anyway. Logistics is a problem. They will be in this spot by dusk." He indicated the Oracle's palace.

"That means the ogres and goblins will meet somewhat to the north of the Oracle," Stile said grimly, tracing the likely paths on the map. "We'd better send a detachment of unicorns to help the ogres. After all, that's right in the path of our decoy effort. We have to take it seriously enough to fool them." He glanced at the golems, who were moving the ball again. "Have them go slowly, maybe pushing the ball farther uphill than necessary, so we can roll it down quickly—in an unanticipated direction. I want to give the enemy every chance to rush its forces to the wrong rendezvous."

Brown gave instructions to a messenger golem, then accompanied Stile on the mock survey excursion. Stile would have preferred to fly, but Sheen's antimagic spell stopped him as well as the enemy Adepts. He had to go on foot, at least until a unicorn arrived. Fortunately he was quite capable afoot. He set out at a running pace, covering each mile in about seven minutes. Brown's big golem steed kept pace with huge strides.

Then the unicorn he had hoped for came into sight. "Clip!" Stile cried. "Thou didst know I needed thee!"

Clip played a saxophone tune of agreement. Stile vaulted to his back, and they were off at a much faster pace. "Aw, the troll told him," Brown said disparagingly.

Of course that was true. In this frame of magic, coincidence was seldom unassisted.

Stile experienced the peculiar wrenching of separation again. They had once more passed outside the zone of juxtaposition, and his soul was all his own. The boundaries of the expanded curtain seemed to be quite irregular. He had supposed north would lead into the center of it. His other self had not intruded, letting Stile handle things his way, but the other's presence was increasingly comfortable, and his absence increasingly jarring. Now the terrain seemed less familiar, for his other self's experience with the land was absent. Also, now the overlapping terrain of Proton was gone; this was mostly barren rock and sand, in the science frame, easy to ignore in the presence of the Phaze vegetation, but still present when one cared to perceive it. Well, at least he would suffer no Citizen malice here; only the enemy Adepts could reach him.

Was there a valid parallel here? His soul was complete only when the geography was complete. Could the land be said to have a soul, perhaps in the form of the special mineral that the Citizens of Proton had depleted? It was odd, in one sense, that the Citizens resisted the transfer of Phazite, since it would dramatically enrich their world. But of course they would prefer to keep the frames partially overlapped, linked by the curtain so that in due course the Citizens could mine in Phaze as well as in Proton. They would equalize the frames by depleting both. The fact that such mining would do to the environment of Phaze what it had done to that of Proton, and also eliminate the remaining magic of Phaze, seemed not to concern the Citizens. There were, after all, other worlds in the universe to exploit, once this one was squeezed dry. Since Stile's transfer of power-mineral would enable the frames to balance, freeing them to separate, that would forever deny the Citizens the opportunity of exploitation. They seemed willfully ignorant of the substantial risk that both frames would be destroyed long before such exploitation could be completed. Stile wondered whether the citizens of ancient Harappa, in the Indian subcontinent of Earth, had had a similar attitude. Had they denuded the land of its necessary resources until it could support their population no longer, so that they weakened and fell to Nordic barbarians in the sixteenth century B.C.? Wealth and power at the expense of nature were an inevitably lethal cancer. But there seemed to be no gentle way to convince cancer to practice moderation.

Well, he, Stile, was fated to have considerable power, it seemed, in the frame of Proton after the separation, and his other self would have it in Phaze, assuming that prophecy had priority over the Blue-be-banished prophecy. The resources of the Oracle-computer, which were obviously considerable, would be at his disposal, and the self-willed machines would cooperate. Those machines would have legal-person status, of course. He would be able to enforce a more sensible restraint on that errant society.

Stile sighed. Somehow the prospect of all that power and responsibility did not appeal to him. All he really wanted was to be in Phaze with his creature friends and the Lady Blue. That was what he could not have.

Would it be so bad with Sheen? Of course not. She was the best possible woman, her origin aside. Meanwhile, in

Phaze, the Lady Blue would have her real husband back. She, at least, would not suffer.

Somehow he was not convincing himself.

Soon they were in sight of the unicorn herd, with a good route for the ball worked out. Stile suffered a pang, realizing that this was probably the last time he would see the Lady Blue. He would have to tell her and bid her farewell—and conceal if he could the way he actually felt about this coming separation. The break was inevitable; it was best that it be clean, without hysterics.

The Herd Stallion met him.

"Lord Blue, I will tell our plan, an thou dost prefer," Brown volunteered. "Do thou go to Neysa and the Lady."

Stile thanked her; she was a most helpful child at times, though somehow he was not eager to do what he had to do. He nerved himself and went directly to the protected inner circle, where Neysa and the Lady Blue awaited him.

He tried to tell himself he was happy to see them, but instead he found himself overcome by misgiving. He tried to smile, but they realized at once that something was wrong, and both came to him solicitously. "What is the matter, my Lord?" the Lady asked. "Does the campaign go ill?"

"It goes well enough," Stile said. He had learned so much so recently and shared so little with her! They had just been on their honeymoon, and now it seemed years past.

"Then what we feared is true," the Lady said, one hand on Neysa's black mane. "I have my child of thee, and thou art leaving us."

Was this the extent of her reaction? He knew she was capable of fierce displays of anger, sorrow, and love. How could she treat this as if it were commonplace?

"The prophecy of thy second husband no longer protects me," he said gravely. "Thou hast conceived, and I am no longer essential. There is another prophecy, that Phaze will not be safe until the Blue Adept departs it. I am now the Blue Adept; I would not put this frame in danger willingly." And he realized as he spoke that the prophecies could indeed make sense; the present Blue Adept had to leave so that the defunct Blue Adept could return. Thus

Blue would both leave and remain, both prophecies honored. "The frames will separate—and I must return to mine own."

The Lady nodded. "Somehow I knew it would be thus. Prophecies care naught for human happiness, only the letter of their fulfillment."

True; fate did not care. "But thou wilt not be alone," Stile said quickly. "The soul of thy first husband, mine other self, survives. He shall have a human body again."

Her composure faltered. "He lives?"

"Not exactly. He lost his body. But I believe I can restore it to him, and he will be the same as he was, as far as anyone can tell."

Her brow furrowed. "But I love *thee* now!"

"And I love thee. But when thy husband lives, my place will be elsewhere. I thought him dead, else I would not have married thee. He gave up his body that Phaze might be saved, and now he must have it back. This is what is right."

"Aye, it is right," she agreed. "It is clear where my duty lies."

She was taking it well—and that, too, was painful. He knew she loved him but would be loyal to her first husband, as Stile would be loyal to Sheen. This was the way it had to be. Yet somehow he had hoped that the Lady Blue would not take it quite this well. Was it so easy to give him up on such short notice?

Suddenly she flung her arms about him. "Thee, thee, thee!" she cried, and her hot tears made her cheek slippery as she kissed him.

That was more like it! She was meltingly warm and sweet and wholly desirable. "Thee, thee, thee," he echoed, in the Phaze signal of abandonment to love, and held her crushingly close.

Then, by mutual resignation, they drew apart. She brought a cloth to his face and cleaned him up, and he realized that half the tears were his own. Through the blur he saw the shimmer of the landscape about them, the reaction of the environment to an expression of deep truth. The unicorns perceived it too, and were turning to look at the couple.

But now they both had control again. They uttered no further words, letting their statement of love be the last.

Stile turned to Neysa to bid her farewell: But she stood facing away from him, standing with her tail toward him —the classic expression of disapproval. The woman might forgive him his departure; the unicorn did not.

He could not blame her. His body, so recently so warm, now felt chilled, as if his heart had been frozen. Had he expected Neysa, his closest friend in Phaze, to welcome his announcement with forward-perking ears? There was no good way to conclude this painful scene. Stile walked silently away.

Clip stood near, watching his sister Neysa. His mane was half flared in anger, and his breath had the tinge of fire, but he was silent. Stile knew Clip was furious with Neysa, but had no authority to interfere. There was justice in it; Neysa expressed the attitude the Lady Blue did not, in her fashion freeing the Lady to be forgiving. The complete emotion could not be expressed by one person, so had been portioned between two.

The Brown Adept was waiting for him at the edge of the unicorn circle. "I told the Stallion," she said. "He'll help." She looked toward Neysa and the Lady Blue. "I guess it didn't work out so well, huh?"

"I fear I'm not much for diplomacy," Stile said. "I don't want to go, they don't want me to go—there's no positive side."

"Why dost thou not just stay here when the frames part?" she asked naïvely.

"I am a usurper here in Phaze. This good life is not mine to keep—not at the expense of mine other self. I was brought here to do a job, and when the job is done I must leave. So it has been prophesied."

"I guess when I'm grown up, maybe I'll understand that kind of nonsense."

"Maybe," Stile agreed wryly.

Stile mounted Clip and they returned the way they had come, setting small markers to show the prospective route for the ball. There was no interference from the other Adepts; they were of course biding their time, since they were unable to strike at him magically at the moment.

They would have their minions here in force to stop the ball, though! The unicorns would have an ugly task, protecting this decoy route. The irony was that this was an excellent path; if there were no opposition, the ball could travel rapidly here.

When they recrossed into the zone of juxtaposition, his other self rejoined him. The personality of Blue assimilated the new experience and shrank away.

"Thou dost look peaked," the Brown Adept said. "Is aught wrong?"

"It is mine other self," Stile said. "I fear he likes not what I have done."

"The true Blue? Speak to me, other Adept."

"Aye, Brown," the other self said. "But surely thou dost not wish to be burdened with the problems of adults."

"Oh, sure," she said eagerly. " 'Specially if it's about a woman. Some day I'll grow up and break hearts too."

"That thou surely wilt," Blue agreed. "My concern is this: for many years did I love the Lady Blue, though she loved me not. When finally I did win her heart as well as her hand, I learned that she was destined to love another after me, more than me. This was one reason I yielded up my life. Now I know it is mine other self she loves. Am I to return to that situation, at his expense?"

"Oh, that is a bad one!" Brown agreed. "But maybe she will learn to love thee again. Thou dost have charm, thou knowest; the Lady Machine's nerve circuits do run hot and cold when thou dost address her."

"The Lady Machine is programmed to love mine image," Blue said. "I admit she is a fascinating creature, like none I have encountered before. But the Lady Blue is not that type. She will act in all ways proper, as she did before, and be the finest wife any man could have, but her deepest heart will never revert. Her love never backtracks."

"Then what good is it, coming back to life?" Brown asked, with the innocent directness of her age.

"There are other things in life besides love," Blue said. "The Lady will need protection, and creatures will need attention. There will be much work for me to do—just as there will be for mine other self in the fabulous science frame. He will be no happier than I."

Stile had no argument with that. His other self was the same person as himself, in a superficially different but fundamentally similar situation, facing life with a woman who was not precisely right. The days of great adventure and expectation were almost past. To lose the present engagement would be to die, knowing the frames would in time perish also as the unrelieved stress developed to the breaking point. To win would be to return to a somewhat commonplace existence—for both his selves. The choice was between disaster and mediocrity.

"I'm not sure I want to grow up, if that's what it's like," Brown said.

They reached the ball of Phazite. Sheen had returned to it also. "Is the other route ready?" Stile asked.

"Not quite. We must delay another hour. But it will be worth the wait."

"Then I have time to make a golem body for Blue," Brown exclaimed. Evidently she had resigned herself quickly to the situation and was determined to do her part even if Stile and Blue were not destined for happiness. "I hope I can do it right. I haven't had much practice with lifelike figures, especially male ones. My golems are mostly neuter."

Stile could appreciate the problem. "Maybe Trool can help. He's quite a sculptor."

Trool appeared. "I model in stone, not wood."

"We'll convert stone to flesh," Sheen said. "All we need is the form."

So while the golems rolled the great ball along its soon-to-be-diverted course, Trool the troll sculpted in stone. He excavated a rock from the ground in short order, his huge gaunt hands scraping the earth and sand away with a velocity no normal person could approach, and freed a stone of suitable size by scraping out the rock beneath it with his stiffened fingers. Apparently the stone became soft under his touch, like warming butter. Stile picked up a half-melted chip and found it to be cold, hard stone. No wonder trolls could tunnel so readily; the hardest rock was very much like putty in their hands. No wonder, also, they were so much feared by ordinary folk. Who could stand against hands that could gouge solid stone? Trool had stood with the Lady Blue against the ogres, Stile remembered, and the ogres had been cautious, not exchanging blows with him. They had been able to overpower him, of course, by using their own mode of combat.

When Trool had his man-sized fragment, he glanced at Stile and began to mold the image. Rapidly, magically, the form took shape—head, arms, legs. The troll was indeed a talented sculptor; the statue was perfect. Soon it was standing braced against a tree—a naked man, complete in every part, just like Stile.

Sheen and Brown were watching, amazed. "Gee, you sure are better at carving than I am," Brown said. "My prede—pred—the former Brown Adept could make figures just like people, but I can't, yet."

"I can't make them live," Trool said shortly.

Then Sheen made magic from the book, and the statue turned to flesh. But it remained cold, inanimate. The Brown Adept laid her hands on it, and it animated—a golem made of flesh. The new body was ready.

"Say—it worked!" Brown exclaimed, pleased.

Stile wondered how this carved and animated figure could have living guts and bones and brain. Presumably these had been taken care of by Sheen's spell. Magic was funny stuff!

But the soul could not yet enter this body. Two selves could not exist separately in the zone of juxtaposition. The second body would only become truly alive when the frames separated.

"Will it be all right until needed?" Stile asked. "It won't spoil?"

"My golems don't spoil!" Brown said indignantly. "It will keep until the soul enters it. Then it'll be alive and will have to eat and sleep and you-know."

"Then park it in a safe place," he said. "And let the harmonica remain with it, so that his soul can find it in case there is a problem." For despite all his planning, Stile was not at all sure he would succeed in his mission, or necessarily survive the next few hours. Little had been heard from the enemy Adepts recently; they had surely not been idle.

Sheen conjured body and harmonica to the Blue Demesnes, which were in no part of the current action. Stile felt another pang of separation as he lost the harmonica; it had been such an important part of his life in Phaze.

The necessary time had passed. They had the golems start the ball on its new course to the south. "But make a spell of illusion," Stile directed. "I want it to seem that the ball is proceeding on the course Brown and I just charted."

"I can generate a ball of similar size, made of ordinary rock," Sheen said.

"And I'll have some of my golems push it," Brown said. "It won't be nearly as heavy, so I'll tell them not to push as hard."

Soon the mock ball diverged from the real one, and a contingent of golems started it on its way. Stile wasn't sure how long this would fool the Adepts, but it was worth a try.

Meanwhile, under cover of a fog that Sheen generated, the main part of the golem force levered the Phazite ball back toward the Purple Mountains. A door opened in the hillside, and they saw the tunnel the trolls had made—a smooth, round tube of just the right size, slanting very gently down. They rolled the boulder to it, and it began to travel down its channel on its own.

"From here on, it's easy," Sheen said. "This tube will carry the Phazite kilometers along in a short time. At the far end, the tunnel spirals up to the top of a substantial foothill; from there it can roll north with such momentum the enemy will not be able to stop it before it crosses into Proton proper."

"Good strategy," Stile agreed. "But can the golems get it up that spiral?"

"My friends in Proton have installed a power winch."

Stile laughed. "I keep forgetting we can draw on science, too, now! This begins to seem easy!"

They followed the ball as it moved, Stile and Clip fitting comfortably in the tunnel, Brown's golem steed hunching over, and Sheen riding a motorized unicycle she had conjured. She was enjoying her role as enchantress.

The ball accelerated, forcing them to hurry to keep it in sight. Even so, it drew ahead, rounding a bend and disappearing.

They hastened on, but the ball was already around the next bend, still out of sight. When they passed that bend, they looked along an extended straightaway—and the ball was not there.

Stile wasn't sure whether he or his other self first realized the truth. "Hostile magic!" he cried.

"Can't be," Sheen protested. "I had it counterspelled."

"Use a new spell to locate the ball."

She used a simple locator-spell. "It's off to the side," she said, surprised.

"That last curve—they made a detour!" Stile said. "Had a crew in to tunnel—no Adept magic—goblins, maybe, or some borers from Proton—they can draw on the same resources we can—the ball went down that, while we followed the proper channel."

They charged back to the curve. There it was. An offshoot tunnel masked by an illusion-spell that had to have been instituted before Sheen's arrival. The enemy Adepts had anticipated this tunnel ploy and quietly prepared for it.

No—they couldn't have placed the spell before Sheen got there, because Sheen had supervised the construction of the tunnel and had her magic in force throughout. Something else—ah. The offshoot tunnel was in fact an old Proton mine shaft. A small amount of work had tied it in to the new troll tunnel, and a tiny generator had sealed off the entrance with an opaque force field. No magic, and minimal effort. Someone had been very clever.

"I don't like this," Stile said. "They evidently know what we're doing here, and someone with a good mind is on the scene. We're being outmaneuvered. While we made a duplicate image of me, they did this."

But there was nothing much to do except go after the Phazite. They started down the detour tunnel, hoping to catch up with the ball before it reached whatever destination the enemy had plotted. Sheen's magic showed no enemies nearby; like her own workers, they had departed as soon as their job was done. The tunnels were empty because the presence of anyone could alert the other side to what was going on.

They heard a noise ahead. Something was moving, heavily, making the tunnel shudder.

Ooops! The ball of Phazite was rolling back toward them at horrendous velocity!

"Get out of its way!" Stile cried. "A hundred and fifty tons will crush us flat!"

But the ball was moving too swiftly; they could not outrun it, and the intersection of tunnels was too far back. "Make a spell, Lady Machine!" Brown screamed.

Sheen made a gesture—and abruptly their entire party was in the tunnel beyond the rolling ball, watching the thing retreat. Stile felt weak in the knees, and not because of their injury. He didn't like being dependent on someone else for magic. Was that the way others felt about him?

"See—it slants up, there ahead," Brown said brightly. She, at least, was used to accepting enchantment from others, though she was Adept herself. "They fixed it up so the ball would roll up, then reverse and come right back at us."

"Timed so we would be in the middle when it arrived," Sheen said.

"No direct magic—but a neat trap," Stile agreed. "They must have assumed that if the book blocked out Adept magic, it would leave us helpless. They didn't realize that a non-Adept would be doing the spells."

"Funny Trool didn't warn us," Brown said.

Trool appeared, chagrined. "I saw it not. I know not how I missed it."

For a moment Stile wondered whether the troll could have betrayed them. But he found he couldn't believe that. For one thing, he had confidence in his judgment of creatures. For another, it was a woman—a young-seeming one—who had been prophesied to betray him, and that had already come to pass before the prophecy reached him. So there had to have been enough illusion magic, or clever maneuvering, to deceive everyone in this case; no betrayal was involved.

"Set a deflector at the mouth of the detour," Stile told Sheen, "so that when the ball reverses again, it will go down the correct tunnel."

She lifted a finger. "Done."

"You sure know a lot of spells," Brown said.

"Robots assimilate programmed material very rapidly," Sheen replied. "The advantages of being a machine are becoming clearer to me, now that I have considered life."

They marched up to the intersection of tubes. The ball had already reversed course and traveled down its proper channel. They followed it without further event to the end.

"Be alert for other hostile effects," Stile told Sheen. "The enemy can't hit us with new magic, but, as we have seen, the prepared traps can be awkward enough."

Sheen held her finger up as if testing the wind. "No magic here," she reported.

They stood at the winch. It was a heavy-duty model, powered by a chip of Protonite, and its massive cables were adequate to the need. They placed the harness about the ball; it fitted with little bearings so that the ball could roll within its confinement. With the pulleys and leverage available, the ball should move up the spiral.

It did move up. There were no hitches. Yet Stile worried. He knew the enemy would strike; he didn't know when and how. Why hadn't they destroyed the winch, since obviously they had had access to this tunnel? "Trool?" he asked.

There was no response from the troll. Probably he was out surveying the situation, and would report the moment he spied anything significant.

The winch cranked the ball of Phazite up the spiraling tunnel, providing it the elevation it would need to roll all the way across the juxtaposition zone to Proton. Once that boulder started rolling, it should be prohibitively difficult to stop. Victory seemed very near at hand—and still Stile worried. He was absolutely sure something ugly was incipient.

At last they reached the top. The winch delivered the ball to a platform housed in earth, surely resembling a mound of the Little Folk from outside. All they had to do now was open the gate and nudge it out.

Trool appeared. "Found thee at last!" he exclaimed. "Take not this route, Adept!"

Stile looked at him sourly. "We have already taken this route. Where hast thou been?"

"Looking all over for thee! There are a hundred traces of thy presence, all mistaken—until this one."

"Diversion magic," Stile said. "False clues to my where-abouts, laid down in advance, so that I become the needle in the haystack. But why would they try to mislead thee?"

"Because I have spied on them. Barely did I reach thee in time to give warning; the goblins have bypassed the giants, indulged in forced marches, and are lurking in ambush for thee here. Thou canst not pass this way, Adept."

"Nonsense," Sheen said. "I detect no goblins within seventy kilometers."

"Thou shouldst get beyond their screening spells," Trool said. "From behind, they are naught. There are maybe five hundred goblins there, armed with Proton weapons and busy making entrenchments. That much did I see; I looked no more, so that I could return in haste to warn thee. But then did I face the enchantment that concealed thee from me. All of it is passive magic, set in place before we came here, yet a nuisance."

"I knew things were too easy," Stile muttered. "They left us alone so we would continue on into their trap. We have perhaps four hours remaining to get the Phazite across the north border of the juxtaposition zone. We can not backtrack now. We shall have to proceed."

"I can neutralize the screen magic," Sheen said. "But that will not remove the goblins. The enemy Adepts will prevent me from performing any mass spell on them."

"So there are, after all, limits to the book," Stile said with a wry smile.

"Yes. It gives me power to stand off all the Adepts—but not to overwhelm them. We shall have to handle the gob-lins physically."

"The animalheads are arriving on the scene," Trool

said. "But they, too, are confused by the shield-spells. If
thou dost eliminate the shields, all will encounter each
other and there will be mayhem galore."

"I don't want mayhem," Stile said. "But if it has to be, I
want to ease the burden on the animalheads. Sheen, conjure me a holophone."

In a moment it was there. Stile called his own dome,
and Mellon answered. His leg had been repaired. "I am
glad to see you back in form, sir," he said.

Stile was sure the call was tapped and might soon be
blocked off. "I'm in a battle situation and need reinforce-
ments," he said quickly. "I can't arrange to conjure large
groups, so they'll have to march. The goblins are enemies
and will slaughter whomever they can; the other creatures,
however strange they may appear, are friends. Can you
arrange anything?"

"Allow thirty minutes, sir." The image faded.

So, just like that, it was done. Mellon would get the
coordinates of Stile's location from the holo and would
send out what he could. Stile's Citizen resources were now
considerable; he could afford a private army, if anyone
could.

He returned to his immediate situation. "If the goblins
have Proton weapons, we'll need Proton defenses. They
are probably making ready to storm this hill. We should
have light, bulletproof armor, laser screens—"

"Personal force fields," Sheen suggested. "They will
handle a combination of attacks, and I can conjure in such
small units without alerting the enemy Adepts."

"And make invisibility-spells for the rest of us," Brown
added. "They'll know we're near the Phazite ball, but
still—"

"Yes," Stile agreed. "Probably they won't want to fire
their shots too close to the Phazite; they won't have effect,
and if they did, what would it be? There's power to destroy
the planet in this dense little sphere; no one would gain if
that energy were suddenly released."

"Most likely they will attempt to wipe us out, and send
the ball rolling back down the spiral tube," Sheen said.
"Then they will blast the entrance closed and wait for the

juxtaposition to terminate. Clef surely can't hold it much longer."

"We're committed to our present course," Stile said, shaking his head ruefully. "They gave us full opportunity to go beyond the point of retreat. I'd like to meet the goblin commander; he's one smart tactician."

"Maybe an Adept is running things," Brown said.

"This smacks more of field tactics to me." Stile brought out his map. "As I make it, the ball has a fairly straight path north from here. All we need to do is clear out a few obstacles in the channel and start it rolling. We don't want to mire it in the lake, unless that's beyond the juxtaposition zone. Trool, where is the north side of the curtain now?"

"It is stabilized north of the lake and north of the Oracle's palace, in this section," the troll replied. "There is some curve in it yet; elsewhere it impinges the White Mountain range, but here it is fairly southerly."

"And where is it in this section?" Stile asked, indicating the place where the Oracle-computer was buried, somewhat removed from the Oracle's palace.

"It slants northwest, passing just south of that region. But that is not a good place to roll the ball anyway; there is a long incline up, with the curtain almost at the ridge there. Much easier to roll it through the valley to the east."

So the curtain was just south of the Oracle-computer. That was why there had been no news of the computer's crossing; Clef's Flute had not been able to broaden the juxtaposition zone enough. That meant the curtain would have to be stretched northward a little—and how would Stile find the creature-power to accomplish that, in the midst of battle?

"Nevertheless, I believe we'll roll it across at this site," Stile said, after reflecting a moment. "I hope the giants arrive in time to help; they'll be able to roll it barehanded."

"I'm not sure," Sheen said. "The ball of Phazite is the same diameter as a giant's finger—but its substance is fifty times as dense as living flesh. Trying to push on it could be clumsy and painful."

"They can use silver thimbles, or roll it with a pool cue," Stile said, smiling briefly.

"And the route," she said. "Why roll the ball across that particular place?"

Stile did not want to express his notion openly, for fear the enemy was somehow eavesdropping. "Because it will be difficult, slow, but certain; the enemy will not have barriers entrenched there, and no special traps, and our time will be running out."

"That's not fully logical," she protested. "The enemy will not guard that region well, because the natural terrain represents a formidable defense. They will have time to regroup while we struggle to push the ball up the hill."

"Maybe," Stile agreed.

"I hope your illogic has some redeeming aspect."

"I think thou art crazy," Brown said succinctly.

"We'll clear a course that curves northwest," Stile said. "They may assume it's another ruse. Then we'll roll the ball along it as fast and far as we can and hope for the best."

Trool faded out for another survey and returned to report that the contingent from Proton was arriving. "Flesh and metal men," he said wonderingly.

"Cyborgs, maybe. Robots with human brains. They can be very effective. It's time for us to move." He looked around the chamber. "I want the golem crew to remain here, to start the ball rolling at my signal. Timing is essential. Brown will supervise them. Sheen and I will sneak out and clear the path. Trool will act as liaison."

"I want to sneak out too!" Brown cried.

"What about me?" Clip asked, in man-form.

Stile had been afraid of this. He had to devise legitimate jobs for everyone. "Thou canst go report to thy herd," he said to the unicorn. "In thy hawk-form and with a spell of invisibility, thou canst get through to tell the Stallion of our situation." Stile turned to Brown. "But thou—if thou shouldst go, who will guard the book?"

Her brown eyes widened. "The book of magic?"

"If the enemy gets its hands on that, we're finished. We dare not take it out to battle. Sheen has memorized the spells she needs; she doesn't need the book with her now. So it is safest with thee and thy golems."

Brown's eyes fixed on the book, round with awe. "I guess . . ." she breathed.

The main reason Stile wanted her here was to keep the child out of the worst danger. Any protective spell they might make might be negated by a specific enemy counter-spell. The book did need guarding, so it was a valid pretext.

He left with Sheen, using an invisibility-spell as well as the protective shields she had fashioned before. He doubted the two of them would remain undiscovered, but with luck, the goblin army should be distracted by the detachments of serfs, robots, and animalheads.

They started down the slope, using conjured spades to eliminate troublesome ridges. This, too, was risky, since the changes they made were visible, possibly calling atten-tion to their otherwise invisible progress. Most of the slope was all right, with a natural channel requiring only touch-ing up.

But as they got away from the ball, the illusion fash-ioned by the enemy Adepts faded. They saw the goblins ranged about the base of the hill, pistols drawn. The mo-ment there was any visible action at the top of the slope, the goblins would start firing.

Even in this hiatus, it was bad enough. Detachments of goblins were building a series of obstructions near the base of the slope, wedgelike barriers with the sharp ends pointed uphill. If the Phazite ball encountered a wall crosswise, it would crash right through; but these wedges were oriented to deflect it efficiently off-course, where it could be further deflected by the natural channels below, until it was stuck in some cul-de-sac, and the game would be lost. That smart enemy commander's handiwork again! "Our work is cut out for us," Stile said. "One misplay, and we lose the ball. Conjure me some plastic explosive and detonators that can be set off by magic invocation. I'll have to mine some of those barriers."

"That sort of thing is not in the book," Sheen protested. "No plastic explosive with magic detonators! But I can get you one-hour timed explosive."

"That will do. Just let me know when the hour is up so I can get clear."

She conjured the explosive. It was high-grade; a kilogram had enough explosive power to blast away all the emplacements they would have time to mine. They walked on down the hill.

The contingent from Proton was marching toward the hill. Stile realized that it was on the wrong side of the illusion-spell and did not perceive the goblin army; the goblins would ambush it, wiping it out before it had a chance to organize. "I can't let that happen," he muttered. "I haven't been much of an organizer; my allies will be cut down, trying to help me. I must warn them!"

"If you show yourself, *you* will be cut down!" Sheen said. "My spells won't save you from attack by the entire goblin army, backed by the magic of all the Adepts."

"Maybe your magic can help, though. Generate an image of me, like a holograph. Then you can jump it around, and no one will know exactly where I am, so the enemy won't be able to attack me."

"Now that might work," she said. "It's risky, but so are the alternatives. Your convoluted organic brain does come up with artful wrinkles." She made a combination of gestures and sounds, sketched a little figure in the dirt—he could see it and her, as the invisibility-spell affected only the enemy's observers—and suddenly Stile found himself standing in the path of the cyborgs. He felt a squeeze on his hand and knew Sheen was with him, and that his consciousness had joined his distant image. This was clever magic; his respect for the book increased.

The leader of the cyborgs spied him and approached. This was an obvious machine, with gleaming metal limbs and chambers for attachments on its torso. But it was no robot; the brain was human, taken from the body of some aging, or ill, living person. Cyborgs could be exceedingly tough and clever. "I perceive you, sir," the machine-man said, orienting a lens on him. "But you have no substance. You are therefore an image. I can not be sure of your validity. Please identify yourself in a manner I can accept."

"I am an image of Citizen Stile," Stile said. "Also the Blue Adept. My employee Mellon should have primed you with key information about me. Ask me something appropriate."

"Yes, sir. Who is your best friend?"

"In which frame?"

"That suffices, sir."

Oh. Clever. It was the type of response, rather than the actual information, that had been keyed. "Let's get busy, then," Stile said. "This region is infested with goblins with modern weapons. I doubt they are good shots, but don't take chances. If you can drive them away from this area, that would be a big help. But don't attack any animalheads or unicorns. There's quite a bit of illusion magic around, so be careful."

"We understand, sir."

"I'm not sure you do. Send out scouts to the base of that slope." He indicated it. "They will pass the line of illusion and see the truth. Pay attention to what they tell you. This is likely to be deadly serious; your lives are in jeopardy."

"Thank you, sir."

They would have to find out for themselves. Stile murmured the word "animalhead" and found himself on a hill where the animalheads were gathered. The elephanthead chief spied him with a trumpet of gladness. "We have found thee at last, Adept!" he exclaimed; evidently Stile's prior spell of intelligibility remained in force. Spells did seem to have a certain inertia about them, continuing indefinitely unless countered or canceled. "We feared ourselves lost."

Quickly Stile briefed the elephant on the situation. "Now I'll be clearing a path for the ball to roll along," he concluded. "In mine own body I'm invisible, but the goblins will quickly catch on and interfere. So if thy force can divert them from this side, and while the cyborgs operate on the other side—"

"Cyborgs?"

"They are combination people, part human, part machine, strange in appearance but worthwhile when—"

"They are like us!"

"Very like thy kind," Stile agreed, startled.

"We are ready," the elephanthead said.

Now Stile was prepared to place the first wad of explosive. But as he returned his awareness to his invisible body, he discovered that Sheen was already attending to it. She had mined two wedges and was on the third. But the goblins were all about, digging their trenches and organizing themselves for the battle.

Stile had always thought of goblins as occurring in undisciplined hordes; these were highly disciplined. They were supervised by sergeants and commissioned officers, their insignia of rank painted or tattooed on their arms.

Despite his indetectability, Stile was nervous. There were too many goblins, and they were poking around too many places; at any time, one of them could make a chance discovery of the plastic explosive. He needed to distract the goblins' attention right now, before the cyborgs and animalheads went into action, lest his game be lost at the outset.

"Goblin leader," he murmured.

He stood beside a command tent. An ugly goblin with an authoritative air was surveying the field with binoculars. "I trust it not," the goblin murmured. "They be too quiet."

"Perhaps I can help thee," Stile said.

The goblin glanced quickly at him, showing no surprise. "I had thought to see thee ere now, Adept," he said. "I be Grossnose, commander of this expedition."

Stile could appreciate the derivation of the name; the goblin's nose was unusually large, and shaped like a many-eyed potato. But physical appearance had little to do with competence. Stile found himself liking this creature, for no better reason than that he must have risen to power in much the way Stile himself had, overcoming the liability of appearance to make his place in his society. "I compliment thy expertise," Stile said. "I had thought thy forces to be intercepted by our ogre detachment."

"We force-marched around the ogres," Grossnose said. "They be not our enemy."

"I prefer not to be thine enemy, either."

"Then hear our terms for peace: leave the Phazite in place, and thy party will be granted safe passage elsewhere."

"Declined," Stile said. "But if thy troops depart in peace, we will not hinder them."

"Now understand this, Adept. If fight we must, we shall be forced to seek the source of thy power. We shall make a thrust for the book. We have held off so far only that it be not destroyed. The book may be more valuable than that entire ball of Phazite, and it were a shame to put it into hazard. But this forbearance makes mischief; already the Adepts be quarreling as to who shall possess that book. I prefer to leave it in thy hands, as thou art least corruptible by power. But I can not allow that demon ball to cross to Proton-frame; that be the end."

"The end of the present order, mayhap," Stile said. "For Citizens and Adepts. They will have to share power more equitably in the new order. Other creatures will have proportionately more power, including thine own kind. Dost thou really oppose that?"

"Nay," the goblin admitted with surprising candor. "But I do serve the present order."

This was an honest, clever, incorruptible commander, the worst kind to oppose. "I regret what will come to pass," Stile said. "If we meet again after this is over, I would like to converse with thee again. But this next hour we are enemies."

"Aye. Go about thy business, Adept. Thou dost know what be in the making."

Stile knew. It was the irony of war that slaughter and destruction came about when both sides preferred peace. He faded out, and found himself back with Sheen.

"We have to move fast," he said. "They are going to go after the book."

Indeed, a troop of goblins were already charging the hill, lasers blazing. But they were met by the animalheads, who sprang from ambush and grappled with the goblins before the latter's modern weapons could be brought into play against this close-range opponent. The goblins' inexperience with such weapons cost the enemy dearly now; the animalheads were wresting them from the goblins and using them themselves.

Simultaneously the cyborgs commenced action—and their weapons were completely modern. Some had stunners, some gas jets, some lasers, and some projectile hurlers, and they knew how to use them. The battle was on.

Stile and Sheen moved hastily along their projected channel, placing the remaining explosive. Their hour was passing, and the plastic would detonate at its assigned moment regardless of their proximity. It was funny stuff, gray-white and slightly tacky to the touch, like modeling clay; it could be torn into fragments of any size, shaped as desired, and it would adhere to whatever it was pressed against. They fitted it into the chinks of stones like mortar, and on the undersurfaces of wooden beams. The goblins should not notice the plastic unless warned about its nature.

The sounds of the battle behind became louder. Stile looked back—and saw a squadron of winged dragons coming from the south. The cyborgs fired bazookas at them. Their aim was excellent—but after the first few dragons went down in flames, the others took evasive action. They dived down close to the ground and strafed the cyborgs with their flaming breath. The goblins who had been engaging the cyborgs screamed; that strafing was hurting *them*, while the metal bodies of the machine-men withstood the heat better. The dragons might as well have been the cyborgs' allies.

"Keep moving," Sheen cautioned Stile. Indeed, he had become distracted by the action, forgetting his own important role. He hurried to place more plastic.

But haste made waste. They ran out of plastic and time before the job was done; several barriers remained. They had had enough of each, and had wasted part of both. "We must move," Sheen warned. "In ten minutes the plastic detonates, with or without us."

"Better head back for the ball," Stile said. "I want to be ready just before the plastic goes off, so we can start the ball rolling right at the moment of goblin disorganization."

They began running back toward the Phazite. New contingents of goblins were arriving from the north; they were swarming all over. Stile saw that the enemy was winning the battle of the hill; both animalheads and cyborgs were being contained and decimated. The goblins were absorbing huge losses, but prevailing because of their greater numbers and overall organization. A new force was advancing toward the Phazite. They would overrun the site before Stile could return.

"Conjure us there!" he cried.

"Can't," Sheen snapped. "The enemy Adepts have focused their full attention on this place, blocking off new magic. They're learning how to impede the potent book spells by acting together. This is the final squeeze, Stile."

"Then send my image there; that's an existing spell."

Suddenly his image was in the chamber. There were the Brown Adept and the troll, holding laser rifles clumsily, trying to oppose the advancing goblins. The remaining golems stood about awkwardly; their hands were not coordinated enough to handle modern weapons, and their wooden minds not clever enough to grasp this rapidly changing situation.

"That's no good," Stile said. "You can't stop a hundred vicious goblins by yourselves."

They looked at him, startled. "We feared for thee!" Brown exclaimed.

"Fear for thyself; they will be upon thee before I can return in the flesh. They want the book, and we must keep it away from them at any cost." Stile pondered a moment. "Trool—canst thou take Brown and the book into the tunnel and shield them with thine invisibility?"

Trool faded out. In a moment Brown faded out too. "Aye," his voice came. "But it is not safe in the tunnel, Adept; goblins are coming from the far end. We have blocked them off for the moment, but—"

"Canst thou fly with her to safety?" Stile cut in. Time was so short! "It need be but for a few minutes, until the explosive we have set goes off. Then will the enemy Adepts' attention be distracted, and we can use the spells of the book to protect ourselves."

"I will try," Trool's voice came. From several feet up, Brown cried, "Hey, this is fun!" Then they were out a ceiling aperture and away.

The goblins burst in, caving in the mound walls with pikes. They spied Stile and charged him—but their points had no effect on his image. On inspiration, he pretended that he could be hurt, and dodged about to avoid the thrusts, so as to distract them as long as possible. He didn't want them working on the Phazite ball, now vulnerable.

The golems were still standing awkwardly. Stile realized that they needed to be told what to do. "Protect yourselves!" he cried. "Golems, fight the goblins!"

Now the golems acted. They were neither smart nor swift, but they were as tough as wooden planks. The goblins swarmed over each golem and were hurled back violently. Yes, it was after all possible to make a decent fight of it!

Abruptly he was back with Sheen, at the base of the hill. The two of them were running through the battlefield, and it was grim. Goblins and animalheads lay dead and dying. This was where the animalheads had been fated to lose half their number, he realized. Some cyborgs were here too, their metal lying twisted and smoking; Stile saw one with its metal skull cracked open, the human brain exposed and shriveled. The odor of carnage was strong.

"We must find help," Sheen said, "to clean out the goblins and get the ball rolling."

"I wish we could save these creatures in pain," Stile said.

"We can't do it now. Once the ball crosses, we can."

Stile knew it was true. They had to move the ball first. Now only seconds remained before the plastic detonated.

They found a bearhead just recovering consciousness. Stile put his hand on the creature's shoulder, breaking the invisibility-spell for this one individual. "We need thee," Stile said. "Follow us."

"Aye, Blue," the bearhead agreed dizzily.

Sheen found a cyborg in the process of self-repair; it had lost a foot, but was affixing the foot of a dead cyborg

in its place. Sheen introduced herself similarly. The four
hurried on.

As they reached the crest of the hill, they smelled
smoke. Something was burning in the mound. "The
golems!" Sheen said grimly.

Stile winced. He knew the wooden golems were not
truly alive, but surely they hurt when they burned. The
goblins had used a devastating weapon, and the Brown
Adept would be mortified.

They charged the mound, staring into its broken chamber. In the smoke of the golem bonfire, the goblins were
trying to push the ball back into the spiral tube. The ball
was shaking, starting to rock. Soon they would get it moving.

The four burst into the chamber. The goblins cried out
and scattered as they saw the bearhead and cyborg, but
rallied in a moment and drew their weapons. Stile and
Sheen, invisible to them, knocked the pistols from the
goblins' hands. Unable to fathom this new menace, the
goblins nevertheless fought bravely, overwhelming their
opposition, both visible and invisible, by force of numbers.

Then the plastic explosive detonated. The barrier
wedges blew up, raining fiery pieces on the heads of the
goblin army. The goblins in the mound disengaged and
dashed out to see what new danger threatened. There was
general disorganization.

"Now we roll it!" Stile cried. The four of them, joined
by a charred but surviving golem, picked up the scattered
limbs of golems and their tools and started levering the
ball forward. They were more disciplined and purposeful
than the goblins had been, and the ball was poised for this
direction, but it was so massive they had just as much
trouble budging it. "We need better levers!" Stile gasped.
But he knew of none within range—and now they heard
the goblins charging up the spiral tunnel. There was no
time for a search.

A hawk flew into the chamber. "Clip!" Stile exclaimed.
"What art thou doing here?"

The unicorn changed to man-form. "I knew thou
wouldst foul it up by thyself, Adept," he said. "Mere men
always do. So I brought some friends to bail thee out."

Now a bee, a hummingbird, and a blue heron flew in, changing to three more unicorns. The third had an iridescent mane. "Belle!" Stile said, recognizing her.

"She was wandering toward the battle," Clip said diffidently. "I could not leave her to such danger, and she does feel she owes thee, Adept, for the manner in which she was used to—"

"Yes, of course!" Stile agreed. "The four of you—help us push this ball down the hill!"

Clip shifted to equine form and played musical directions on his sax-horn. He was answered by a violin, tuba, and ringing-bell tune of agreement. The four put their horns carefully down into the crevice between ball and floor; then, musically coordinated, they levered up and forward.

Just like that, the ball moved. The unicorns repeated the process, working it over the dirt and rubble and outside. It was a slow, difficult task, but they worked well and kept the ball crunching forward.

Goblins burst in from the spiral tunnel. Stile, Sheen, and the bearhead, the cyborg, and the remaining golem turned to face them, protecting the unicorns' flanks. The goblins, seeing only three motley opponents, charged—and discovered the hard way that there were five. In this cramped, littered space, it was a fair match.

Then the ball nudged over the brink and started rolling down the slope in the direction Stile had dictated. The unicorns, their task done, turned to face the goblins—who suddenly lost their eagerness to fight, seeing the odds shift so substantially.

"Mount!" Stile cried, trusting the unicorns to cooperate. "Follow that ball!" And he leaped onto the nearest steed—who happened to be Belle. She spooked, never before having borne a rider, but heard Clip's musical clarification and immediately settled down. Sheen took the golem and mounted Clip, and the bearhead and cyborg mounted the remaining two. They charged down the slope.

For an instant Stile was daunted by the improbability of it all: a man, a cyborg, a robot, an animalhead, and a wooden golem, all riding unicorns through a battlefield strewn with goblins and dragons, pursuing an invaluable ball of power-rock that rolled along a channel cleared by plastic explosive. What a mishmash!

Mishmash? No—this was juxtaposition. The complete mergence of magic and science. He should enjoy it while it lasted, for it would not last long. Already he thought he felt the influence of the Platinum Flute weakening, as the strength of the Foreordained became exhausted.

Belle was a fine steed, running smoothly and swiftly, her lovely mane like silk in his grasp. But of course she was smooth; she had won the Unolympics dance event! "Belle, I thank thee for this service," he breathed, knowing she heard him despite the rush of air and booming of the passage of the Phazite ball, for her left ear rotated toward him. "I will try to do thee some return favor, when I can." And she made a faint bell-melody in response.

Meanwhile, the ball was gathering velocity. It crunched down the hill, leaving its smooth, small channel. Where bodies were in the way, they too were flattened. The Phazite was ponderous and inexorable, crushing everything in its path. The live goblins, seeing its onrush, scattered out of its way in alarm. This was the sensible thing to do.

The four unicorns galloped after it, losing headway as the ball rolled down the steepest section of the slope. All the goblins were watching it now, seeing its passage through the erstwhile barriers. For them, this progress was disaster.

But Stile knew the war was not over. Several barriers remained in place, and the slope reversed farther to the north. Stile's big gamble was with the giants and the route. If he had judged all aspects correctly, he would win—but at this moment he was in severe doubt.

The ball encountered the standing barrier wedges and blew them apart. They had not diverted it perceptibly, and seemed not to have slowed it, but Stile knew crucial impetus had been lost. Would the ball carry far enough?

Now the terrain was gently rolling, largely clear of trees. Stile had planned this carefully on the map. The ball sailed up the slope, and down, and onward. It was right on target. But it was slowing, as it had to, for the incidental resistance of the miles was cumulative.

The Proton-frame terrain, unobtrusive so far because of its barrenness, suddenly became prominent in the form of a cluster of force-field domes. The isolated estates of Citizens, perhaps occupied at the moment, perhaps not. There was a peculiar appeal to such technology set in such an absolutely barren environment, a nugget of complete wealth in complete poverty, like a diamond in sand.

Strange that he should see it this way, Stile thought—then realized that it was in fact the perspective of his other self, to whom the entire frame of Proton was a novelty, much as the frame of Phaze was to Stile. What was commonplace to Stile was a miraculous new discovery to Blue.

The ball was rolling toward a linked trio of small domes. The connecting tubes arched high, leaving sufficient clearance below to pass the Phazite—but the ball eschewed that obvious passage to crash right into the westernmost dome. The dome disappeared as its force-field generator was taken out, leaving the serfs gasping in expectation of the sudden decompression. But there was the Phaze atmosphere, here in the juxtaposition; they discovered to their surprise that they could breathe quite well outside. It was every bit as real as the ball, of course.

One serf ran blindly out in front of Stile's steed; Belle tried to swerve, but the serf's erratic course made avoidance uncertain. "Serf—turf!" Stile sang, willing the message. He wanted the man to be removed to a safe spot, suitable turf. Nothing happened, and he realized that Sheen's repressive enchantment against Adept spells remained in force. Fortunately Belle managed to miss the man, and they galloped on past the domes. Just as well the magic hadn't worked; the enemy Adepts would be casting spells furiously now, trying to sidetrack the Phazite, to conjure imposing barriers or trenches in its path, and Sheen's counterspell was the only protection against this.

It was not hard to keep up with the ball now as it slowly lost velocity. Had Stile started it at a different angle, it could have proceeded down a long valley and maintained speed. But he had elected to go the more difficult, surprising route, gambling the fate of the frames on his hunch. The giants should be arriving soon, and the other thing—he would not say, lest it be overheard.

The slope changed, and the ball slowed more definitely. This was the beginning of the rise he knew would balk it. No goblins were in evidence; he had at least been successful in fooling them. Probably there was a huge concentration at the other route and many barriers, pits, and various obstructive things. If the giants arrived in time, there would be no trouble.

At last the ball stopped, settling into a soft pocket so firmly that it was obvious that their present force could not budge it. They rode up and paused beside it. "What now, Stile?" Sheen inquired with a certain unrobotic edge.

"You unicorns change suits and fly up and see if you can spot the giants," Stile said. "They should be close now. Tell them we need help in a hurry."

The four unicorns shifted immediately to their airborne forms and zoomed into the sky. "I'll check too," Stile said to Sheen. "Project my image in a fast survey around the area."

She did. Soon he verified that the goblins were indeed massed at the valley route in horrendous number—but already they were marching toward the ball's present location. It would not be long before they got there. The giants just had to get there first!

The unicorns were successful. In a moment, three of the towering giants appeared, striding across the horizon, their heads literally lost in the clouds. They had been following the progress of the ball with giant field glasses, so had been ready to intercept it when it was stopped.

Stile had Sheen terminate their spells of invisibility and protection against attack, as these were no longer useful or necessary. Now Stile needed to be seen, to help organize the giants for their giant effort.

Soon the giants were using huge metal canes to propel the ball forward, up the slope, following the route Stile dictated. The giants enjoyed this; it was like a giant game of pool, knocking the tiny but extremely solid ball along. If they did it improperly, their pool cues broke, which was inconvenient.

The first elements of the goblin army arrived too late; the ball was well on its way. Stile and his companions were galloping after it.

Now, Stile thought, was the critical time. If the canny goblin commander did what Stile expected him to—

"There's no way the goblins can stop the giants," Sheen said. "We've won! Clip says the other side of the curtain is this side of the crest of the hill. We're nearly there!"

But another contingent of goblins was arriving at the hill. They did not try to oppose the giants; instead they marched ahead, as if clearing the way, which was strange. The giants, unperturbed, kept pushing the ball, taking turns with their cues. Even for them, it was very heavy, and progress slowed as they tired and their cues broke.

"The line should be right about here," Sheen said.

"Not any more," Stile told her. "The goblins are moving it."

Now she caught on. "No! We aren't gaining at all, then!"

"Oh, we'll get there," Stile said. "This only means delay. The giants are tired; it will take longer to crest the hill."

"I should think so," she agreed, eyeing the steep, almost cliff-faced crest. "You anticipated this? Why did you come here, then? The giants could have pushed it around the hill and across the curtain much faster, and we could have won the game by now. As it is, the enemy will have time to set up something worse."

"Yes," Stile agreed gravely.

The giant currently taking aim at the ball paused. He shook himself, and sweat flung out from him like rain.

"You'll have a workers' revolt soon," Sheen cautioned. "You've got to have some reason for this foolishness."

But Stile was listening for something. Now at last he heard it: an abrupt intensification of the faint Flute music in the background.

"The Oracle has just crossed the line," Stile announced. "Or rather, the line has crossed the Oracle. That computer is now within the zone of juxtaposition. From there, it can use its own stored moving equipment to transport itself the rest of the way to Proton."

"The Oracle!" Sheen exclaimed. "It had to cross to Proton to complete the exchange. To be able to make its vast expertise available for the reorganization of the Proton economic complex."

"The goblins have just enabled it to do that," Stile agreed. "Now we can tip the ball over the crest, roll it down across the line—and Clef can let the curtain collapse into singularity and vanish."

"You did have a cunning notion! You knew the curtain had not spread far enough, that the Oracle was hung up here, right under this mound, so you—"

"We still have to get the ball across," Stile reminded her. "We haven't won yet."

But now the giants renewed their efforts. The ball was shoved up over the cliff face with a convulsive joint effort, and began its inexorable roll down toward the curtain.

They charged up after it, scrambling for handholds at the brink, feeling the exhilaration of victory. As they crested the ridge, they saw the opposite slope blackened with goblins; all the rest of that army had force-marched here for the final confrontation.

The individual goblins could not stop the massively rolling ball, of course; they plunged desperately from its path. The slope was so steep that even the giants would be hard put to halt the ball before it crossed the curtain halfway down.

On the horizon Stile now spied the ogres, who had just arrived on the scene. They were ready to fight, but were understandably hesitant about wading into so vast an army of goblins. But it seemed the ogres would not be needed now.

On the next hill to the north was a device Stile recognized only from his researches into planetary warfare—a nuclear cannon. Powered by atomic fusion, this pre-Protonite weapon could fire a solid projectile into deep space—or into any object in its viewfinder at a lesser range. Stile knew the canny Grossnose would have it loaded with a half-ton slug of Protonite—the only substance that could have a proper effect on the rolling ball. The goblin commander had devised his strategy to counter Stile's strategy without pause.

"Get back over the ridge!" Stile cried. "Down, giants! Now!"

The earth trembled as they obeyed, trusting his warning.

Giants, unicorns, and others all huddled in the shelter of the ridge.

The cannon fired. The Phazite ball exploded into thousands of fragments and a great cloud of dust. Phazite rained down around them in the form of stones, pebbles, gravel, and sand.

Sheen jumped to cover Stile's body with her own tougher one, and the cyborg did the same for the bearhead. The unicorns changed to their flying forms and huddled under the same shelters. But the giants were in some discomfort; they swatted at the pieces that struck them, as if bitten by gnats.

Now the great goblin army went into action, obviously rehearsed. Each goblin ran to pick up one fragment of Phazite and carry it south, away from the border of the juxtaposition. "No!" Sheen cried. "Fragmentation doesn't matter, so long as it gets across the line to Proton-frame. But this will finish us!"

Grossnose's final ploy had been a brilliant one. Once more the goblin had outmaneuvered Stile, giving up a lesser thing—in this case the Oracle—for the sake of a greater one. The ball had had to crest the hill to come into range of the nuclear cannon.

But Stile refused to give up. One hope remained. "Troll! Brown!" Stile called. "If you hear me—use the book! Do something while the enemy Adepts are relaxing in victory!" Did they hear? Could Brown locate a spell and use it in time? Stile was afraid not.

Suddenly there was a strange wrenching, as of vastly potent magic gone astray. Then the world stabilized, seemingly unchanged. The goblins still charged forward with their burdens, seeming slightly dizzy but hardly incapacitated.

Sheen looked at Stile in despair as the last of the sandfall cleared. "We can't possibly stop them all," she said. "We have ogres and unicorns, but there are too many goblins, too hard to catch. The book-spell failed, or was blocked by the other Adepts. Lady Brown simply lacks the experience to use that sort of magic properly."

"I don't know," Stile said. "That didn't feel like blocked

magic." He was getting a notion what it might have been, but decided not to say. It could not make a difference at this point. "Let the goblins be; no sense getting ourselves in trouble in a futile effort."

The giants and unicorns turned away from him in disgust, but left the goblins alone. Soon virtually all of the Phazite was gone, carried away in pieces or in bagfuls. The battle was over.

Commander Grossnose strode over the crest. "Congratulations on an excellent campaign, Adept," he said graciously. "Thou didst trick me on crossing the Oracle—but I countered with the cannon. The power of the Oracle in nonseparated frames becomes moot. But if thou wouldst be so good as to answer a point of curiosity—"

"Certainly," Stile agreed.

"What was the nature of that last great spell thou didst attempt to perform? I felt its vasty power—but naught happened."

Trool and the Brown Adept appeared, she with the book of magic clutched in her arms. "We can answer that, goblin," she said. "It was reversal."

Grossnose's constricted brow wrinkled. "Reversal? I understand that not."

"Thou knowest—changing directions. So west turns east, and north turns south—or seems to. The Oracle told us to do it, once it got into jux and could use its holo—hologramp—its magic pictures to talk to us. That's one smart machine!"

"North turns south?" the goblin asked, dismay infiltrating his face.

"Yep. Thine army just carried all the Phazite the wrong way—north across the line."

The goblin commander stood for a long moment, absorbing that, grasping the accuracy and import of the statement. All of them had been deceived, for it had been an extremely powerful spell of a quite unanticipated sort—as it had needed to be, to avoid interference by the enemy Adepts.

Grossnose turned again to Stile. "Congratulations on a better campaign than I knew, Adept," he said gravely, as gracious in defeat as he had been in victory. "The final ploy was thine." He marched back up the slope, his troops falling in behind him.

The victory had been won; juxtaposition could end, and the frames could safely separate, never to intersect again in this region of the universe. Stile could see the glimmer of the curtain contracting, closing more rapidly from the south so as to finish at the site of the Oracle beneath them. Or was that from the north it was closing? It was hard to be sure, with that reversal-spell. Beyond that line, north (?) was the verdant world of Phaze; at the crest to the south(?) was the barren desert of Proton. Only the directions were reversed, not the terrain, somehow; the goblins had marched the wrong way home. Not that it mattered; they were creatures of Phaze who would remain there regardless, just as the robots and cyborgs would remain in Proton.

Stile himself would now return forever to Proton, to settle his debt to Citizen Merle, marry Sheen, and work with the Oracle-computer to reform the existing order. His alternate self would reanimate to be with Neysa and Clip and Stile's other friends of Phaze and the Lady Blue. How much better off he would be!

"Thy life seems not dreary to me," the Blue Adept thought. "The sheer challenge, the strange and fascinating bypaths of politics, the marvelous Game, and the ladies in Proton—no woman could be better than Sheen. Thou hast far the best of it, methinks."

"Just do thou wrap up my commitments in Phaze," Stile thought back sourly. "Petition must be made to the Herd Stallion to release Clip to pair with Belle; that is best for both of them. And it is in my mind that Trool the troll, with his integrity and skill at sculpture, should be given the book of magic and become the new Red Adept, fashioning useful magic amulets for—"

"That was *my* thought, fool!" Blue thought. "Of course I will—"

Then the closing curtain caught them. "Ah, the reversal!" Blue thought, amazed, as his other soul was drawn from Stile's association. "Farewell, self!"

Stile blinked. Blue had caught on to something Stile had

not, it seemed, and now it was too late to ascertain what. That, and the whole wonderful world of Phaze, were gone. He felt the bitter tears of loss. Never to see the Lady Blue again, or Neysa—

But he could not afford self-pity. He had things to do in this world. He opened his eyes.

He was lying on a bed in a chamber of the Blue Demesnes. The Proton replica, of course. He must have lost consciousness, and Sheen had brought him here and left him to recover in decent privacy. Sheen was certainly the perfect woman; too bad she had not been able to remain in Phaze—but that would have been too complicated anyway.

He got up, felt momentarily dizzy with the sudden rising, and quickly squatted to let the blood return to his head. It was as if he had been lying here a long time, his body unused; he felt somewhat awkward and unsteady, but now was recovering rapidly.

He stared at his knees with slow amazement. They were fully flexed, without pain. His injury had been cured!

Oh—of course. Sheen had taken advantage of his unconsciousness to have him in surgery, and now he was better. Though he really would not have expected her to do that without consulting him first.

He walked to the door. The short hall was dark, so he sang a spell: "Right—light." Immediately there was light, though only half as bright as he had intended.

Wait—he could not do magic in Proton!

He glanced back—and saw the harmonica lying on a table beside the bed. Blue's harmonica, left with the—

Then he heard a light tread on the floor, probably someone alerted by Stile's own motion. He recognized it immediately: the Lady Blue. Sheen's step was quite different.

He knew with a shock of incredulous joy that something had gone wrong. The reversal had sent himself and his alternate self to the wrong frames! Stile's soul had gone to the golem body, whose knees were good, while the Blue Adept had left Phaze—

Phaze would not be safe until the Blue Adept departed it forever. The prophecy had been fulfilled after all. *Stile* was in Phaze, not the true Blue Adept, who had been here all along, in the harmonica, until this final separation. The Brown Adept, unacquainted with the book of magic, prompted by the all-knowing Oracle, had made the reversal-spell too comprehensive, and thus—

And the other prophecy, which he had thought had come after the fact—that Stile would be betrayed, for his own good, by a young-seeming woman. Brown seemed as young as they came. That mixup had been no accident! She had perceived more clearly than he where his true future lay, and had acted to make it come true. How neatly it all fit together now! The Blue Adept, loath to live with a woman who no longer loved him, and fascinated by the marvelous world of science and the beautiful, loyal, deserving creature Sheen—who was as much intrigued by Blue, a person in Stile's own image and spirit who had left his love for the Lady Blue behind—

Now the Lady Blue came into view, breathtakingly lovely and somber. Her face composed, she approached Stile. "My Lord, thou knowest I will serve thee in all things with grace and propriety," she said sadly. "What is to be, must be."

She thought he was Blue, of course—and she loved Stile. She had the mettle to carry through, to bear and raise his son, with no word of regret or reproach—but this time she would not need it.

"Beloved," Stile said. "I have news for thee, thee, thee . . ."

About the Author

It was not necessary, in England in 1934, to name a baby instantly; there was a grace period of a number of days. As the deadline loomed, the poor woman simply gave all the names she could think of: Piers Anthony Dillingham Jacob. The child moved to America, where it took three years and five schools to graduate him from first grade, because he couldn't learn to read. It was thus fated that he become a proofreader, an English teacher, or a writer. He tried them all, along with a dozen other employments —and liked only the least successful one. So he lopped off half his name, sent his wife out to earn their living, and concentrated on writing. That was the key to success; publishers would print material by an author whose name was short enough.

He sold his first story in 1962 and had his first novel, *Chthon*, published in 1967. His first fantasy in *The Magic of Xanth* Trilogy, *A Spell for Chameleon*, won the August Derleth Fantasy Award as the best novel in 1977. He has written approximately forty novels in the genres of science fiction, fantasy and martial arts.

He was married in 1956, right after graduating from college, to Carol Ann Marble. Their daughter Penny was born eleven years later, and their final daughter Cheryl in 1970. That was the beginning of a whole new existence, because little girls like animals. In 1978 they bought nice horses, and that experience, coupled with knee injuries in judo class, became *Split Infinity*. Piers Anthony is not the protagonist—he says he lacks the style—but Penny's horse Blue *is* the mundane model for the unicorn Neysa.